PRAISE FOR A

"Abby Brooks is a wizard with Beyond Us—entertaining and pure enjoyment!"

ADRIANA LOCKE—USA TODAY AND WASHINGTON POST BESTSELLING AUTHOR

"A masterful blend of joy and angst.

PRAISE FOR *ABBY BROOKS*

"As a voracious reader it is not unusual for me to read 5-7 books per week. What is unusual is for me to be thinking about the writing and characters long after I've finished the book. With just the perfect amount of angst and remarkable character development, Abby Brooks has crafted a masterpiece..."

PRAISE FOR *BEYOND WORDS*

"Once again Abby Brooks creates a world filled with beautifully written characters that you cannot help but fall in love with."

PRAISE FOR *BEYOND LOVE*

"A lovely story of growing beyond your past, taking control of your life, and allowing yourself to be loved for the person you are."

MELANIE MORELAND—NEW YORK TIMES BESTSELLING AUTHOR, IN PRAISE OF *WOUNDED*

"Abby Brooks writes books that draw readers right into the story. When you read about her characters, you want them to be your friends."

PRAISE FOR ABBY BROOKS

FAKE

A HUTTON FAMILY ROMANCE

ABBY BROOKS

Copyright © 2024 by Abby Brooks

All rights reserved.

No part of this book may be reproduced in any form or by any electronic or mechanical means, including information storage and retrieval systems, without written permission from the author, except for the use of brief quotations in a book review.

Cover image copyright © 2022 by WANDER AGUIAR PHOTOGRAPHY LLC

Cover design by Abby Brooks

CONNECT WITH ABBY BROOKS

For more books and updates:
abbybrooksfiction.com

- facebook.com/abbybrooksauthor
- instagram.com/xo_abbybrooks
- tiktok.com/@abbybrooksauthor

Books by

ABBY BROOKS

THE HUTTON FAMILY SECOND GENERATION

Fate

Fire

Fake

WILDROSE LANDING

Fearless

Shameless

Reckless

THE HUTTON FAMILY

Beyond Words

Beyond Love

Beyond Now

Beyond Us

Beyond Dreams

It's Definitely Not You

The Hutton Family Series - Part 1

The Hutton Family Series - Part 2

A BROOKSIDE ROMANCE

Wounded

Inevitably You

This Is Why

Along Comes Trouble

Come Home To Me

A Brookside Romance - the Complete Series

WILDE BOYS WITH WILL WRIGHT

Taking What Is Mine

Claiming What Is Mine

Protecting What Is Mine

Defending What Is Mine

Wilde

THE MOORE FAMILY

Finding Bliss

Faking Bliss

Instant Bliss

Enemies-to-Bliss

THE LONDON SISTERS

Love Is Crazy (Dakota & Dominic)

Love Is Beautiful (Chelsea & Max)

Love Is Everything (Maya & Hudson)

The London Sisters - the Complete Series

IMMORTAL MEMORIES

Immortal Memories Part 1

Immortal Memories Part 2

AS WREN WILLIAMS

Bad, Bad Prince

Woodsman

ABBY BROOKS

ONE

Mina

"You've got this, Mina. This is the first day of the rest of your life." I blow a puff of air past pursed lips and flex my hands against the steering wheel. On the other side of my windshield is a large stretch of undeveloped land—trees, beach, ocean—the site of my next project and today's meeting with the two men I'll be working with for the next several months. Both larger than life. Both wildly successful. Both wealthy and sought after in their respective fields.

And me?

I am just Mina Blake. Simple. Hard working. Counting every dollar and hoping life will finally cut me a break with this new interior design contract. I so do not belong with the two men I'm about to meet.

"But I'll fake it 'til I make it," I say to myself.

It's my battle cry, one that brought me this far, and the woman staring back at me through the rearview looks positively ferocious.

I arrived a respectable fifteen minutes early to the meeting, expecting the same from my soon-to-be colleague and our very famous client. However, twenty minutes have passed and I'm still pep talking myself all by my lonesome, so I pull up our group chat to verify the address the client sent last night. Definitely at the right spot. Still, nerves get the better of me, so I send a quick text as a get out of jail free card.

> This site is gorgeous! Can't wait to talk ideas for the build!

If I am in the wrong place, I'll find out soon enough.

A black Tesla whines to a stop beside me. The most beautiful man in the entire world glances my way and smiles, which only amps up the wattage on his allure. With effort, I close my mouth, gulp down my libido, and lift a hand before climbing out of my twenty-year-old Honda to meet the man *Architectural Digest* named "One to Watch" for five years running before basically crowning him King of Architecture.

Benjamin Bancroft. Smart. Talented. And sexy as all get out.

Chocolate hair hangs playfully into dark eyes. Tight jeans hug an ass I'd love to sink my teeth into and a worn T-shirt clings to broad shoulders, screaming, "I'm too cool for business attire. Look how easy and breezy I am, arriving for a meeting with a famous client in casual clothes." A worn khaki messenger bag bounces off his hip in agreement.

My thrift store blouse, slacks, and heels don't stand a chance next to him, vintage vibes be damned. I smooth the front of my pants then close the car door, the ancient hinges groaning in complaint.

Mr. Hot, Cool, and Talented gives a quick scan of my dated clothes and vehicle as he closes the distance between us. I brace for impact. These wealthy types can be difficult to deal with once they know you're not in the same class. There's no hint of judgment, another check in his favor.

"Hey there! I'm Benjamin Bancroft," he says, in a voice as smooth as a warm slice of chocolate lava cake. "You must be Mina Blake. I've heard good things about your work."

My grin widens until I remind myself to crank it down a notch or seven. I may be slightly in awe of the man. I know all his projects by heart after obsessively following his career as I was building mine. Which possibly, maybe, led to a teensy tiny crush. Totally innocent and understandable, especially after seeing him in person. How is it possible he's better looking in the flesh than on the cover of a magazine? Even the sun shines brighter in appreciation, bringing out beads of perspiration at my temples. Florida heat is not to be trifled with.

"It's such an honor to work with you." I extend a hand to the living legend. "I promise to do whatever it takes to live up to these good things you've heard."

"With an attitude like that, I'm sure you will." Benjamin chuckles, a low sultry rumble that's yet another check in his favor. Could he be more perfect? "Though, between you and me, I wouldn't get my hopes up about this project. I've heard Mr. West can be difficult to please."

"Da da dunnnn..." I hum the international theme song for danger before my brain has time to analyze the appropriateness of said action. Which it does. Quickly. Then sends a panicked rush of adrenaline through my system, slamming the abort button.

Dear God. Make it stop. Sincerely, Mina Blake.

Thankfully, Benjamin laughs again, then indicates the shore with his chin. "I'm gonna wander the site and get my bearings before Mr. West arrives." He takes a few steps before pausing to turn over his shoulder. "Stick with me, kid. We're gonna do good things together."

There are so many good things I'd like to do with

the man in front of me. Business. Pleasure. The mind boggles with options. I try not to swoon as he saunters away, dictating notes into his phone.

Hormones aside, working with someone like Benjamin Bancroft could be the professional break I need. I haven't spent a lot of time with people who can afford interior designers and architects for their private builds. They have money to spare and time to waste and I've never had much of either. Try as I might, they sniff out my 'poor as dirt' background faster than a police dog searching for a donut.

While I stare after Benjamin, a second vehicle rumbles to a stop beside me. Sleek. Black. Drenched with the understated pretension of generational wealth. A tall man climbs out, affording me my first look at our client live and up close. Nathan West, firstborn son of Collin and Harlow West, pop culture icons who retired right here in the Florida Keys to be near Harlow's family, the Huttons.

The man is a checklist of privilege. Everything I wanted while growing up in a teeny apartment with Mom, he had. And then some.

Nathan stretches his back, showing off a physique that puts Benjamin's to shame. Sunlight glints off dark hair, revealing streaks of mahogany, and he rakes a hand across a jawline that could cut glass. His mouth curves with a smirk and the sun catches his eyes, highlighting their brilliant green before he slides a pair of sunglasses into place. Strong shoulders. Stronger arms. The muscles flex and twist in a hypnotic dance beneath the black T-shirt he's paired with ordinary looking jeans and work boots.

"Holy wow," I murmur, smoothing the front of my pants again.

Sure, I expected Nathan West to be hot. I'm no dummy. I did my research the second his offer hit my inbox.

And by research, I mean I let my best friend, Fallon Mae, tell me everything she knows. Which is a significant amount, considering her past, present, and imagined future.

Fallon fell madly in love with Nathan the day she saw him onstage at his parents' benefit concert for The Reversal of Fortune Foundation—a charity for underprivileged children started by Nathan's aunt. For years, Fallon swore she would grow up to be Mrs. West until Nathan started showing up in the news again, still hot, but making decidedly questionable decisions.

Since then, it's been her mission to remind him who he really is by publishing articles on her gossip and entertainment blog that point out every bad choice he's made in the last several months. For example, the article Fallon's publishing today will mention the house Benjamin and I are designing for Nathan. She says comparing Nathan West to an antihero will help him see what he's become, and she'll have him back to his old self in no time. I've never really gotten my head around how she thinks that will work, but who am I to judge good intentions?

So yes, I know Nathan West is the first-born child of singer-songwriter duo Collin and Harlow West. I know he was raised wealthy by his famous parents. I know that up until very recently he was a freaking unicorn of goodness. Kind. Caring. Humble. Giving. He's dedicated his life to charity, using his privilege to help children who were dealt a difficult hand. And yes, thanks to Fallon, I also know he hasn't been that man since he broke things off with his girlfriend.

There's been a lot more drinking.

And sleeping around.

All the typical douchebaggery you'd expect from someone with unlimited time, money, and zero consequences for bad decisions.

Frankly, it's disappointing, though not all that surprising. Money breeds greed and power. Nothing good comes from that combination.

"This is it," I murmur to distract myself from focusing on the negatives. "This is the day everything turns around. You've got this. You know you've got this. You're strong and confident and talented and capable. You belong here. This is your time to shine."

Painting on my best smile, I glance Nathan's way and find him staring. Hard. And not in a, "Wow, I sure can't wait to meet my interior designer!" kind of way. He looks like he's trying not to swallow his tongue. Or like he's gotten a whiff of a stench so revolting he wants to be anywhere but here. I smooth back the wisps of ebony hair that have fallen free from my ponytail and do a quick BO check. Fresh as a daisy despite the Florida heat.

I take a step Nathan's way and a wave of disbelief hits me. Is this really my life? Mina Blake, hobnobbing with the rich, famous, and uber talented. My phone buzzes and I take a quick glance, smiling when I see a response to my text in the group chat.

> BENJAMIN BANCROFT
>
> Ms. Blake is correct. This site is overflowing with potential.

Nathan, however, scoffs and shakes his head as he stares at his phone.

Okay...not exactly the exuberance I hoped for.

But confidence fixes everything, and I'll fake it 'til I fix it, despite the nerves his grumpiness set loose in my belly.

After one more deep breath, I smooth the front of my pants, shooting an exuberant, "Good morning, Mr. West!" over the roof of my car.

"Morning," he grumbles, glaring at his phone, his thumbs tapping the screen in a sharp staccato.

Unfazed, I cross in front of the hood, hand extended. "I'm Mina Blake and I—"

"I know who you are," Nathan barks, declines a call, then holds up a hand, looking contrite. "I'm sorry, I—"

His phone buzzes again and tension tightens his jaw.

"I have to take this," he says, then strides away, shoulders hunched, chin dropped as he whisper-yells at the poor soul on the other line, probably an assistant who got his coffee wrong or the woman he was out with last night getting dumped. From what I hear, he doesn't keep them around very long.

I scowl as Nathan walks away, then shake my own hand, murmuring, "It's a pleasure to meet you, Ms. Blake. You came highly recommended. Oh! Why thank you, Mr. West! It's a pleasure to meet you as well. My best friend's a huge fan! Fallon Mae? Maybe you've heard of her..."

Nathan glances over his shoulder, and I drop my hands to my side before he can see, then hurry after the man with the power to make or break my future clenched between his teeth. When I catch up, his sunglasses are dangling from the neck of his shirt and he's cordially shaking hands with Benjamin, his phone tucked into his back pocket.

"Benjamin Bancroft. It's great to finally meet you in person." Ben's gaze jukes to me, and damn. That smile. How does he do it? "As I said in the group chat," he continues, "this site is brimming with potential. I see great things here."

"The pleasure is mine, Mr. Bancroft," Nathan replies, and would you look at that? He sounds downright cordial. "The body of your work speaks for itself. I can't wait to hear what you and Ms. Blake have in mind for my new home."

His voice reminds me of the ocean, soft and soothing, yet churning with the constant threat of turbulence, and hinting at unexplored depths.

I stop beside them, hand extended, smile in place, determined to make a good impression. "Mina Blake," I say again. "It's an honor to meet you, Mr. West. And yeah, this site is amazing."

His eyes should be warm, like foliage in springtime or reeds in the breeze. Instead, they're sharp and cutting like overgrown thorns. He has the gall to check his phone before he extends a hand like the thought of touching me repulses him.

"Miss Blake."

Okay. Nice to Benjamin. Rude to me. Gotcha. I glance down at my high-waisted slacks and white blouse with the cute cap sleeves and Victorian style buttons. Compared to the jeans and T-shirts spackled on my companions, I'm overdressed for the occasion. Maybe he's turned off by formality?

You know what? It doesn't matter.

I'm turned off by people who can't introduce themselves with a modicum of decency.

"I am so excited to work with someone as talented as Mr. Bancroft. Especially on a project like this. This is basically a dream come true for me."

Nathan's thorny eyes sweep over me with...is that disdain? "You mean a project with an unlimited budget."

Fallon's right. Nathan West has officially entered his villain era. I drop the pretense and speak to him on a level he'll understand.

"An unlimited budget will let us flex our creative muscles to your heart's content. A man like you deserves to get what he wants."

By that, I mean everyone deserves a life of happiness and ease, but that's not the way he'll take it. These rich and famous types think they deserve a bigger slice of the pie. Why? Because they're better than the little guys, the working class, the people who keep the world running, of course!

Nathan's face hardens. The muscle in his jaw pulses and his eyes flash like the embers of a fire raging back to life. He's unreadable and unpredictable— terse heat wrapped in a scornful sneer.

A sneer?

Who sneers at a perfectly pleasant woman they just met?

Nathan freaking West, that's who. The man I hoped would be a dream come true but has his heart set on being my worst nightmare.

"Why don't you walk us around the site and tell us about the house as you envision it?" Benjamin says, situating himself between me and Nathan like some kind of human shield. I could just about hug him for that kindness.

Nathan gives Benjamin his full attention, wandering the site and rattling off his wish list in a voice so quiet, I can barely hear. Almost like he's leaving me out on purpose. Like he took one look at my bargain bin clothes and car and decided I wasn't worth his time. Another wave of disappointment sweeps over me. I'd hoped Fallon was wrong about him, but Nathan West is just another pretty face and bloated bank account.

Flustered, I scan the area—a secluded cove with a wide stretch of private beach, hidden from the road by a mixture of oak trees and slash pines that open to a view so magnificent it's like it was painted to order. Nathan's future house appears before my eyes, building itself from the foundation to the rafters, with large windows and sweeping rooms that are sophisticated, but lack pretension. It's not too small, not too big. There's a giant library filled with more books than a person could read in one lifetime. Fiction. Non-fiction. Rare first editions sitting beside pop culture new releases. There's a chef's kitchen and a large deck overlooking the ocean, a perfect place to curl up and watch the sunset.

With a sad smile, I realize I just built my mother's dream house. The one I hope to surprise her with some day after...well...*after*.

I make a few mental adjustments to the build, adding masculine shades of blue, green, and gray that perfectly offset Nathan's mahogany hair and thornbush eyes. There's a billiard room and a bar and I'll probably keep the deck and library because something tells me he might like them. Considering his villain era vibes, I add an office with an imposing desk, a hulking leather chair, and a secret passageway lurking behind enormous bookshelves.

"Wow," I whisper. "This is really gonna be something."

When I look back to my companions, Nathan is

staring at me with open disdain, and I don't know what I've done to earn it.

I promised myself I'd make the best of this situation, but we're twenty minutes in and one thing's for sure:

I don't like Nathan West.

TWO

N<small>ATHAN</small>

It's a gorgeous day. A handful of clouds float through an azure sky. Sunlight glimmers over the ocean that's soon to be my backyard and a breeze dances through the air.

I'm too hungover to appreciate any of it.

Damn Dominick Taylor and his ability to short circuit my common sense by dangling wealthy donors in front of me. I court them while he scandalizes their daughters, nieces, and mistresses. It's a mutually beneficial deal...unless I have an early meeting.

I pull up to the site of my future home and curse. Not one, but two cars are parked and waiting, morning light slicing off their windows like knives into my brain.

Any other day I would have gotten here first, but

my head was throbbing and the world was spinning and funny thing about that, it tends to slow a person down. I'm better with a chance to process my surroundings before other people arrive. A chance to plan what I want to say, and, most importantly, a chance to plan my escape for when conversation inevitably turns to how cool it must have been to grow up with Collin and Harlow West as parents.

And it was cool, just not for the reasons people expect. They want stories of fame and fortune, of drunken parties with celebrities and gallivanting around the globe in private jets, not solid parenting, a stable home, and the knowledge that our wealth doesn't make us inherently better than anyone.

I kill the engine with a sigh.

I am so not in the mood for this.

The meeting hasn't even started and I'm ready for it to be over, which is a shame because, thanks to Dom and his coaching, I'm actually excited about having this house built. It'll be nothing like my current home, one that suits my needs and nothing more. Nothing extravagant. Everything practical. My old place basically begs the world to see me as normal.

I've been afraid of my money. Afraid to enjoy the finer things in life.

No more. This new house will be an ode to things I never knew I wanted. To the lifestyle the rest of the world thinks I already lead. It's like Dom says, "People love a good show. Why not put on the costume and play the role they expect?"

I park beside an older Honda. Well cared for but limping close to the finish line of usefulness. A woman leans on the hood, nodding emphatically as she talks to herself, a sleek black ponytail bouncing as she bobs her head. Fair skin. A cute nose, pretty smile, luscious curves wrapped in black slacks and a filmy white blouse. Perky gestures punctuate her sentences. She's really giving herself a talking to. Probably about her choice of shoes. Who wears heels to a build site?

I laugh and it feels good, though foreign.

I need to remember to do that more.

Turning that thought into a promise, I swing open my car door, stretching my back and turning my face to the sky before slipping a pair of sunglasses into place. I'd hoped my headache would be better by now. No luck there. A bolt of shame twists in my belly. Nathan West doesn't get sloppy drunk and he sure as hell doesn't show up to meetings hungover.

But that was before my girlfriend cheated on me.

Before I realized people see me as a resource rather than a person.

Before I decided it was time to do whatever it takes to expand the foundation.

So, I drink more than I used to. And I don't trust

people to be who they say they are. And I work so much my family worries, especially now that I've caught the attention of Fallon fucking Mae, the gossip and entertainment blogger from hell.

I don't know what I did to that woman, but she hates me.

And after weeks of being her favorite punching bag, the feeling is mutual.

I run a hand over my jaw, inwardly willing away the icepick in my temple as the hint of stubble *scritch-scratch against* my palm. I'm done drinking like that. I'm done feeling like this.

It's time to stop acting like an asshole and start acting like myself again.

Whatever that means.

The woman leaning on the car beside me is still talking to herself. Her personal pep talk is endearing, though she'd probably die of embarrassment if she caught me staring. Which she does, meeting my eyes as if she can hear my thoughts. She laughs lightly—a quick toss of her head makes that ponytail dance—then smiles and waves like she isn't embarrassed at all.

I used to respect confidence like that. It was one of the things that attracted me to my ex, Blossom. But now, brazen confidence makes me instantly question a person's true motivations. No one's that assured without a hint of narcissism, a dash of sociopathy, or a streak of ulterior motive running through everything they do.

My phone pings.

I give the woman a quick wave, then check my notification as a distraction. There's a message from the architect in the group chat, quickly followed by one from Dom. I dismiss the first—better to talk face to face since we're all here—and open the second.

> **DOM**
>
> Fallon fucking Mae strikes again.
>
> She just posted a new article with pics from last night
>
> You look good
>
> I look better
>
> The girls? Fucking delicious, brother
>
> But head's up
>
> She says you've entered your villain era.

Villain era? *Villain era?*

Sure. That's what this is. I've dedicated my life to The Reversal of Fortune Foundation, spending my days behind my desk and my nights with Dom, schmoozing the charitably inclined so I can expand our scope of benefits. Dominick gets the girls. I talk to their wealthy parents...

ROF's future isn't just children in need, but all people in need.

But the damn paparazzi always manage to find the one photo, with just the right angle, where it looks like I'm drunkenly hitting on a woman, while in reality the interaction was completely benign. Polite laughter over a cheesy joke. An apology over a spilled drink. That kind of stuff.

> **DOM**
>
> She says you spend all your time with spectacular and dazzling women
>
> She must have us confused
>
> You've got a hard on for rich old men

This is the wrong time to read the damn article. Not as the woman—undoubtedly Mina Blake, my interior designer—heads my way, calling a polite "Good morning, Mr. West!" over the roof of her car.

Distracted, I return the greeting as another text comes in.

> **DOM**
>
> She even insinuates you're Bruce Wayne, building a lair out on a secluded cove
>
> Which isn't a bad look for you
>
> We can work with this
>
> Villains are popular nowadays

A choked laugh grinds up my throat. A lair...

That woman has no clue who I really am.

My phone rings with a call from Dom as Ms. Blake crosses in front of her car to introduce herself, hand extended, an unsure smile casting shadows in eyes so blue they put the sky to shame.

Seriously. How does anyone have eyes that blue? Especially with hair so dark and silky it's like midnight melting...

Fuck. Thoughts like that are off limits. I'm not doing the dating thing. Hell, I'm not even doing the one-night fling thing, especially not with someone who's clearly hurting for money. Not after Blossom.

And if all that wasn't enough to get me to hard fucking pass, she's my interior designer. Business and pleasure do not mix, never mind my newly appointed villain status.

"I'm Mina Blake and I—"

"I know who you are," I bark as I decline Dom's call, then immediately feel bad. It's not Ms. Blake's fault Dom can't stand to be ignored. It's not her fault Fallon fucking Mae needs to get her head out of my ass. It's not her fault I'm too hungover for any of this. I hold up a hand in apology. "I'm sorry, I—"

My phone rings again, another call from Dom. He won't give up until I hear what he has to say. If there's any hope of focusing on this meeting—

"I have to take this." I storm out of earshot from Mina before answering the call. "What?" I grind out through a jaw so tight I'm lucky my teeth don't crack.

"You read it yet?"

"No time. I'm ten minutes late to my meeting to plan the Bat Cave."

"Come on. You have to admit, that's pretty funny." Dom laughs to prove his point.

"There's nothing funny about being serially misrepresented by this woman. Villain era? Really?"

"You can't let stuff like that get to you, brother. You know what they say about publicity, and Fallon fucking Mae has that covered for you." Dom sucks his teeth. "You meet your dream team yet?"

"I was just incredibly rude to my interior designer, if that counts. Thank you for that, by the way."

"What's she like?"

I pause and glance over my shoulder to find Mina glaring daggers at my back...and talking to herself again. She doesn't seem to be a Nathan fan, though she does have this gutsy, effervescent quality to her. Like she never met a situation she couldn't find her way out of. She seems a lot like someone I'd like to know better. But Dom doesn't care about that. I give him the details he's fishing for.

"Cheap clothes. Cheaper car. Pretty face. Great body. She's talented too," I add, to mitigate the guilt of reducing a human being down to a superficial checklist of finances and physical attributes.

"So, she's in a bad financial situation, not afraid of work, and she's hot. Basically your Kryptonite."

"You're mixing your superheroes. I'm Batman, not Superman, remember?"

"What you need to remember is *don't date down*. If you learn one thing from Blossom, let it be that women like them see you as a paycheck. Not a person. A paycheck."

That is exactly the lesson I learned from my ex. Hence my resolve to focus on work.

"Not everyone is Blossom."

"More are than aren't. Mark my words. Your hot little interior designer will say something about 'a man like you' or 'a person in your position.' She'll make it clear she sees you as *other* within the first ten minutes of your meeting."

Blossom used to say it all the time. *A man like you should get what he wants*. Like I'm somehow better than the rest of the world. Why? Because I have money?

It felt like a manipulation. Like she was trying to pull a sleight of hand by soothing an ego that doesn't exist.

"Gotta go," I say to Dom. "Thanks for the heads up about the article."

I end the call and shove my phone in my pocket, then stroll towards a man in tight jeans and a T-shirt that begs someone to acknowledge his gym time. The man named "One to Watch" by *Architectural Digest* for five years running glances up as I approach.

He shakes my hand. Firm grip. Likable smile. "Benjamin Bancroft. It's great to finally meet you in person. As I said in the group chat, this site is brimming with potential."

"The pleasure is all mine, Mr. Bancroft," I reply as my phone vibrates like a goddamn buzzsaw in my pocket. Probably my family complaining about me dragging our name through the mud when they really should be tracking down that awful journalist and talking to her.

I refocus on Bancroft, slipping off my sunglasses and hooking them into the neck of my T-shirt. "The body of your work speaks for itself," I say, mirroring his smile despite my raging headache. "I can't wait to hear what you and Ms. Blake have in mind for my new home."

My phone stops alerting me to texts and switches to calls as Ms. Blake arrives beside me. Her hand's extended. Her smile is plucky, like she refuses to be ignored, kind of like whoever the hell is blowing up my phone.

"Mina Blake," she says and damn it, if my phone

doesn't stop ringing, I'm going to throw it in the ocean. "It's an honor to meet you, Mr. West. And yeah, this site is amazing."

I pull out my phone, glare at the slew of notifications, and silence the damn thing before I shake the woman's hand. "Ms. Blake."

She's beautiful.

I mean, you know, in an everyday kind of way. Softer than the rail thin socialites Dom flirts with night after night. Ebony hair glistens like onyx in the sunlight. She's overdressed for the occasion in a pair of tailored black pants and a delicate white top that hugs her chest every time the wind whispers through. The outfit looks worn, though well cared for, like her car. Money's tight for Mina Blake. Her face is guarded, but her lips twist into a mischievous smile when she glances at Benjamin.

"I am so excited to work with someone as talented as Mr. Bancroft. Especially on a project like this. This is basically a dream come true for me." Mina's eyes meet mine, sparkling with enthusiasm, which should be a point in her favor, but after my conversation with Dom, I'm afraid they're sparkling with dollar signs.

"You mean a project with an unlimited budget." I shoot her a scathing glance that's really meant for the Blossoms of the world, then swallow hard, preparing an apology, but Mina speaks first.

"An unlimited budget will let us flex our creative muscles to your heart's content." The temperature of her voice drops several degrees. "A man like you deserves to get what he wants."

A man like me...

Fuck. Dom was right. Five minutes of conversation and there it is.

I can't trust Mina Blake.

THREE

Mina

"Oh my God. Fallon! It was awful!" I collapse onto my friend's orange velvet couch, curl into a ball, and pull a shaggy chenille throw over my head. "I'm never coming out from under here. This is where I live now."

"That's fine. You're welcome to stay there as long as you like." The couch shifts as she sits beside me and pats my thigh. There's a soft *thunk* of something heavy being set on the coffee table with the unmistakable *clink* of wine glasses following behind. "It *will* make it harder for us to share this bottle of vin santo rosso, but I'm sure you're okay with that."

Damn her willingness to exploit my love of sweet red wine!

"I can drink under here just fine, thank you very

much." I slip out a hand to reach for my glass, but Fallon scoffs.

"You absolutely cannot drink wine under there. It's red. My blanket is beige. And you, while sweet as can be and I love you to pieces, are a klutz with a capital K when you drink."

"Wow." I sit up and wrap the blanket around my head and shoulders, insulating myself from the memories of Nathan West glaring at me like I didn't deserve to breathe the same air as him. "Way to kick me when I'm down."

"Honey, there are certain truths we need to own about ourselves. Drunken klutzhood is one of yours." Fallon carefully unwraps the blanket from my head and folds it before draping it over the arm of the couch in a seemingly haphazard way that's effortlessly stylish, just like the sleek black hair that falls gracefully down her back, highlighting a flowing, off-the-shoulder floral top. Add in high-waisted, wide-legged white linen trousers and it's hard to believe she works from home.

"Now. Talk. Spill." Fallon playfully flutters her eyelids, showing off a daring shade of eyeshadow while smiling widely. "Give me everything you have on 'Welcome to my villain era' Nathan West, then we can switch to what really matters, Benjamin Bancroft."

"He's so nice," I say dreamily. "And a thousand times better looking in person, if you can believe it.

They both are, assuming you can get past Nathan's attitude." I reach for the bottle of wine sitting on the coffee table. "I can't get past it, by the way. I mean, I have to for the job's sake. For Mom's sake. But, well, you know. Rich assholes just aren't my thing. Especially when they emphasize the asshole part."

Fallon plucks an oversized wine glass off the designer coffee table she was so proud to bring home and holds it out for me. I fill it to the top. She widens her eyes when I do the same to mine. "How is your mom? Any better?"

"So much better. This treatment center is going to be everything she needs. I can feel it."

"And once you get paid, you can afford it." Fallon arches a brow.

She wasn't a fan of my decision to enroll Mom in the clinic before the money from Nathan's project came in. But I couldn't watch her wither away. Not when help is available. His retainer fee was enough to get her started and I have room in my design schedule to add more clients. I'm not afraid of hard work and I don't need much sleep. I'd rather be broke and tired, but know she's taken care of than sit on a pile of money like a dragon protecting its hoard. Besides, it's not like I do much with my evenings and weekends. Why not fill the time with work?

I arch a brow in return. "Which is why I'm not letting Nathan West bother me."

"You might consider asking him for your full fee up front. Or at least part of it."

"Sure. Right. The man is every bit as awful as you made him out to be, and it's already clear he judges me for being poor. So I should definitely ask him to give me money before the work's been done, even though our contract clearly states I'll be paid at the end unless I need to make purchases along the way."

"You're the one who enrolled your mom in the program before you had the money." Fallon holds up her hands. "I know. I know. Her condition was deteriorating. She couldn't wait. No judgment."

I cock my head. "I mean, some judgment."

"I just worry because I love you." She sighs dramatically before taking a large gulp of wine then says, "I still think you should consider asking him for an advance."

I pout as I bring the sloshing glass to my lips and take a hefty swallow. "Can't," I say, then take another sip for good measure, "he's a narrow-minded asshole who was nice to Benjamin and rude to me."

I drink again, caught up in the unfairness of the meeting. Fallon raises her eyebrows and takes another large gulp herself.

"Nathan West used to be as kind and chivalrous as

you could imagine. Hot, but humble. Rich, but generous. Smart, but down to earth. Driven, but, well, you get the point." She shakes her head as she stares into the distance. "I'm telling you, Mina. Anyone who ended up with him would have won the relationship lottery. But something happened with that girlfriend because he went downhill fast after they broke up. I haven't figured out why yet, but I'll keep digging... unless you happen to hear something and feel like passing it on."

"We've been over this. I'm not snitching on my client. It's wrong and you know it." I say, blinking to refocus my eyes before taking another swallow of wine from a glass that is becoming decidedly difficult to handle. I wrap both hands around it and bring it to my lips like a bowl to take another slurp. "Besides, you're supposed to be making me feel better, not turning me into a spy. Let's talk about anything but stupid Nathan West and his stupid self being nice to stupid Benjamin but not me."

Stupid men and their stupid stupidness.

"Except Benjamin's not stupid," we say in unison, then burst into laughter.

"He's nice," I say, thinking of Nathan cutting me off halfway through my introduction, those broad shoulders blotting out the sun like the villain he is.

"And he's talented," Fallon adds.

I nod, remembering the way Nathan glared with those thorny eyes. "And Benjamin's smile feels like sunshine. I like being around people that feel good."

Fallon finishes off her mega glass of wine and pours another. "And he's already made a name for himself with the kind of clients you want to add to your roster. Leveraging this relationship could be a big break for you, Meens."

"Maybe."

Her words float around my vin santo rosso filled brain and several seconds pass before they bump into my conscience. "Yeah, but I want to focus on how hot he is, not what he can do for me. He's a person not an opportunity. It's better to objectify him than to scheme ways to use him to my advantage, right?"

"Give me your phone." Fallon holds out her hand expectantly.

"What? Why?" I ask, already passing it her way.

"It's nothing." Her smirk says it's definitely something as she holds the phone up to my face to unlock it, then starts tapping away at the screen.

"What are you doing?" I ask, nervous now.

"Playing Cupid." She's typing, her smile growing more and more mischievous.

"Fallon. No. Give me back my phone."

"You're right. It's better to objectify him...especially if he knows it's happening."

"I have to work with this guy!" I stand and grab for my phone. She jerks it away. "Stop playing Cupid!"

"I want you to know I've had a crush on you for a long time," Fallon reads as she types, twisting out of my grasp. "You're hot. And smart. And sweet. And talented. And I think we could really be something together. PS—Is it wrong if I dream about sinking my teeth into your ass?"

"Do not send that text." I make another move for the phone and she holds it away, wriggling it playfully. "Fallon...be careful..."

"I'm not gonna send it, you goof. I'm drunk, not dumb." She gives the phone one more wriggle as she hands it over. It slips from her hands, but I catch it with my catlike reflexes. Okay, my fumbling, bumbling, just-drank-a-bowl-of-wine reflexes. I drop it two more times before I finally get a good hold on it, then laugh as I plop back onto the couch.

"How's that catch for a drunk klutz like me, huh? Where's that capital K now?"

I unlock the phone to delete the text, but the chat box is empty. My heart stops. My jaw drops.

Why is it empty?

Where did the text go?

I blink several times and find the missing message, right beneath Benjamin's reply...*to the group chat with our super important but not at all nice client!*

A man who just hired me for a job that pays enough to finally get Mom the help she needs.

A man who already doesn't like me for some inexplicable reason.

How the hell am I going to explain this?

"Oh, shit." I look to Fallon, feeling the color drain from my face. I never knew that was something you could feel before now.

Her brows furrow into a look only a best friend can give. A look that says she knows exactly how much trouble I'm capable of getting myself into.

"Oh shit, what?"

"I sent it."

"You *what* it?"

"I sent it."

Her jaw drops. "You didn't."

"I did! I must have hit send when I caught my phone! Oh my God! I *am* a klutz!" My eyes widen as the full ramifications of what just happened sifts like dust through my wine-numbed brain.

My phone rumbles with a text. I've never heard a more ominous sound. Biting my bottom lip, I read Nathan's response. A single question mark.

I might be sick.

"That text didn't just go to Benjamin," I say, biting my thumbnail as the full weight of what just happened lands. "That went to a group chat. With Nathan West. Fallon!"

And now I know what it looks like to watch color drain from a face. "Oh my God! Meens! I'm so sorry. This is all my fault."

"What am I going to do?"

There's a moment of stunned silence and then, just like that, an idea forms.

"I don't like that look," Fallon says.

"What look?" I ask, pulling up Nathan's contact info.

"The one that says you think you know how to solve a problem but maybe should talk this idea of yours through before you do something impulsive."

Still chewing my thumbnail, I stare at the call button, then, after a quirk of my head to my best friend, I stab the thing and put my phone to my ear.

FOUR

Nathan

**Alert:
Search term "Nathan West" mentioned one time online:
Holy Villain Era, Batman! Former Do-Gooder Nathan West Builds Lair on Sketchy Cove. You'll Never Believe What He's Up to Now!**

I sit at my desk, staring at my laptop, flicking through Fallon Mae's latest hit piece on me while sipping whiskey, the "never again" promises I made myself this morning overpowered by the indignation of yet another shitty article from a woman who sounds like she hates me. My head throbs from the growing realization that I owe Mina Blake an apology after our meeting this morning. Probably Bancroft too, though I think Mina took the brunt of my frustration.

What would Fallon say if she knew I was home alone tonight, instead of out with another "dazzling and spectacular" starlet?

In my modest house?

At my modest desk?

Worrying what my interior designer thinks of me instead of living some insane lifestyle of the rich, famous, and potentially evil?

Does that sound like a man entering his villain era? Not to me. And I should know. I've been spending time with that type a lot lately.

What would Fallon say if she knew all those nights out were calculated moves to secure donations to expand the Reversal of Fortune Foundation, the charity I've worked at since high school? What would she say if she knew the women were for Dom? That I've deemed myself damn near celibate after being taken advantage of by Blossom? Would she still condemn me? Or would she be more understanding? Or maybe my famous parents negate the fact that I'm a human being with feelings and imperfections.

I know Fallon's type. She grew up poor and resents all the opportunity I had, that she didn't. And you know, I could understand that resentment, if she channeled it into something positive. A drive for more. A desire to better herself or, better yet, the world around her. Instead, she turns everything I do into a failure, publishes it for the world to see...and sounds gleeful while doing it.

My phone buzzes and I grab it out of habit. I'm not in the mood to talk to people tonight. I'm not in the mood for much of anything tonight. I almost put it right back down on my desk, but Mina Blake's name catches my attention. The hot mess express I caught pep-talking herself this morning. It would have been cute if it hadn't been so hopeless. Endearing, if she hadn't immediately lumped me into a box labeled "other" with that comment about a man like me deserving to get what I want.

There's something about the woman that makes me...what?

She sets off my internal alarms...but why?

Something tells me I should stay far, far away from her.

Despite that being true, curiosity wins and I read

Mina's message anyway, one that came into the group chat with Benjamin, the architect my cousin Mason recommended after giving me a dissertation on the wonderful, up-and-coming interior designer he adores working with.

"What the fuck?" I murmur, bringing the screen closer to stare at a text talking about crushes, drinks, and biting asses. My mind instantly supplies an image of Mina's luscious rear end and I chase it away with a swig of whiskey.

"Hello, hot mess express," I whisper, reading the text one more time before sending a single question mark in response.

It's not like she left me a lot of options with that one.

Seconds later, my phone buzzes with a call from Mina. I let it ring once. Twice. A third time. Once more and it'll go to voicemail, which is definitely the best outcome.

I accept the call at the last minute.

"First of all, please let me apologize for my unprofessional behavior," Mina says after I answer. "I can assure you; this is not typical of me."

Her words are too bright. Her optimism forced. She's panicking, and...drunk?

"And second of all?" I prompt, then cringe. That came out harsher than I intended. I'm swimming in uncomfortable waters here. Dom knows how to handle situations like this. Not me. I shouldn't have answered the phone.

"I, uh..." There's a long pause followed by a deep sigh and then, "I have a favor to ask you."

"A favor?"

"Yeah. Yes. Um. A favor. I was wondering if you could pretend that text was for you." Mina's words are slurred and fever pitched. They hit me hard enough that I pull the phone away from my ear.

"I'm sorry, you want me to do what?" I ask, slowly.

"That text. The one in the group chat. I didn't mean to send it and it's going to create a lot of trouble and if you could just—"

"Ahh, yes. The 'I didn't mean to send the text' chestnut." I lean forward, elbows resting on my desk, intrigued. So, Mina has a crush on Benjamin. Something about the thought of them together bugs me, though I couldn't say why. Probably the lack of professionalism.

Mina half-sighs, half-groans. "No, really. This was truly an accident. I'm having drinks with my friend and I was talking about how awful our meeting went and—"

"You thought our meeting was awful?"

Damn it. I knew I owed her an apology. I sip my

whiskey, hoping it'll burn away whatever is making my stomach twist and turn and sink into my feet.

"Yes! Oh my God it was so awful!" Mina blows a puff of air into the phone. "You're supposed to be my dream client, and you were so rude. But only to me. For some reason you were super nice to Benjamin and—"

"And that made you want to admit your crush on him in a group chat and invite him for drinks so you can bite his ass." I sit back and rest my ankle on my knee, ice clinking in my glass as Mina Blake, Hot Mess Express, huffs a sigh.

"You have no idea how embarrassed I am right now. I swear to you, this is not like me, and all I want from Benjamin is a professional relationship. So, could you please pretend that text was for you? I know it's a big ask, but..." There's the murmur of another voice in the distance and Mina grunts in frustration. "Shh. Damn it. Leave me alone."

"Which is it?" I ask, a half-grin slowly lifting one cheek. "Should I leave you alone? Or pretend that text was for me?"

"I wasn't telling you to leave me alone. I was talking to my friend who seems to think I'm making a hot mess of this entire conversation." There's a quick whispered argument that has me laughing.

God, it feels good to laugh.

I really do need to do that more.

And I've done it twice in one day thanks to Mina Blake, Hot Mess Express—even her friend agrees.

"I bet I'd like this friend of yours. We seem to think along the same lines."

"Of course you would. She's awesome and she loves you. But you're distracting me from the point. Again. Please. *Please*. Just respond to my text like it was for you."

"Now why would I do that, Hot Mess?"

"Because I've followed Benjamin's career for a long time and I'm kind of in awe of working with him and my friend decided to play Cupid but I dropped my phone and, you know what? None of that matters. What matters is that Benjamin and I will work really well together and you're going to love the house we come up with for you."

"Will you be biting his ass when he designs my home? I won't love having that image in my head every time I walk through the door."

Mina groans and the sound goes straight to my dick. Okay. Was not expecting that. It must not be as big a fan of this celibacy idea as I am.

"I know I'm making a terrible impression," Mina says, "but please, hear me out. I *may* be a few too many. I mean... I've had a little drunk. I mean..."

"Easy now. Don't hurt yourself."

"And this isn't like me at all. I'm really excited

about this project, and I would hate to lose an opportunity like this because Benjamin gets the wrong idea from a joke he wasn't supposed to be part of. Believe me, I regret everything that's happened in the last twenty minutes and I swear to you, this is not typical of me."

"As you've said."

"If you could please pretend that text is for you," Mina continues, as if she didn't hear me, "I promise I will do everything in my power to make this process as smooth as silk from this point forward."

I close my eyes and pinch my forehead, my dick enjoying the phrase 'smooth as silk' more than I'd like. "Are you done?"

"Yes. I think so." Mina takes a deep breath. "Well, no, there's one more thing I should say. I'd like to thank you for your time and consideration," she finishes proudly while laughter twinkles in the background. "I do not sound like an overly formal email, thank you very much," she whisper-hisses before returning to her normal voice. "Will you please help me?"

My impulsive answer is yes. This woman is asking for my help, and it would take very little effort on my part to give. But these are the situations I'm trying to avoid, the kind that end with me being taken advantage of in ways I never saw coming because I'm blind to narcissism, sociopathy, and ulterior motives.

So I grit my teeth and give an answer that makes me instantly uncomfortable. "No."

"No?" Mina sounds as appalled as I feel.

"No." I switch the phone to my other ear. "I've made it my official policy to leave hot messes alone to do their thing. Effective immediately."

"You are so incredibly disappointing. I know, I know," she says to whoever's listening to her end of the call. "It's his villain era. You're right. I should have known better."

Fucking villain era. The words tighten my jaw, my fists, my throat. Did the whole world read Fallon Mae's article this morning? "Good night, Miss Blake," I say, sorry I answered the call.

"Wait!"

I pause, finger hovering over the 'end' button despite myself.

"Did you hang up? Oh, man! He hung up." Mina sounds so crestfallen, I put the phone back to my ear.

"I'm waiting, as requested."

"I'll…I'll drop my fee by ten percent."

The argument on the other end of the phone increases by a decibel or two. Mina's shrieking friend confirms my suspicion. Money is tight for Ms. Blake.

Old Nathan would tell Mina paying me isn't necessary, but what should New Nathan say? She's so ready to cast me in the role of the villain,

I'd hate to disappoint her more than I already have.

I pinch my forehead and say the first thing that comes to mind. "Make it ninety and I'll consider."

Good God. Did that really come out of my mouth?

"Ninety percent?" Mina sounds appropriately offended. "I think you know exactly what to do with that offer. And I sincerely doubt you would have said anything like that to Benjamin."

"I doubt Benjamin would find himself in this position."

"I need this money, Mr. West," Mina continues, ignoring my game winning point. "And more than that, I'm worth this money."

"What do you need more?" asks the villain. "The money? Or a chance to convince Benjamin Bancroft it's my ass you're drooling over instead of his?"

There's a long pause and then, "You really are The Prince of Darkness, aren't you?"

She sounds even more disappointed, and I don't like the way it feels, but I shut it down by throwing back the rest of my whiskey. If it's a villain she wants, it's a villain she gets.

"Take it or leave it, Miss Blake."

"Fifty percent," she counters, despite a less than quiet argument from her friend.

"Seventy."

"Sixty."

"Done. Have a better day, Hot Mess." I end the call and stare at the group chat, chewing my lip as I reread Mina's text. Who types something like that into a chat as a joke? And worse, who accidentally hits send while dropping a phone?

Sitting back, I stare at the ceiling while I think, then grin as I come up with the perfect response to earn the sixty percent discount I just negotiated on Miss Blake's interior design services.

> Dear Hot Mess Express... As I've mentioned before, discussing your lifelong crush on me is inappropriate, especially in group chats.
>
> Let's move this to a private thread.

Chuckling to myself, I close my laptop and head to bed, my mood inexplicably brighter than it was twenty minutes ago.

FIVE

Nathan

Muffled voices outside my office door drag my attention from the proposal I've been working on for the foundation's upcoming charity gala. I need one more quiet hour to put the finishing touches on this thing, but the hubbub sounds like someone out there has big enough balls to go toe to toe with my assistant.

My intercom buzzes with her voice close behind. "I'm very sorry to bother you, Mr. West, especially after you specifically asked not to be disturbed." There's a long, passive aggressive pause and if I know Rita MacDonald, there's a matching look shooting through her Elton John worthy glasses. "But I have a Mr. Dominick Taylor here for you," she continues. "He claims it's urgent."

If anyone is a match for Rita, it's Dom. He doesn't believe the word "no" applies to him.

So much for finishing that proposal.

"Send him in."

The door swings open and Dom steps in. He's dressed in white slacks, a light blue button down with the top three buttons undone, and a dark gray blazer with loafers, no socks. Very trendy. Very expensive. He claims the look makes him ready for business or pleasure at a moment's notice and so far, he's been right. Dom never looks like he's working but is always in the middle of seducing someone out of their money...or their clothes.

He closes the door and leans on the wall, hands shoved in pockets, dark eyebrows raised. "You spend too much time in this office."

Great. It's gonna be one of those days where I get lectured on my dedication to work.

"I can't wish this expansion into existence." I tear my focus from the screen and sit back. "The work has to get done."

"The work can get done elsewhere. If you weren't chained to your desk, I wouldn't have to battle that walking spreadsheet you call an admin to tell you Frederick Chantal is hosting a reception tonight." Dom pauses as if he's relayed sufficient information for me to understand the reason behind his visit.

"Good for Frederick Chantal." I highlight a worthless line in the proposal and smash the delete key. "And be nice to Rita. I'd be lost without her."

"You'd be lost without *me*. Come on, Nathan. Leave the office for the worker bees and spend time with people who like spending money. That isn't wishing the expansion into existence. That's being smart enough to use the tools at your disposal."

"Tell me why I care about Frederick Chantal?"

"Because he's new money." Dom quirks his lips in distaste. "He made his fortune in tech under some seriously shady circumstances. Now he's looking to prove he isn't the asshole the media's making him out to be."

"Good for him." I type the beginning of a new line, hate it, delete it, and glare at the screen. "I love hearing these success stories. It's inspiring to know humanity is so generous and altruistic."

"Do I really need to spell it out for you?" Dom scoffs. "Don't you think making a large donation to a well-known charity might be exactly the proof our friend Frederick is looking for?"

"He doesn't sound like the kind of friend I'm looking for." I get enough shit from the family for hanging out with Dom. He's not a bad guy, but he's not necessarily a good one either. That's enough for the people in my life to write him off.

"Damn it, Nathan. I despise these moods of yours.

If you really want to save the world, you're gonna need money. And it's time to face facts. Nothing is as perfect as you want it to be. People are people. We do shitty things from time to time, brother." Dom pushes off the wall to lean on the desk. "Bring a date to Frederick's thing. Might fix this permanently bitchy mood of yours."

"Not gonna happen."

After Blossom took advantage of me, I wrapped my bleeding heart in barbed wire. No one, and I mean no one, will mistake my kindness for weakness again. The first step to making sure that stays true is that healthy dose of self-imposed celibacy my dick didn't seem so interested in last night.

Dom eyes me, then sighs in relief. "At least you didn't give me the barbed wire speech again," he says, then pauses, looking disappointed. "But you were thinking it, weren't you? Come on, Nathan. You're young. Rich. Attractive. You were dealt a winning hand. Play it, for fuck's sake." Dom straightens. "I'll send you the details so we can talk about it when you're not being a stubborn ass."

"Gee, Dom. Love you too," I say as he leaves, passing my cousin Nick Hutton on his way out.

On paper, they're nearly identical. Both men come from wealthy families, both have personalities that demand respect and are driven to make their mark on the world. Both are tall, with dark hair and strong builds, but that's where the similarities stop. Nick's Marine training makes him more physically imposing, but only until you strike up a conversation and get a taste of Dom's razor-sharp intellect. Nick sees the good in everyone he meets, while Dom can suss out an ulterior motive in seconds. They exchange a lukewarm greeting for my benefit.

"My God! He lives!" Nick gives Rita a knowing look before he steps into my office. He's always felt more like a big brother than a cousin. Younger me looked up to him like the sun rose and set on his shoulders, and if I'm honest, older me still does. He's just one of those guys you want in your corner.

I stand to offer a back thumping hug. "Was there any doubt?"

Nick runs a hand over freshly cropped dark hair—a clear sign he's frustrated—then chews his bottom lip—a sign he's trying to hide it. "Seeing as you only leave this room to give that journalist ammo for her articles, there's been talk we might need to stage an intervention at your birthday party this Friday."

With a deep sigh, I drop back into my chair. "Not funny."

"I agree." Nick swipes a hand over his mouth. "Self-destruction didn't need a new poster child, man."

I rest my ankle on my knee, arms crossed in defiance. This might be the first time I *don't* want him in my corner, if that's how he sees me.

"Self-destruction? Really?" I fire back. "I'm pouring myself into work—a charity, mind you—because I might be onto something that could make a difference for a lot of people. Gosh, Nick. I think you're right. I do need an intervention instead of a birthday party."

Currently, ROF's focus is on supporting underprivileged children, but with the economy crushing the middle class there are more and more adults who need help too. People are sick and unable to afford care, even with medical insurance. People need jobs. Or education. Or hell, a roof over their head and food in the fridge. I want to expand the foundation's scope to include anyone who needs a reversal of fortune—young, old, and in between.

Because Dom is right.

I was dealt a winning hand.

And this is how I intend to play it.

Nick pulls out his phone, unlocks the screen, and reads, "Nathan West's fall from grace is punctuated by dazzling women decorating his arm, spectacular starlets whose fame insulates them from the dumpster fire that is the former philanthropist's entrance into his villain era..." He glances up, one eyebrow arched. "Villain era, Nathan. This isn't you."

Fucking Fallon Mae. If I ever meet her, I'll ruin her. And while I'm at it, I'll take down anyone connected to her. Friends, family, even distant cousins will feel my wrath.

"This isn't my villain era."

Though Mina Blake would disagree. Only a villain would charge an obscene amount of money just to send a text.

Nick pulls out a chair and takes a seat. "You're building some kind of lair—"

Fuck me. Apparently, my cousin disagrees as well.

I sit back in my chair and scowl. "It's not a lair."

"You're drinking. Spending nights out with women—"

"The women are for Dom."

"You grunt and scowl and sneer..."

I fold my arms over my chest and huff. "I do not grunt," I say through gritted teeth.

"You just did!" Nick glances up as our aunt Maisie appears in the doorway. Her blonde hair swoops down her back in casual waves, offset by a smart pair of black slacks, a fitted blouse, and heels that look like they could kill a person.

"You heard that, right?" Nick asks, with a wide grin. "Nathan grunted to prove he doesn't grunt."

"And he's scowling," Maisie replies, smiling

through sad eyes. "Maybe everyone's right about this whole intervention thing."

I drop a hand on my desk and my companions jump. "I don't need an intervention! I'm not doing drugs. I'm not self-destructing. Blossom cheated after using me for my money, and I'm channeling my disappointment into building something better for the people who really need it. I don't see how what I'm doing is wrong!"

"The late nights, the drinking, the questionable company." Aunt Maisie glances at Nick, who nods in sage agreement, which makes sense since she bullet-pointed everything he said two minutes ago.

I laugh to myself. What will they think after I spend an evening with Frederick Chantal?

"Your actions are tainting the reputation of the foundation. The reputation I've spent decades building." Aunt Maisie's features aren't designed for judgment. It sits uncomfortably on her pretty face as she seeks out my gaze. "How are we supposed to help those who need it when every time there's a headline with your name on it, we lose credibility?"

"Fallon Mae is misrepresenting me." And if anyone should know that it would be the people standing across from me.

"Maybe that would be easier to believe if you surrounded yourself with less..." Maisie glances at

Nick. "What did she call the women he's out with all the time?"

"Dazzling and spectacular." He says the words like he's describing a criminal enterprise.

Maisie flares her hands. "You don't need dazzling and spectacular to secure donations."

"The women are for Dom. Not me."

"That's not the way it looks in the pictures, Nathan," she continues, her posture softening from that of the CEO of a deeply respected charity, to the aunt who hosted sleepovers and taught us to build blanket forts. "You are so much better than the way you look online."

"Maybe if I wasn't being misrepresented," I grumble, then hold up my hands because they won't leave me alone until I concede. "But I hear you. I'll try to keep myself out of the headlines."

"Good." Aunt Maisie closes her eyes and clears her throat. She glances at the floor, then meets my gaze and I don't like what I see there. "Because the charity gala is in a few months. If you can't get your act together, I don't want you there, especially if there's going to be anyone dazzling or spectacular on your arm."

There's a charged moment where everyone seems to want to say something but chooses silence instead. With a sigh, Maisie turns and leaves the room.

"I'm not a villain," I say, more for my benefit than anything.

"Don't read any of Fallon Mae's articles or you're in for a rude awakening."

I grumble something about Ms. Mae being in for a rude awakening if we ever meet and Nick shakes his head.

"Just try to hear what we're saying. The whole family's worried. There are good women out there and you'll find one when the time is right. Just because Blossom is a parasitic nozzle muncher doesn't mean everyone works that way."

Fuck finding another woman. That's not gonna happen. Ever. I almost launch into my speech about wrapping my heart in barbed wire but stop myself before Nick can make fun of me too.

"I'm listening," I lie.

"That's all I ask. Opportunity will present itself. Something good is coming your way. Keep your eyes open so you recognize it when it walks in. In the meantime, pick yourself up, dust yourself off, and get back to being Nathan Fucking West."

"Pretty sure that's what I'm in the middle of doing."

Nick sighs deeply and shoves his hands into his pockets, chewing on a thought he's not sure he should express. "Friday? Your birthday party?" he finally says. "If you bring a date—"

"I'm not bringing a date." Maybe I should have hit him with my barbed wire speech after all.

"Okay, fine. But if you do, it might put everyone's mind at ease if she wasn't the kind of woman who'd catch Dominick Taylor's eye."

We say our goodbyes and I sit there, replaying the last couple days in my head, Dom insinuating I'm squandering a winning hand, Aunt Maisie telling me to skip the charity gala when it's my favorite part of the year, Mina calling, drunk and desperate...

Huh.

Look at that.

Maybe the opportunity Nick mentioned already presented itself in the form of an accidental message and a drunken request. Maybe I can keep that barbed wire around my heart *and* put my family's mind at ease.

I'll ask Mina Blake to pretend to be my new, non-dazzling or spectacular girlfriend.

It'll be a little "extension" to our business relationship.

After the utterly dickish move of cutting her fee to send that text, I'll have to offer to pay her.

But that could actually work in my favor.

That would make it a business arrangement, bound by professionalism.

What could go wrong?

SIX

Mina

A heady mix of guilt and excitement hits my belly as I pull into Shady Cove Restorative Clinic. I'm always glad to see my mom. She was my first best friend. My rock. She worked her ass off to take care of me after Dad left and was the perfect blend of "shoulder to cry on" and "get your butt in gear." She was strong and beautiful and held her chin up no matter what life threw in our direction.

When I was thirteen, she sold the house she bought with my father. It was a handyman's dream and they planned to pour time and attention into it over the years until they ended up with the kind of home they deserved. Only, Dad was the handy one in the family and Mom couldn't keep up with the repairs after he left. Rather than trying to pay someone she couldn't afford to do the work, she moved the two of us into an apartment.

When I was fifteen, she took a second job. She never said why, never once complained, though I know she took on the extra work to pay for my driver's ed classes and to start saving for my first car.

When I was sixteen, I got a job within walking distance from home so I could buy that car myself. I tried to help pay for other things around the house, but Mom wouldn't take my money. Thankfully, I inherited my father's stubborn streak and stocked the fridge anyway. Bought my own clothes so she wouldn't have to. Picked up little extras I knew she wouldn't buy herself.

When I was seventeen, she told me about the money she was saving for my college tuition and by the time I was eighteen, I'd earned a full ride so she could keep it for herself.

I swore I'd earn my degree and become so successful, she never had to struggle again. I'd build her a house and pay her bills and give her the life she deserved.

She's struggling now more than ever, but I'm doing everything I can to put an end to that.

A smile lifts my lips as tears well in my eyes. I brush them away, smooth the front of my shirt, and stride through the front doors, pausing to sign in at the front desk before navigating the hive of brightly colored hallways to find my mother. If it weren't for the patients in wheelchairs, or trundling by with IV stands, you wouldn't know this was a medical facility. It looks more like an upscale community center.

When I finally duck my head through the door of room 208, I find Mom propped up in bed, eyes closed, breathing deeply as Spanish guitar flows through speakers on her bedside table. Fresh flowers bloom on the counter in the tiny kitchenette. Sunlight pours through the curtains she brought from home. Pictures adorn the walls, some she's had for years and others she made in the art therapy classes here at Shady Cove.

She's humming to herself; more content than I've seen her in a while. I lean in the doorway and watch, lost in memories of her grabbing me by the hand and spinning us into a dance in the kitchen while she hummed whatever song filled her heart that day. Mom worked long hours, followed by a race home to cook dinner because she promised me I'd never feel alone after Dad left. She kept that promise until I learned to cook and kept it for her. That's what we did. We took care of each other.

And I'm going to keep on taking care of her until she can do it herself again.

I sniffle and Mom jumps, turning to me with a

gasp. "Mina! Sweet Jesus!" She covers her heart with her hand then starts laughing. "How long you been there?"

"Long enough to see you need some of these." I heft a bag of fresh mangoes from a nearby farmer's market. "They're not mango fritters from Tineil's Bakery, but they're the next best thing."

Mom's crooked smile springs to life and she waves me over, her eyes filled with vitality for the first time in a long time. "They're organic right? You know how Shady Cove is about pesticides and stuff."

"Organic. Grown locally. I wouldn't dare go against your doctor's orders." Perching on the edge of Mom's bed, I wrap my arms around her and bury my face in her shoulder, breathing deeply. Her floral perfume soothes tension I didn't know was hiding in my neck and jaw.

She cups my cheeks. Smooths my hair. Her eyes literally glisten with love. "I was just about to make some burdock root tea. I'll make enough for both of us, and you can tell me all about your meeting with that fancy architect and new client."

"Yum?" I wrinkle my nose, mostly in jest. The dieticians have Mom eating and drinking some strange concoctions, trying to meet her unique dietary needs so her body can finish healing. Burdock root tea is just another entry in a string of unusual food.

Mom pushes into a sitting position and swings her legs off the bed, then closes her eyes and takes a shuddering breath, gripping the mattress like her life depends on it.

I spring into action like the seasoned pro I am, clutching her shoulder in case she falls. "Here, Mom. You sit. I'll make the tea."

Two years ago, Mom got sick. Just your ordinary, run of the mill, spend a day or two in bed with the sniffles and then life goes on kind of sick.

Except life didn't go on.

Mom got worse and worse, too tired to feed herself. Too weak to sit up. Pain wracked her body and confusion stole the sassy spitfire who raised me and left an old woman in her place. After countless trips to the ER followed by visits with every specialist in the area, they slapped her with a diagnosis of chronic fatigue syndrome, told us there was no cure, and that was that.

It might as well have been a death sentence. She was alive, but she wasn't living. I refused to believe that was the best the world had to offer.

I spent hours researching online, devouring patient testimonials and the latest medical research, desperate to find something to bring her back to herself. I even called Dad, though to this day I don't know what I expected from that. Whatever it was, I didn't find it.

Then I found Shady Cove, an inpatient facility

with medical, functional, and integrative doctors onsite, claiming to treat the individual, not the symptoms. The success stories had hope blooming in my heart for the first time since Mom slipped into bed and never slipped out.

But the best care comes with a price tag to match.

I made it my mission to find the money, which the universe graciously provided with Nathan West's project.

And now she's here.

And she's going to get better.

Though the discount The Prince of Darkness negotiated last night threw a serious wrench in my gears. Finances were tight before my brush with the villain. Now? I'll have to say yes to every financial opportunity that comes my way, no matter what it is. I may even have to pick up a second job for evenings and weekends in addition to the extra clients I'm adding.

Whatever it is, however strange, however unappealing, if it pays, I'll do it.

For Mom.

"No, no." My mother waves me off. "They want me moving around more. This is nothing but a little bout of dizziness. Doc Morgan says it's my overactive nervous system trying to keep me safe, and I need to remind myself that I'm already safe." Mom closes her eyes and takes several measured breaths. I watch as color returns to her cheeks.

"See?" she says, just as I decide to help her back into bed and choose another day for a visit. "All better. I just got back from PT, so I'm a little tired, but I have a massage to look forward to later. And my neurologist will be by after that to discuss my medications and supplements. Every time she tinkers with those, I feel a little better."

"I should have picked a less busy day for a visit."

"I can't tell you how good it feels to be able to have a busy day." Mom hits me with a smile I haven't seen in a long time. She stands and shuffles towards the kitchenette, looking pleased as punch. Six months ago, she couldn't go to the bathroom on her own. A month of dedicated treatment and she's making me tea.

I was right to secure her place here the moment I accepted Nathan West's offer, even though I couldn't afford it yet.

I was less right to negotiate away the money he owes me so he'd send a shitty text, but that's what I get for drinking bowls of wine with Fallon.

But... I'm resourceful and determined.

Mom won't lose this momentum. There's a way to afford the full round of treatment and the second I find it, I'll snatch it up lickety-split. In the meantime, there's room on my credit cards and I'm sure I'll qualify for a loan if we get there.

"Tell me about this meeting." She fills her tea kettle with filtered water and places it on the stove. "Was it everything you hoped it would be?"

"Yes and no." I don't usually keep things from Mom, but I don't want to tell her my new dream client is rude. She'd worry. Just like if I told her how much it cost for her to be here, she'd worry. And if she knew I was spending money I didn't already have, she'd worry.

And worrying isn't good for her.

"That is not the enthusiastic answer I expected. What went wrong?"

"Nothing, nothing. Not really. Benjamin Bancroft is every bit as talented as the magazines made him out to be. And he's even better looking in person. And so easy to be around. I have no business working with someone like him—"

Mom holds up a hand. "You do though. You might not have the name yet, but you're every bit as talented as this guy."

"I hope that proves true. If he likes working with me, this could really be a jumpstart to my career. Plus, he's so very, *very* pretty."

Nathan West is prettier, whispers a grinning voice in the back of my head.

As long as you like assholes, I reply, then realize part of me must, since I'm the one who brought it up in the first place.

Mom pulls two misshapen mugs out of a cabinet with a sheepish grin. "I made this one in pottery class last week," she says, pointing to a chunky blue mug with a slight lean to the left. "It's hideous, but I love it and I swore my next one would be better but..." She lifts a green one that looks like it's melting. "Maybe I'll do better next time?"

I take the thing in my hands, laughing as I turn it over. "Does it even hold liquid?"

She snatches it back, eyes wide with good humor. "Of course it holds liquid! Just because it's not perfect doesn't mean it's worthless. Now tell me about this other guy. The one I suspect is the reason you're not as excited as you should be."

"He's not exactly easy to be around."

"People who can afford designers and architects usually have a chip on their shoulder."

"He had a full concrete block on that thing. He's rude, Mom. Just plain rude."

"Good thing your hot architect makes up for it, huh? Focus on him, on his positivity, and don't even let the client into your headspace. He's a means to an end, that's all."

I dip my chin, not ready to concede her point. I

want to believe in the fairy tale version of Nathan West, the one where he's good instead of bitter and if I make a snap judgment I'll miss out on a wonderful connection.

"Learn from my mistakes, Meens," Mom says with a look that says she knows what I'm thinking. "Life is harsh enough without letting harsh people in. I knew from the get-go that your dad was wrong for me, but I saw this glimmer of goodness in him and focused on that instead of who he really was. Your client? He's not worth your energy. You give him the time he pays you for and nothing more. Like I said, he's a means to an end. That's all."

"A paycheck," I reply, hefting my melting green mug.

The most important paycheck I've ever earned.

SEVEN

Mina

The sun is bright. My coffee is just the way I like it, warm and creamy and sweet. The sky is blue, Mom's getting better, and Benjamin Bancroft doesn't think I want to bite his ass, thanks to Nathan West and his meanspirited, expensive text. All that alone would add up to a wonderful Friday, but there's a bonus on my schedule that makes this a fantastic intro to the weekend.

"Miss Blake?" Tad, my too hot to be real assistant, pops his head into my office. "Mason Channing is here to go over the plans for the custom bookshelves on the Maharishi project." The twinkle in Tad's eyes as he leans against the doorframe says this meeting is the bonus in his schedule too.

Not only is Mason Channing dark-haired and dark-eyed, with muscley arms and strong hands, but he's smart and funny and one of the most talented carpenters I've collaborated with, eclipsed only by his father, Joe. Together, they run Channing Construction and I've had the pleasure of working with both father and son on multiple projects.

Mason doesn't flirt and neither do I. Not really. Or, not seriously. He's just so good looking and so funny that sitting in the same room with him for twenty minutes is enough to make me smile for the next hour. He's one of those people who feel like sunshine—the complete opposite of Nathan West, Prince of Darkness. A man who grunts and growls and builds a villain's lair on a secluded cove just because he can.

Sixty percent off my fee just to send one little text! And that's after negotiating! What happened to him?

I smooth my hair and check my breath, cross, then uncross my legs before I settle on leaning my elbows on my desk and perching my chin in my hands. "Thank you, Tad. Please send Mr. Channing in."

"Wilhelmina! How's my favorite interior designer?" Mason steps into my office with a broad smile and a gleam in his eyes.

I stand and extend a hand, almost giddy as his firm grip envelops mine. "I don't know how many times I have to tell you that I'm just plain Mina."

"About as many times as I have to tell you there's nothing plain about you." He pulls out a chair and takes a seat before proposing some changes on the custom-built wall bookcase Rajesh Maharishi wants added to his home office. The meeting is fast and fun, and the changes Mason introduces are smart as well as economical. As suspected, it's the feather in the cap of my already fabulous morning.

"Oh, hey!" Mason pauses as he stands from his chair. "I heard you're working with Nathan West on his new house."

"Don't get too excited for me," I say, assuming he's about to congratulate me on my good fortune. "I was so excited when I got the offer, I wanted to throw a party for whoever recommended me to him. But then I had my first meeting with Mr. Nathan West and, well—" I lean forward conspiratorially "—he's kind of an asshole."

Mason grimaces. "He's also kind of my cousin."

Dear God. Please remind me to stop shoving my foot in my mouth. Sincerely, Mina Blake.

"I'm sorry, he's your what now?" I ask, then bask in the glow of my eloquence.

"My cousin. I'm the one who recommended you to Nathan and I totally expect that party in my honor," Mason says with his characteristic smile.

Of course they're related. I mean, not of course. I

can't think of anyone who would connect those dots on their own, but of course I insulted Mason's family to his face.

"Don't get me wrong," I blubber. "I'm really thankful for the opportunity. He's just... Um... Nathan's..."

Say something nice, Mina. Anything at all will do!

"The exposure is going to be wonderful and the site is simply beautiful and I'm so excited to work with a legend like Benjamin Bancroft let alone someone as famous as Nathan West and..." I run out of platitudes and move in with the truth. "I'm sorry, but are you sure you're cousins? You're nothing alike."

Mason makes a face I can't quite read, one that might mean he agrees with me. Or...he may never want to work with me again.

"Nathan and I have more in common than you might think."

"Really?" I ask before realizing I might want to stick my foot back in my mouth to stop myself from talking.

"He's going through a bit of a rough patch, and has been a little, I don't know..." Mason chews on his word choice.

I have several I'd like to suggest. *Horrible. Rude. Stuck up. Self-centered. Judgmental.* Just off the top of my head.

"...withdrawn," Mason finally says. "But I didn't think he had it in him to be grumpy with someone as nice as you or I would have warned you before you accepted the project. I'll talk to him about it."

"Oh, God no." That's the last thing I need. "Please don't. I'm sure we just got off on the wrong foot."

Probably the one I keep shoving into my mouth.

"Well," Mason says, bracing his hands on his thighs to stand. "You let me know if you change your mind. I'm happy to slap some sense into him."

We say our goodbyes and I lean in the doorway to watch him make his way through the office toward the front door, basking in the afterglow of his warmth and hoping I didn't offend him enough to ruin the relationship.

"They just don't make 'em like that anymore," Tad says, eyeing Mason's exit from his desk.

"They really don't." I throw back the last of my coffee and frown. I never drink the last swallow. It's always a bitter disappointment.

Speaking of bitter disappointments...

"I have an hour before the meeting with Mr. West, correct?"

Tad's face falls and he swivels back to stare at his computer screen, looking like he swallowed a fly.

"I know that look," I say, drumming my fingers on my empty coffee cup.

"What look might that be?" Tad's nonchalance only solidifies my fear that the day is about to take a turn for the worse.

"Don't you 'what look' me. What you're doing with your face right now says there's something you've forgotten, and you just now remembered, and I'm not going to like hearing about it at all."

He grins sheepishly. "You say that like you know me."

"You say that like you're surprised," I say with a sigh. "Out with it, Tad. If you're going to ruin my day, I'm a 'sooner rather than later' kind of woman."

"Mr. West called this morning to move your meeting forward by forty-five minutes." Tad grimaces, his shoulders coming up to meet his ears like he's bracing for impact.

"By forty-five...? Tad! That's like ten minutes from now!" Thankfully, I spent most of last night tweaking my proposal and finishing the mood board, so I'm prepared. I'll only need a few minutes to go over the materials and get my head on straight. Which is good because a few minutes are all I have.

Tad chews his bottom lip and my heart sinks.

"Oh, for heaven's sake. What else do you need to tell me?"

"Mr. West also requested you meet him at Red Stiletto for lunch instead of him coming here. And I was sure you'd be prepared because you always are, so you could go over your notes before the meeting with the charming Mason Channing, then skedaddle on over to the restaurant as soon as it was over...except I forgot to tell you about the change."

"Yes. Yes, you did." I glance at the time and all I can do is laugh. "And now, I have to race across town to meet a client, showing up late and underprepared."

A client I'm already on shaky ground with, thanks to a certain drunken text and embarrassing request on my part.

A client who agreed to help, but only after negotiating himself a sixty percent discount off my design fee.

A client who really is The Prince of Darkness. I shiver as the last bit of Mason's sunshine bleeds out of my body.

Tad flashes me his most winning smile. "It's a good thing I'm so amazing every other part of the day or you'd fire me, right Ms. Blake?"

"Oh, Tad. I could never fire you." I pat his cheek. "You're just too pretty."

My assistant beams. "I love working for a woman who appreciates my strengths."

I dash into my office and shoot Mr. West a quick text.

> Sorry. Running late. Will be there ASAP.

I watch for signs of a response, but when nothing happens, I swipe my tablet off my desk, slide it into my bag, then head for the door.

EIGHT

Mina

The beautiful, cloudless day has turned my car into a sauna. It's so hot, I can barely breathe and I'm sweating under my arms, my boobs, and at my temples before I make it out of the parking lot. I hit every red light on the way to Red Stiletto, which gives the air conditioner a chance to stop me from melting, but by the time I find myself seated across from a bristly Nathan West, I'm almost half an hour late.

He's wearing a black T-shirt that clings to his upper body and offsets the mahogany in his dark hair. The glint in his eyes skews a little more summer forest and a lot less thorns and brambles, an improvement over our first meeting.

I think.

The Prince of Darkness is hotter when he's friendly and I'm not sure what to do with the way my lower belly clenches at the sight of him. Combine that with a dusting of scruff on the hard lines of his cheeks and jaw and I'm swallowing a sigh of appreciation.

Maybe I misjudged him at our first meeting.

Maybe he was having a bad day.

Maybe he deserves the benefit of the doubt and a little grace on my part.

"I am so sorry, Mr. West," I say, breathlessly tucking a lock of hair behind my ear. "I assure you this is not typical of me."

"Oh, come now, Hot Mess. I feel like I've heard that somewhere before."

And that might be the end of the grace I have for him.

If his snarky grin didn't make me bristle, the stupid nickname sealed the deal. I'm willing to put our bumpy start aside. He should be too.

"And please," he continues as if he didn't just insult me, "call me Nathan."

How can someone so pretty be this rude?

"I'd rather stick with Prince of Darkness," I retort with a sweet smile, then drop my jaw, realizing I'm in a business meeting...

...with a client...

...and after showing up half an hour late...

...I insulted him.

I clamp a hand over my mouth. "I'm so sorry—"

"Let me guess." Nathan coolly arches a brow. "You can assure me this isn't typical?"

He's got me there and we both know it, but I won't give him the satisfaction of admitting it to his smug face. After pausing to place my order—the cheapest salad I can find because this place is expensive with a capital E—I slide my tablet out of my bag. A quick flip through the screens brings up the project I put the finishing touches on last night. "This is my mood board for your build—"

Nathan's eyebrows imitate a rocket trying to break through the atmosphere. "Mood board?"

Great. He's one of those. A stick in the mud who rolls his eyes at all things creative. I bet he'll fight me at every turn. Second guess every color choice. Every fabric recommendation. Ten bucks says he'll struggle to grasp that the pictures I included are about the feeling and the vibe, not actual design suggestions.

Why hire a designer if you don't respect the craft?

But, rather than firing off another insult, I refresh my smile and do my best to explain.

"You know. Images, materials, and text that evoke

the feelings and design I think are best suited for your home." I angle the tablet so Nathan can see the screen. "I'm thinking dark blues, soft grays, and warm browns. Take the richness of this library here and combine it with the serenity of this lake. And while your outward vibe suggested metal and glass accents like these—" I point to a picture of an ultramodern skyscraper next to a surprisingly pretty close up of barbed wire covered in frost "—there's something about you that calls for this greenery here. Something fresh and alive and…"

I trail off.

Nathan's just sitting there. He's not nodding or making any sounds of agreement or understanding. He's just…

…staring…

…his eyes hardening on the image of the barbed wire.

Really?

How did that offend him? Tell me he doesn't think he's a sunshine and daisies kind of guy.

I slide the tablet away. "If this is the wrong direction, I can scratch it. Start over with new ideas. New feelings. New everything if you'd like."

"No." He tears his gaze from the picture to lock on mine. Something intense swims between us. Something charged and uncomfortable and I like it better when his eyes look like thorns because whatever this is feels vulnerable and that's not good. I've watched enough movies to know being vulnerable with the villain leads to heartbreak.

"I hired you because I heard you're a hidden gem," he says, the intensity increasing. "I just wasn't prepared for you to see me so clearly after only one meeting."

I furrow my brow, expecting a trap. "But..." I prompt as I lean forward and cock my head.

"But what? I like it. Approval granted." Nathan waves a hand through the air. "Start shopping or designing or whatever it is you do at this point."

"I honestly didn't expect you to make things this easy," I say, reaching for my water. "You seem more..."

Cranky. Controlling. Egotistical.

I take a drink before I stick another foot into my mouth.

Nathan lifts a brow and gestures for me to continue. "I seem..."

Like the type of guy who wouldn't like hearing what I truly think of you.

Nope, shouldn't say that either.

Dear God. A little help, here? Yours, Mina Blake.

"Let's say I don't make a habit of calling my clients The Prince of Darkness."

The last bit of warmth in Nathan's smile fades. I take it back. I definitely prefer the summer forest vibe to thorns and brambles. The way he's glaring at me makes me want to fidget—a nervous habit I can't quite crack. His scrutiny makes me feel electrified. Like I'm standing in line for an amusement park ride I'm not brave enough to try.

Like I'm falling, or flying, or...

"Maybe you don't see me as clearly as I thought," Nathan growls, jerking me away from wherever the hell those thoughts were heading. "There's a lot you don't know about me, Ms. Blake."

I almost tell him that isn't true. I happen to know a lot about him, thanks to Fallon's constant updates on his life. But our food arrives, and the moment passes. Silence sits strangely between us as we fiddle with napkins, seasoning, and silverware. Sharing a meal implies a deeper connection than we have and eating in front of a client I can't stand just feels weird. Especially when he's being oddly magnanimous today. Something tells me there's more to this meeting than mood boards and giant mansions, but I couldn't guess what it is. I keep waiting for the other shoe to drop, but it's just hovering a few feet off the ground.

I meet Nathan's eyes and glance away. Dig my fork through my salad, then look up only to glance away again when I discover he's staring. Tuck my hair behind my ear, untuck it, then tuck it again before stabbing aimlessly at a bite of chicken. This is almost as uncomfortable as our first meeting and that's saying a lot. I can't believe this is Mason Channing's cousin.

Though, Mason did say Nathan is going through a rough patch. And Fallon swears he used to be amazing. Maybe I should cut the man some slack.

Smiling awkwardly, I put my fork down and fold my hands in my lap. "I assume you have something more you'd like to discuss, since we're here, stuck eating together instead of at my office where you could make a hasty exit."

Nathan stares for a long moment, then scrubs a hand over his mouth and shrugs. "Our meeting overlapped my lunch. This kills two birds with one stone."

Nope. Not buying that.

There's an ulterior motive here and he's stalling. I'm sure of it. Maybe a little self-deprecating humor will lighten the mood enough to bring it out.

"I'm surprised you're willing to be seen with someone who isn't dazzling and spectacular," I quip, referencing Fallon's favorite way to describe Nathan's type. "From what I've heard, 'hot mess' isn't exactly the company you keep."

A muscle in his jaw ticks and his nostrils flare. There's a flash of fire in his eyes. Did I hit another nerve? Talking to this guy is like tiptoeing through a minefield covered in Lego blocks...barefoot. And naked.

An image of a naked Nathan West flashes through my mind, all hard lines and taut muscles, glaring as he strides closer. My nipples pebble and I cross my arms over my chest.

Traitors.

Nathan leans on the table, those mercurial eyes on mine. His hair falls into his face, and he flips it away, one finger lazily brushing through the condensation on his glass. For a moment, I imagine that finger brushing my cheek.

I break eye contact to regain my sanity.

Nathan takes a long drink before, "Un-spectacular company is exactly what I'm looking for."

"Umm...thanks?" I swipe up my fork and hunt down a bite. Apparently, his ulterior motive is to kill any hope I have that this project will go smoothly.

"You know what I mean," he replies, brushing away my frustration like a bit of dust in the air.

I shove food into my mouth and chew ferociously to keep myself from another snarky response.

You need this job. You need this job. You need this job. Do not insult your client again, Mina!

"Someone down to earth," Nathan continues. "Normal. Someone who drives a Honda and lives paycheck to paycheck and wears cheap clothes. Someone boring. Someone safe."

And just like that, the slack Mason earned him runs out.

"Boring? Hey, yeah, that's not insulting at all. I feel so much better now. Thank you for clearing things up." I yank my napkin from my lap and drop it on the table, flagging down our waiter to request a to-go box. I didn't budget for lunch, but the leftovers will serve as dinner, mitigating the cost a little.

"Wait, wait, wait." Nathan puts his hand on mine and adrenaline dumps into my bloodstream. This hum of...*something*...roaring through my veins.

I'm falling again. Flying again.

I scowl until he removes it.

"I have a favor to ask of you." He might as well be flipping through junk mail, he's that nonchalant.

"Seeing as the favor *I* asked of *you* is the most expensive thing I've purchased for myself lately, I'm not sure what to make of that."

"Your favor put the idea in my head," Nathan says, and he's so detached I think he stopped blinking. "I could really use your help here."

"And you chose to insult me as your opening salvo," I shoot back. "That's a bold move."

"Says the woman who called her client The Prince of Darkness to his face."

Well, hell. Neither of us look very good here. Time to hunt down the last drops of patience in my body.

"We do bring out the worst in each other, don't we?" I take a deep breath, convinced I'm going to regret my next statement. "Tell me about this favor."

Nathan crosses his arms and scowls. "I want you to pretend to date me."

The restaurant is busy. Customers talk and eat while music plays gently over speakers. The murmur of servers taking orders blends with the chaos of the kitchen. Behind me, a table of young businessmen erupts in laughter.

Surely, I misheard the man across from me.

I lean closer. "I'm sorry, you want me to what, now?"

"Pretend to be my girlfriend." There's no hint of shame or embarrassment. No 'please.' No 'thank you.' No explanation. None of the things you'd expect from a normal human being. You know, the kind with a soul.

"Why would I do that?" I shake my head and hold out my hands as a better question comes to mind. "Why would you *want* me to do that?"

Nathan mumbles something about his family, work, and an ex-girlfriend, then nods like it's a done deal. "Your accidental text the other night sets it up perfectly. Benjamin believes there's something going on between us and I'm asking you to roll with it. We'll just make things more public than we originally thought."

"You want me to roll with it." I prop my elbows on the table and my chin in my hands. "Like you did? When I asked for my favor?" I ask sweetly.

"Exactly." Nathan looks smug. He clearly doesn't remember what an asshole he was that night.

That's fine. I'm happy to remind him.

"No." I sit back, folding my hands in my lap, too proud of myself for my own good. "I will not pretend to date you."

Nathan's lips part. His brows jump. His head cocks and his eyes narrow until they smolder into mine. "I thought you were going to roll with it."

"Right. Just like you did." I laugh as realization tightens Nathan's jaw.

"Funny," he says with a sneer that doesn't look funny at all. "In case your memory is as chaotic as the rest of you, I did pretend your idiotic text was meant for me."

"You sure did. For a *spectacular* and *dazzling* amount of money. No 'good guy' points for you on that one. But let me see..." I drum my fingers on the table and the way Nathan's eyes lock with mine makes me feel alive for the first time in a long time. I lean closer, hoping to grab hold of the feeling. "What could you do to make me more inclined to consider this *idiotic* idea of yours?"

I grin, pleased for throwing not one, but three of his words in his face. Maybe I should consider a villain era of my own. I'm better at this than I should be.

"Subtlety isn't one of your finer points, is it?" Nathan leans in and I can't help myself, I lean even closer, drawn into his orbit like a sun-diving comet.

"Atta boy," I retort with a sly smile. "Keep insulting me. That'll convince me to pretend to be your girlfriend, for what? One night? A week? Longer? What are you asking for here?" I swipe my water off the table, sit back, and take a dramatic draw on the straw while Nathan scowls.

"Longer."

"And why would I want to do that?"

"We negotiated sixty percent off your design fee for my text to Benjamin. Let's make it twenty instead."

I snort so hard water comes out my nose. "That's a joke, right?" I ask, choking on the rest of my drink. I grab my napkin and cover my mouth as I cough, then pull it away when Nathan doesn't laugh. "You're joking?"

"I'm the villain, right? Why would I joke about something like this?"

Right. Duh. Rich assholes never joke about money. How silly of me to hope an offer that offensive wasn't real. Too bad I need every dollar I can get my hands on, or I'd storm out of Nathan West's life forever. No amount of money is worth this kind of humiliation.

But Mom is.

I do some quick math in my head, then bring Nathan back into my sights.

"Seeing as anything less than a hundred and ninety percent of my original price is clearly a joke, you can see why I'd wonder." Adding that much money to our contract would mean I could pay off Mom's treatment and still have a little left over for myself. Not enough to get me out of that crappy apartment, but a start.

Nathan sits back, folding his arms. His eyes narrow as thoughts tick across his face. For a moment, I wonder if he's about to say something profound. Something that helps me see the man Mason expected me to meet when he gave his cousin my name.

But then Nathan smirks, and I remember who I'm dealing with. "You realize that means I'd be paying you to date me."

"Seems appropriate," I reply with a smirk of my own. "As that's the only way anything would happen between us."

"And is basically illegal," he counters, his eyes narrowing wickedly.

I summon every villainous thought I've ever had—most of them centered around people like him—and let them linger in my smile. "No, that's prostitution and trust me. We're fine. You don't have to worry about us having sex. Ever."

A passing waitress glances over in surprise, takes stock of Nathan, then looks sorry for him. Not me, the woman who's being asked for a ridiculous favor. Him, the man who can ask that favor without blinking an eye. I get it. He's pretty and I'm raving about prostitution. But if she'd been around for the rest of the conversation, she'd drop her tray in his lap to high five me.

"A hundred," he says, chewing his lip in defeat. "We'll call it a favor for a favor."

"I have to pretend to like you, so your favor is bigger than mine. A hundred and twenty percent."

Nathan's eyes harden. His smile dies. He stares just long enough to make me uncomfortable. "Fine," he says in a voice that isn't. "A hundred and twenty percent."

I reach across the table, and we shake on it. "When do we start?"

"My family is throwing a party for my birthday. I'd like you there." A smile lifts Nathan's lips and for one brief moment, he feels like sunshine. Like eyes closed, sitting on the beach with nothing to do but breathe and let the waves crash and recede, crash and recede…

"You should do that more," I say before I think better of it.

"Do what more?"

"Smile. You have a nice one and it makes you so much easier to be around."

And just like that, black clouds boil over the horizon, the ocean churns and the sun disappears. "Careful, Hot Mess. It's not too late for me to change my mind."

As much as I'd like that to happen, I promised myself I'd take every financial opportunity that came my way. No matter how outlandish or bizarre. Mind you, I was thinking bizarre might be something along the lines of professional pet food taster or water slide tester, not fake girlfriend to a rich asshole. But here we are.

"I'm sorry. Those are inside thoughts," I say, tapping the side of my skull. "They won't make their way outside again. When is this birthday party?"

Nathan's smile reappears, but there's no sunshine in sight. This is one that belongs to a villain.

He makes a show of checking his watch, then sits back, looking...mildly concerned?

No.

No way. That's giving him too much credit. The Prince of Darkness wouldn't look concerned. Why would he, when he always gets his way?

That look right there is smugness.

"Well Hot Mess, I kinda hate to say it, but we've got roughly four hours. Party's tonight."

"Four hours?!" My jaw drops. "You want me to pretend to be the kind of date you bring to a family gathering and all we have is four hours to prepare? Are you insane?"

Nathan sits back, arms crossed over his chest, looking at me like I'm a money hungry bottom feeder. "In my defense, I didn't expect you to agree so fast. I thought I'd have to dangle money in front of you for a couple days at least, but you just snapped it right up, didn't you?"

Tutting in disappointment, I tuck a strand of hair behind my ear. "I hate to break it to you, but some of us have to accept creepy financial offers to afford our boring, Honda-filled lives."

A slow smile warms Nathan's face. "After this conversation, I've realized 'boring' is the wrong word to describe you."

"Yeah?" I lift my chin. "How would you describe me?" I brace for a barrage of insults. Chaotic. Frenzied. Master of Disaster. Coming from him, it could be anything.

But Nathan is as unpredictable as ever.

"You're fascinating," he replies, surprising us both.

There's an undercurrent to the admission, one that threatens to pull me in, pull me close, pull me under. I break eye contact and switch to safer ground. Facts. Data. Not whatever the hell that was.

"I'll call my assistant and have him clear my schedule," I say with a resolved sigh. "We'll spend the rest of the afternoon learning to pretend we like each other."

"That's gonna take more than one afternoon," Nathan murmurs, then checks his phone. His brows furrow as he reads a text, then shakes his head, laughing humorlessly. "Shit."

"Everything okay?"

"I have to go." He pulls his napkin out of his lap and places it on the table.

"You have to what?" Shock raises my voice an octave or two. The businessmen at the table next to us look sorry for Nathan. How is everyone at this restaurant misjudging our situation?

"The timing isn't ideal but..." Nathan smiles gently as he reads another text. "This is important." He waves his phone as if that explains everything, then lifts a hip to slide it in his pocket. "I have to take care of it."

"What could possibly be more important than this?"

"Believe it or not, there are more important things than figuring out the best way to lie to my family." He stands and pushes in his chair, gripping the back to lean close. "This shouldn't take long," he says. "As soon as I'm confident everything's under control, I'll give you a call."

I watch in shock as he turns to leave.

"At least tell me what to wear!" I call out and he pauses long enough to toss me a pained look over his shoulder.

"Come on, Hot Mess. It's not that hard. It's a birthday party. Look it up on the internet if you have to."

NINE

Nathan

Sunlight blinds me as I leave Red Stiletto. I shield my eyes while digging into my pocket for my sunglasses, then round the corner into the parking lot to reread the texts from Ricky Valdez, one of the most talented—and least confident—ten-year-olds I've ever met.

> **RICKY VALDEZ**
>
> im freaking out mr west
>
> i cant do this im not good enuff for the talent show
>
> i know you said i am but im not

A couple years ago, I started a weekly guitar class for the foundation kids. I fell in love with teaching, but more importantly, I fell in love with the children. Watching their eyes light up when they nail a song they've been struggling with, or their little faces tighten with concentration while we master a new skill has taken my love of music to a new level. These kids, they've had hard lives. Broken homes, shitty parents, not enough of anything to go around. Some of them jump in fear every time the door opens unexpectedly. Or flinch when I reach out to shake their hands. Some hide behind their parent's legs when we first meet, peeking out with distrust baked into eyes too old for such young faces.

Mom always said music can heal, and I see that truth for myself every week. Slowly but surely, these kids learn to trust again. Not just the world at large, but in themselves as well. And that's what really matters.

Though poor Ricky Valdez has a long way to go on that last one, courtesy of a mom who criticized every move he made, verbally abused his father, then divorced the man when the company he worked for went under and he lost his job.

I check the time. School let out fifteen minutes ago and Ricky has another hour and a half to drive himself crazy before the talent show. I pull up his contact info and call as I walk to my car. He answers after one ring.

"I'm sorry I bothered you, Mr. West," he says breathlessly, "but I'm seriously freaking out."

"We can't have the best guitarist at Oceanview Elementary freaking out. That's just not right." I climb into the car, ignite the engine, and crank the AC. Mina was a sweaty mess when she arrived at the restaurant. I assumed it was because she was late, but the weather probably had more to do with it. Punctuality and discipline don't seem to be high on the list of things that matter to the Hot Mess Express. Nor do privacy and a general sense of right and wrong, given her liberal use of the words "dazzling and spectacular" made it clear she reads Fallon fucking Mae's bullshit clickbait gossip blog. No wonder Mina expects the worst of me, even though her mood board had me thinking she might see the real me.

That picture of the barbed wire...

How on the nose can you get?

"I shouldn't have called..." Ricky's little voice brings me back to the problem at hand. "Dad said not to bother you because you're very busy doing an important job and I'm just a kid and you probably only gave me your number to be nice and I really shouldn't take advantage—"

"Hey now, buddy. If I didn't want you to call me, I wouldn't have given you my number. That's just the way I work. Now. What's going on?"

Ricky runs down a list of imagined failings, starting with his complete inability to play the song he perfected months ago and ending with a teary rendition of, "They're all gonna laugh at me."

The kid is way past freaking out. He's nearing a full-on panic attack. As much as I need to go back into that restaurant, smooth things over with Mina, and make plans for the evening so we can sell this asinine lie, Ricky needs me more.

When I arrive at Oceanview Elementary Ricky is waiting at the front door, his gig bag strapped to his back as he paces back and forth, his sneakers slapping the pavement as he runs his hands through hair almost as black as Mina's. When we first met, his clothes were a size too small and the boy himself was rail thin—his father even thinner than that. Now, Ricky's cheeks are round, his clothes are new, and his little face lights up when he sees me. We find a child-sized table and chairs near the playground. We sit and he plays, frowning deeper with every strum of the strings.

"See?" he says, squeezing his eyes shut and shaking his head. "I can't do this."

"What are you even talking about? I just watched you do it."

"Yeah, but not good. I suck."

"Ricky." I arch a brow.

"I know, I know. Don't say 'suck.'"

"Not when it's not true. Show me C again."

Ricky arranges his fingers and strums.

"Now G."

He deftly switches positions and strums again, then frowns. "See? The E string keeps buzzing."

"I hear no buzzing. And it's almost like I know enough about guitar to be your teacher or something."

"Funny." Ricky's tight laugh encourages me to crack another joke.

"Don't forget to tip your waitresses. I'll be here all week."

His brows furrow in confusion. "We don't have waitresses. Unless you mean the lunch ladies?"

One of these days I'll learn to stop when I'm ahead.

A text comes in and I take a peek. It's Mina, wondering where I am. It's a fair question, and I'm sure if I explained she'd understand, but she's so quick to assume I have villainous intent, I don't feel like giving her an explanation. I don't need to justify myself to her.

My God. Is this really who I want to be? What version of Nathan West *isn't* willing to offer a simple explanation for his actions? The one that's spent too much time listening to Dom and his cynical views on the world, that's who. Is it his influence that made me think this whole pretend girlfriend thing was a good idea in the first place? It was all I could do to keep a straight face when I made the proposition. Mina's shocked expression was so on point, and me? I worked so hard to play it cool I don't think I even blinked...

"See!" Ricky grimaces. "I knew I was bothering you."

Fuck. Enough worrying about Mina. You're here to help, so help already. "Ricky—"

"Mom always said I'm too needy and—"

I put a hand on his arm and those watery browns meet mine.

"What does it mean if a plant's leaves are drying up and turning brown?"

The out-of-context question short circuits Ricky's meltdown. "That it hasn't been watered enough?"

"Exactly. Would you call that plant needy and tell it to deal? Or would you grab a watering can and get to work?"

"I'd water it."

"That's what I'm doing here." I shrug as I let my point sink in.

Ricky smiles softly and stares at his feet. "Can I play one more time?" he asks quietly. "Will you listen?"

Every minute I spend here is one less I have to get my story straight with Mina, but there's no way I can leave Ricky. Not until I'm sure he won't psych himself out of playing tonight. If he doesn't get on that stage, his confidence may never recover. Keeping the promises we make to ourselves is the most important step in mental health. It doesn't hurt to have someone at our side, cheering us on when we falter. I need to ensure both happen for this kid today.

"I'm here as long as you need me."

Ricky's eyes light up. "Really? Will you stay and watch the show? It starts real soon, and I play first."

I do some quick math. I should be able to watch Ricky, pick up Mina, and still have time to get to the party, but I'll be cutting it close. "I'll have to leave as soon as you're done playing..."

"That's okay. I just would feel so much better to know you're here."

A text from Mina comes in and she's understandably uncomfortable. I answer her question to the best of my ability, then silence my phone and give my full attention to Ricky before his nerves get on top of him again.

TEN

Mina

Nothing about today has turned out the way I expected. I thought I'd have a quick meeting with Nathan at my office to talk about my ideas for his build. Now I'm pretending to be his date at his birthday party. I thought I'd hear from him hours ago so we could get our stories straight. Now it's time to get ready and I haven't heard squat.

I have no idea what to expect tonight. No clue how many people will be at this party. Nathan's family is well known for their philanthropy, which means they might be good people but they're also swimming in money, which means they probably aren't. How is someone like me supposed to fit in, given my boring life and budget friendly wardrobe he so kindly pointed out? I wait as long as I can, then finally open my messaging app, which says Nathan has silenced his notifications, with an option to force my message through if it's urgent. This seems urgent to me, so I select that option and angrily type in a text.

> We still on for tonight? We're running out of time to have any kind of conversation about "our relationship." I don't know where you are. I don't know where the party is. I don't even know what to wear. And you call me the hot mess…

Seconds later, a curt reply.

THE PRINCE OF DARKNESS

busy

party at my parents' house

I'll call you as soon as I can about the other stuff

> But we're still on?

yes

> A little more info would be a lot of help

I wait for a response. And wait…
And wait…

> Hello?

Nothing.

> Is this thing on?

After several minutes pass, it's clear our communication has come to an end.

Nathan didn't come close to giving me enough information, and if I didn't need this money, I'd tell him where he could shove this ridiculous favor of his. But I do need the money because I really don't want to juggle a second job as a waitress along with my new clients, so I turn to the internet for inspiration, doing a search first on Nathan's parents, then his extended family. My search expands and I find pic after pic of Nathan and another obviously wealthy man who is never without gorgeous women dangling off both arms. Their dresses probably cost more than what Mom made in a year when I was little. Make up expertly done. Not a hair out of place. If that's what he's used to...

I need someone down to earth. Normal. Someone who drives a Honda and lives paycheck to paycheck and wears cheap clothes. Someone boring. Someone safe.

You know what? Screw boring. To hell with being safe!

I can do dazzling and spectacular just as well as the rest of 'em. Nathan and his family won't know what hit them. After some deliberation, I put on my red dress. The one that goes perfectly with my fair skin and raven hair, the one I wear when I intend to leave an impression. And I'm looking forward to watching The Prince of Darkness choke on that impression, though I'm sure I'll still be underdressed compared to the rest of his family. Wealthy people can't help but add a dash of pretension to everything.

After an hour fussing with my hair and makeup, I pace from my bedroom to the kitchen, my heels clicking on the outdated tile, my gaze tracing chipped and stained grout out of habit. Growing up in a series of ever more economical apartments, owning a home seemed like the epitome of success. The fact that I'm a full-blown adult with a career in interior design paying rent instead of a mortgage sits on my shoulder and whispers "FAILURE" on repeat.

I have dreams of buying an older place and renovating it room by room, turning something forgotten into something beautiful.

And I will.

But Mom's growing pile of medical bills and the insane balloon in the cost of housing means that dream is on hold—at least until Nathan pays me.

Assuming his silence isn't a sign he bailed and forgot to tell me the deal's off.

I grab my phone from the counter and shoot him a text.

> Helloooooo....
>
> We're officially out of time here. What do you want me to do?

With anyone else, I'd be worried he was in some sort of trouble. But not The Prince of Darkness. Chances are good he changed his mind and decided I wasn't worth a phone call.

I pace a path between the front door and the kitchen a few more times before Nathan finally responds.

> **THE PRINCE OF DARKNESS**
>
> That took longer than expected but I'm done now. Meet me at this address.

No apology. No plan. Just an address that, according to my GPS, is going to take me to a bar instead of his parents' house. Sure. Yeah. This is gonna work out just fine.

I have never met someone so infuriating. So selfish. So completely and utterly chaotic. Every interaction we have leaves me wondering what the hell just happened. As if that's not troubling enough, my underserved libido suddenly seems to have a thing for handsome, growly men. What if my hormones take control while we're pretending to like each other? What if he tries to kiss me? What if I let him?

What if I like it?

I take a deep breath and dig my phone out of my purse to call the whole thing off, but the memory of Mom making tea stops me in my tracks. Nathan may be the most difficult and disappointing person I've ever met, but I can't jeopardize our working relationship. Not when he's dangling much needed money my way.

With a heavy sigh, I swallow my pride and make the drive to the address he gave me.

When I pull into the parking lot, Nathan's leaning on the side of the building. His dark hair falls into his eyes, making his chiseled face seem less imposing. He's still wearing the jeans and T-shirt he had on at lunch. By comparison, my form fitting red dress and heels are overly formal and completely ridiculous. I pull to a stop beside his car and he pushes off the wall, looking mildly apologetic as he opens my door.

"The afternoon took an unscheduled detour." He clears his throat and laughs humorlessly, almost daring me to challenge him as I stand, and he closes the door.

Laughing to myself, I pinch the bridge of my nose and stare at my feet. "You've got to be kidding me."

"I'm really sorry. I know this puts us in a difficult situation, but this afternoon was important." There's a vulnerability in his voice I'm not expecting. An almost gentle energy sits in his half-smile and softens my outrage. Suddenly, Nathan seems less like a villain and more like...

Hold on now, Mina. You're falling right into his trap. I square my shoulders and lift my chin, adding as much outrage to my voice as possible. "More important than this?"

"Yes. More important than—" Nathan finally looks at me and his lips curve into a gentle smile that transforms the atmosphere of the parking lot. "Woah."

His voice is hushed. His nostrils flared.

I meet his eyes for a few uncomfortable seconds before looking away. "Everything okay?"

Nathan's gaze traces my face, trailing across my cheekbones, caressing the divot between my collarbones. My breath catches and a blush warms my cheeks, my throat, then flames across my chest. I wanted him to choke on his impression, but I didn't expect it to feel like this.

My heart races as a smirk twists his lips.

"You're wildly overdressed."

"If only there was something you could have done to save me from this predicament. Something like staying at the restaurant to talk through the evening..." I tap a finger against my lips. "No...that must not be it. That would be asking too much of you, I'm sure."

"Are you done?" he asks.

"With you," I reply, then immediately wish I could stuff the words back in my mouth. "I'm sorry. I'm done now."

"Get it all out of your system?" Nathan lifts one playful eyebrow.

I nod sheepishly. "First things first, I guess. Your jeans and my dress work together just about as well as you and I do." Though he does look damn good in them. That is an ass I'd like to sink my teeth in, for sure. "Should I change? Should you? Assuming we're still doing this thing..."

"We're doing it. And honestly? I'm not that worried about us having a solid story. My family probably won't talk to you much anyway. They're not exactly interested in me being in a relationship."

"Then why am I even here?" I pop a hand on my hip as a couple rounds the corner, drawing up short when they see us. I don't know if it's the clash in our attire or the tension thrumming between us that puts them off more.

Nathan takes my arm and leads me to his car, leaning close. Secretive. Intimate.

"We're planting a seed," he says in a low voice.

"They think I'm sleeping around. I'm tired of them thinking that way."

"Maybe if you just stopped sleeping around…" I find myself saying, then bite my tongue. I promised I was done with the snark and promises mean something to me. "You know what? It's fine. Whatever happens tonight, happens, but if I end up humiliated, you owe me. Big time. Like maybe an extra couple percent big."

Nathan's smile disintegrates. The light in his eyes fades. It's like watching a cloud cover the full moon, plunging the night into oblivion.

"Of course." His voice is hard and distant. "I'll tack another five percent onto your fee, if that makes you feel better."

And suddenly, I'm dealing with The Prince of Darkness again. Every ounce of vulnerability I thought I saw in the guy disappears and I'm left standing next to a cold-hearted jerk. Wordlessly, he opens the passenger door on his car with an air of expectant exasperation.

This is gonna be a long night.

ELEVEN

Nathan

Nick specifically told me not to bring a dazzling and spectacular woman to my birthday party tonight. So of course, Mina shows up looking like someone hanging on Dom's arm. Her red dress is a feast for the eyes. Her silky black hair begs for my fingers. Her ass is round and luscious and I want to grab it with both hands as I bury my face in her neck and breathe in her citrus perfume. I don't like her, but my dick doesn't care. There's no doubt I'm attracted to her. At least I won't be lying to my family on that count.

Mina pauses as we approach my parents' house, her gaze wandering the premises with what I hope is appreciation. I try to see my childhood home through her eyes. It's big enough for our family of six, but not overly so. It's elegant without being pretentious. But I grew up here. Maybe I don't see it the way the rest of the world does.

"Everything okay?" I ask, shoving my hands in my pockets to keep from brushing them against the small of Mina's back. I don't know what it is about that dress, but my hands want on her body. Even knowing she's only here for the money can't dampen the desire.

"This house." Mina's brows draw together, and she chews her bottom lip. "It's not what I expected."

"Tuck in, blue eyes. My family doesn't exactly fit into a box."

Dom says people are most comfortable when everyone plays their expected roles. If Mina's outfit says anything about her expectations, she's in for an uncomfortable evening. I take a gross amount of pleasure in that thought. When did I get so mean?

"Plus," she says with a crooked smile, "I'm about to meet Collin and Harlow West. I grew up listening to them. I mean, they're icons, right? And I'm just gonna spend an evening in their home. No biggie."

Great. Not only does Mina bring out the absolute worst in me, but she's a lifelong fan of my parents' music. Probably one of those wackos who dissolve into tears the moment she meets them. Lord knows I've had enough of that to last a lifetime.

"They're also just people. Come on. The faster we

get this over with, the better." I wrap an arm around her waist and draw Mina close as we near the front door. She tenses and peeks up at me, clearly uncomfortable. I get it, but we have a lie to sell.

I lean down and tuck a lock of hair behind her ear. The intimate gesture sends a jolt of desire through me. I linger longer than I expect. Longer than I should.

"Game face on, Hot Mess," I whisper, breathing in her citrus perfume. "Time to pretend you like me."

"Believe me," she whispers back, "my game face has been on since lunch, Sweet Prince." Her smile says I'm the love of her life, though her eyes look mildly murderous.

We pass through the foyer into an open floor plan barely large enough to fit my extended family. My cousins, aunts, uncles, brothers and sister all greet me, calling out happy birthday and raising glasses as we pass. Inevitably, their smiles fade when they see Mina. She's wildly overdressed. To their eyes, the epitome of the shallow women I've been swearing were for Dom, instead of me. My parents catch sight of us, exchange a concerned glance, then quickly cross the room. I get the distinct impression they're running defense.

Mom wraps me in a tight embrace, tossing Mina a polite though chilly smile. She smells like lilacs and her silver-blonde hair is swept off her shoulders in a messy updo. Even though she's wearing jeans and a loose-fitting linen top, she pulls off an understated sophistication I've always appreciated. Mom gives me the onceover, motherly love glistening in her blue eyes before she cups my cheeks, the star tattoo on her wrist blurring in front of me.

"Happy birthday, Nator Tot! I was just starting to wonder about you. You're not the kind of guy who runs late."

Fuck me.

"Mom. Please. With the nickname."

I glance Mina's way, silently begging her not to have heard it.

The wicked grin lifting her lips says she not only heard it, but she'll have no qualms dragging that arrow from her quiver if the need arises.

Dad gives me a back thumping hug and wishes me a happy birthday, his gaze flicking to Mina. He's not happy to see her, though he'd never let her get wind of that. He spent too much time feeling unwelcome in some of his foster families to pass that feeling on.

"Mom, Dad, I'd like you to meet Mina Blake. Mina, these are my parents, Collin and Harlow West."

I brace for the gushing. The teary-eyed revelations of a lifelong fan that shift the atmosphere from cordial to awkward in a heartbeat.

I know all your music by heart!
Your songs are the soundtrack to my life!

I have the lyrics from Ice Princess tattooed on my ass!

It's one of the reasons I dread bringing anyone to meet my parents. Apparently, it can be easy to forget they're human, just like the rest of us.

To her credit, Mina keeps it together. "It's a genuine pleasure to meet you both," she says, then lets out a shuddering breath, tucking a strand of hair behind her ear then crossing and uncrossing her arms before letting them fall uselessly to her side. "I grew up listening to you guys and have heard such wonderful things about you from Nathan. You have a lovely home, by the way."

Fidgeting notwithstanding, she's cool. Calm. Collected. The perfect blend of recognition, admiration, and levelheadedness. Nothing like the Hot Mess I've come to know and dread. The four of us chat easily for a few minutes until my cousins Angela, Micah, and Nick join us. The men run big in my family, and Micah, Nick, and I prove that rule. Micah is physically the biggest, with a personality to match. His dark hair and eyes make him look more imposing than he actually is—though he does run into burning buildings for a living, so what do I know.

"I didn't know you were bringing a date," he says, tossing an arm around my shoulder in that way that used to signal an incoming noogie.

I duck out of reach, glaring to remind him I outgrew that more than a decade ago. "I thought I'd surprise you. Mina and I...we're..."

And this is the part where I lie to the people I love most in the world. Oddly enough, deceit does not roll off my tongue.

Thankfully, Mina doesn't share my crisis of conscience.

"We're having a lot of fun together." She lays her head on my shoulder and grins like she's infatuated.

According to the chain reaction of worried glances passing around us like some psychic game of telephone, the statement doesn't sit well with my family. Given that they think I'm fucking a new woman every night, she could have said she's using me for money and it would have gone over better.

"How did you two meet?" Angela asks with a careful smile my way.

"I'm Nathan's interior designer," Mina replies, helpful as ever. "We just clicked from the moment we met, didn't we, Sweet Prince?" She beams adoringly into my eyes.

"We sure did." I cup her cheek while I fight the urge to growl. She's enjoying this too much. "The *chemistry between* us was immediate."

And by chemistry, I mean hatred and loathing.

"And normally I wouldn't date a client, but Nathan insisted." Mina giggles and I narrow my eyes.

"Now don't make me out to be the villain here, Hot...Mehh...Hot Stuff." I wrap an arm around her shoulder and give a little shake to shut her the hell up. "I distinctly remember a phone call where you begged me to go out with you."

"I mean..." Mina pats my chest a tad too hard, "with charm like this, who could blame me?"

I force a laugh while my family looks uncomfortable. "Let's hit the bar and get a drink," I say before we make matters worse. "Anyone want anything?"

I glance at my cousins and parents, each of them with drinks in hand and confusion on faces. They shake their heads and everyone, myself included, visibly sags in relief as we move away.

As soon as we're out of earshot, Mina turns to me with a raised eyebrow. "Really?" She hisses. "I begged you to go out with me?"

"You're saying you didn't? Because my memory of that night is crystal clear..." The glint in my eyes sends a spark of fury down her spine.

"Maybe the next time the topic comes up, I'll share the part where you were so eager to date me you offered to pay for the privilege."

I scoff, then give in to the growl I've been holding back. "I didn't offer to pay you."

She forced me to.

"Hmm. You sure?" Mina laughs like I said something hilarious before leaning close to whisper, "Because that's the way I remember it..."

"Fucking hell. It's going to be a long night." I scrub my face in frustration, then snatch her hand and storm off in the direction of the bar.

TWELVE

Mina

I just met Collin and Harlow West. I'm in their house. I'm drinking their booze and holding hands with their son. And I just stood in front of them and had the most awkward conversation of my life like it was no big deal.

Me in my red dress and heels and them in jeans.

How is this real?

Nathan and I each down a drink at the bar while side-eyeing each other, order another, then find our way back to the clump of cousins he never actually introduced me to. I hold out my hand to a pretty redhead with a smile that lights up the room. She wears a loose-fitting, sleeveless linen blouse in a soothing pastel pink. Paired with high-waisted shorts in a light floral pattern, the outfit exudes both style and comfort—and makes me look downright slutty in comparison.

"I'm sorry," I say, with a pointed glance Nathan's way. "I didn't catch your name."

"Angela Cooper, at your service. I'm Nathan's oldest cousin."

"But only by a day!" A tall man with a military-straight spine bumps her shoulder. Strength and confidence emanate from him and a head of dark, neatly cropped hair complements his chiseled features. His piercing gaze and well-defined jawline speak to a determined and disciplined spirit.

"I'm Nick Hutton, Nathan's second oldest cousin," he says to me. "But only by a day," he reiterates, giving Angela a playful grin.

With a physique that belongs on a fitness inspiration video, Nick carries himself with authority. Despite his rugged exterior, his friendly demeanor and warm smile make me feel like we've known each other for years. How is it that Nathan's entire family feels like sunshine while he's...him?

"Nick's always felt like being born second meant he had something to prove. Hence his dedication to the Marine Corps and all that protecting freedom nonsense. Micah Hutton, by the way." A tall man with dark, tousled hair offers his hand. "It's nice to meet you."

"Says the firefighter." Nick scoffs then rolls his eyes, leaning close to whisper conspiratorially, "If you ask me, he's the one trying to prove something."

"My dad's a Marine," I blurt, before I remember Dad's not a story for strangers. "Or, he was..."

Nick crosses beefy arms over a proud chest. "I wouldn't say that around him. They say 'once a Marine, always a Marine' for a reason."

"My dad is the exception that proves the rule. He was injured in the line of duty—"

"So was my dad!" Angela grins like we just discovered we're long-lost sisters, then points to a striking man across the room. Broad shoulders. Imposing presence. The man has military written all over him. "He still has shrapnel in his hip," continues Angela. "The airports love him! He was clinically dead for a couple minutes, but then he met my mom, and she brought him back to life."

"I think the doctors had more to do with that part," quips Nick.

"There's a difference between surviving and living, thank you very much." Angela rolls her eyes and takes a long drink. "Mom is the one who actually brought him back to life."

"My dad never really recovered. I mean, his body healed, but his mind…" I shrug, wondering how to bring the conversation back to safer ground. "He was medically discharged then made it two more years before he hit the skids and left me and my mom to fend for ourselves."

I try to present the information like it has no weight. Like it's a piece of data and nothing more. But I still hear my parents fighting in those awful years leading up to his disappearance.

"My mother raised me alone," I continue, going for nonchalant and failing, "working crazy hours to make sure I had the life she thought I deserved. I mean, right up until I was old enough to get a job, then I insisted she let me contribute, much to her dismay." I swallow a lump in my throat and force a smile. "And now I'm doing everything I can to return the favor."

Everyone bobs their heads in that way that means I've wandered out of comfortable small talk and fallen into too much detail. I wonder how they'd react if they knew that when I said I'd do everything I can for Mom, that includes pretending to date their cousin.

Nathan stares for a long moment, his dark eyes bouncing across my face like he's seeing something he didn't expect. Hopefully, he'll take the conversational ball and give me time to remove these stupid feet from my mouth.

Alas. I should know better than to expect help from a villain. All he seems capable of doing is glaring. At me. His cousins. His drink. Just a ray of sunshine, that one.

"But that's enough of that," I say, giving Nathan a withering look. "I didn't embarrass myself too badly with your parents, did I? I mean, considering I can sing every one of their songs..."

"Do you sing?" asks Angela.

"Badly." I chuckle. "I've heard babies who sound better than me. And cats."

"Speaking of kids and music," Micah says, swatting Nathan on the arm. "Nell said she saw you at the talent show this afternoon."

Wait...

This afternoon? That was the super important meeting he couldn't miss? A talent show?

Nathan glares at the spot his cousin hit and arches an annoyed eyebrow. "One of my kids was performing."

Micah pulls his lips into an exaggerated frown. "I didn't know you got that involved with your students."

Across the room, someone laughs loudly, then turns up the music. I want to hush them because I don't want to miss one word of this explanation. Nathan West, The Prince of Darkness, has students?

There are people who actually let him near their children?

"I usually don't," Nathan says. "But this guy is incredibly talented and has the worst self-esteem. He started to panic and was going to pull out of the show. He texted me for help. What was I gonna do? Leave him high and dry?"

"That's so you." Angela beams with nothing short of adoration. "You're always the one who drops everything to take care of the world."

That's so him?

We know very different versions of Nathan West.

"You were at a talent show this afternoon?" I ask, incredulously.

"Yeah." Nathan frowns, eyeing me like he wants to beam information into my brain. "You know. I told you about Ricky. He's in my guitar class at the foundation?"

So much to digest.

Nathan plays the guitar...

He shares his knowledge with underprivileged kids...

He makes house calls when they're nervous...

And here I pegged him as one of those guys who hates all things creative and growls at passing children. I stare at the man across from me, trying to fit this new puzzle piece into the image I've built. He's rude. He exploits small infractions like an accidental text message for big financial gains. He's willing to fake a relationship and lie to his family rather than make better choices.

And he's a role model?

I guess even villains have a tender side.

"Oh. Right. Yeah. Ricky." I clear my throat and search for words that might form an actual sentence. "Of course I know all about Ricky. How could I have forgotten Ricky?"

"Nell said he was really good." Micah gives me a funny look, probably because he's wondering how many more times I'll say the name Ricky. "You must be doing something right."

Nathan holds out his hands and feigns shock. "You all heard it, right? Someone mark the calendar. Micah actually gave someone else credit for doing a good job."

"Uncle Nator Tot!" A little girl with golden blond hair bounds up to the group and leaps onto Nathan's back. He grunts, then twists back and forth, waving his arms like he's trying to brush her off.

"What the...?" He spins wildly, then stops, craning his neck to look over his shoulder. "Is there something on my back?" he asks me, his eyes gleaming, his smile wide and toothy and absolutely stunning.

Look at me, breathless again.

Wow. I mean, just, *wow*.

The little girl giggles, burying her face in his neck.

"There's no kids here and I'm bored. Will you play with me? Grandma says there's strawberry ice cream, just for us."

"Strawberry ice cream just for us?" Nathan asks excitedly, pivoting back and forth like he's looking for something. "Where? Point me to it!"

The girl digs her heels into his side, pointing to a table set up on the other side of the room. "That way, Cap'n!"

Dear God. Ovaries have exploded. Cuteness overload disabling common sense. Stop me before I do something stupid. Desperately, Mina Blake.

"That's enough, Nell," says Micah. "Hop off Uncle Nathan and let him say hi to everyone before you commandeer him for the evening."

"Nell Bell?" Nathan cranes his neck to meet the giggling girl's eyes. "Is that you?"

"Who else would it be?" She slides off his back, then stands in front of him, her little chin lifted. "You knowed it was me the whole time."

"Maybe," he says with a grin, then shakes his head as Nell skips away and disappears in the crowd.

"So that's my daughter," Micah says to me before turning to his cousins. "She's desperate for a cousin or seven, if any of you would like to get on that it would be very helpful."

The group chuckles and cracks a few more jokes

while I acclimate to a Nathan who doesn't feel like The Prince of Darkness.

"I'm gonna finish saying hello to everyone," he says, during a lull in conversation. "So Mina can meet the whole crew."

We say our goodbyes and make our way around the room. He introduces me to so many people I'm dizzy with names and faces. Dinner is delicious, the cake is huge, and damn if the smile on Nathan's face when he blows out the candles feels like sunshine. We sing. We eat. We help ourselves to cocktails from the bar.

And then, we dance.

Nathan's arms are draped around my waist, his eyes locked on mine. I'd almost buy that he adored me if I didn't know the truth. And if I'm being honest, I wouldn't mind being adored by the man I met tonight. I don't know which version of him is real. The grumpy rich asshole who charges obscene amounts of money for a favor? Or the man giving piggyback rides to his niece and making house calls to nervous students because he's the guy who drops everything to save the world?

"You are uncomfortably good at this," I say with a sigh.

"At what?"

"Pretending to like me."

He cocks his head and grins like I said something to

melt his heart. "I'll admit, it's taking more energy than I thought it would."

Of course, then he says things like that and I remember everything about tonight is an illusion. Grumpy rich assholes can be good with kids *and* awful with everyone else.

Nathan's hands slip lower on my back, almost brushing my ass for the third time since this song started playing.

"Touch my butt one more time. Go ahead. I dare you," I say, pressing my cheek to his chest.

"It's a great ass."

"It's an off-limits ass."

"You didn't have to wear a thong."

I pull back, my brows lifted into twin stop signs. "I see. You're one of those men."

Nathan slides his hands a few inches towards safety. "And what kind of man do you think I am?"

"One who blames a woman's clothing for his lack of self-control. A proud member of the 'she asked for it' crew."

He stops in his tracks. "A man is responsible for his actions. Always." His eyes are intense as they hold mine and there's a flicker of something dancing in my belly.

Something that feels like we're having a moment.

And I'm not interested in having moments with Nathan West.

So, I do the only reasonable thing. I slide myself back into his arms, press my body against his, then take both his butt cheeks in my hands and squeeze.

He jumps. Yelps. Then pulls back and now it's his eyebrows reaching for his hairline. "What the hell are you doing?"

"Just in case what you said was bullshit, I thought you'd like a turn at feeling objectified."

Nathan shakes his head and laughs lightly.

"What was that?" I ask, dropping my jaw in astonishment.

"What was what?"

"That sound you just made."

"I didn't make a sound."

"You did. From anyone else, I'd say it was laughter, but I didn't know The Prince of Darkness knew how to do that."

"Very funny," Nathan replies in a voice lacking the sarcastic edge I've come to know and hate.

"You should do that more. It's, uh, well it's very appealing." A blush burns across my cheeks. Did I really say that? Out loud?

"I'll take that under advisement." His gaze slips over my shoulder, and when his eyes meet mine, there's a spark of something I don't have a name for. "My cousins are staring."

"Good?"

"Just warning you what's about to happen." Nathan reaches for me, lightly drawing his finger down the side of my face and along my neckline. His touch is gentle yet electric, sending shockwaves through every inch of my body. His fingers whisper across my skin, lower, lower, until they rest just above the swell of my breasts.

I'm shocked.

I'm speechless.

I should be outraged, no, I *am* outraged but I'm hypnotized as he moves closer, then closer still. Our lips are almost touching. My senses captured. I'm surrounded by the scent of sandalwood and whisky and the musk of his skin. Surprisingly, I don't hate it. I don't hate it at all.

Eyes on my mouth, he tilts his head and thank God for small miracles, I snap out of whatever spell he's cast on me before I allow him to do something we'll both regret. I am so not ready to be kissed by The Prince of Darkness.

I turn my face and press my cheek to his chest, wrapping my arm around his shoulders and holding him close while I catch my breath...

Only I can't.

Not with his dick thickening, lengthening, and pressing against me, a long line of warmth neither of us can ignore.

No matter how much we might want to.

Nathan dances us into a dark corner, out of the middle of the room, then steps back. We stare for several long moments, my chest heaving, his eyes heavy and hooded and filled with something that sets my heart racing.

"Sorry," he murmurs. "I had a lot to drink."

"Me too." I swallow hard. "I mean, obviously that's the only way something...like that...would happen." I glance pointedly at his crotch, which sends my libido into a happy dance of expectation, then drag my focus back to his face. I thought that would be safer ground, but it's not. The heat in his gaze threatens to light me ablaze.

Nathan frowns. His jaw tightens. Brows furrow. "Obviously," he says, crossing his arms over his chest. "Listen, I—"

"Wilhelmina!" booms a familiar voice. "You are the last person I expected to see in Nathan's arms. After our conversation this morning?" I turn to see Mason Channing, drink in hand, sunshine engaged.

It might be the first time I'm not happy to see him.

"You know I'm just plain Mina," I say, hoping I don't sound as discombobulated as I feel.

"Not in that dress." Mason flares his hands like the statement is obvious. "So, which is it? My cousin's an asshole? Or you're dating?"

"Both," I say with a shaky laugh and a glance at Nathan, whose face is maddeningly unreadable.

After tonight, I know one thing for sure:

I don't know the real Nathan West.

THIRTEEN

Nathan

The party ends, I sober up, and drive Mina back to her car. All in all, the evening didn't go too badly. Hot Mess Express or not, Mina Blake is beautiful. She wears the hell out of that red dress. It begs my hands to explore every curve. Her smile is a gentle white wine, a light rain after a scorching summer day. Her rich black hair hangs straight and shines like moonlit midnight over water. Her lips are candy, sweet and baited.

I want to taste them. And damn it, I almost did. Worse, I'm disappointed I didn't.

There's something to her. Something I didn't expect.

She's funny.

And strong.

And won't take my shit.

Mina doesn't like me. And she has every right not to. I've been rude. And selfish. And impulsive.

Hell, *I* don't want to like *her*.

But part of me does.

And that is a big ass problem.

When people like Mina look at me, they see an opportunity. Not a human being with hopes and dreams and feelings.

And because Blossom opened my eyes to that truth, I've wrapped myself in barbed wire, frozen like that damn picture Mina included in her mood board this afternoon. I'm not supposed to like being seen or understood. I'm not supposed to let Mina's smile lower my guard.

This is a woman who would do anything for money, including pretend to date a man she thinks is an evil, villainous, Prince of Darkness. Her old car and worn clothes tell me she's hurting for money, and me? I'm a fucking bank.

How can I believe anything she says or does around me is real?

I can't. Simple as that.

"You're awfully quiet," Mina says as I pull to a stop beside her car. Streetlamps illuminate the parking lot, light diffused by humidity tumbling through the window to brighten her face. "Having second thoughts about this whole fake relationship thing?"

Her tepid smile tells me she definitely is.

"Something like that." I roll my lips together and stare out the windshield, watching bugs flit around the streetlights.

"If this is a bad idea, we could end our little experiment and no one would think twice."

"No." I speak too quickly. Too sharply. My voice is intense. Mina's gaze darts my way and she frowns, then holds up her hands.

"Fine. Fine. No worries. I said I'd do a thing, so I'll do the thing. I'm just getting weird signals from you and honestly, this whole day's got me wondering if I should be looking for hidden cameras or something." She finishes the sentence with a shrug and silence charges the atmosphere of the car.

My jaw pulses in frustration. With myself. With her. With everything that's happened in the last several months. She's waiting for me to explain my strange behavior. Hell, I'm waiting for me to explain my strange behavior.

"I've had a lot to drink," I finally say, even though we both know I was perfectly sober before I got behind the wheel.

Mina lifts her chin like she's assessing the statement, then shakes her head and lets it pass. Now it's her turn to watch the bugs dancing under the streetlights.

"Maybe that explains it."

She doesn't sound convinced. Her brows furrow as she sighs deeply.

"I know it's none of my business—"

I snort. "But you're going to make it your business anyway?"

She huffs a sigh and shakes her head. "...but whatever you're trying to run from isn't going away on its own. You're not letting yourself feel whatever it is, which means you're not processing, so it's just sitting in there, festering. It's only going to get worse."

Scowling, I glare out the window. "Who says I'm running from something?"

"Maybe you're not, but after watching you with your family, something tells me you are. And call me crazy, but I hate to watch anyone self-destruct. Even The Prince of Darkness." She offers the name with a smile. Not a barb, but a friendly jab.

I swipe a hand down my face. "I'm not self-destructing."

And I'm tired of people saying I am. I'm setting boundaries and making sure they don't get crossed. I'm doubling down on doing good work for people who deserve it. Feels more like self-preservation to me.

"All right, then." Mina gives me one of those looks

you save for awkward situations with people you don't want to offend. "I think it's probably time to call it a night."

"You're probably right." I grip the steering wheel and sigh.

Mina puts a hand on my arm, and that jolt of what-the-holy-fuck stops me in my tracks. "Think about what I said," she says, her voice soft. "I think there's more to you than smirks and snark and all this villain era BS. I think maybe you're working through something and, well, you don't have to work through it alone."

I start to thank her, but I've already blurred my boundaries too much tonight. I close my eyes and clear my throat instead.

"I can take care of myself," I growl.

With a sad shake of her head, Mina blows a puff of air past her lips. "Says the man who paid his interior designer to go to his birthday party rather than deal with whatever's going on in his life."

Her eyes flash and she shoots me a grin that says, "So there."

I put in a request for a scathing comeback that my brain completely ignores, so after a few silent seconds, I guide her back to her car, leaning down before I close the door. "Good night, Hot Mess."

"If you say so, Sweet Prince." Mina lifts her hands

and waves as she pulls out of the spot. I return the gesture as her words replay in my mind.

...you don't have to work through it alone.

As much as I'd like that to be true, tonight has shown me one thing for sure:

I can't trust myself around Mina Blake.

FOURTEEN

Mina

"Oh my God, Fallon. You'll never believe how awful tonight was." Perched on the edge of my best friend's couch and still wearing my red dress, I drop my head into my hands, then spread my fingers to peep at my friend's reaction.

"I've got a huge case of déjà vu." Fallon sits beside me, hair up, PJs on. We look just as mismatched as I did with Nathan at the party. Well. Not just Nathan. His entire family was significantly more casual than I expected. I stuck out like a sore thumb. A bright red, very sore thumb. Which was only the beginning of my humiliation.

"How can you have an awful night when you look

that good?" Fallon frowns. "And how is it that you look that good and I don't know why?"

Everything happened so fast today, I didn't call her after lunch to tell her about my new fake relationship. She'd make a bigger deal out of it than it is, maybe try to talk me out of it, or maybe I was just embarrassed by the whole thing. Even now, I'm a tad hesitant to fill her in, and that doesn't seem right. Maybe it's because I know how she feels about him. Whatever it is, it's time to get over it.

"I was with Nathan..." I begin, but the rest of the sentence sticks in my throat.

"Nathan? As in Nathan West? You look like that because of Nathan West?" Fallon waves her hand over my face and body, looking intrigued.

"You are so not prepared for this."

"Something tells me whatever happened tonight is gonna make my readers go crazy when they read about it. My sub count has grown so much since I started talking about Nathan West." Her gaze shifts toward the ceiling, her eyes glazed and faraway. She's already trying out headlines and that isn't going to work. I might not like Nathan, but that doesn't change the definition of right and wrong.

"Nope. No way. Hard stop. You either promise this is protected by best friend code, or I keep the story to myself," I say, holding up a finger. "You absolutely cannot publish any of this."

Fallon blinks. Frowns. For a moment, I wonder if I misjudged the power of best friend code, but then she bobs her head and shows her palms. "Done. Your secret is safe with me."

"Nathan and I had a meeting scheduled this afternoon to talk about some of my ideas for his house, and you will never guess what he asked me." Stalling, stalling. Why do I keep stalling? Does some part of me not trust Fallon with this information?

"To come up with an entirely different scheme, using colors that will clash with his personality and ruin the flow of the space." She speaks with the confidence of someone who's listened to me complain about work too many times.

"It's worse than that," I respond with a laugh. "Way worse."

Fallon puts a hand to her heart and drops her jaw. "Tell me he didn't decide to go with the architect's functional placement for the staircase rather than your more aesthetically pleasing idea?"

See? This is Fallon. There's absolutely zero reason to feel weird about sharing this story with her.

"I mean, that sounds exactly like something he'd do, and bless you for listening to me enough to know that's even a thing. But no. It's worse than that. Best friend code?" I ask, arching a brow and cocking my head.

Fallon mimes zipping her lips. "This information is protected by said code and shall go no further."

I explain lunch with Nathan and his request for a fake date, his sudden disappearance and me deciding to use the internet for inspiration on what to wear.

"Which turned out to be a total bust, by the way. Imagine meeting Nathan's family, who are all perfectly sweet, pretending like I'm falling in love with this guy that I barely even know and what I do know, I don't like. All while wearing this dress while everyone else was super casual." I flare my hands down my body, remembering the way Nathan trailed his finger along the swell of my breast. My body throbs its approval while I shove the memory into a dark corner to evaluate later. Or never. Whatever's better for my mental health.

"Oh, Mina." Fallon flops back, resting her head on the headrest and her feet on the coffee table. "You always, *always* meet up before the first date and get your stories straight. You know, set ground rules."

She speaks with such authority, I wonder how many fake relationships she's been a part of, but we'll circle back to that later.

"You mean ground rules like no groping?" I ask. "Or making comments on my underwear choice?"

I flash to the look of contrition on Nathan's face when I called him on it, then the look of shock when I grabbed his butt. My cheeks twitch into a smile that Fallon wipes away by hitting me in the arm.

"He did not grope you and talk about your underwear!"

The arch to my eyebrow asks her why I'd lie. "His hands. Headed for my butt. But I returned the favor and that seemed to set things straight." I explain what happened and I can't believe it, but I've finally rendered Fallon speechless.

"This..." she finally manages, "is exactly why you need ground rules."

I stand and move to the kitchen, my heels clicking across her tile floor until I stop and kick them off with a sigh of relief. "We were supposed to discuss things before the party," I say as I yank open the fridge. "But he..."

I don't even know what I'm looking for. I'm not hungry. Or thirsty. And a reason to avoid telling Fallon Nathan ditched me to play White Knight for a little kid isn't sitting next to the ketchup. If I give her this tidbit of kindness on his part, she'll be sure her plan to shame him back into his old self is working and I'm not sure that's true. I don't want to encourage her.

"He what?" she asks from the doorway, clearly finding my behavior suspicious.

I lean farther into the fridge. "He had something come up."

Fallon's head pokes in beside mine. "Something came up. Are you kidding me?"

"It's not that big of a deal. Especially because I negotiated the rest of my design fee back, plus twenty percent." I straighten with a little swagger in my step, then swing the fridge door shut like the badass I am.

"Twenty percent." Fallon does not look impressed. "You gave him a sixty percent discount for one measly text, and he can only fork up twenty for an entire fake relationship? Oh, Mina..."

"That twenty percent is gonna help Mom."

"That twenty percent should have been eighty. Or ninety." Fallon sighs deeply. "I was going to go for the ice cream, but I think this situation calls for a drink. This man does not have your best interest at heart. And you..." She shakes her head. "You're so kind and loyal, you expect the same thing from everyone you come across. You dismiss giant red flags because you see this little nugget of goodness, like your mom did with your dad."

I frown. I've worked hard to build a better screening process than my mother's, but challenging Fallon's point will do no good. Once she decides she's right on a topic, she'll fight to the death over it.

Fallon grabs a bottle of wine and her giant glasses,

filling them to the brim. I remind myself to sip carefully tonight. The last thing I need is another drunken mishap.

"You're gonna need some insurance," she says, sliding a glass my way. "In case Nathan turns on you."

"Turns on me? What's that even mean?" My feet are still aching, so I hop onto the counter while Fallon stares into space. She does that when she's brainstorming new ideas. She once described it as watching mind-movies.

"That's the thing with these guys," she says, her eyes still far away. "You never know. Nathan's so rich, his grandchildren's grandchildren won't need to work. That kind of money comes with power." She hops onto the counter beside me and lets her legs swing, shaking her head at the blight of generations living to excess while others struggle.

"But what's he going to do with that power?" I lean in, caught up in her vision and her eyes snap back into focus.

"How am I supposed to know that?"

"You're the one who brought it up." And spoke with so much confidence, I was sure she knew what she was talking about.

"I just think you need a little leverage. In case things get squirrely."

Leverage? What in the world does she think is

gonna happen? Nathan's going through something, and he's not always easy to be around, but he's not actually an evil asshole. Not by a long shot. I'm not in any real danger. Not unless death by annoyance is a thing. Though with Nathan and his Jekyll and Hyde mood swings, it just might be.

Fallon hefts her wine glass to her lips, then freezes, a grin blooming. "I know! I'll write an article about the relationship being fake. 'It's Fake, Folks!' That's such a catchy headline, I'd grab more subscribers for sure."

"No. I already told you this whole thing is protected by best friend code. You will do nothing of the sort."

"You're not seeing the bigger picture here." Fallon's grin continues to grow as she turns to me. "If things go off the rails or you're in a bad situation, I'll publish the article to give you a little breathing room."

"That's a bad idea." And I'm seriously starting to regret letting her in on this secret.

"Worse than pretending to date a man you know nothing about and can't really stand, without spending time to lay some ground rules?" The arch to Fallon's brow says she thinks she has me.

"I don't know..." I drag out the last word, hoping to buy time for a catchy comeback that doesn't arrive. "But I'm sure we won't need leverage."

"Why? Because Nathan's been such an upstanding guy since you met him?"

I can't get away from the image of him carting his niece around on his back. Or the way his whole demeanor changed when he was around his family. Fallon herself has said Nathan used to be this amazing guy. Why assume he'll stay in this grumpy state? He probably just needs time to work through whatever he's working through and meeting bad energy with more bad energy isn't helpful.

"I just don't like it, that's all. I just met the guy. I'd like to give him a chance to prove my first impression wrong before we start planning ways to bring him down."

"We don't even have to use it. We'll write it tonight. Just in case. I'll save it with my drafts and if things go off the rails, we'll have it."

"Nope. Not happening, Fal."

Fallon hops off the counter and takes my hand. "If only you'd been this resistant when you were at lunch with Nathan. He was the one with the bad idea. I'm the one looking out for your best interests. Villain," she says, waving her hand toward the door. "Best friend." She places her hand to her chest. "And, you know, bonus for me, my readers would just gobble the story up. I might actually cross the one million subscriber mark."

"Good thing it's not about that," I say as she leads me into the living room and plops on the couch.

"Of course not. This is about protecting you."

"Double good thing I won't need protecting. Nathan's a jerk, but…" I shrug and plop down next to my friend. "I can't imagine a situation where I'd, what? End up in danger?"

Fallon snorts. "With this new version of Nathan West, there's no telling where you'll end up."

"It's a no on the article." I lift my brow and stare until she lifts her hands in defeat.

"Fine, fine. I hear you. No article. Just promise me you'll remember it's an option if things go off the rails."

Try as I might, I can't see a scenario where having leverage would do me any good.

"You really expect the worst from people, don't you?" I ask with a frown.

"No, my friend. I expect people to be people." Fallon cups my cheeks and almost looks sorry for me. "You, dear sweet Mina, are too idealistic for your own good."

FIFTEEN

Nathan

**Alert:
Search term "Nathan West" mentioned one time online:
Nathan West Seen with Tech Villain Frederick Chantal. Shocking Proof Former Good Guy is Feeling the Power of the Dark Side.**

If Mina's office had a mood board, there would be pictures of Victorian homes with wrought iron fences. Foggy fields with dew glimmering in the earliest rays of a brilliant sunrise.

The walls are painted a soothing palette of soft grays and muted blues. Large windows adorned with sheer curtains allow natural light to filter in, illuminating the room and giving it an open and airy feel. The desk is a sleek modern piece, no nonsense and clutter-free, except for an orchid arching near her computer in a burst of vibrant purple. The mood board she made for my home is pinned on the wall next to a bookshelf filled with design books and architecture magazines, along with a few photographs and trinkets.

In one corner of the office, plush chairs circle a low coffee table adorned with design catalogs and a chic vase of fresh flowers. The area is perfect for Mina to present her ideas and sketches, fostering a collaborative and inviting atmosphere.

This is not what I expected from the Hot Mess Express.

I scrub a hand over my mouth to wipe away a smile.

It's been a week since my birthday and I still haven't unraveled everything that happened. Mina and I haven't seen much of each other, an unspoken agreement that we needed some space. I almost kissed her. And she almost let me.

And then, in the car, she may have offered to be there for me while I work through whatever is bothering me. And I liked the way it felt, thinking she saw through all the shit posted about me online to who I really am.

And I'm not supposed to like shit like that, especially with someone like her.

So yeah, space was necessary.

"Would you like a cup of coffee? Maybe a bottle of water?" asks Mina's ridiculously good-looking assistant, lingering in the doorway, eyeing me like he's prepared to defend his boss's honor if I make one wrong move.

"I'd love a coffee," Mina replies, sitting behind her desk, back straight, prim, proper. Our eyes meet and my heart thumps a wild rhythm.

What the fuck is that about?

I've never met anyone who made me feel so out of control.

I hate it.

"Mr. West?" she prompts, and I swallow hard.

"Coffee, please. Strong and black."

Tad nods, pushes off the doorframe, and then Mina and I are alone.

"Look, I—" I begin at the same time she says, "I think we should—"

There's an awkward laugh and some dodgy eye contact before I let out a short breath. "You first."

Mina crosses her legs, then promptly uncrosses them. Folds her arms over her chest, then licks her lips and finally settles on clasping her hands in her lap. "I asked you to arrive early so we can talk freely before Benjamin gets here. After the catastrophe that was your birthday last week, I think we—"

The door swings open and in breezes Tad, sporting two coffee mugs and a grin the size of Texas. "Here's a hot, sweet, and basically white for Ms. Blake and a broody, dark, and bitter for Mr. West."

He sets the mugs down in front of us, then pauses at the door. I feel his eyes boring into the back of my head like a guard dog alerting to danger before he closes the door and once again, Mina and I are alone. She takes a drink of what looks more like a milkshake than a coffee, and I sip a rich, dark brew. Her outfit is demure today, a cream-colored blouse buttoned up to her throat and a form fitting blue skirt that stops just below her knees. It's a stark contrast to the red dress she wore the other night, but my hands still ache to be on that body.

Mina rests her elbows on the desk and her chin on her hands. "As I was saying, if we're going to pull this fake relationship off, we need to be better prepared than we were at your parents' house. We need a story and we need a plan, Mr. West. A good one."

"Before we get to that, you need an apology, Ms. Blake. A good one." I smile as I mimic her no-nonsense speech pattern. "I wasn't myself that day. I haven't been myself for some time now and I assure you, you won't deal with that version of me again."

"So, you're saying that behavior isn't typical for you." Her eyes glimmer with ball busting glee. She's given me that excuse more than once and looks thrilled to throw the words back into my face. I hate that I gave her the ammunition but respect her for using it. It will, however, be the last time Mina Blake gets the better of me.

I glare into my coffee before meeting her eyes. "Since you called me in early, I assume you have ideas on how we should prepare, which would be strange because planning ahead seems out of character for the Hot Mess Express."

There. That's better. A return to equilibrium. It's better when we bicker.

"There's a hot mess in this room, but I don't think it's me." With a crooked grin, Mina cups her mug in both hands and sits back to cross her legs. "In no particular order, we need an end date on this relationship. We need parameters in place regarding physical contact, number of dates we'll be going on, what those dates will look like, and who pays for what while we're out. We need our stories straight about how we met and why we like each other because what happened last week was humiliating."

I take another pull of coffee to hide my smile. "That's a comprehensive list."

She nods, pleased. "I think you'll find me most thorough."

I flash to her naked, on her knees, her mouth on my dick while I wrap my fist in that silky hair. How thorough would she—

What the actual fuck?

What is wrong with me?

Mina and I have a business agreement. There's no room for her lips on my dick in a business agreement. Not even when it happens in my head. And especially when we don't even know each other.

Or like each other.

Mina. In the car. Watching bugs dance through streetlights. "I think maybe you're working through something and, well, you don't have to work through it alone..."

I scrub the memory away.

"All right," I say, like I didn't just mentally fuck her mouth. "An end date." I stare towards the ceiling and pluck the first one that comes to mind. "My cousin Nick received orders and will ship out soon. He'll be home in six months. We can stage a breakup after we've been to the party my family is sure to throw in his honor."

"Six months?" Mina arches a brow, probably wondering if she can stand to be around me that long.

"Six months," I say with a decisive nod.

"It'll take about that long to finalize the plans for your house. So, the timing works in more ways than one." She jots a note on her tablet. "What about physical contact? I can't have you groping me whenever you feel like it."

I lean forward, forearms on her desk, drunk on the scent of citrus. "As I remember, you're the one who groped me. I simply readjusted my hands on your back."

"And commented on my underwear." Mina sips her coffee, then mimics my posture, her gaze locked on mine. Her blues meet my greens and I swear she's daring me to say otherwise.

Obviously, that solidifies my need for the last word.

"Did I?" I cock my head. "That doesn't sound like me."

"Oh, you better believe you did. Like it was my fault that you can't control yourself. Who in their right mind would blame someone else for their own bad judgment?" Her eyes flash with surprise and it sounds like she's working herself up to righteous indignation, so I hold up my hands in defeat.

"Okay, okay. You're right. I'm very sorry about the underwear comment and won't do anything like that again." At least not out loud. When it comes to Mina Blake, my mind seems happy to wander into filthy territory on its own accord.

She sits back, satisfied. "I'm glad we both agree. Also, no more unplanned butt touching."

I surprise myself by laughing. "Honestly, that should go without saying."

"Right?" Mina quirks her head and laughs to herself. "Anyway, we obviously need to do some of that stuff in public if we want people to believe we're in a relationship. We can definitely hold hands."

"And you can lean into me." She did that at the party. It wasn't awful.

"And you can wrap your arm around my waist or put your hand on my low back as long as you adhere to the no butt touching rule."

"That seems like all the appropriate touchy-feely in public stuff."

"Exactly. No need to go any farther than that."

There's an awkward moment of silence while I wonder about "farther." If we're really going to sell a relationship that lasts six months, we'll have to do more than light touching at some point. My dick throbs its approval of that idea.

Mina bites her lip, eyes downcast. Is she wondering about "farther" too?

We agree on two dates a week. "I'll pay my half," she says like it's a done deal.

"First of all, no." I bite off the sentence a little harder than I intend.

She recoils. "And second of all?"

"Hell no." I put on what I hope is a friendly smile. "If this relationship was real, I'd be paying for our dates. It would look strange if you're the only woman I expect to split the bill."

Mina jots another note on her tablet then reads for a few seconds before glancing up. Gone is the fidgety woman who didn't know how to arrange her body and in her place is a force to be reckoned with. It's hard to reconcile the two.

"Any special events we want on the calendar? Birthday parties? Holidays?"

"Obviously there's the welcome home party for Nick, but I don't know exactly when it'll be. There's a charity gala at the foundation around that same time frame. I'll want you there with me." And hopefully, by then, my family will be off my back enough that Aunt Maisie won't object to her being there.

Mina starts to respond, but her desk phone rings and she yanks it to her ear. "Yes?" she asks then takes a deep breath and lets it out, shaking her head. "Send him in, Tad," she finishes before whispering, "Game face on. Benjamin's here."

Saying his name rattles her right back to fidgety. Her gaze darts to the door. She bites her lip and furrows her brow. Sitting back, she tucks her hair behind her ear and takes a deep breath. *This guy makes her nervous and I don't know why.*

Though actually, I do.

The crush that inspired that stupid group text.

For some reason that annoys me. Probably because it will be harder to sell our relationship when she's got the hots for another man. Or maybe I want them focused on my build, not each other.

Definitely not each other.

"Easy now, Hot Mess. Don't hurt yourself trying to impress the guy."

Mina rolls her eyes and settles back in her chair, looking poised, polished, and astonishingly beautiful. Benjamin Bancroft enters the office, freezing when he sees me already seated at the desk.

"Am I late?" he asks, adjusting his messenger bag to check his watch.

When we met at the build site, I instantly liked the guy. He's friendly without being cloying. Professional without being stuck up or rude. You'd have no idea he was at the top of his field. Today, watching Mina's cheeks blush when she shakes his hand, I like him a little less. It's not so much her reaction as it is his. His eyes shouldn't linger on her lips. His handshake shouldn't be so...touchy.

I offer him my hand. Linger on that, asshole. "Mina and I had some personal things to discuss before you arrived."

"Oh. Right. The butt biting text. Should I leave?" Benjamin jerks his thumb over his shoulder. "I can sit out there until you're ready."

"There's no need," Mina says. "I think we've just about gotten everything we needed to talk about out in the open."

I should just agree and leave it at that. Move on. Talk about the house. The build. But I don't like the way Benjamin looks at Mina. If anyone else sees him looking at her like that while she blushes like a schoolgirl, it will be really fucking hard to make people believe we're together.

That's gotta be it.

"There's something else we need to get out in the open," I begin with a glance toward Mina. Her face transforms into a minefield of dismay but she catches herself before giving into another fidget outburst.

Benjamin pulls out a chair and sits beside me,

slightly concerned and entirely interested. "Is there a problem?"

"I should hope not." I reach across the desk to take Mina's hand. "Though a lot of that rests on your level of professionalism. Mina and I are in a relationship. A pretty serious one. And I know I should apologize but I'm not sorry, because I'm starting to think she's the best thing that ever happened to me."

I beam sappily into her face and a genuine smile morphs her pretty features into something beautiful. Fuck. I wasn't prepared for that.

And apparently, neither was Benjamin Bancroft.

"Oh. Wow. Yeah. Okay then. That's wonderful. I guess I assumed, you know, your text made it sound like you guys weren't all..." He points back and forth between Mina and me, then tugs at the strap on his messenger bag like it's strangling him.

"Nathan has that way about him," Mina replies. "He can be hard to read until you get to know him, and then he's just...well...we're very happy together, aren't we Sweet Prince?"

"You better believe it..." I almost call her Hot Mess but catch myself just in time. "...HM."

"HM?" Benjamin cocks his head.

"Her nickname isn't exactly work appropriate, if you get my drift."

He nods. "Oh. Right. Yeah. That's funny," he says even though it's clear he's clueless. His gaze turns upward as he mouths "HM" like he's trying to decipher a code.

SIXTEEN

Mina

I always enjoy being at work after hours. The hum of activity dissipates, leaving the cubicles and desks in shadows. My office becomes a haven—an island of light in a hibernating atmosphere. Which is a good thing, given that I've taken on so many new clients, I'd be smart to turn my sitting area into a sleeping area. The bill for Shady Cove is due. Technically, it's past due, though Glenda in the financial office is an angel and gave me some leeway on the stipulation that I didn't tell anyone. I almost had everything under control money-wise until one of my clients, a happily married couple looking to spice up their living space, decided to get divorced instead. How's that for spice?

I'm going to have to figure out something, because

as sweet as Glenda is, that leeway will have a limit and I can't risk Mom losing her place at Shady Cove. Maybe I should ask Nathan for the advance Fallon suggested when this whole thing started. I cringe, then question the reaction. Maybe going to him for help wouldn't be as bad as I fear.

After weeks of feigning a relationship with Nathan, we have settled into a strangely pleasant rhythm. We go on three dates a week instead of the two we agreed on and I'm not even sure how that happened. I think it just feels nice, pretending to be falling in love. Mostly, we have dinner and drinks at The Pact, a bar and grill owned by his aunt and uncle. Nathan likes being there because we're most likely to be seen together and inspire family gossip. I'm a fan because I love everything about the place. The ambiance captures the essence of island living with its laid-back charm. There's a pool table and a dart board. A jukebox adorned with colorful neon lights that perpetually plays good music. The décor reflects the coastal vibe, with nautical accents, wooden furnishings, and walls adorned with local artwork as well as the pact the owners wrote when they first became roommates, swearing they'd never fall in love. Funny how that turned out.

Everything on the menu is mouthwatering, inspired by local flavors and seafood. From conch fritters to grilled mahi-mahi tacos, I've yet to find something I don't like. The bar serves an array of tropical cocktails, craft beers, and signature drinks. I leave slightly tipsy and totally full most nights.

Our time together has been spirited, to say the least. Nathan and I pretend to flirt while actually picking fights in round after round of one-upmanship. Though lately, we've been running out of things to argue about and have stumbled into actual conversations that give me glimpses of the man his cousins know. The man his students know. Kind. Caring. Giving. But say the wrong thing or make the wrong move and Nathan shuts that down. Hard. He's trying to draw boundaries. Or recreate himself. Or something. Whatever it is, he's going about it all wrong. Maybe someday we'll talk about it.

Even though we promised we wouldn't go farther than arms around shoulders and hands on waists, the moment we get together, that all goes out the window. He'll touch my cheek and electricity courses through my body, so I return the favor by rubbing my thigh against his. My libido riots when his eyes go hot, heavy, and hooded, then obviously, he lets his hand linger on my hip until one of us says something to irritate the other and then we're rat-a-tat-tatting to see who gets the last word.

Bicker. Flirt. Bicker. Flirt. Everything between us is fire and flash.

I sit back in my office chair and stretch. My aching muscles thank me for the movement. According to the tension in my neck and shoulders, I've been hunched over my desk longer than I thought. I have a meeting with Benjamin in the morning to discuss our preliminary plans for Nathan's build and I stayed late so I could be prepared, not exhausted.

My phone lights up with a call as I check the time.

I huff in surprise when Benjamin Bancroft's name fills the screen. Did I summon him with my thoughts? Might be a beneficial skill, seeing as I've loved every minute of working with him so far. He's talented. Driven. The design in my mind blends perfectly with the structure in his. At least that's the way I see it. Maybe to him, I'm the young pup biting at the ankles of a titan.

I accept the call and put the phone to my ear.

"Speak of the devil," I say, then grimace. Weird much, Mina?

"I hope we're speaking good things." Benjamin sounds like he's smiling. Or flirting. No...that's ridiculous. He wouldn't be flirting. He thinks I'm dating Nathan. I must be getting my signals crossed.

"I was thinking about you more than speaking, I guess." I blink several times, quickly, then slap my cheeks to knock the cobwebs loose. If that doesn't sound like flirting, I don't know what does. "I'm at the office, preparing for our meeting tomorrow," I clarify, in my most professional voice.

"I thought that was your car in the lot." Benjamin huffs a laugh, almost embarrassed. "I was working late too, saw your car, and thought I'd take a chance that you'd like to work late, together. I'm kind of right outside your building."

He's here?

Now?

I peer through my office door toward the front of the building while Benjamin continues, "I do some of my best thinking while driving. It was chance that brought me your way." He sounds nervous, which makes me giddy.

Is the man named "One to Watch" five years running worried about what I think of him?

"I actually know that about you," I say, then hurry to explain. "I read an article about you...okay, I've read lots of articles about you, but this one explained how you like to 'drive down the ideas.' I tried it, hoping to get some Bancroft level inspiration, but I'm more visual. I need to move things around in CAD and see the effects of the changes."

"You know, if you wanted, you could let me in and

we could have this conversation face to face. Not that I mind standing out here or anything."

"That, sir, is a solid point," I say, then drop my head into my palm.

Dear God. Send help. Yours truly, Mina Blake.

I push out of my chair and hurry for the door, sending a stack of papers on Tad's desk into the air. I slow my pace as they float to the ground like confetti for a celebration I didn't know was happening. Nathan's words from weeks ago echo in my head.

Easy now, Hot Mess. Don't hurt yourself trying to impress the guy.

My infatuation with Benjamin seems to annoy him, though everything about me seems to annoy him, so I'm not sure it's that big of a deal.

I restack Tad's papers, then make my way through the quiet building. Wouldn't you know, Benjamin's right where he said he'd be, leaning against the wall, messenger bag resting on his hip, looking more handsome in the dimly lit entrance than he has any right to. He lifts a hand when he sees me and I turn the lock, pushing open the door and stepping aside as a muggy blast of air hits me in the face.

"Hey," I say, brushing flyaways behind my ear.

Benjamin's smile softens. "Hey."

He steps inside and the door closes behind him. Suddenly the meditative quiet takes on a life of its own, swirling between us and highlighting that I have no idea what to say or do from here. I'm standing next to a legend.

A legend who drove by my office late at night, saw my car, and stopped because he *wants* to work with me.

And this is after I met Collin and Harlow West. Actually had drinks in their house.

My life is the coolest right now...and I have Nathan to thank for it. I guess even villains can't be all bad all the time. I inwardly grimace at the joke. Nathan isn't a villain. I should stop thinking of him that way.

Benjamin glances around at the interior of Fuller Design and I try to see it through his eyes. The empty reception desk with the vining plant trailing off the edge. The scripty logo on the wall behind. The handful of cubicles leading back to the offices. I've been happy here, but knowing he works out of his home studio instead of for a firm makes me very aware of my modest place in the design world.

"This doesn't look like the kind of place that inspires the design magic you're capable of." He looks pleasantly unimpressed as he leans over the reception counter and peers at the mess Gina considers an organizational system.

I hold out my hands like a realtor showing a home she knows is beneath her client's standards. "Well, see, my magic happens back there. In my office. Not to brag, but I have a door and everything."

Benjamin straightens. "Fancy."

"Follow me and prepare to be amazed." We head for my office, and I'm acutely aware of him behind me. My heart flutters for a moment, and I silently curse the timing of things. Why couldn't the man I've been crushing on forever show up at my office, out of the blue, in the middle of the night, when he didn't think I was dating our rich client?

We step into my office and Benjamin makes an approving face. "Now, see? This? This is where magic happens. I loved this space the first time I was here, and I love it even more now. You're smart with your design, Mina. It shows."

I beam at the compliment. I tried to make the space as inviting as possible without overwhelming the design concepts I present to clients. Clean lines. Clean surfaces. Comfortable seating. Though tonight, my desk is strewn with sketches, fabric swatches, and notes on Nathan's build, with several others I'm working on neatly stacked in the corner.

"Wanna talk about the ideas you're trying to drive down?" I ask, steering the conversation toward a professional tone. "Got some groundbreaking designs keeping you up?"

He chuckles, a sound that warms the room. "If I'm honest, I couldn't wait until tomorrow to see you."

Benjamin looks at me, a flicker of something in his eyes—a question, an invitation. My heart races, unsure of how to navigate this unexpected tension.

While I'm trying to figure out what the hell is going on, Benjamin realizes what he said and hurries to clarify.

"We're good together," he adds, like that makes it all better.

In any other situation, this would be a dream come true. But I'm supposed to be dating Nathan, which makes this kind of a problem.

I step back, palms lifted. "Look, I'm sorry if I gave you the wrong impression..."

"I mean, professionally. We're good together professionally." Benjamin chuckles nervously. "I couldn't stop staring at the preliminaries for Nathan's build and they're good, Mina. Really good. Do you know how many arguments I've had with designers about load bearing walls? They never take things like that into consideration. But you do. You and I make quite the team. I had to get in the car to settle myself down, saw you were here, and well, you know the rest."

I am such an idiot. Of course Benjamin Bancroft wasn't here to hit on me. Why in the world would I jump to that conclusion? And why does knowing he's here professionally make me feel relieved? All this fake flirting with Nathan is messing with my head. I'm seeing things that aren't there. Feeling things that don't exist.

"Do I get to see these magical plans?" I ask.

Benjamin pulls a laptop out of his messenger bag, opens it on the desk and I literally gasp when I see the visual representation of our brains coming together. These designs are only preliminaries and they're damn near perfect.

"I'm not even going to have to argue with you about the staircase placement!" I meet his grin with wide eyes. "That literally never happens."

"I extended the living room by a few feet to make space for one more window," he says, tapping the screen, "maximizing natural light in the morning as per your suggestion. That meant the stairs fit better here..." Another tap.

"Which completely opens up the flow of the first floor." I lean in for a better look. The influx of natural light will transform the feeling of the living room, and after spending so much time with The Prince of Darkness, there's one thing I know for sure...

Nathan West could do with more light in his life.

"This is amazing." I straighten and lean a hip on the desk. "I would have needed a drive to settle myself down after seeing it too."

Benjamin stands close, pointing out several other exciting design features that I totally miss because there's a warm line of contact between us, his shoulder, arm, and hip brushing against mine. Talk about mixed signals! I know he's not flirting, but it sure as hell feels like he's flirting.

I can see the scowl on Nathan's face, hear the gravel in his words. If he saw us now, he'd be upset.

I shift, putting space between me and Benjamin.

That's strange. The man of my dreams is possibly coming onto me, and I can't stop thinking about Nathan. What am I supposed to do with that?

Benjamin leans a hip on my desk, the picture of boyish charm. "Can I ask a personal question?"

I suddenly have a terrible suspicion I'm not gonna like where this is going.

"Sure."

"You're talented. Intelligent. Beautiful. Nathan's, well, he was rude to you at our first meeting and his response to your text that night? The ass biting one?"

I nod and pray Benjamin moves on quickly.

"It didn't give me the warm fuzzies," he finishes. "I know I'm way out of line here, like pushing every possible boundary of our professional relationship out of line, but how do you get from that to being in a serious relationship? Are you sure you want to be with him? Is there a chance the crush you've had on him for years might be blinding you to what's really going on?"

I almost correct him and say that he's the one I've had a crush on for years, but catch myself just in time and exhale all the breath in my lungs in one quick huff. "That is definitely personal," I say instead.

"I don't mean to be rude and you can tell me to shut up and I will, but I hate to see people accept less than they're worth and, something tells me that's what's happening here."

I disintegrate into a fidget fest and search for something to say. Anything at all will do. Unfortunately, I couldn't form a sentence if my life depended on it.

Benjamin straightens, shaking his head and reaching for his laptop. Eyes averted. Cheeks flushed. "I'm sorry. I'm way out of line. I've made my career by following my instincts, but people aren't as straightforward as blueprints. I should know by now not to stick my nose where it doesn't belong."

He shoves his laptop in his bag, and I put a hand on his arm. "It's okay. I appreciate you looking out for me. I do. It's incredibly sweet and thoughtful and I wish more people went out on limbs like that for others. Nathan's..."

Normally a litany of negative descriptors would be clamoring to rocket out of my mouth, but the only word I have tonight is, "...misunderstood. I called him The

Prince of Darkness when we first met. To his face even. When you get past that, he's..."

I search for a word to describe what's underneath Nathan's bristly exterior, but Benjamin holds up his hands.

"You don't have to explain. If you're good, great. Just...if you're not good, I'm here to help."

That's the kind of support I'd expect from Fallon, or my mom, not a business associate whose career is lightyears ahead of mine.

"How are you single?" The question's out before I have time to evaluate its conversational worthiness. Thankfully, Benjamin doesn't so much as flinch.

"I'm a perfectionist who hyperfocuses on just about everything. Great for architecture. Not so great for human interaction. Add a penchant for saying exactly what I'm thinking and oddly enough, that narrows down my dating options." Benjamin swings his messenger bag over his shoulder. "Forgive me?"

"There's nothing to forgive."

Other than the fact that I almost found myself standing up for Nathan.

We say our goodbyes and Benjamin sidesteps his way toward the door, eager for an exit I'm glad to let him take.

SEVENTEEN

Nathan

Mina's ass rubs against my cock as I lean over to adjust her grip on a pool cue. I swear to God, she's doing it on purpose. This sexy little sway back and forth, back and forth, like a cat swishing its tail as she lines up her shot. There's no way she doesn't feel what she's doing to me, so I have no qualms about doing it right back to her.

"You want to hold the stick like this." My breath moves past her ear, lips whispering against the delicate skin at the nape of her neck. My body blankets hers. She shivers, exhaling sharply before glancing over her shoulder to meet my eyes.

We're face to fucking face. Those blue eyes holding me in a death grip of seduction.

"Like this?" Mina readjusts her grasp, giving her focus back to the pool table and wiggling those lush hips against me again.

"Just like that," I growl, though if she doesn't stop, we're going to have a very real, very obvious problem on display. I straighten to let her take the shot, surreptitiously eyeing the patrons at The Pact to see how many people give two shits about our cliché attempt at looking like a couple.

My aunt Hope drops me a knowing wink before disappearing into the office she shares with her husband. She's happy for me, which makes me a dick for selling her a lie, but at least Mina and I are convincing. It's been a while since anyone has mentioned me needing to get my shit together, so the family rumor mill is obviously doing its job.

The crack and clatter of pool balls scattering across felt catches my attention. Mina gasps, then whoops in excitement, lifting her hands over head and wiggling in the spiciest celebratory dance I've ever seen. I adjust my pants and try not to stare, though the guys a few tables over don't join me in the effort. I clear my throat and cock my head, mean-mugging them until they get the message and look away. Assholes.

"Bet you regret teaching me how to play pool now, don't you Sweet Prince?" Mina wiggles her way towards me, eyes blistering with heat.

Fake heat, I remind myself. Though she's getting too good at faking it and my body is getting tired of fighting it. Another jolt of desire strikes like lightning. It's very, *very* real.

Each date we've gone on, the flirting has gotten hotter, the eye contact heavier. We talk about stupid things, argue about everything, but somehow, someway, I feel less like she sees me as a bank account and more like she sees me. Not the villain. Nor the wealthy philanthropist.

Me. Not the...the...trope.

I actually look forward to our nights out.

Instead of stepping away—which is what Mina's expecting—I move into her space, backing her against the pool table and caging her with my arms. My nose brushes hers. Her breath warms my lips.

"Gettin' a little cocky for someone who still needs me to set up her shots."

"Oh, big bad scowly man." She brushes the tip of my nose with her finger. "Maybe I only let you think I still need your help. Maybe I like it when you touch me, and I play dumb so you won't stop."

The twinkle in her eyes could mean anything. Maybe she's telling the truth. Or maybe she knows she's getting to me and is proud of herself.

Only one way to find out.

I grab her by the waist and pull her close, our

bodies crashing together, my hand strong and possessive against her back. "You mean touch you like this?"

Mina gasps, her eyes wide and dilated, her chest heaving. "Yes," she whispers on an exhale, voice shaking, "like that."

I swallow hard as all things Mina invade my senses. Her scent. Her touch. I consider kissing her and in that brief moment I think she considers kissing me, but I release her before either of us can make that mistake.

What the hell is wrong with me? I'm playing with fire, touching her like that.

The question is echoed in Mina's eyes as she puts some distance between us to set up her next shot. She licks her lips, a sign she's working up the courage to say something she's nervous to have out in the open. Everything about her demeanor changes. I don't know if it's because of what just happened or what she's about to tell me.

"Benjamin came to see me last night."

I scowl. What possible reason would he have to drop in outside of work hours? Whatever it is, I'm not a fan.

"At home?"

"At the office." Mina sights down the cue, her tongue caught between her lips, then sighs and straightens. "He was prepping for our meeting this morning, went for a drive, saw my car, and stopped in because he was so excited about the plans for your build, he couldn't wait to show me."

Or, he was so excited about the beautiful woman all alone after dark that he couldn't pass up a chance to see her without anyone else getting in the way. Benjamin is attracted to Mina. I have no doubts about that. Who wouldn't be? Obviously, I am. As are the guys at the table next to us. And if the way our waitress keeps stopping by to stare means anything, she is too.

So why is this Benjamin conversation making my jaw clench?

"Your house is gonna be beautiful, Nathan. I can't wait for you to see it."

"With you at the helm, I'm sure it's just about perfect." Strangely enough, that's not bullshit I'm spouting to make our relationship feel real. Mina is truly talented.

"That's very sweet of you to say, but it's a team effort. Benjamin said it himself. He and I are great together. Our brains just click. It's a partnership made in heaven, and I have you to thank for that. Not only am I working with my hero, but he likes my work." She beams and I chew the inside of my lip.

I should be celebrating that my interior designer and my architect are a great fucking match, but it feels more like a splinter I can't get out. An itch I can't scratch. An irritation I can't solve. I start to ask if she's still attracted to Benjamin, but Mina speaks up again, clearly nervous.

"So, uh, I have a favor to ask."

"How much is this one going to cost me?" I joke, but she doesn't laugh. Instead, she braces for impact. Damn. And here I was just starting to think she didn't see me as a bank account.

"No more than you already owe me. But I was hoping maybe you could pay me sooner? Or in installments? I know our contract states I'll be paid after services are rendered but..." She flares her hands, eyes meeting mine with no small amount of trepidation.

Something's not right. The car. The clothes. The apartment. I used to think she was bad with money but the Mina I've come to know is more meticulous than I gave her credit for.

"Of course. Yeah. I can cut you a check first thing tomorrow if that would help." I fold my arms over my chest and try to end the sentence right there, but my mouth has other ideas. "Are finances tight for you? Do you need more money?"

Mina's lips part. Her gaze bounces across my face, filled with questions, with confusion, with gratitude and embarrassment. My heart clenches, something in my soul unlocking, unwinding...

Shit.

Look at me, running to the rescue yet again. I know

better than to let myself care. I know better than to get involved. I'm supposed to be playing the villain and here I am, donning my white armor to fight for Mina's honor. Everything we are to each other is a lie. She's not my girlfriend and has feelings for someone else. Even if she needs to be rescued, I'm not the man to do it.

Mina inhales, about to speak, but I hurry forward to cover my mistake. "I mean, that's how a boyfriend would respond, right?" I whisper with a conspiratorial smile.

"Ahh." Understanding streaks across her face. "Right. Yeah. Very smart. Thank you." She clears her throat then takes a long drink, looking embarrassed before hopping off the stool to distract herself with the pool table.

I need to get my act together and remember why I'm doing this.

This is a fake relationship.

I'm the villain, not the prince.

I can't be caught up by the way she moves her ass. Or dream up ways to protect her from problems I'm not even sure exist. This relationship is a business venture that ends in just under five short months.

Nothing more.

Something about that makes me incredibly sad.

EIGHTEEN

Mina

Nathan is a much better actor than I gave him credit for. I actually thought he was concerned for me. For this precious moment, he looked like he genuinely cares about me. Like he could tell I'm going through something and wanted to help.

And I *liked* him looking that way.

After an hour of feeling my core tighten and my nipples pebble every time he leaned over me to adjust the pool cue, maybe that makes sense. I've never had someone flirt so suggestively, so thoroughly, pulling out my chair for me, opening doors, deep, intense eye contact whenever I talk, followed by questions that suggest he was actively listening.

He makes me feel appreciated.

He makes me feel beautiful.

He makes me feel wanted, no, *needed,* like he's seconds from lifting my skirt, ripping my undies to shreds and burying himself to the hilt. And then, when we're finished, we'd spend the whole night on the beach. He'd play his guitar for me, and we'd laugh and talk and *connect* until the sun shimmered across the sea.

No wonder I'm confused.

Attention like that would be hard for anyone to resist.

I line up a shot, half wishing for the warmth of his body pressed against mine, the brush of his lips against my ear, when Nathan's phone dings. I glance over in time to see his eyes darken. His jaw tightens. His lips press into a thin line and his shoulders slump. All the light that had brightened his scowl drains away. He is The Prince of Darkness once again.

"Damn it," he mutters, then locks the screen and banishes his phone to a back pocket with a gritty apology.

"What's wrong? Is Ricky having another guitar emergency? Do you need to go?"

Nathan brushes off my question. "It's nothing bad. Nothing good either, but it can wait," he says, his scowl deepening.

"You sure?" I ask, concern tightening my chest.

His mood has done a full one-eighty. Whatever just happened is more bad than good. I cock my head in question and wait to hear more.

He doesn't make me wait long. "I have an alert set for whenever my name gets mentioned online. Apparently yet another article has been published about me."

My initial response is full of long-standing biases. Something along the lines of: *Why am I not surprised? Of course he needs to know the second someone mentions him. His ego demands dopamine from spotlights and attention.*

Though, that doesn't jibe with the man I'm starting to know. Nathan West doesn't need approval from others the way I assume everyone with fame and money does. And if the pulsing muscle in his jaw has anything to say about it, he's not riding high on a much needed dose of dopamine.

He's pissed the hell off.

Go figure. I can always count on The Prince of Darkness to find a reason to be grumpy.

Meanwhile, my belly tingles with a heady mix of excitement and worry. Fallon said she would mention me in her next article. I've been giddy ever since. Maybe this is it.

"What's it say?" I ask, aware that my excitement clashes with his frustration and consciously take it down a notch. The chances that this has anything to do with Fallon's article are small. I doubt she's even a blip on his radar.

Nathan scrubs his face, then shakes his head. "Nothing good, I'm sure. They never do."

I cringe, thinking of Fallon's mission to make him see how much he's changed. "*None* of them?"

"Not lately anyway." Nathan sighs, then runs a hand through his hair. It flops into his eyes, transforming his scowl into a smolder before he shakes it back into place. "And it's mostly just one blogger. She's relentless. If I so much as step into the crosswalk a second early, she's there. Yammering away about my villain era."

I inwardly cringe. Fallon's been calling this his villain era too. I've always questioned the validity of her idea to "bring him back to himself." How can pointing out someone's mistakes, without context or caring, spur positive change? If his reaction to this other blogger is any indicator, he has enough people calling him out. I'll have to tell her how much it bothers him so she can take it down a notch.

Nathan sucks his teeth before sitting back and crossing his arms over his chest. His muscles flex and my libido shouts its approval. I imagine him hefting me onto the pool table, spreading my knees with strong palms sliding up my inner thighs, stepping close, heated gaze, rough touch...

Enough already! His response to me asking for an advance should be enough to shut down all physical reactions from this point forward.

Isn't that what a boyfriend would say?

Dear Mina. This is fake. Sincerely, yourself.

I drag my focus back to Nathan's face and look for something to say, but he sits forward, gesturing as he continues.

"And on the one hand, I get it. A lot about my life has changed, but this woman...she crosses lines. Everything I do, and I mean *everything,* she twists into something terrible with these clickbait headlines. She's profiting off my misery. Fucking vulture. She has my whole family thinking I'm out drinking myself stupid and sleeping with a different woman every night. I tell them it's not me, it's my friend, but they'd rather believe her. It's the whole reason I came up with this fake relationship idea in the first place, to help them see she's the problem, not me...just see for yourself." Shaking his head in disgust, Nathan shifts one hip to slide his phone out of his pocket, then freezes. "You know what? Never mind. It doesn't matter. Whatever Fallon fucking Mae has to say about me can wait for later. I don't need to drag you into this more than I already have."

Fallon...? She's the reason he's paying me to date him?

"I kind of thought you'd be used to being in the public eye, after growing up in a family like yours."

Nathan picks up his empty glass and glares into the bottom before plonking it back to the table. "There's no way to get used to invasions of privacy like this. This woman can blow a cup of coffee into a three-act tragedy. And then? When something bad does happen? It's blasted to the world, without any context. I'm imperfect, just like everyone else. I'm good and bad and right and wrong. I just get to go through it all with public commentary."

I catch myself chewing my lip and take a drink instead. Damn nervous habits sneaking in to ruin my aura of confidence. Being friends with Fallon makes me feel complicit in his misery. He's so much deeper than she gives him credit for. He's not a two-dimensional character on a TV show. He has nuance and feelings. I need to tell her to back off.

"Humans weren't designed to have this much attention," Nathan continues. "Fucks with your head." His green eyes flash with anger, followed by sympathy. "If this headline is any indicator, you'll see what I mean soon enough."

"Why?" Adrenaline dumps into my system, twisting excitement with concern. This must be the article Fallon told me about. "What's it say?"

And why didn't she let me read it first?

Nathan pulls his phone out of his pocket to read, "Serial dater Nathan West adds another girl to his lineup—and she's a little different from the rest." He rolls his eyes and puts the device on the table. "I promise you, it's better if you don't pay attention."

"That's not bad, though." I smile, curious about the rest of the article, though I'm sure my best friend made me sound ten times better than I am. "I don't mind being a little different."

"That's what I said the first time Fallon Mae put out an article about me. 'That's not so bad. It's almost complimentary.' Everything went downhill from there. I should have warned you about the possibility of being in the media before I asked you to pretend to date me."

"It's okay, Nathan. It really is. I was aware of the risks."

Mostly because this particular risk comes in the shape of a close friend, but I'll explain that uncomfortable little coincidence later, after I've told her to stop talking about him on her blog and he's less angry. Bringing it up now feels...complicated.

We finish dinner and he pays the bill, then stops to chat with his aunt and uncle. They're the kind of people who feel like sunshine, like Mason, like Angela. I lean close to Nathan just to be close to them, wondering if I'll ever feel like sunshine for someone else.

Nathan says his goodbyes, then walks me to his car, one hand placed firmly on my lower back as he always does. Over the last few weeks, I've grown used to the warmth of his palm, the gentle pressure, the intimacy of his touch.

I know I shouldn't like it.

But I do.

A lot.

We step into a glorious evening and Nathan slides his palm from my back to take my hand. The moon is full and the air is warm, the breeze caressing my skin as it moves through my hair.

"This is my favorite time of day," I say, watching the stars shimmer and shine. "When it's dark out but the energy is high. Expectant. There's no pressure to be or do or conform, but there's this...anticipation...like anything could happen. One minute, you're living your life and the next, everything's different."

There's a heartbeat of silence. Then another. One more and I start to feel judged. Why did I think Nathan would care about my favorite time of day? What's more, why do I want to share that bit of myself with him? This relationship is transactional. It's not real. Getting emotionally involved is a mistake.

But then he stops, tugs my hand to turn me around, then pulls me close, slipping one arm around my waist and nuzzling my nose with his. The look in his eyes is bright, like the moon, filled with promises and anticipation, and maybe he cares more than I thought.

Maybe this isn't an act.

Maybe he's falling.

And I'm falling.

Maybe we aren't faking it.

Maybe, somewhere along the line, this started to become real.

"What are you—"

Nathan tips my chin and brushes his lips to mine. I return the kiss, helpless, hopeless, tentative then insistent. I grip his back as he cups the nape of my neck, his tongue teasing my lips, then meeting my own. He tastes of whiskey but feels like fire, ready to devour me until there's nothing left but smoke and ash and this one perfect moment.

I groan, relaxing into his strong embrace. Humidity hangs in vaporous clouds around us, softening the moonlight. Crickets chirp and someone opens the door to the bar, letting a rush of laughter escape before silence descends around us.

This is another one of those things I don't want to like.

But I do. Oh, but I do.

His touch is strong yet gentle, confident without being demanding. His tongue dances in luxurious circles and I'm melting. Relenting. Walls come down and barriers shift. Our kiss is filled with the anticipation of endless possibilities, matching the energy of the night, without pressure or expectation. My nipples pebble and my core clenches and I was so not prepared for how much I like kissing Nathan West.

This isn't fake. The attraction is real. His. Mine. I'm losing control of this entire situation and...

A throat clears beside us. "Wow, Nathan. In a parking lot? Classy."

Nathan freezes, pulls back a fraction of an inch, his hand still cupping the nape of my neck as he turns to grin sheepishly at his cousin Angela and her husband whose name I've completely forgotten.

"Oh, Angela..." Nathan says with a sarcastic chuckle. "I'm feeling genuinely sorry for Garrett."

Ah. Yes. Garrett. I commit the name to memory while Angela furrows her brows and leans into her husband.

"And why is that?" she asks with a pout.

"Don't you remember being so overcome with passion that you don't care where you are or who can see? You've obviously let the fire burn down."

Garrett throws an arm around Angela's shoulders and pulls her close. "There's no need to feel sorry for me. Our fire is doing just fine."

Nathan dips his chin and shows his palms. "I'm just saying."

His hair falls into his eyes again and his grin comes fast and easy. This is the real version of him. I know it. The villain is a mask. I wonder how hard it would be to help him remove it...

Angela studies her cousin's face, grinning incredulously. "You know, I've been hearing all these stories about how much happier you look now that you're with Mina and I have to say, I didn't think it was true. But look at him," she says to Garrett. "There's not a glare or a growl anywhere. That might even be an actual smile. It's amazing what falling in love with the right person can do."

Angela pokes Nathan's cheeks and he ducks out of reach. "It's a little early to be talking about love."

His gaze locks onto mine and a jolt of electricity blasts through my veins. His eyes are storm-thrashed, filled with...longing? Loathing? I don't even know.

"Yeah, for you," Angela retorts, "but as an interested third party, I can point out the obvious without making it too weird. And maybe this leads to a conversation that will deepen your relationship and growly Nathan might be gone for good."

The look on her face suggests she thinks I'm a saint or miracle worker. I better set her straight before she expects more than I can deliver. "I promise you; he still glares and growls and snorts..."

"I do not snort," Nathan says, following the statement up with a derisive snort while the rest of us burst into laughter.

"That was just bad timing," he says, trying to look serious, but giving in to a chuckle.

"Bad timing, perfect timing, potato, po-tah-to." Angela bumps her shoulder against Nathan's. "You know we love you, right?"

"Is that what you call it? Because I've been a little iffy." Nathan wraps an arm around my waist. He's relaxed. His boundaries are down. His whole vibe is warm and inviting without a frozen barbed wire to be found. I could fall in love with this version of him.

If only he's willing to take off the mask...

"Are you guys coming or going?" Angela asks with a bob of her head toward the entrance to The Pact.

"Going." Nathan's thumb traces my hip, and a tremble of excitement clenches my core.

"Oh, I see, that make out moment was the lead-in to a night of passion—"

"You really could use a filter, you know?" Nathan puts his hands on Angela's shoulders and turns her towards the entrance of The Pact. "Why don't you go inside before you ruin the moment more than you already have."

"Going. Going!" She pivots, walking backwards as her husband guides her. "Hey! We're taking the boat out tomorrow. You two should come with us. I need to get to know the woman who's putting Humpty Dumpty back together again."

Nathan huffs a laugh and shakes his head. "We'll be there, as long as you promise never to say something like that again."

After Angela and Garrett disappear into the restaurant, Nathan steps away from me. "I don't even know what to say other than I am really, really sorry."

"It's fine." I wave away the apology, my lips aching from his kiss. No. That's not quite right. My lips are aching *for* his kiss.

I lick them in case that helps. "I'm fine to add an extra date to our schedule. It's not like we've been sticking to our two-date agreement anyway."

"What?" Nathan pulls back, confusion drawing his brows tight. "No. I mean yes, I'm sorry if I should have talked to you about going out tomorrow first. But I was apologizing for the kiss. I saw them coming and really wanted to sell us being in this relationship and I just kind of did it."

Oh.

Right.

Obviously, that's what I should be upset with him about.

The kiss.

Not a spur of the moment double date with his cousin.

"You don't have to apologize for that," I say, still a little breathless and hoping he doesn't notice. "I mean, it was going to happen eventually, right?"

"Right. I just, wasn't prepared for it to be…" He rakes a hand across his mouth and my brain rapid fires ways to finish that sentence.

Amazing?

Hot?

Intense?

The start of a torrid affair I'll tell stories about from my rocking chair when I'm eighty?

"For it to be today," he finally says.

"At least we got it out of the way." I laugh and it comes out all high-pitched and awkward.

Dear God. Kill me now. Yours truly, Mina Blake.

"Exactly. Now we know what to expect." Nathan clears his throat, his eyes darting towards his car, plotting his escape.

"Right. Now we know." I nod decisively, then let my gaze creep up his handsome face to find him glaring down at me. "You're pretty good at that, you know. Kissing."

A smile quirks his lips and he tilts his head my way. "You know what? So are you, HM. So are you."

After tonight I know one thing for sure:

I really, *really* like kissing Nathan West.

NINETEEN

Nathan

What the hell was that kiss? Mina's fingers threading into my hair, her breasts pressing against my chest. Her lips were supple and soft but stoked the fire we lit at the pool table.

I ruminate over it the entire drive home, then some more as the garage door closes behind me and I let myself into the house. My cock throbs and shudders. I pause, leaning against the kitchen counter to give it a moment to remember who we're talking about here.

This is Mina Blake. My interior designer. Hot Mess Extraordinaire. We have a business relationship. Nothing more.

Except it sure feels like more. Like I can talk to her about anything and she'll listen. Like she sees through the stupid barbed wire I've wrapped around my heart to the man I used to be. Like she wants to help me be that man again. And when I'm with her, I want to be that man again.

Except I'm paying her to date me for shit's sake.

And I promised I'd cut a check for it tomorrow.

Sure, most of the money is for her design services, but there's a financial aspect to our relationship that I can't ignore. It's a devil on my shoulder, whispering, ridiculing...

I'm struck by the memory of Mina's shocked face at Red Stiletto the day I proposed this crazy idea.

No, she said, *that's prostitution and trust me. We're fine. You don't have to worry about us having sex. Ever.*

But, when my hands met Mina's waist tonight, she pulled me closer and held me tight. Nothing about her said no and everything about her said yes...

Said every rapist ever.

My eyes blink open and I push off the counter.

What the fuck, man?

What's going on with me?

And for that matter, if a little contractual flirting turns me on this much, how in the hell will I handle Mina in a bathing suit tomorrow—with even more contractual flirting on tap? If our next kiss includes skin on skin contact...

Maybe she isn't a bikini kind of woman.

Maybe she's into the sleek black one-pieces favored by athletes.

Or better yet, considering her vintage vibe, maybe she'll show up in one of those turn of the century deals that covers every inch of her body...

Right. And maybe Dom will text tomorrow to inform me he's entering a monastery and completely approves of my choices of late.

I am so fucking screwed.

I pour myself a drink, assistance to get Mina off my mind.

The whiskey goes down smooth. Too smooth to drown the thoughts of her, so I pour myself another. No help there, either. I place the empty glass in the sink and head upstairs for a shower, but she's waiting for me there, too. On her knees. Lips pink and parted as she beckons me forward. I blink away the image as I crank on the water and strip, but my dick has a different idea. As water sluices down my face, my chest, my abs, I imagine her lips wandering the same path, kissing and licking and staring up at me with those fucking baby blues. I take myself in my hand, rolling my palm over my crown, tilting my head back in ecstasy.

In my mind, Mina smiles and takes me to the back of her throat and then I'm pumping and shuddering and fuck, my fist in her hair, those perfect tits bouncing as she sucks me, moaning and groaning and oh damn she's glorious. Pull her to her feet and bend her over. Slap that ass and spread her thighs, then bury myself balls deep as water pelts her back, my chest. Her hand pressed against the cool tile, steam gathering around us, her pussy clenching and quivering and fuck fuck fuck! She's screaming my name, her voice breaking as it echoes off the bathroom walls.

My fist pumps and my breath speeds and then I'm coming harder than I remember and all I see are blue eyes, soft skin, and hair so black it's like midnight over the water...

The light blazing through my window is unforgiving. One eye cracks open, then the other, then the icepick inserted at my temple does a viciously twisting dance. After my self-love extravaganza last night, I had another drink. To wash away the shame, I said. Drunk and disorderly me continued to wander back to thoughts of Mina. Some about sex, others about what life would be like if our relationship was real. So I had another.

I cover my face with my hands and groan.

The shame is still there and has joined forces with a righteous hangover that pounds against my skull. I know better than to listen to drunk Nathan. He does stupid shit.

Dragging my palms down my face, I press up on my elbows and take stock.

Headache? Check.

Nausea? Not as bad as it could be.

Grumpy as fuck? That's an affirmative.

I check my phone and find a text from Dom.

> **DOM**
> Thought I warned you about dating down

> wtf you talking about

> That blogger told the world about your interior designer/girlfriend. When are you gonna learn it's better if you just take my advice?

> Don't worry, though

> Dr. Dom to the rescue

> Come out with me tonight

> Can't.

> Why?

> Her?

> Yep

> I'm telling you brother, you're making a mistake on this one.
>
> She ask you for money yet?

Fuck this shit. I don't have it in me for this conversation.

I chug coffee then shave and get dressed before stopping in the office to cut Mina a check. My teeth grind as I sign the damn thing.

No. That's prostitution...
She ask you for money yet?

Is this who I am now? A man who pays for a relationship? A man who ignores his friend's advice while the warning signs he's pointing out flash in my face?

I'm aware of the check's presence in my pocket as I make the drive to Mina's apartment. I pull into the parking lot, grimacing as I bump over one of many potholes dotting the crumbling concrete, then park beside her ancient Honda. Considering I know exactly how much her design services are worth, her living arrangements confound me. She should have a nice home, a new car, designer clothes. Instead, she lives in the cheapest apartment in a fifty-mile radius and asked me for an advance just last night. It doesn't add up. Is Dom right? Is she using me for my money? Is everything I'm starting to feel for her predicated on a lie?

Her shitty living situation makes me even grumpier.

"Pull yourself together," I growl, then kill the engine and sigh, closing my eyes tightly. Unfortunately, shower Mina is waiting, smiling that sultry smile and reminding me how willing I am to cross the boundaries I put up for my own protection. Maybe I'm more of a villain than I want to admit. Lifting my sunglasses, I give my face a quick scrub, then head for her porch and ring the bell.

"Good morning!" Mina exclaims as she throws open the door, her face falling when she sees me. "Oh no. What's wrong?"

"Long night," I mutter, trying to conjure a dismissive smile and failing. Her neighbor's door creaks open as Mina steps outside to lock up.

"Good morning, Ms. Markowitz!" Mina calls brightly to a woman who could be anywhere between fifty and a hundred and twenty, clutching a cat in one hand and a coffee mug in the other.

"You're awfully chipper for someone who had to listen to the Dietzes fight all night." The woman's eyes light on me and a knowing smile twists her lips. "Though I'd be chipper too, if I had someone like that knocking on my door."

Mina blushes. "If it's not the Dietzes, it's Marius revving his engine or the frat boys coming home drunk and trying to break down my door because they forgot which apartment is theirs. I just tune out the noise."

Ms. Markowitz sits on her top step and arranges the cat in her lap. The feline closes his eyes and lifts his face to the sun like the light isn't an icepick twisting son of a bitch. "I wish I could be as chill about it as you,"

"She shouldn't be that chill about it," I retort, teeth grinding. "She shouldn't have to deal with it at all. Neither should you. I don't know what you did to end up in a place like this..."

But you deserve so much more, I finish in my head while Mina's eyebrows raise and her jaw sets.

"Maybe you should worry more about your life choices and less about mine." Her tone is a warning shot. She's not a fan of my mood or what I have to say.

Yeah, well, neither am I. And it's her fault I feel this way.

"Maybe if you weren't surrounded by assholes, I could do that." I lift a hand at Ms. Markowitz. "No offense."

"None taken. I have to like someone to care about their opinion," she replies with a sweet smile before giving her attention back to her cat.

"What's gotten into you?" Mina hisses.

You. You got into me, and you weren't supposed to.

Outrage dances in those baby blues and that feels so much safer than what I saw in them after the kiss.

It's better if she doesn't like me.

For both of us.

"Like I said, long night." I turn my back, stomp down the steps, yank open the car door, then plop into the driver's seat and wait. Mina pops her fists on her hips and shakes her head before following suit. Slowly, with her chin held high.

"Are you hungover?" she asks once the passenger door closes behind her.

"I was a perfect gentleman while we were together."

"And after?"

"After is not in our contract."

She frowns, then disappointment softens her outrage. "I guess that's true. I just thought..." She's quiet now. I've hurt her feelings.

Damn it. I don't want to play the villain with her anymore.

"You know what?" she says. "It doesn't matter."

Her focus is out the window, her lip caught between her teeth and in that moment, I realize that somewhere along the way, she stopped hating me and I stopped hating her. Inexplicably, our fake relationship has blurred into something real, and I've been an absolute dick this morning...because I'm angry at myself for liking her.

I pinch the bridge of my nose. "You just thought what?" I ask, trying to erase the bite in my voice.

"It doesn't matter," Mina replies, amping up the bite in hers.

"It does matter. Look, I'm being an asshole and I'm sorry. I'm grumpy and I don't like knowing you live in this cheap apartment, and I like it even less knowing you're surrounded by dick weasels who keep you up all night and that makes me uncomfortable because we aren't, you and I, we're not supposed..."

I'm not supposed to like you, but I do.

I'm not supposed to want you, but I do.

I shake my head and almost growl but refuse to give her the pleasure. "Can we start over?"

Mina stares like I've lost my mind.

I get out of the car, cross in front, open her door to take her elbow and pull her out with me.

"What are you doing?" she squawks as I drag her up the steps and stop in front of her door while a stunned Ms. Markowitz and her cat watch with enough interest to be Fallon fucking Mae drafting her next headline.

Wouldn't that be a kick to the gut?

If Fallon Mae turned out to be Mina's neighbor

and she didn't think that was something I should know?

"Unlock it." I rattle the doorknob to make my point.

"What?" Mina steps back, eyeing me like I might be dangerous. "Why?"

"Please," I add, as gently as possible. "Just unlock it."

Frowning, Mina does as I ask. I open the door, tenderly shove her inside, then close it between us while she squeaks in dismay. With a deep sigh, I remove my sunglasses, scrub my face, and conjure a smile before smoothing my shirt, squaring my shoulders, and ringing the bell.

The door flies open to reveal a distraught Mina. "What the hell, Nathan?"

"Good morning, HM," I say. "You look absolutely gorgeous as usual."

"What the hell do you think you're doing?" Arms crossed. Chin jutted. Brows furrowed. Eyes glittering.

I have a way to go to earn her forgiveness.

"Treating you the way you deserve to be treated."

"Does that mean I get to treat you the way you deserve? Because I don't know how much you'll like that." That ball-busting glee is back in her eyes, right where it belongs.

"You be you and all will be good."

There's a pause followed by a strange smile, Mina steps back outside and locks the door again. With my hand firmly on her lower back, I guide her to the passenger side, open the door, then close it gently once she's safely inside.

"It was nice to meet you," I say to Ms. Markowitz as I cross in front of the car for the fourteenth time. She nods, petting her cat and watching with curiosity.

After the last twenty-four hours I know one thing for sure:

I want to be a better man for Mina Blake.

TWENTY

Mina

I woke up this morning excited to see Nathan. Listening to the Dietzes scream about who is failing who all night long made me realize that feeling truly seen and understood by a partner is rare. As Mrs. Dietz hollered about video games and Mr. Dietz bellowed about the lack of sex and Mrs. Dietz retorted that she had to respect someone to be attracted to them, I kept flashing back to how I feel when I'm talking to Nathan. He listens. He cares. He doesn't want to, but he does. And that kiss...

People write poems about kisses like that. Books make millions over kisses like that. And it just happened to me in a parking lot, with a man I'm supposed to hate, even though somewhere along the way, I think we both stopped faking whatever this is and missed the message.

Then I opened the door on a bridge troll dressed in Nathan's clothes. Dread took the place of excitement and I realized I'd spent the whole night fooling myself. This is The Prince of Darkness, the man my best friend claims has started using his powers for evil, the guy who'd rather lie to his family than fix whatever's broken in him.

After his whole 'starting over' display, the only thing I know for sure is that his bad mood is contagious. What he said and did was sweet, but can I trust it was genuine? There was an audience, after all.

Which version of Nathan is real? The bridge troll with a hangover dropping red flags like a mad man? Or the Romeo trying to be 'what I deserve?' Would he have said or done any of that if we were alone? Or did Ms. Markowitz and her cat watching have something to do with his change in attitude? I could ask him, but I'm not sure which answer I'm hoping for. I opt for silence instead and Nathan seems fine with that decision.

Which pisses me off.

I try to talk myself out of anger while he quietly navigates us away from the rundown neighborhood surrounding my apartment. With each click of the turn signal, the price tags on the homes gain a few more zeroes and that doesn't help my mood. I'm a good person—mostly—and my mom is a freaking angel. Why do we struggle while others have luck and abundance raining down on them?

The game is rigged.

Or I never got the rule book.

Or...something.

"Wanna explain the hangover?" I cross my arms and twist in my seat to glare at the man who has everything but still can't be happy.

Maddeningly, an unreadable smile lifts his lips. "Not particularly."

"How about why you were so rude this morning? Feel like explaining that?" I bite into the words and it feels so damn good, I lift my chin in righteous fury.

Anger is safer than everything else I'm feeling. I'll hide here for a while.

"I thought we already covered the fact that I'm hungover." His voice is calm, his face composed.

I roll my lips together before shooting back, "And didn't you just say I deserve better?"

"You're right. You do." Nathan runs his hand through his hair. "I just don't know if I have better in me."

"That's bullshit and you know it. You spent a lifetime being better until whatever happened to make you bitter instead."

His eyes narrow. "You don't know me well enough to say things like that."

"That's bullshit too. We've been hanging out long enough for me to know you're not the guy who showed up this morning. You're just not. I see you, Nathan West. You're the guy who carries his niece on his back. Who drops everything to help a troubled student. You're the guy whose family knows will drop everything to save the world. That's you. Not this guy. This guy is an asshole."

I give my attention back to the road before I say something I regret. The sky is blue and the ocean peeks out between the houses, glittering in the morning sun. Palms bend in a gentle breeze. Given the atmosphere in the car, I'd expect arctic winds and rumbling thunder, but the world doesn't care about petty dramas like ours.

Nathan clears his throat, then risks a quick glance my way. "Kissing you bothered me."

His voice is low, almost tortured. I tear my gaze off the idyllic landscape and focus on the storm-ravaged man beside me. The muscle in his jaw clenches and he looks ashamed.

Here I was, daydreaming about million-dollar kisses and he was what? Grossed out?

"Okay. Wow. I'm..." I fling my hand around,

looking for something to say. "I'm sorry it was so awful for you."

Dear God. Looking for a lightning bolt here. Yours, Mina Blake.

There's a dreadful moment of silence where I consider telling him to turn around and take me home. How can I get through another day of charming Nathan when this is the reality?

But then, "It bothered me because I liked it."

His words send my heart into overdrive. My confusion trips over itself, oh so helpfully offering ten different reasons it might bother him that he liked kissing me.

He's secretly gay.

He's in love with someone else.

He's embarrassed to be seen with me.

I have terrible breath.

His family prefers arranged marriages.

Nathan glances over, brows furrowed, and I realize that now I'm the one letting horrible silences linger.

I tuck my hair behind my ear. Suck in my lips. Glance at him and start to apologize, but I have no idea why. Finally, I murmur, "I liked it too."

"I liked it so much I went home and jerked off, thinking of you." His eyes burn with the admission. My core throbs and I lick my lips as my nipples pebble. I picture him, dick in hand, eyes closed, head back, lips parted...

All because of me.

"And I know I shouldn't have done it," he continues, "and I definitely shouldn't have told you, but that's why I'm hungover. Whiskey was the only thing stronger than you."

"I..." What am I supposed to say? I'm flattered? I want you too? I wish you'd do it again and let me watch?

But Nathan isn't waiting for a response. He's a man at confession, head bowed, tortured by his sins.

"And all of that bothered me because of this." He digs in his pocket and pulls out a folded check. He hands it to me, and that dreadful silence descends again. I take the money, pinching it between my thumb and forefinger like I'm afraid to touch it. This complicates everything, but I can't not take it.

"Nathan, I..." I swallow hard, ready to tell him about my mom so he understands why I have to take the money, but he flips on his turn signal and pulls into a driveway filled with his cousins and their spouses.

He stops the car and stares for a long moment. His lips part and he takes a breath and the look on his face is a warning. What he just said changes everything, but what he's about to say scares him even more.

"That check is for the design work. Not the dates.

Not the kiss. Not our time together. Those are mine." Nathan's gaze is intense as his cousin Angela pulls open his car door.

"There you are! I do miss the days when you were always on time instead of constantly running late." She leans in and waves.

I've never been so disappointed to see a friendly face.

TWENTY-ONE

Nathan

Garrett's boat glides through the water. Mina leans on the rail, watching the horizon. A warm breeze lifts her hair off her shoulders, and she turns to catch me staring. The sky matches her eyes, bright and blue and clear. The corners of her lips twitch upwards and she drops her gaze before giving her attention back to Angela and Micah's wife, Ivy.

What the hell was I thinking?

Not the dates. Not the kiss. Not our time together. Those are mine.

Who says something like that? Worse, who says something like that right after admitting he jerked off and right before it becomes impossible to talk about either thing?

What a stupid, stupid move.

What's Mina thinking?

What happens next?

Where do we go from here?

There's no undo. No going back. No claiming my actions were for show or that she misunderstood or I was caught up in the moment. By admitting how I'm feeling, I irrevocably changed things between us. For better or worse, that's yet to be seen.

Micah claims the seat beside me, shit-eating grin fully engaged, elbows on knees, already half laughing at whatever he's about to say.

"What?" I growl with a shake of my head. "Why are you looking at me like that?"

"It's nothing." His grin intensifies.

"It's something or you wouldn't look so proud of yourself."

"I can't believe you're the same asshole who bailed on my wedding. That's all."

"He did what?" Mina turns to us, surprise dancing across her face. Turns out she is not a vintage bathing suit kind of gal and favors red and skimpy instead. Something I should have expected, considering the dress she wore to my birthday party.

"Micah's making it sound worse than it was," I say quickly. "I didn't bail. I was there for the wedding and most of the reception."

"Most." Micah runs a hand over his head, then gives his attention right back to Mina. "He claims to have seen us cut the cake and stayed for our first dance, but I didn't see him. He was too heartbroken to stick around."

He's got me there. I had just discovered Blossom was cheating. I was drinking a lot. Wallowing more than that. I wanted what Micah had with Ivy and felt too broken to ever find it. I was going downhill fast, until I had the idea to expand the foundation. Throwing myself into work saved me.

But spending time with Mina saved me more. Our eyes meet, her blues as soothing as cool water on a summer day. I smile despite myself before giving my attention back to Micah with a snort.

"You were too enamored with your new wife to care if I was there or not."

"She's easy to be enamored with. No doubt." Micah holds out his hands to Ivy. When she takes them, he pulls her into his lap and nuzzles her hair and rubs his hands over a barely there baby bump while she squeals in delight.

Mina leans her back on the rail, hair dancing in the breeze, her focus on me and me alone. "Why were you heartbroken at his wedding?"

Her eyes hold mine. They're soft. Concerned and

questioning. There's so much we don't know about each other. Something I want to remedy.

My God, do I want to remedy it. I want to know her. To explore her. To understand her.

I swore never to be involved again and the first woman I meet changes my tune. I'm either an idiot or extremely lucky.

I lift a hand to dismiss Mina's question, but Micah surfaces from kissing his wife to open his big fat mouth. "Because of Blossom. He'd just found out she was cheating..." He bites his lip then turns to me with a frown. "Am I saying too much? I assumed she knew. I mean, it seems like something you guys would have covered by now."

Does it? At what stage does one disclose the "I'm a moron who fully supported a manipulating narcissist and her daughters for two years" story?

Well, hell.

If Micah thinks Mina should know, then I'll roll with it and hope she's ready to roll with it too.

"You remember," I say, my eyes locked on hers like I can beam the information into her brain. "I'd just found out Blossom was cheating, and she'd said all that awful stuff about only being with me for my money, which was super clear retrospectively because I'd been supporting her and her daughters for two years..."

Mina's brows lift with surprise which she quickly

hides by sucking in her lips and bobbing her head. "Oh, right. Yeah. Of course. She was cheating on you. After using you for your money." Thoughts tick across her face, like she found the missing piece to a puzzle and she's fitting it into place. "Which was really hard for someone who dedicated his life to making the world a better place."

She softens even farther.

Uncomfortable, I shrug off the observation. "I wouldn't go that far."

"I'd go that far," Ivy replies with a gentle smile. "You've spent your whole life trying to apologize for being born into a wealthy family and only doubled down on that after the whole Blossom thing."

"There was talk you were trying to work yourself into an early grave." Garrett leans back in his seat. "Not that I think that's actually possible."

"Between the long days at the foundation and the late nights with all the 'dazzling and spectacular' women, it wasn't looking good for our boy Nathan." Micah shakes his head and sighs dramatically.

How many times do I have to defend myself on this?

"As I've said many times before, the women were for Dom. I tagged along to secure donations from their wealthy relatives."

"Speaking of donations!" Angela claps her hands

under her chin, grinning widely. "Mina should totally take part in the auction for the gala! I'm assuming she'll be there. Why wouldn't she when she makes you look like that?"

"Like what?" I shoot my cousin a glance, warning her to tread carefully. She shoots one back, informing me she'll do what she wants.

"It's the way I look at Garrett and it's the way he looks at Ivy" –Angela points to Micah— "and now it's the way you look at Mina and it makes my heart glad."

"I'm glad I'm not the only one that sees it." Micah chortles. "It's a relief, after you went around swearing off love and relationships and doing the cold and bitter thing. You're just not that guy, Nathan."

I meet Mina's gaze. A blush works its way up her chest and throat, then pinks her cheeks. Her eyes are filled with questions.

There is too much left unsaid between us, too much up in the air, for what Angela and Micah are insinuating.

I want to murder my cousins.

"Anyway," Angela continues, before I get the chance, "every year, we auction off dates at ROF's charity gala. It's no big deal, just an evening out with the winner, and there's a contract to protect us from any funny business, which you really don't have to worry about because usually the people with enough money to throw away on something like this are older and just looking for some conversation and a break in routine. The proceeds go to ROF and it's a lot of fun. The whole family gets involved and I think it'd be awesome if you did too."

Mina licks her lips. "I doubt anyone would spend good money just for an evening with me."

"Don't be too sure about that," I say with a growl, the thought of Mina with another man twisting in my gut.

I have no right to feel possessive.

But that doesn't change the fact that I do.

Angela gives me an odd look but doesn't call me on my strange reaction. "Too bad Nick won't be home in time. He always pulls in a hefty donation."

"I don't know," says Garrett. "The timing is awfully close. His leave might start just in time for him to make it to the gala."

"Nick's the Marine, right?" Mina draws her brows together. "My family is so small; I don't know how you guys keep it straight."

"Yep!" Angela grins, brushing a lock of red hair out of her face. "He's the second oldest of us cousins—"

"By one day!" Micah rolls his eyes in the way he always does when Angela goes out of her way to point out she's the oldest.

"That doesn't make it less true," she shoots back, crossing her arms over her chest.

"Nick's more like a big brother than a cousin," I say to Mina, trying to help her make sense of my family tree.

"The best big brother," Micah offers with a grin. "Kind and protective but never one to take shit from any of us. He kept us in line, didn't he?"

Angela nods her agreement. "Our parents were so close; we all basically grew up like siblings."

"That sounds wonderful," Mina says. "I always wished I had a brother or a sister. Built in friends, you know?"

"It's just you and your mom now, right?" Garrett asks.

"Yep. Just us." Mina smiles, but it's not hers. It's forced. Troubled. "Mom was an only child. Her parents passed away before I was born."

"Are you guys still close?" Ivy asks. "You and your mom?"

Mina chews her lip, something heavy settling onto her shoulders. "Very. I'd do anything for her. Her health has…" She shakes her head and drops her gaze. Smooths back a strand of hair that's fallen from her ponytail. Crosses her arms. Uncrosses them.

She only fidgets when she's upset.

Her eyes settle on me, and she tenses even more.

"That's a topic for another day." Mina refreshes a sad, sad smile and every instinct I have demands I run to the rescue.

"I totally respect that," Angela says, "but if you ever want to talk, we're good listeners, though you have Nathan, so you're good to go in that department." She looks to Ivy, Micah, and Garrett, who nod their agreement. "But just so it's out there, our hotels offer an entire health and wellness package, massages, nutrition, guided meditations, if that's something your mom is into. I can get her set up with the whole deal if you want."

"That's incredibly kind of you." Mina's smile continues to weaken. She chews the inside of her lip, and I add one more item to my Things About Mina Blake That Drive Me Crazy list. A list that used to be exclusive to things I couldn't stand but has recent additions like the fact that I can't stop thinking about her, or the adorable way she looks at me when she's made a point. The fact that the list has expanded at all is actually an item on the list.

And now there's today's addition:

She's in trouble and I want to help...and I'm tired of telling myself I shouldn't.

I am who I am. I protect and care for the people

that matter and for as much as Dom likes to remind me people like Mina see me as a bank account, it's not true. Mina is kind and hardworking and if I can do something to help, I will. I just have to figure out what's wrong first.

TWENTY-TWO

Mina

> **MOM**
>
> Glenda from billing just stopped by to ask about a missing payment. Should I worry? I don't want you digging yourself into a hole just so I can be here

>> Absolutely do not worry. I'm good. Money's good. Wires got crossed, is all. Everything will be straightened up tomorrow.

> That's what I told Glenda
>
> Now.
>
> Why do my 'Mama Senses' keep telling me you're seeing someone?

> Your mama senses are on point as always

> Please tell me it's the nice architect guy you've had a crush on forever. You deserve good things, Meens. Hot, talented, and kind fits the bill

> No...though it is someone I met through work

> As long as it's NOT that rude client

> I mayyyy have misread him that first day

> Oh Mina...be careful. I didn't like your dad when we first met either, but I ignored all those initial red flags and got involved anyway. You know how that turned out...

> That's not what's happening. I promise. I'll explain at our next visit, but please the most important thing is that you don't worry. All is fine

---

I shove my phone back into my bag and find Nathan watching me. Intensely. Which pretty much describes everything between us now.

That check is for the design work you've done. Not the dates. Not the kiss. Not our time together. Those are mine.

What did he mean when he said that? Are we dating for real now? Does it mean he has feelings for me? I want to think it does but am afraid to assume anything.

We've barely touched since we got out of his car, but I feel his eyes on my body, trailing across my bare skin like the whisper of his fingertips, exploring...

...claiming...

And it's not like I haven't returned the favor. Nathan in swimming trunks is a gift to the female population at large. Strong shoulders. Perfect pecs. Abs that trail into that goddamn V at his hips that always does me in.

It's just the two of us. Micah and Garett are in the water, swimming, splashing, and laughing while Angela and Ivy sun themselves at the front of the boat.

"Everything okay?" Nathan's voice is quiet. Personal. Like he already knows the answer to his question. When he handed me the check, I was ready to unload my worries about Mom and money. But now is not the time and until I know what we are to each other, I'd be a fool to share that story. Our entire relationship, whatever it is, hinges on money.

If it's fake, he's paying me.

If it's real, he shouldn't.

How do I talk about the financial pickle I'm in and not make it weird?

So, I shove it all into a box in the back of my mind and focus on the easy stuff.

"How could things not be okay when I'm surrounded by this?" I wave my hand around to encompass the boat, the view, the companionship. "Your cousins are wonderful. I'd love to call them friends. And if younger me heard I'd be on a boat like this one day? She wouldn't believe it."

"You fidget when you're upset." Nathan half-smiles and I'm touched he's been paying that much attention. "Whatever happened on your phone wasn't good news."

What am I gonna tell him? I'm depending on the money you owe me for a fake relationship that might not be fake anymore? I'm contemplating a second job so I don't have to take advantage of Glenda's kindness again? I'm so tired of not quite making ends meet that I'm ready to scream?

It all feels like too much information given where we are. Or where we aren't.

"That was my mom," I say, swallowing the urge to unload it all. "She's in an extended care facility and the admin staff bothered her about some clerical stuff after I specifically asked them to come to me instead of her.

Stress isn't conducive to her recovery, by their own admission."

"How sick is she?" Nathan sits back in his chair, resting his ankle on his knee. The wind rustles in his hair as the sun dips behind a cloud. His focus is lasered in on me, like we're the only people in the world and his very existence hinges on what I say next.

"That's hard to answer." I glance at my hands, then at him. "It isn't terminal, but at her worst, she's unable to care for herself. Every '-ologist' she's been to hasn't had a lot of hope she'll ever have her life back. They make it sound like we should be grateful she's not dead. But existing the way she was might be worse than death." I shake my head, overcome with grief for what she's lost and hope that she'll find it again. "What she's doing, it isn't living."

I explain the fear and confusion when Mom couldn't form sentences. When all she could do was lie in the dark, hovering on the line of consciousness. I tell him about helping her to the bathroom and feeding her meals and sitting by the bed in tears, praying and hoping and wishing for something better for the woman who raised me.

"When I got into college, I promised myself Mom would never struggle again. I saved every penny I earned so I could build her a home. Like an actual house. It was a start, you know? To pay her back for everything she did for me after Dad left. Thank God I had that money saved. It's all gone into her medical bills."

That's close enough to the truth. He doesn't need to know any more. Not when things are so complicated between us. Not when I can't trust what's real and what's not. I stare at the man beside me. His eyes are inviting, like morning in springtime, his hair soft and hanging in his face the way I like. He smiles gently, totally different from the bridge troll who knocked on my door a few hours ago. Which only makes everything more confusing.

If this is who Nathan really is, I could fall in love with him. I might be halfway there already. But if he's determined to stay The Prince of Darkness, I'd be a fool to breathe life into those feelings.

Nathan leans his elbows on his knees and stares at his feet. "So now you know what happened with Blossom and I know why you live where you live and drive what you drive."

"Is it so bad, getting to know each other?"

"Yes." The word is hushed yet harsh. A deep truth with roots sunk into his heart. "And no."

I stand and grasp the rails, staring out at the horizon as another cloud covers the sun. A cool breeze sends a shiver of goose bumps across my skin as the boat rocks in the waves.

I listen as Nathan stands. Close my eyes when his hands grip my shoulders. Soften as he turns me to face him. He's close enough that I feel the warmth of his body. His eyes hold mine and he brushes a strand of hair out of my face.

"Why do you make it so complicated?" I whisper.

"Because you scare me."

"*I* scare *you*? Me? The woman who talks to herself and fidgets when she's nervous and drives a Honda and wears cheap clothes...she scares the famous philanthropist raised by super stars?" I huff a laugh and drop my gaze. "I don't think you understand the situation."

Nathan lifts my chin with the tip of his finger. "You're beautiful. And smart. And I can't stop thinking about you. Can't stop wanting you. And I'm not supposed to feel any of that. I'm not supposed to make myself cum while imagining you on your knees in front of me. You're not supposed to be the first and last thing on my mind each day."

"Because we're pretending?" I ask in a voice so quiet it's nearly lost beneath the churn of the sea.

His gaze drops to my lips. Heavy and hooded. Another breeze slips between us, cold against the sweat at my temples. My breath hitches as Nathan cups the back of my head and presses his lips to mine, his warmth erasing the chill creeping into the air now that the sun is hidden behind clouds.

"Did that feel pretend?" he whispers, his lips brushing mine, his fingers in my hair.

"Not to me."

"Not to me, either." He presses his forehead to mine. "I don't want you to date me because I'm paying you. I just want you to date me."

Garrett's head appears over the rail as he hauls himself back into the boat, water streaming from his trunks and puddling at his feet. He slicks his dripping hair back as Micah follows him up the ladder, shaking seawater out of his brown locks.

"Weather's changing," he says, jerking his chin toward the sky. "Probably best to call it a day before things get worse."

Nathan steps out of my personal space and I shiver, though I couldn't tell you if it's because of the chill in the air or the lack of his body next to mine.

TWENTY-THREE

Nathan

> DOM
>
> Please tell me you've got a date to the ROF auction
>
> And please tell me she's high-class and deserves you

Mina deserves me

> Annnnddd...you're right back where you started when I found you
>
> What is it with you and these charity cases
>
> Chances are you're nothing but a giant fucking dollar sign to her
>
> You know that, right?

> Need I remind you of the shitshow known as Blossom?

>> You're tiptoeing close to a line you shouldn't cross.

> Fine. Fine. This is me, stepping away from the line

> But...

> Let me ask one question

> To make my point clear

> What's she gonna wear? The thrift shop bargain bin shit she always does? What about her hair? Her jewelry? Her makeup?

>> Your point makes you sound like an asshole

> That was never in dispute

I slam my phone down on my desk. I don't know who I'm madder at, Dom for making the point about Mina's clothes, me for not seeing it first, or Mina for...

What?

Why would I be mad at her?

It's not her fault finances are tight. Her dad abandoned her. Her mom got sick. Mina's doing everything she can to keep her family afloat.

Despite the logical side of my brain recognizing

that truth, I still feel a great deal of agitation in her direction. I don't like knowing she's scrimping and saving. I don't like knowing she lives in a cheap apartment surrounded by assholes. I don't like her driving a shitty car. I don't like her wearing thrift shop clothes. She deserves so much more.

For as wrong as Dom is, he's also right. I can't let her show up to the gala in anything she currently owns. She'll stand out like a sore thumb. I already did that to her once at my birthday party. I won't let her be humiliated again. A quick text to Aunt Maisie gets me the name of a reputable women's clothing store that carries dresses of a certain quality. And then I call Mina.

"I was just thinking of you," she says and the warmth in her voice goes straight to my dick.

"I'm pretty much always thinking of you," I mumble, then swipe a hand over my mouth. Dom's wrong about her. I know he is, because I know her. But I thought I knew Blossom and I promised myself I'd never let someone catch me off guard like that again.

But Mina's not like that. She's not keeping things from me. And I can't be a jaded fuck the rest of my life.

"I'm taking you shopping tonight," I say with a smile.

There's a long pause and then, "Shopping?"

"You need a dress for the gala."

"I have dresses."

"Not like this. There are certain expectations about presentation at these things."

"And you don't want me to let you down."

Why does it sound like she's offended?

"No, dammit. I don't want to let you down. I want you to feel like you belong there."

"Nathan..." Again with the pregnant pause, the silence too heavy for a fucking shopping trip. "I'm not comfortable with you spending money on me."

"Let me do this for you." I close my eyes. "I want to do this for you."

The admission drips with meaning. I want to take care of her. I want to make her feel beautiful. I want to shove Dom's words in his face. I want Mina to be as good and true and honest as she seems. I want her to step onto that stage and for everyone to gasp because they see how truly spectacular she really is. For once in her life, I want her to have more than enough.

Mina takes a breath and I brace for a fight. "Nothing too expensive."

"No promises. I'll pick you up at seven."

I end the call just as an alert on my name comes in.

Playboy Nathan West Spends Day on the Water with His Hot New Girl. Sources Say Things Got Spicy! How Long Until the Villain Ruins Everything?

"You know what?" I murmur as I delete the message. "I'm in too good a mood to care about Fallon fucking Mae."

I bump to a stop in front of Mina's apartment a few minutes early. She's sitting on the top step of the porch and stands when she sees me. Her hair is down, the ends lifting off her chest in the evening breeze. Her eyes find mine like a thunderclap. I'm out of the car and pulling her to me before I know what's happening. My hands slide up her back and into that midnight hair as I press her luscious body to mine and kiss her deeply. Her lips part and she tastes of strawberry and smells of citrus and feels like fucking heaven.

"I've been looking forward to seeing you all day," I whisper, then kiss her again. I'm giddy with the thought of spoiling her. She's lived her whole life never quite having enough and tonight, I'm changing that. She'll have everything she could possibly want.

Our first stop is Blush. My aunt said the clothing is expensive but worth it and that's enough for me.

Mina gawks at the storefront as we near the entrance. "I can't go in there."

"Of course you can."

She steps back, like she's thinking of running. "I'll set off the 'you're too poor to be here' alarm."

"Oh, wow. I didn't even think about that. Thank goodness you remembered that's a thing because, oh wait, it isn't." A car rumbles by on the street behind us, filled with teenagers laughing, music loud, energy high. The world is theirs for the taking. I remember feeling that way. With Mina here, I still feel that way.

"Go ahead," she says, pressing a hand to my chest. "Laugh it up. You've clearly never been judged by how you look and what you wear."

I almost laugh in her face but choke it back. My entire life, people have judged my clothes, my parents, my privilege and wondered how they could use me to their advantage. For Mina, when a stranger judges her on the street, she's just a nameless face, quickly forgotten. Me? I have people like Fallon Mae pointing out all my flaws—both real and imagined—with my name, my face, my business, *my family* attached. The damage is real and lasting. The stakes are higher.

One look at Mina's face says she's not in the mood for truth like that.

"You don't have to worry about money," I say, brushing a lock of ebony hair out of her face.

"I wish that were true." Brows furrowed. Lip caught between teeth. Deep sigh.

"I'm sorry. I meant to say you don't have to worry about money tonight."

Before Mina can argue, I press my palm to the flat of her back and open the door. She smiles up at me as she passes and that's it. I'm done for. I'd do anything to have her look at me like that every hour of every day.

The walls are adorned with soft blush tones, accented by touches of gold and silver, casting an inviting glow throughout the space. Crystal chandeliers hang from the ceiling, sending shimmering reflections dancing across Mina's awed face. Plush velvet curtains frame the large display windows, and a musician plays classical guitar in a corner. His eyes are closed, enraptured with his own music and I take a moment to join him. A salesclerk approaches. Dressed in black. Hair slicked back. Her makeup is expensive yet polished. Her look designed to be a blank canvas. One that allows the customer to imagine her to be whoever she wants.

"You must be Mr. West and Miss Blake. Your aunt told me to expect you and has filled me in on your needs. I've pulled several dresses that might interest you, though you're free to look around at our other options. Help yourself to the coffee bar over there, or would you prefer a glass of champagne?"

Mina gapes at me, unused to luxury shopping

experiences. I tell the clerk we'd like to start with champagne, then ask to see the dresses she set aside.

"Of course, Mr. West. Right this way." She leads us to a private room, with subtle lighting and plush armchairs. A rack of dresses sits in the middle near a dais placed in front of elegant full-length mirrors.

"There's a changing room there," says our sales clerk, pointing to a closed door in the back. "My name is Nora and I'll return shortly with your champagne."

As soon as the door clicks shut, Mina turns to me, jaw dropped, eyes wide. "This is too much, Nathan. Private rooms? Personal shoppers? I can think of a hundred better ways to spend this money."

"I don't want you to think about the money at all."

"How can I not?"

She's panicking and I don't understand it. I have money I want to spend on her. Why is that a problem? I lower myself into one of the armchairs and drape my ankle over my knee. "Because you're going to try on the dresses Nora picked for you and leave the money worries to me."

"Nathan..."

I love the way she says my name. I want to make her scream it.

Nora arrives with two glasses of champagne, hands them to each of us, then leaves without a word. People who sell luxury know how to read the room.

Mina raises the glass to her lips, her eyes locked on mine. "Okay then," she says after she swallows. "If his royal highness insists."

"He insists."

She pulls a dress off the rack and presses it to her body, swinging her hips back and forth to make the skirt sway.

"Like that one?"

She checks the price tag and her face blanches. "Not that much," she says, hanging the dress back on the rack without a second glance.

Mina flips through the dresses, eyeing them appreciatively until she comes to one the color of champagne. She holds it to her body, eyeing her reflection almost reverently, then reaches for the tag.

"No more looking at prices," I say, arching a brow.

She meets my eyes through the mirror, takes a deep breath, then drops the tag. "That's a deeply ingrained habit, but I'll do my best."

"That's all I can ask," I reply with a smile. "How about that one? Like it?"

"It's so pretty," Mina gushes, "but I don't think I can pull it off."

"There's only one way to find out." I point to the door in the back of the room and Mina disappears inside.

Minutes later, the door cracks open and her head pokes through, her body hidden. "I can't pull it off."

"I'll be the judge of that." I crook my finger, beckoning her out of the room. Mina hesitates, then swings the door open and steps forward.

Pearlescent silk hugs her frame, cascading over her breasts, her peaked nipples holding my attention until I follow the curve of her waist to her hips and then back up again. Thin straps sweep over her shoulders, exposing pale, delicate skin. Mina turns to inspect her reflection and my dick throbs as I'm afforded a view of her ass draped in silk.

Fuck me. I'd love to have that dress pooled on the floor at the end of my bed. Mina naked, waiting, legs spread for me as her dark locks fan across my pillow. My cock swells.

"It's so pretty, but I don't think I have the body for it." Mina glances over her shoulder, worry furrowing her brow as she smooths the fabric at her belly and waist.

I stand and cross the room. You don't appreciate a masterpiece from a distance.

Mina watches me approach, her eyes locked on mine like she can read the dirty thoughts parading through my head.

"Do you like it?" she asks, returning her attention

to the mirror, smoothing her hands over her hips once again.

I fucking love it. I can't stop staring. I want to be the one running my hands along that body.

"It's fine," I manage.

She bites her bottom lip. "I knew I couldn't pull it off."

"Mina." My voice comes out harsher than I intended.

She turns, those beautiful eyes wide. Lips parted. Chest heaving.

I brush a strand of hair off her face, then turn her back to her reflection. "You're stunning."

Her smile is fleeting at first, then so bright it warms the whole damn room. "You're just being nice."

"Since when have you thought I'm capable of being nice?"

"Since I've gotten to know you better." She presses a hand to my cheek and there's a moment where I think she's going to kiss me, but then she drops her hand and turns back to the mirror. "I'd never wear something like this."

"You're wearing the hell out of it right now. That's the one. Go change and I'll let Nora know you've made your decision."

Mina disappears back into the dressing room, and I

perch on the edge of the chair. The best of me can't wait for her to see how people react at the gala. The worst can't stand the thought of sharing her with whoever makes the winning bid. Maybe it should be me. Maybe I should place the winning bid, so I don't have to share her with anyone.

The more I think about it, the more appealing I find the idea. I force myself to change topics.

What else will Mina need to feel like the most beautiful woman at the ball?

Jewelry? I'm sure my mother has some to loan her.

Shoes? I could ask Nora to recommend a store...

"Nathan?" Mina's panicked voice precedes her head popping out of the dressing room. "I'm stuck," she whispers.

"Stuck?"

"I can't get the zipper down."

"I can call for Nora..."

She shakes her head frantically and waves me in. "Just get in here and help me."

Apprehensively, I step into the dressing room. Mina's clothes are folded neatly on a chair, her bra and underwear laid neatly on top. Fucking black lace. And if it's on the chair, it's not on her...

I yank my gaze back to Mina but that isn't any better. She's clasping the dress to her breasts while trying to reach behind to the hidden zipper in the back.

"The silk is caught, and I don't want to tear it." Her blues lock onto me. "Do you think you can get it?"

Nodding, I turn her away from me, then grasp the zipper clasp, my fingers brushing her spine. Goose bumps flare across her skin as I use my other hand to tug gently at the silk. And then, like magic, the zipper releases. I slowly draw it down and the dress gapes, revealing her bare back, waist, and hips.

She glances over her shoulder. Eyes blazing. Chest heaving.

Using just my pointer finger, I slip first one strap off her shoulder, then another. She releases her grip on the dress, and it pools at her feet.

She turns and just like that, Mina Blake is naked before me.

She's more dazzling than a sunrise over the ocean. More spectacular than a sky full of stars.

I drag my thumb across her lips. She gasps. A sound so full of longing and want that I'm crashing into her. My mouth devouring hers. Tasting her tongue. Her throat. Her neck and shoulders. My hands sweep into that midnight hair, angling her head to better access her sweet as candy lips.

I bow to her, sucking a rose-colored nipple into my mouth, capturing it between my teeth, then suckling away the pain. She moans, deep and low in her throat, and my dick pulses, throbbing with envy.

"Nathan..." Her voice is a whisper, yet wild and wanton. "I don't... Do you... Should we..."

Lust blazing through me. An unencumbered wildfire. I slide a finger down her belly, between her folds, and press the bundle of nerves that sends her hips bucking against me.

"Quiet now, Mina," I murmur, my lips grazing her throat, and she freezes.

"I like it when you say my name."

I press a finger to her lips, then nibble her ear with my teeth. "Mina."

I slowly lower to my knees, looking up into those beautiful blues. "Mina."

I hook a leg over my shoulder and lower my face to her, drawing my tongue across her clit. "Mina."

And then I'm licking and sucking and Mina is writhing and moaning. Her orgasm comes fast and hard, like she's been waiting for me for days. She tastes like heaven and feels like—

"Ms. Blake?"

I freeze, my mouth hovering over her cleft as Mina covers her mouth with her hand.

Footsteps thump ever closer to the dressing room. "Ms. Blake?"

I jerk my head to the door, my drawn brows screaming, *Say something!*

"Yes?" Mina's voice is thin and trembling. I blow lightly on her clit, and she gasps.

"Is everything okay in there?" asks Nora, right on the other side of the door.

I draw my tongue across Mina's slit.

"Fine!" she whimpers. "Everything is fine."

"Fine?" I mouth, sliding a finger past her entrance.

"I mean great! I think I found something I really like." She smiles down at me, her eyes dancing with delighted panic. She's wild. Undone. I fucking love it.

I smile back. I've found something I really like too.

"I just wanted to make sure you didn't need any assistance. Mr. West seems to have abandoned you."

"He, uh, went to the bathroom."

"I didn't see him—"

"Maybe you weren't looking very hard!" Mina cries out as I stroke her inner walls with my fingers. "I'll uh, I'll uh, I'll finish up in here and see if I can locate him."

Nora's footsteps recede and I lower my lips once again, bringing a new meaning to the words 'finish up.'

TWENTY-FOUR

MINA

There are defining moments in any relationship. Nathan kneeling at my feet in a dressing room is one for us. Which is weird because we aren't in a relationship. Or maybe we are. How crazy is it that he did what he did, and I don't know what we are to each other.

He said he doesn't want me to date him because he's paying me. He just wants me to date him.

Is that what we're doing? Dating?

Nathan grins. Wipes a hand over his mouth. Stands. I can't tell what he's thinking. Is he as confused as I am? Is he upset? Does he want to do it again?

I want to do it again.

My body clenches its approval of the idea.

"I... Well... What do you..." Nathan's voice is low. His eyes search mine. He adjusts his pants to make room for an impressive erection, laughing quietly as he runs a hand over his head. "I clearly have no idea what to say. Should I apologize?"

I shake my head and press my palm to the mirror to steady my suddenly wobbly legs. "No."

"Good." A secret smile. Made for me and no one else. "Should I go?" He jerks his chin toward the door.

A growing part of me votes I make Nathan as naked as I am so we can finish what we started and the bulge in his pants suggests he's as game as I am. But Nora could return any minute.

Besides...

Going further would only confuse things more.

So I lick my lips, cover my breasts, and say, "Probably."

Nathan nods to himself, balls his fists and moves to the door, then pauses, turning to meet my eyes. "Was that a mistake?"

The question charges the air.

If things between us are supposed to be fake, then yes, that was a mistake.

But if what I'm feeling is real...

If what I think he's feeling is real...

Then no. That was beautiful. Meaningful. And so freaking hot I can't believe it happened.

I work to untangle my twisting thoughts and wait too long to respond. Nathan misinterprets my silence. He drops his gaze. Shoulders slumped. Head nodding as if he understands what I haven't said.

But he doesn't.

He can't.

Not when I don't understand it myself yet.

"I don't think that was a mistake," I finally say, desperation speeding through my words.

Nathan steps in my direction, his eyes softening. "I don't want it to be."

"Me neither," I say and mean it.

"Good." A quick smile dashes across his face, filled with boyish, gleeful energy, and he pulls me in for one last kiss before he cracks open the door and slips outside.

I sag against the wall, staring at the stranger in the mirror. Her cheeks are flushed. Her lips swollen. Her eyes are wild, and her hair is a mess. I smooth it back into place, my gaze memorizing the path of Nathan's mouth, gasping slightly when I find a purple mark on my breast. I trace it with my fingers and a shiver of pleasure sends goose bumps prickling across my skin.

"So that happened," I whisper, and the stranger in the mirror grins.

"Hot damn, Meens!" Fallon turns to me with wide eyes. "*This* is the dress Nathan bought you?"

I meet her gaze through my vanity mirror. It was my grandmother's, once upon a time. I like to imagine her sitting here on the bench-style chair, fussing with her hair in the mirror with the floral crown molding, pulling toiletries out of the drawers, fingers pinching the vintage ring-pull handles, maybe getting ready for her day, or maybe a night out with a hot date. I never got the chance to know my grandma, but sitting here, where she sat as a young woman, helps me feel connected.

Fallon lifts the dress from its place on my closet door and holds it against her body. "No wonder you had him on his knees. *I'd* be on my knees, and I prefer a little more penis in my relationships than you have to offer."

"You promised we wouldn't talk about that."

I didn't intend to tell Fallon what happened in the dressing room at Blush. I wanted to spend tonight with Nathan, to talk about where things are going, to get a feel for how we are together. I don't need her thoughts and feelings tangling up with my thoughts and feelings and making this more difficult than it already is. But I had to explain the dress, and once I started, I couldn't stop. The story needed out whether it was a good idea or not. Though I did make sure to remind her about best friend code, since the last time I didn't, she published that stupid article about the day I spent on the water with Nathan and his cousins. Nothing in the story was bad—

I take that back.

The headline was downright cruel and a total violation of the trust I've placed in her.

I won't make the mistake of sharing stories without invoking best friend code again.

"We need to talk about that." Fallon hangs the dress back in place, the silk rippling through the air before settling. "First of all, do you know how many times I've had men give me an orgasm and call it a done deal? Just leave himself hanging? Never! Mina! The average male is too selfish for dressing room shenanigans like that."

"Nathan wasn't hanging, believe me." I point my elbow at my crotch and extend my arm straight out to emulate his erection, eyes wide. "He was very much... and very big..."

I shake my head and run my fingers into my hair trying not to imagine the impressive erection. My nipples pebble and my lower belly clenches when I do it anyway. The low thrum of desire rolls through me, and Fallon lets out a long sigh.

"Which is why I have to bring up my second of all," she says, perching on the edge of my bed, gripping the mattress like she's afraid to fall off.

I pivot to meet her eyes, stomach dropping. Whatever she has to say isn't a 'through the mirror' conversation. "Why do you have your bad news face on?"

Fallon looks at me like I've lost my mind. "Because this whole thing is bad news, Meens. Nathan said he doesn't want to 'pay you to date him.'" She makes air quotes and sneers as she drops her voice in a shitty imitation. "Does that mean you're going back to your initial contract, with your original fee? Or are you still getting the extra money you negotiated to fake this relationship with him?"

I gape at my friend, trying to imagine how that conversation would go.

So, uh...I'm happy to date you but are you still gonna pay me for it, or what?

"How am I supposed to ask him something like that?"

"How can you not?" Fallon widens her eyes and scoffs. "You need that money! You've filled your design schedule with so many new clients I'm surprised you don't sleep in your office. Even with that, you're still considering a second job to pay for your mother's medical expenses while he's spending a small fortune on a dress you'll never wear again. Not to mention, crossing sexual boundaries that shouldn't be crossed if your relationship still has a predetermined end date."

"You just went on a tirade about how amazing he was for what he did in the dressing room. Now it's crossing a boundary?"

Her jaw drops and she huffs a harsh laugh. I've never seen her look so disappointed in me and I can't for the life of me understand why.

"If you heard me call him amazing, you missed the point entirely." Fallon stands and paces to a window, sneering at my dress before she crosses the room to kneel at my feet. "Men don't act that way. Think, Meens. How many times has a guy done anything regarding sex if there wasn't something in it for him?"

I arch a brow, inviting her to clarify her point. "Never for me, which is why I assumed the point of your tirade was to illustrate how awesome Nathan is."

Fallon's face falls. "Did it ever occur to you that he's trying to make this relationship seem real so he can get out of paying you, only to break things off after he has what he needs?"

Now I'm the one huffing in disapproval. "Nathan isn't like that."

"Are you sure?"

"Without a doubt."

Fallon stands and runs her hands into her hair. "If he isn't like that, then why did I say from the very beginning that you needed a protection plan in place? That Nathan West wouldn't have your best interest at heart? Why did I want to write an article to use as leverage in case we ended up in a situation just like this one?"

"I didn't agree with you then, and I don't agree with you now. Nathan's not that guy. In fact, you need to stop calling him a villain in your articles. Actually, you need to stop with your whole 'make him realize how much he's changed' experiment. I get that you think you're helping him, but it's not working the way you want it to, and half the stuff you publish isn't true in the first place."

No matter how much Fallon wants it to be. As long as Nathan's a womanizing villain, she has something to write about. The moment that's not true, she's the villain, profiting off lies. I almost say as much, but I'm not sure she's thought that deeply about it and she sure isn't prepared to think about it now.

"You need to talk to him." Fallon drops back onto my bed, her eyes pleading with me to pay attention while she completely disregards my point. "And you need to do it with your bullshit detector on, so you catch any shady shit he's throwing your way. Or hell, maybe I need to talk to him as an objective third party."

"For one, you're not objective and for two, he doesn't know we're friends." I hang my head, feeling like an asshole. I keep meaning to tell him, but there's enough going on between us without trying to broach the 'My Best Friend Is Your Archenemy' conversation.

Fallon's entire body recoils as she objects to my objections. "And that matters, why?"

"Because your articles piss him off and I should have told him I know you a long time ago but haven't found a good time yet. And, while I'm on the topic, please, *please* hear me and stop calling him a villain."

If I'm not gonna be brave enough to tell him I'm friends with the blogger he calls a vulture, the least I can do is make sure she stops publishing lies.

"I'm glad I'm pissing him off! That's the whole point!" Fallon shakes her head. "And the fact that you don't feel like you can tell him about me, or your overfilled schedule, *or* your need for a second job, *or* ask a simple question about finances, that should tell you something. You're in over your head. You're too kind. Too genuine. You believe everyone operates like you and that just isn't true."

"You don't know Nathan the way I do. You don't know what happened or what he's actually doing. He's not a bad guy."

"Ask your mom what happens when good people make excuses for bad people."

My jaw drops and I stare. Who is she to think she knows anything about my parents, let alone compare Nathan to my father? I had the grace to stop myself from hitting her where it hurts. She can't do the same for me?

"That's a low blow, Fallon."

"If that's what I have to do to make you hear me..."

I pull open a drawer and retrieve my brush. "I need to look gala ready in a couple hours and you swore you'd help. This isn't helping."

"Right. Silly me, trying to protect you." Fallon crosses her arms over her chest. "You know I only brought this up because I love you and don't want to see you hurt."

"I know."

There's so much more I want to say, excuses to make, questions to ask. I know what I see when I meet Nathan's eyes, and it isn't a power-hungry asshole using me for personal gain. He's genuine. I know it.

But I won't convince Fallon of that. Not tonight. And I'll be fidgety enough this evening without being in a fight with the only real support system I have.

I hold my brush out like a peace offering. "Will you please help me with my hair?"

Relief softens her posture. "Will you please think about what I've said tonight?"

I press my lips together and lift the brush again. "As long as you promise to think about what I've said."

The next several hours pass quietly, the two of us lost in thought as I transform from boring and basic Mina Blake into a woman I barely recognize. A woman wearing a spectacular dress, with Harlow West's diamonds dripping from her ears and sparkling at her wrist. They dazzle me when they catch the light.

The silk is so thin and fits so perfectly to my body, that even a thong showed through, transforming the classic lines of the dress into something slutty. After trying too many undergarments to count and all of them ruining the effect, I finally opt to go commando, then slide on a pair of strappy heels, and stand in front of the mirror.

Dear God. Pinch me because I must be dreaming. Yours ever so truly, Mina Blake.

"Are you sure it's not too..." I ask, twisting to look at my butt.

"Oh it's 'too' all right." Fallon laughs gently. "Those stuffy charity people won't know what hit them."

TWENTY-FIVE

Mina

Fallon leaves at quarter after two and Nathan arrives an hour later. The gala starts early, with the auction happening first thing, leaving the rest of the night free for the winners to spend with their dates for the evening. With a deep breath, I pull open my door and there he is. The man I can't stop thinking about. The man Fallon thinks is so evil he would lie about his feelings to get out of paying for a fake relationship. The man she compared to my father.

Low blow followed by lowest blow.

Nathan's hair is effortlessly swept back to frame his chiseled cheeks and jaw. His eyes are bright, and the steep angle of the setting sun casts half his face in shadow. Fallon would call it symbolic but that's the writer in her, ascribing meaning to shitty lighting. A tuxedo hugs broad shoulders and a slim waist I want to wrap my legs around. The subtle glint of silver from his cufflinks catches the light and I realize I'm silently staring as seconds tick into minutes.

"Hi." I lift a hand, then use it to steady myself on the doorframe. I'm suddenly unbalanced. Everything I thought was real and true in the world has come undone.

How can The Prince of Darkness look at me like I'm a goddess?

How can Fallon think she knows him when she's never even spoken to him?

How can I be this awkward with him when I know how his tongue feels pressed against me? The way his hair feels fisted in my fingers? The way I wanted to scream his name and ride his face and now we're just standing here and—

"Hi." Nathan's smile is inscrutable as always. "Ready?"

"As I'll ever be." I grab my clutch off the table near the door then step outside to lock up, fully aware of Nathan standing behind me, his body so close to mine. This thin line of expectation…

Of possibility…

"I thought I imagined the way you look in that dress," he says, drawing his fingers across my bare shoulder. "That I'd built it into something magnificent to excuse the way I behaved in the dressing room."

I slowly turn to face him, my breath racing, and press myself against the door to give us more space. "And?"

"I didn't imagine it. You are stunning, Mina Blake. Any man would be lucky to have you on his arm. I'm honored that tonight, it's me."

Nathan presses a hand to my lower back and I glance up at him, waiting for the punchline. The hint of evil to vindicate Fallon's concerns.

All I see is the boyish charm I've come to know and love.

He looks completely genuine.

The car waiting in the parking lot isn't Nathan's. This one is sleek and black and belongs in movies, not parked outside my apartment. Ms. Markowitz steps outside to stare, as do the Dietzes, and the frat boys a few doors down, all of them whispering excitedly as the driver emerges to open a door for me. This isn't typical for Lime Tree Bay Apartments. If I wasn't the one climbing into the car, I'd be staring and whispering too. Nathan tosses me a knowing grin as he lowers himself into the seat beside me.

"I probably should have warned you about the car and driver." The crook to his smile says he doesn't mean it.

"Why didn't you?"

"I wanted to see the look on your face."

If Fallon could see this version of Nathan, she'd take back everything she said. His eyes shimmer like dew on blades of grass, bright and warm as they hold mine. Gone are the thorns and frozen barbed wire.

"Was it worth it?" I ask.

"Completely," he responds, threading his fingers with mine as the driver pulls out of the lot.

The car slows to a stop in front of The Hutton Hotel, which, according to Fallon, started as a sprawling colonial style house on the beach with more rooms than family members when Nathan's mom was a little girl. The extra space disquieted Nathan's grandmother—Rebecca Hutton—a woman with a heart big enough to love the whole world and the brains to know a business opportunity when she saw one. It didn't take long for the extra rooms to become a bed and breakfast, and for the bed and breakfast to become a full-blown resort. Last year, the family opened a second hotel in Bliss, South Carolina with Angela and Garrett spearheading the project. Fallon says it's as charming as the one in front of me and just as successful.

Behind the old house, the ocean stretches out until it kisses the horizon. Several tents have been set up on the beach, with temporary walkways and flooring to accommodate fancy footwear. A string quartet plays quietly, the music dancing in and out of the ocean waves crashing rhythmically against the sand. After the auction, a live band will take their place to allow for dancing. There's an open bar where servers load trays of appetizers and champagne to float fluidly through the crowd once the guests arrive. There are tiki torches and strings of lights and the view is so striking it doesn't look real. How does someone like me end up in a place like this, wearing what I'm wearing, on the arm of a man who grew up thinking any of this is normal?

It's elegant and excessive and I don't want to think about what it costs. Events like this are what placed a giant chip on my shoulder the first day I met Nathan. Growing up poor, I resented those who had money to burn. But this entire evening is dedicated to raising money for a charity that helps little kids dealt a bad hand like me.

Maybe I was wrong to judge. To assume. To lump people into groups and categories without taking the human factor into account. None of us fit neatly into boxes.

Nathan and I make our way toward the bar and are instantly enveloped in a herd of Huttons. A man I don't recognize hangs back, arms crossed, glaring at me like I'm an unwelcome addition to the group. He's as tall as any of the men in Nathan's family but lacks the feeling of warmth I've come to expect from the Mason's and Angela's...hell even Nathan himself. If ever there was a Prince of Darkness, it's this guy.

"I thought I said you'd be better not to come at all than to show up with a dazzling and spectacular woman on your arm," an older woman says to Nathan. She sounds stern but looks friendly and is downright stunning. Her blonde hair is swept up and back, with tendrils framing her face. She's wearing black pants with wide legs, a fitted blazer, and sky-high heels.

Having those two words aimed at me sends my heartrate into overdrive. I grip Nathan's arm, smiling weakly as I decide if I'm supposed to respond.

"Breathe, HM." He presses a kiss into the top of my head, inhaling deeply. "Aunt Maisie is simply confirming what we already know. That dress looks amazing on you."

The gesture is so sweet, so familiar, so easy, I do exactly what he said and breathe a sigh of relief.

"You need stronger adjectives, son. 'Amazing' doesn't begin to describe what's happening here."

Nathan's mom gestures between us and I get the distinct impression she's not talking about the dress. That maybe, just maybe, she's talking about *us*.

Nathan presses his palm against my lower back, his thumb brushing lightly against my spine. I lean closer, smiling despite myself.

"Is this her? The one who's bringing our dear, sweet Nathan back to life?" A young woman with a mess of dark curls, a shit-eating grin, and a short black dress with fabulous red heels appears at my side. She's several inches smaller than everyone else with a personality that towers above us all.

"Mina, this is Garrett's little sister Charlie, down from New England," Angela says. "Charlie, this is Mina the miracle worker."

Charlie waves over a passing server to grab a champagne flute. "Angela told me you're putting yourself up for auction. Believe me, you're not going to regret it. I did it last year and it was an absolute blast. It's the whole reason I flew down again this year."

"We all know the real reason you flew down is still deployed right now." Garrett smirks at his sister. "There was a real chance Nick would be home in time to be here. You rolled the dice and now you're here and he's not."

"Hey!" Charlie drops her jaw and slaps his arm.

"Do I like flirting with a hot Marine? Yes! Who wouldn't? But do you really think I'd spend this much on a dress and fly to Florida simply to flirt with Nick Hutton? Sheesh. Big brothers. Am I right?" She gives me an exasperated eye roll before continuing. "I'll tell you, growing up in a small town, with a single dad doing his best and failing, I never *ever* saw this in my future. But Garrett made all this money and one thing led to another and here I am, reaping the rewards of his success."

"Reversals of fortune." Maisie Hutton smiles gently. "It's why I named the foundation what I did. Younger me would never have believed this could be my life. I didn't have it easy growing up and through a combination of hard work and good luck, I'm here. I want to do everything I can to pay it forward."

This is so not the way I've pictured people with money. This entire family is trying to sprinkle some of their good luck onto the world. If only I could catch some of it for myself, I'd use it on Mom in a heartbeat.

"I've thought the same thing so many times since I met Nathan," I say. "Younger me wouldn't believe this is my life. I wish I could share some of it with Mom."

"Have you given any thought to letting us spoil her here at The Hut?" Angela asks. "And before you tell me you can't afford it, we'll give her the friends and family discount. The whole package, totally on the house."

And there's the rub. This relationship, this...whatever it is...with Nathan is too new for me to profit off his wealth. I'm not going to be someone else who takes from him, or his family. "I can't let you do that."

"Would she qualify for Nathan's new adult program at ROF?" Garrett asks. "Forgive me for making assumptions about your mother's situation, but if she's unemployed due to long-term illness and drowning in medical bills, she sounds exactly like the type of person he's trying to help. And since you kind of have an in..."

"Oh, no, no," I say as the tall man I haven't been introduced to yet shoots Nathan a disgusted glance. "Mom and I are gonna be okay."

I just have to work a little harder for a little longer to get us there.

Nathan breaks eye contact with the stranger and meets my gaze, thoughts ticking across his face.

Who is that guy? What's he doing here? Why do I get the distinct impression he doesn't like me?

The group chatters, tossing banter around like confetti while I hang on Nathan's arm. I'd hoped we'd have time to talk about us, maybe figure out who we are to each other, but that seems more and more like a pipedream. Though the night is young, the company is fabulous, and the view is straight out of a movie. Maybe I should worry less about putting pressure on the evening and let myself enjoy this once in my lifetime experience.

TWENTY-SIX

Nathan

I didn't imagine the way Mina looked in that dress. It wasn't a story I told myself to rationalize what I did in the dressing room at Blush. Her waist begs for my hands. Her breasts call to my lips, my teeth. I want to revel in her. To steal her away from my family and lock us in one of the rooms at The Hut. I'd be on my knees again. Then she'd be on hers, those lips wrapped around my cock.

Instead, Angela whisks her away with Garrett's sister, Charlie, to go over paperwork and details before the auction. Our little group dissipates, leaving me with Dom standing a few feet away, looking wholly unimpressed. His clothes are expensive, his posture casual yet self-important. He's the kind of guy who comes to a charity auction to boost his image, not help those in need, and he looks the part. How could I stand to be around him for so long?

"Did you hear that?" Dom lifts a judgmental eyebrow. "Mina's mom sounds like a perfect candidate for your new program. What a lucky break for her that the two of you found each other just as you're ready to accept your first round of applicants."

I slide my hands into my pants pockets and shift back on my heel. "The timing's a coincidence. This is the first Mina's heard about my plans to expand the foundation."

Dom scoffs. "How can you know that?"

"Because I haven't told her." There's an edge to my voice he's not used to hearing. One that says *back the fuck off*.

But Dominick Taylor does what he wants.

"How much did you spend on her dress?" he asks.

"None of your fucking business," I bark, then step closer so I can lower my voice. The last thing I need is a public argument that fuels a round of gossip. For all I know, Fallon Mae is lurking nearby. Or the person who's feeding her information. Either way, the headlines would not be kind.

"Look, brother," Dom says without a care in the world who hears. "Don't hate me because I'm running defense for you when you should be doing it yourself."

"I don't need anyone running defense," I reply through a jaw tight enough to bend steel.

Dom scoffs. "You just got out of this exact situation with Blossom and you're letting it happen all over again. It's the classic story between the haves and have nots. They're in it for what they can get from you. You're fooling yourself if you think otherwise."

"Who hurt you?" I grimace, then refresh my 'party face' as a server wanders by, pretending not to eavesdrop. "Mina isn't Blossom. And if you'd get your head out of your ass long enough to talk to her, you'd realize what a fucking dick you are for everything you just said."

"You keep calling me names like I don't know who I am. I am an asshole, Nathan. It's one of the reasons you like me. It helps when I'm distracting pretty young ladies so you can schmooze their rich fat uncles. I play my role so you can play yours, just like *Mina* is gonna play hers. The rules won't change just because you wish they were different."

No wonder my family has been worried about me. If this is who Dom really is and I'm just now seeing it, that says something uncomfortable about who I've been.

"Hear me when I say this, Dom. Stop dogging

Mina. Get to know her better, get on board, or shut the fuck up."

"I'll take it under advisement," he says, then heads for the bar, leaving me alone with my thoughts.

The guests begin to arrive, and Angela returns Mina to me in time to greet the more generous donors on our list. We chit and we chat and laugh and smile and all I can focus on is her.

I remember her moans. Her sighs. I remember her taste and the way the dress hit that floor, a cascade of fluttering silk and there she was, bare to me. No bra. No underwear. Just her.

And I suspect the same is true tonight. No bra. No underwear. She's just there, waiting for me to claim her and it's driving me fucking crazy.

Mina and I dance. We laugh. We talk with friends and family. We find Benjamin Bancroft standing on the outskirts, watching everyone with interest, and chat with him until Angela finally arrives to steal Mina for the auction.

"She's something, isn't she?" Benjamin asks me, unable to take his eyes off Mina's back.

She's everything.

I swallow hard, watching as she disappears with Angela.

"She is more than I bargained for, that's for sure."

Benjamin lifts his glass, his eyes on Mina. "Here's to finding happiness in unexpected places."

There's something strange about him tonight. Something tense. Or expectant. The usually friendly architect seems reserved. Before I can decide if I'm imagining things, Aunt Maisie steps onto the stage my uncle Joe and cousin Mason built specifically for this event. With long strips of sheer fabric draping from arching timbers, its simple elegance is striking. I say goodbye to Benjamin and grudgingly take the nearest open seat...right next to Dom. He spares me a cool glance, then glues his attention to the stage as my aunt explains the rules for the auction. There's a light spattering of applause when she finishes, and the games begin.

Several ROF employees take the stage. My assistant, Rita MacDonald. David Doughtry, one of our best caseworkers, an older man we affectionately call Keto Santa. After we cycle through employees, we move on to family members. Micah. My sister Maren and her twin Joshua. Angela. Charlie. Even Uncle Lucas and Aunt Cat.

And then Mina.

There's a collective gasp as she steps into the spotlight. That champagne colored dress. Her red lips, pale skin, and ebony hair. Aunt Maisie starts the bidding at one thousand dollars and several hands hit the air. The price rises, but so do hands, strangers fighting for a night with the woman who came with me.

"Do I hear twenty thousand?" asks Maisie with a conspiratorial smile for Mina.

Twenty-five.

Thirty.

Dom raises his hand. "Fifty."

"What the fuck are you doing?" I whisper.

"Taking your advice and getting to know her," he responds and my jaw clenches.

Before I can say anything, a voice calls out from the back, "Seventy-five thousand dollars."

The audience gasps. Mina's jaw drops. And I turn to see Benjamin Bancroft lowering his hand with that strange look still on his face.

Dom crosses his ankle over his knee and sits back, eyeing Mina like he wants to dissect her. "Seventy-six."

"Eighty," I say without thinking.

A murmur rolls through the crowd like waves preceding a storm. They know Mina came with me. They know I'm bidding on my own date. I look like a territorial asshole, but I don't care. I can't let Dom buy a night with her. Not after everything he's said. Not when he won't think twice about saying it to her face.

"Eighty-five," counters Dom.

I glare and set my jaw. "Ninety."

"One hundred thousand." Bancroft's voice comes from the back.

"Do I hear a hundred and one?" Aunt Maisie looks like she can't believe she's asking for that much money and Mina seems downright distraught.

Dom scoffs and rolls his eyes. I wait an eternity before Maisie cries, "Sold! And that's an ROF record, ladies and gentlemen!"

TWENTY-SEVEN

Mina

"What just happened?" I step off the stage after the most surreal experience in my life and gape at Angela.

"Someone paid one-hundred-thousand dollars for a night with you," she responds, looking as shocked as I feel. "I've never seen the bidding go that high."

That someone is Benjamin Bancroft, the super hot, super nice, maybe a little awkward but incredibly talented architect I've had a minor crush on for most of my career. Of all the things I saw happening tonight, that did not make the list.

"But did Nathan bid too?" I ask, even though I know the answer to that question. My heart raced to hear his voice. My breath caught when I saw the determined look on his face and then caught again when I realized I wanted him to win. I didn't want to spend the evening with the glaring man beside him, throwing bids my way like he intended to kidnap me afterwards. Nor did I want to spend the evening with Benjamin.

I want to share this beautiful, perfect night with Nathan.

"He most definitely bid on you too." Angela nods, smiling broadly. "Right after his friend Dom came out of nowhere for what were sure to be nefarious reasons."

"Dom." I furrow my brow. Have I ever heard Nathan talk about a friend named Dom before? I don't think so. But that guy sure seemed to have heard about me and if the look on his face means anything, he didn't like what he heard.

But if that's true, why would he bid so high?

Angela pats my cheek. A friendly gesture that warms my heart.

I guess that's what we are now. Friends.

"I'm gonna go ahead and assume you're as relieved as I am that you don't have to spend an evening with that Jerky McJerkerson," she says as Micah saunters our way. "He's a special breed, that one."

Micah grimaces, clearly not a fan of this Dom character, either. "Nathan bidding on you really didn't make sense until I saw Dom. He was saving you from a terrible night with a terrible person. That's Nator Tot's thing. Swoopin' in. Damsel in distress. Saving the world, one good deed at a time. Don't tell him I used that nickname, by the way. I promised I'd stop." Micah grins at me. "You must be feeling pretty badass right now. One hundred thousand dollars?"

Everyone's acting like I should be flattered, but I'm not. I'm a little disgusted and a lot uncomfortable. That much money could change someone's life, but Benjamin just threw it away for a few hours with me. What does it mean? Surely, he's not the kind of man who makes a play on someone else's girlfriend. Or does his bluntness extend far enough that a dramatic gesture that big doesn't seem off to him?

"I'm feeling...confused," I say. "That really happened? It doesn't even feel real."

I glance up and there's Benjamin. He smiles gently and waves, almost shy. Behind him, Nathan lurks, glaring in my direction. He sighs when our eyes lock, then cocks his head in Benjamin's direction and saunters away. I have no idea what to make of that, but it doesn't matter because suddenly we're signing contracts and Angela's reciting the rules, grinning like the whole thing's just the best thing ever instead of the confusing mess it really is.

Benjamin scribbles his signature first, then mine hits the dotted line. He offers me his arm. I drape my wrist over his elbow, and he leads me back into the gala while I search the crowd for Nathan. The string quartet has left and the band has taken their place, the lead singer cupping the microphone as he croons a popular love song. Heads turn as we pass, people whispering, grinning, wondering. In a sea of dazzling and spectacular people, I'm suddenly the most interesting person here. How does anyone know what to do with this much attention?

"I want everyone to see the hundred-thousand-dollar girl," Benjamin says as he parades me through the crowd. "I want them to wonder who you are. I want them to talk. I want your name on their lips."

"Benjamin..." I begin, growing more uncomfortable by the second. "I feel like I need to tell you—"

He places a finger against my mouth with a conspiratorial smile. "Hush now, Mina. I'll explain once everyone has seen you."

If I was confused before, I'm downright baffled now. "Explain?"

"You're not very good at hushing, are you?" he whispers, then boops the tip of my nose.

After he's certain everyone has gotten a look at us, we stop at the bar for drinks, then find a secluded table under the stars. He pulls out my chair, then takes a seat next to me. Our backs are to the party, the ocean in front of us catching fire in the setting sun. The music is muted by distance. The waves are constant and a breeze slips across my shoulders. I cross my arms on the table, except that feels too much like I'm leaning close and I don't want to give any accidental nonverbal cues, so I uncross them and put them in my lap, but that feels too expectant, so I take a nervous sip of my champagne and wait.

Benjamin leans back, throwing an arm over the back of his chair as he rests his ankle on his knee. "A while ago, I told you I worried that Nathan might not be good for you."

I tense. Of all the times for him to make his move, he chooses now? In a grand gesture worthy of a movie, nonetheless. A couple months ago, I would have swooned right into his embrace. Now it just seems so...

...so...

...selfish.

I haven't given any hints I was interested. I'm with Nathan. What could Benjamin possibly think would happen tonight?

"You did tell me that." I twirl my glass between my hands, meeting his gaze, waiting and worrying about what he'll say next.

"And you told me everything was fine."

I nod, hoping I look calmer than I feel. "I did."

"I didn't believe you." He takes my hand and meets my eyes.

I brace for him to make his move. It's coming next, I'm sure of it. "That was pretty obvious."

"I do now," he says with a wide grin.

"Benjamin, I—"

Hold on.

Wait.

He said what, now?

"You believe me?"

He nods.

"Then why in the world did you spend a small fortune for a few hours with me?"

Benjamin swipes his drink off the table, fighting laughter. "It's all part of my grand plan."

I harrumph back into my chair. "I figured that much out, but I'm looking for some clarity as to what that plan might be."

"For one, I promised myself at the start of my career that if I made my fortune, I'd give freely, as often as possible. What's the point of being wealthy if you can't spread goodness around where it's needed? Hence, my very large donation to a reputable charity this evening."

That's admirable enough and more in line with the man I thought I knew. I sigh in relief knowing I won't be rebutting his advances tonight. "So, it had nothing to do with me."

"Not so fast, princess." Mischief glints in Benjamin's eyes. "It had everything to do with you."

All the relief that had been seeping through my bones freezes. I press my lips together and study the man across from me for a tense second, my hands balled into fists before I cock my head and hit him with some pent-up truth.

"Now I'm downright confused," I say, shaking my head and holding up my hands. "And frankly, I'm getting tired of being confused because nothing in my life makes sense or is what it's supposed to be and if you can just clear things up for me sooner rather than later, I'd really appreciate that because I need something to be firm and defined before I lose my mind."

Benjamin lifts a brow. "We're going to circle back to all that at some point, but I need to finish the speech I started or I'll lose my place and skip something important. The house we designed for Nathan West will be the best thing I've ever produced, and that's no accident. That's because of you."

My jaw drops. "Me?"

Considering the worst thing he's ever produced is still award-worthy, that's a hell of a compliment.

"The way we work together is a rare and singular gift. A partnership like this doesn't just happen and we would be negligent not to act on it. I've recently been contacted by a high-profile client, and I want you to work with me on her project. In fact, I want you to be the only interior designer to work with me from this point forward. I want to go into business with you. Bancroft and Blake Design." Benjamin waves a hand through the air like he's reading from a sign, then cocks his head. "Though the name is open for revisions."

I blink in the darkness, my heart tripping over my stomach to see who makes sense of his proposition first. Both of them land flat on the ground and refuse to get up. There's no sense to be made here. This is surreal stacked on absurd with a twist of dream come true.

"You paid one hundred thousand dollars just to get me alone and make a business proposal?"

"Yes." Benjamin sips his drink, watching me over the rim of the glass. "And also no. I could have called you tomorrow and met you at the office and did all of this there. But!" He holds up an exclamation point of a finger. "Think of the buzz I just created. How many people are asking who you are? How many people have our names on their lips right now? After Nathan's house is complete, we'll catch even more attention. And even more after our next project. Everyone will want to hire Benjamin Bancroft and the Hundred Thousand Dollar Girl."

A quick glance over my shoulder proves his point. At least half the guests are pretending not to stare in our direction. The other half aren't bothering to pretend. I give Benjamin an approving nod and pick up my glass.

"That's savvy," I say and heft my champagne his way.

He clinks his glass to mine. "I might be too blunt to interact with most people, but that ability to see through bullshit makes me an excellent marketer."

"I'm impressed."

"Like I said, stick with me kid. We're gonna do good things together."

We drink to that. Then drink again. Then suddenly it all lands. I just got offered my dream job while drinking champagne on the beach in a dress that makes me feel beautiful. Somewhere back there, my super rich, super hot, boyfriend—because I think that must be what we are to each other—is waiting with his family that feels like sunshine. When they hear what's just happened, they'll be almost as happy for me as I am for myself.

How is this my life?

"So, what now?" I grin, catching on to the fun of the game. "Are we going to sit out here all night, whispering over drinks? Let people talk and wonder?"

"Nope." Benjamin smiles gently. "As much as it pains me, I'm giving you back to Nathan before his eyes burn hate holes into the back of my head. Not only will people wonder even more, but you deserve some time to think about my offer before you agree."

I turn and there he is. Arms crossed. Thorn and bramble gaze piercing the night. I smile and he glares and won't he think it's funny when he learns what just happened.

"To the many, many good things we'll discover together." Benjamin presses a kiss to the back of my hand before returning me to Nathan. "Thank you for letting me borrow your date. She's quite a woman."

With that, he saunters away, head held high, smile in place as people watch and whisper.

"I bet that made your night," Nathan growls, barely meeting my eyes.

"In a string of surreal days, this one takes the cake."

He's jealous. There's no hiding it. I should put his mind at ease, but there's something fun in drawing it out. I won't make him suffer long, though.

Nathan rakes a hand through his hair. "The whole reason we're...whatever we're doing...is because you had a thing for Benjamin and your drunk friend tried to play Cupid."

"I did have a thing for him." I place my palm to Nathan's cheek and meet his eyes. "But it pales in comparison to the thing I have for you."

A slow smile creeps across Nathan's face as he

leans into my touch. It's like watching the dawn chase away the shadow of night. A thawing. A warming. And then, the sun in all its blinding glory.

He kisses me, his lips gentle then commanding, his hands whispering up my back, slipping over silk to find skin. His body presses to mine, strong and hard, and mine answers, supple, clenching, a low, throbbing need burning in my belly.

Nathan pulls back, brushing his forehead to mine. "Is that why he gave you back so early? Your thing for me?"

One kiss.

Another.

People are watching and I'm suddenly shy.

"Apparently this was all a big marketing scheme."

"Marketing...?" Nathan cocks his head. "What the hell, Mina?"

"This is pretty much the best night of my life for a number of reasons." With the man beside me being the biggest of those reasons. I can't stop smiling and the look in his eyes is like coming home. Like becoming whole. Like knowing all is right in my world.

Nathan glances at the gathered crowd, then leans close to whisper, "Why don't we get out of here and you can tell me all about it."

And suddenly all I want is to be alone with him, so I can finally *be* with him. I want to tell him I stopped faking weeks ago and I want him to agree. I want him to touch me and take me and fulfill the promise he made with that first kiss in the parking lot at The Pact when the moon was full and expectant and hinted at wonderful things.

I nod and he smiles, then takes my hand and we wind through a crowd whispering questions as we leave.

There's one thing I know for sure:

I want more time with Nathan West.

TWENTY-EIGHT

Mina

I tell Nathan about Benjamin's offer in the car. My words trip over each other, each one more eager than the last to get out. "Bancroft and Blake Design. I mean...how awesome is that?"

"That's amazing, Mina. I'm so proud of you and not at all surprised. You're so incredibly talented. Benjamin would have to be blind not to see."

He hasn't let go of my hand since we got in the car, his thumb brushing my knuckle in a soothing dance. Everything's shifted now. The nerves I felt when he picked me up have dissipated, burnt off like morning fog giving way to the sun, dewdrops glittering. A surge of anticipation effervesces through my bloodstream as Nathan's driver pulls to a stop in front of a modest two-story house on the water. It's so much smaller than the one Benjamin and I are designing for him, smaller even than his parents' house, that I don't immediately unlatch my seatbelt, certain there's been a mistake. But Nathan climbs out of the car and the driver steps out to open my door, so this must be where we're supposed to be.

I emerge into a night filled with expectation.

It pulses through the air.

The stars glimmer with it.

The sea roars with it.

I'm bursting with it.

"This isn't the house I imagined for you," I say, as Nathan crosses in front of the car to take my hand once again.

"Had something more lair-like in mind? Something better suited to The Prince of Darkness?" He grins as he brushes a strand of hair behind my ear, his thumb brushing my cheek. He can't stop touching me and I don't want him to.

"It's a quarter the size of what Benjamin and I designed for you."

"I've only recently decided to take Dom's advice and play the hand I was given. Let myself enjoy being rich." With a familiar hand on my back, Nathan leads me towards the steps.

I pause as I reach for the handrail.

"*Are* you enjoying it?" I ask, though what I really want to know is what now? What about us? Who is Dom and why does no one like him?

"I haven't enjoyed much of the last couple months." Nathan takes the stairs, then slips his key into the lock, pausing to look at me. His eyes simmer with heat, with meaning, with something that has me stepping closer.

"That's not true." His voice is low. Personal. "I've enjoyed my time with you very much."

Nathan gestures for me to enter and I step inside his home, aware of how close he is as I pass. Being here with him feels more intimate than having him on his knees for me in the dressing room. This is his space, filled with his things, a personal glimpse into who Nathan West really is and what he values.

I enter into an open living room with a straight path to a dining area. Windows and a sliding glass door to my right reveal a covered deck that overlooks the water—a spectacular view if I've ever seen one. To my left is what looks like an office. The furnishings are expensive, though a few years old. Three gorgeous guitars with gleaming wood line one wall with several paintings hanging above, all by the same artist.

"My mother did those," Nathan says, brushing his fingers against my bare shoulder. "Those two, she did while she was pregnant with me. The others happened throughout my childhood."

I step closer to one done in the exact shades I imagined for Nathan's new house—blues, grays, browns, and greens. Focusing on the paintings gives me a break from the tension smoldering between us.

"They're beautiful." I glance his way, stoking the fire. "They capture your essence perfectly."

"Mom's good at everything she does. Wine? Whiskey?" he asks, then heads toward the kitchen without waiting for a response, almost as if he's feeling the same way I am. Like we're constantly resisting a pull that will eventually overpower us.

"Wine would be nice," I say, then follow, taking in my surroundings, surprised by how normal everything feels. When I first met Nathan, I'd pegged him as one of those Hollywood trust fund types. A man used to having everything he wants, whenever he wants it. Spoiled. Entitled. The kind of man who hires the best of the best to build a house that could fit three families rather than just one person.

This feels more like the man I've come to know. Thoughtful. Kind. Lacking pretense.

"I picked up a bottle of vin santo rosso. Seemed to be something you enjoy." Nathan slides off his jacket and loosens his bow tie, then pulls a corkscrew out of a drawer and a bottle of wine off the rack. "Kept thinking you might be here someday. Then I kept thinking that was pretty stupid of me, right up until it happened."

Nathan pours wine for me and whiskey for him, then pauses before handing me the glass. "You don't have to stay. In case that needed to be said. I can drive you home or call for a ride or whatever you want."

Energy sizzles between us. He's giving me an out I don't want.

"Do you want me to stay?"

He tosses back his whiskey and puts the glass on the counter without looking at me. "Only if you want to."

"Nathan." I put a hand on his, craning my neck to meet his eyes. "Do you want me to stay?"

The question hits the conversation like a sucker punch. His jaw pulses and his hands ball into fists and I'm standing here, waiting for an answer that shouldn't be this hard to find. An answer I have to have before anything else happens.

We started out hating each other but that isn't true anymore.

Something's shifted.

Something important.

And before I let myself think thoughts like that, I need to know. Does he want me? Is this real? Or is Fallon right and I'm falling for an illusion?

Nathan takes the wine glass from my hand and places it beside his whiskey. "I want you to stay."

"Because if I stay, we'll..." I pause before I suggest he finish what he started at Blush.

"I want that too." His voice is husky. It rasps into the room, drenched in need. "I've wanted it every day since we first met."

And then Nathan's lips are on mine, kissing away the confusion. This chemistry isn't fake. Neither is the way he touches me, so reverently. He brought me here tonight because he wants me for himself.

And I want him just as much.

I slide my hands up his back, reveling in the corded muscles under my hands and oh my God when did this start to feel so right? When did I start needing him to touch me? To lick me?

When did I start wanting him to want me?

Nathan grips my hips, then skates his hands over my ass. "That's what I fucking thought," he growls. "No panties."

"We agreed not to comment on each other's underwear." My lips drag across the stubble on his jaw, his throat. I slip my hands under his jacket and push it off his shoulders. He lets it fall, then brings his hands right back to my body.

"I also agreed I wouldn't touch you without an audience," he says, grabbing my ass in both hands and pressing me against an impressive erection. "Are you saying you want me to stop?"

"God no. I'm saying I want more."

More, Nathan. More.

Now, Nathan. Now.

I slide his bowtie from around his neck, then pull his shirt out of his pants, undoing his buttons because he's seen me naked and now, I need to see him. He watches me work, his eyes on my fingers, and then, when the last button is free, he's kissing me before I have time to appreciate what I unveiled. We're a tangle of limbs, desperate to feel everything, all at once. Months of chemistry boiling to a head.

To this moment.

The two of us finally giving in.

Nathan hooks his arms under my hips and I wrap my legs around his waist. He carries me past the kitchen to a first-floor bedroom that looks like it's been plucked off my mood board for his new house. He places me on the edge of his bed, then kicks off his shoes and lets his shirt fall to the floor. I trail my fingers down his chest and abs, tracing the smattering of dark hair that disappears into his pants. He's had me moaning in pleasure and now it's my turn to return the favor. I work the button at his waist but he takes my hand, kissing each finger before he kneels in front of me to work the strap of my shoe, his thumb caressing my ankle. His lips kissing my calf.

First one.

Then the other.

Then the zipper of my dress and the one in his pants and he's climbing on top of me, his knees spreading my thighs as he lowers me to his bed. "I'm gonna be greedy this time," he whispers, "but I'll be generous afterwards."

"Be greedy," I say, reaching between us to wrap my fingers around his cock.

He groans, a guttural sound that has my legs draping around his waist, heels digging into his ass. I want him inside me, thrusting, hips rocking, bodies sweating.

"Condom," he murmurs as I grip his length, pumping him toward my opening.

"I'm on the pill."

Nathan's gaze captures mine, hooded, heated, hungry. He presses his crown against me, stretching me as he slides agonizingly into place. My mouth opens, my jaw thrust forward, eyes locked on his as I adjust to his girth. I'm panting, close to exploding, and he hasn't even started to move. Just having him inside me is a masterclass in pleasure.

"Fuck, Mina. You're perfect."

And with a single roll of his hips, our worlds shift,

moving inexpressibly closer. Intermingling. Unifying. A blessed harmony.

I gasp and moan as he braces his hands on either side of my head, his lips crashing over mine. Our skin slaps and his pace speeds and I clench around him because oh holy fuck I didn't know it could feel like this.

"Mina..." My name tumbles from his lips, into my heart.

I rake my fingers into his hair and press my forehead to his. "I love it when you say my name."

"Mina..." Nathan groans, panting as he stares into my eyes.

I'm floating. Disintegrating. Coming undone and being made whole in an infinite loop. His lips are a necessity. His touch an inevitability. He brands me with his energy. He is everything and I am more than I've ever been and a flutter starts low in my belly then rises through me. For no reason and every reason, I realize my entire life was driving me to this point. Into his arms. His bed. His body hitting mine like a live wire.

I clench and I buck.

Coming apart.

Coming back to life.

Nathan nips at my throat. My jaw. "I warned you I'd be greedy," he rasps. "I've wanted this too long."

I'm beyond answering. Beyond caring. I am sensation and pleasure. I throb and scream, my hands on his ass, his name on my lips, my teeth on his shoulder.

With a guttural growl, Nathan finishes, spurting inside me with one last thrust as his eyes squeeze closed and my body holds him tight.

TWENTY-NINE

Nathan

Holy fuck.
Oh hell.
What the shit.
I collapse beside Mina, my lungs on fire. My head clear of the roar of questions and worries that have been my constant companion for weeks. Maybe my entire life.
I close my eyes.
Whatever happens next, this was worth it.
Mina was worth it.
I am not made for barbed wire and raised defenses.
I am made for her.
After this night, there's one thing I know for sure:
I was stupid to think I didn't like Mina Blake.

She lays her head on my chest, tracing designs on my belly with her fingernails. "I think we just violated every single rule we set for ourselves at the beginning of this. Maybe a few extras. I don't know."

I wrap an arm around her shoulders, fully relaxed. Completely sated. Sliding into sleep with her body pressed against mine. "Fine with me."

The words slip into the room as my eyes close. So this is what contentment feels like. A complete lack of urgency to be anywhere but where I am or do anything but hold her close and breathe her in.

Mina presses a kiss to my chest, my throat, the soft spot beneath my ear. "But you're in your villain era," she whispers. "And I'm the sweet damsel caught in your trap. Shouldn't I be afraid?"

I'm the one who's caught. I'll never not want you again. Why doesn't that scare me?

No time for thoughts like that. Not now. Not yet. They can wait until tomorrow, when I have it in me to care about right and wrong. When I can wonder how Mina slipped through the barbed wire wrapped around my heart.

I run a hand through her hair. "Is that what happened? I trapped you?"

"That's what I'll tell people when they ask. Even though I can't think of anywhere else I want to be" She giggles into my skin. It's like oxygen. Like taking my first full breath after a deep dive. Like stepping out of the ocean in winter and warming myself by the fire.

"I can see the headlines now. 'Nathan West falls for owner of ancient Honda. She's more than dazzling and spectacular. She's extraordinary.'" I wave a hand through the air as if I'm reading the article off my ceiling.

The joke sours my mood. I don't want to think what that stupid Fallon Mae will say about this. She twists everything I do into something awful, and I don't want that to happen to Mina. She's wonderful. She's everything. She's the light I've been searching for.

"No, Nathan. That's you. You're the one who's extraordinary. You're kind and give so much of yourself. You're smart and strong and so incredibly sexy I sometimes can't hear what you're saying because I'm too busy staring. Me? I'm just plain Mina," she says, still tracing her fingers across my skin, driving me fucking mad with lust.

I'd rather focus on that then the what ifs and what nows circling my head like vultures.

In one swift movement, I roll Mina onto her back, caging her with my arms. She shrieks, giggling as I lower my lips to suckle a breast.

"What are you doing?" she moans.

"There's nothing plain about you, HM. Nothing at

all." I nip at her throat, then whisper in her ear, "I was greedy before. Now it's time to be generous."

Who knows how long later, Mina and I are back in the kitchen. She's wearing one of my shirts and nothing else. It grazes her thighs and whispers of familiarity. I like it more than the dress she wore here. She finishes her wine while I sip on whiskey, the light above the sink illuminating the room. There's something comfortable about having her here with me. In my home. The whole world asleep except for us.

Mina swirls a finger along the rim of her glass, her hips swaying as she leans against the counter. "The day we met, if someone told me I'd end up drinking wine in your kitchen at three in the morning, I'd have laughed in their face."

I mimic her posture, side by side, shoulder to shoulder, a long line of contact between us. "Your first impression that bad?

"God yes." She leans her head against mine. "Not only were you exceptionally rude that day, which would have been enough to put me off all by itself, but I called you that night, drunk and desperate, *after* accidentally hitting send on a text that never should have seen the light of day. I was stupid and you were mean. Not exactly a recipe for whatever we just did in your bedroom."

"No, I guess it isn't." I press a kiss to her head, caught in the memory of that day.

The first time I saw Mina, she was giving herself a pep talk, probably pumping herself up to battle the nerves she felt before meeting her idol and a famous client, now that I think about it. Watching her made me laugh for the first time in a long time, and I got out of my car promising I'd do it more. That I'd stop being an asshole and go back to being myself.

But that didn't happen.

Not until Mina reminded me who I really am simply by being with me.

"I'm sorry I was rude that day." I swirl my whiskey and take a sip. "I wasn't at my best, which is putting it lightly," I finish with a smirk.

So much about my life has changed since then.

So much about *me* has changed since then.

"I got the feeling you were going through a lot and forgave you a while ago. Of course, at the time, I thought you were just another rich prick who thought he deserved more than the rest of us. But I see now that's not who you really are. That was a mask you put on to hide behind after Blossom."

I flinch, uncomfortable with how close she is to the truth.

There's a second of silence, laden with anticipation. The condenser on the fridge hums to life and I drop my gaze to my fingers gripping my glass. "Maybe," I finally manage.

"That's okay." Mina pats my hand, smiling gently as she straightens. "You don't have to talk about it."

She's disengaging. Assuming my terse answer has something to do with her when really, it has everything to say about me. I don't want her to know the side of me that's weak. The side of me that not only let Blossom into my head, but then allowed her to burrow in, claws hooked deep into my psyche.

"It's not that I don't want to talk about it," I say. "It's just..."

I don't know how to finish that sentence.

The pause lengthens, the silence lingers.

"Not with me. I understand." Mina drops her gaze, seeking her escape, even as she smiles again to make me feel better.

"You don't though."

"You could enlighten me." Her head is cocked, her heart wide fucking open in front of me. She slides herself into my arms like she was designed to fit there.

And that's the key that unlocks everything.

Because I'm starting to think she *was* designed to fit there.

With a slow sigh, I wrap my arms around her, close my eyes, and let her in. "Micah and Angela told you about Blossom. My girlfriend."

"Oh my God." Mina draws back, surprise lifting her brows. "Is The Prince of Darkness really going to shed light on his origin story?"

Everything in me bristles at her joke. "Do you want to hear this or not?"

"I do." She mimes zipping her lips, then gestures for me to continue.

"So—"

"Wait, wait, wait." Mina unzips her lips. "Time out. Pause."

"I thought you wanted to hear this..."

"Something tells me this story shouldn't be shared standing in the kitchen." Taking my hand, she leads me into the living room and pushes me onto the couch, then hands me a pillow before sitting next to me, smiling expectantly.

"What's this for?" I stare at the thing like I've never seen it in my life.

"You put it in your lap. And hug it. Like this." She grabs the other pillow, crosses her legs underneath her, and wraps her arms around it. "It's the classic posture for difficult stories."

With a roll of my eyes, I put the pillow behind my head, throw my arm over the back of the couch, and invite Mina to cuddle in, where she belongs.

"You're right. That's a much better idea." She lays down on her back, her head in my lap, staring up at me with a heartwarming grin. "Okay. Now. Hit me with this origin story."

I trace my fingers along her features, memorizing the feel of her cheeks, her brows, the gentle upturn of her nose. My thumb drags across her bottom lip and I better start this story soon, before I'm too distracted to continue.

"I met Blossom through the foundation, which crosses all kinds of ethical lines, I know. Hear me out before you judge."

"Who says I'm judging?"

"Everyone judges, HM. Day in, day out, we're judging everyone we see. Just imagine if we spent half as much time working on ourselves as we do complaining about other people."

"That's a lovely existential point, but you're stalling, your highness."

I'm not, but I move on, rather than distract us by disagreeing. "Blossom has two daughters. She came to the foundation because she wanted them to have a better life than she could provide. She was right on the line of qualifying for assistance. Like right there. In fact, if two other families with greater needs hadn't applied at the same time, she probably would have qualified and none of this would have happened. It's only because she didn't qualify that I started talking to her as a person and not a client."

I've spent too many sleepless nights wondering what would have happened if she had qualified for assistance and I hadn't asked her out. If she hadn't come into my life to use me, I wouldn't have decided to push the world away. I wouldn't have leaned into playing the villain, enjoying my money instead of trying to make up for having it in the first place. I would have just been my normal happy-go-lucky self, living in my modest house...

...and I probably wouldn't have met Mina. Six months ago, a life without Blossom was my favorite daydream. Now, I can't imagine missing out on my Hot Mess Express. Mom always said life's greatest difficulties turn into blessings once you're on the other side. I'm starting to see her point.

"Anyway," I say, running a hand through Mina's silky hair. "I have this tendency of seeing the best in people."

"You?" She laughs, twisting to meet my eyes. "You think you see the best in people."

"I do. Or at least I used to. And didn't you promise to stay quiet?"

She sits all the way up, eyes twinkling. "How can I stay quiet in the presence of such bullshit?"

"Fine. Storytime's over." I drop the pillow into my lap and give it a hug. Turns out, it is a surprisingly comforting posture. "You happy now?"

"Nope. Totally discontent. Zero stars. I will not be returning to this establishment."

Annoyed by how much I like hugging the pillow, I put it back where it belongs and scooch my butt to the edge of the couch. "See if I ever open up to you again."

"I'm kidding, Nathan." Mina pushes on my shoulders until I sit back again. "I've been around you enough to know you probably did spend most of your life seeing the best in people. I'm teasing because I feel safe with you. Safe to be myself. Safe to be a little silly. I'm sorry if I hurt your feelings."

My heart swells to the size of the sunrise over the ocean and I draw her into my arms and kiss her deeply. "I like that you feel safe with me."

"Good. Now show me that you feel safe with me."

I tell her about Blossom. About the way she presented herself as a victim of a difficult childhood, trying to do better for her kids. "She'd blow up at me over the smallest things. Or expect me to do everything for her, even be a parent for her girls when we weren't even living together. I took it in stride because I thought all she needed was a little kindness to grow into the best version of herself. The part that was hiding from the light or whatever."

She was so fucking awful to me. I'd bring her to family gatherings and we'd end up alone somewhere, her yelling at me for abandoning her or not paying enough attention to her if I so much as talked to a cousin. And then her kids would do something shitty and it was my job to fix it. It was humiliating and I kept letting it happen, which made me feel weak and worthless. I share all that with Mina, my voice gritty with truth.

"And then you found out she was cheating." She shakes her head like she can't believe what she's hearing. I haven't even gotten to the hard part yet.

"When she told me, she was proud of herself. She wasn't sorry for hurting me or using me or letting me into her kids' lives. She gloated. Like she was so glad to take the mask off and let me see what a dumb fucking asshole I'd been. She told me she'd never loved me, just my money. She used to say, 'a man like you deserves to get what you want.' I wanted it to be a compliment, but it was a way of distancing herself from me. Like I'm somehow *other* because of my money. You said it that first day we met, and it didn't help my impression of you."

"I said it because I thought that's what wealthy people wanted to hear. No, worse than that. I believed that's how wealthy people saw themselves. I can imagine how it landed, now that I know you better."

Everything about Mina softens. She sees all of me now. She knows me now. And I promised I would never let that happen again, but with her, I'm not afraid.

At least not yet.

"And then, to make things worse, we had this rush of applications at the foundation. All from people who had more than enough money to provide for themselves but were happy to steal charity from those who genuinely need it. Everywhere I looked, I saw greed and selfishness. So, I decided to fight it by expanding the foundation, which led me to a man named Dominick Taylor. He's got a nose for money, but he's a cynical fuck. He's been telling me from the start that people like you only see dollar signs when they look at people like me. That I need to lean into my wealth. To accept my role. To play the hand I was given. So that's what I've been doing. In fact, I was on the phone with him during that first meeting and he was going on and on about how I should avoid you."

I flare my hands because there it is. The truth. The reason I withdrew from the world. Now that it's out, the story doesn't sound as devastating as it did when it was trapped in my head.

Have I been just as self-centered as the people I'm retreating from?

"That would be enough to make anyone a little bitter."

"A little?" I arch an eyebrow then surprise us both by laughing.

"Okay, fine. You were a lot bitter." Mina returns my smile. "I don't see you as a dollar sign, by the way. I see you. Nathan West. A man who only needs a glimmer of goodness in someone to trust that's who they really are. I'm sorry if I ever gave you reason to believe otherwise." She grabs both my cheeks and kisses my forehead. "Forgive me?"

"There's no need to apologize. You haven't done anything wrong."

"Are you sure? Because my apology was going to come with a blow job. You got on your knees for me. The least I can do is get on my knees for you."

"Shit, woman. What are you waiting for then? Apologize!"

THIRTY

Mina

"Oh my God, Fallon! It was the best night ever!" I plop onto my friend's orange velvet couch with a dreamy sigh, then frown. "I think that's the first time in a long time I haven't shown up at your apartment specifically to complain."

Fallon picks her nail and arches a knowing brow. "There's been a lot of awful in your life since you met Nathan."

"Not recently," I shoot back, annoyed. As my best friend, she should know that. "And not last night," I continue. "The whole thing was surreal. And magical. And beautiful. But awful? No. It wasn't that."

I pull Fallon's chenille throw off the back of her couch and stand, wrapping it around my shoulders like a hug. A big, fat Nathan hug with his warmth and his strength and the goodness that goes right down to his bones. Right down to his *family's* bones. Kindness is genetically coded in his DNA.

The chances this conversation will go well are slim. Fallon has dug her heels in on Nathan being an asshole and won't change her mind easily.

Thankfully, I have all the ammunition I need to prove she's wrong about him.

"Best friend code engaged?" I ask and she waves a dismissive hand through the air.

"Sure. Yeah. Best friend code engaged."

Grinning unabashedly, I unload the entire night, from the limo and driver with our audience murmuring on their porches, to how comfortable I feel with Nathan's family. From the ambiance and atmosphere to his creepy friend glaring at me from a distance to the champagne and music and elegance of a night under the stars in evening wear. I tell her how nervous I was to step on the stage for the auction and how strange it felt for people to fight to pay money just for a few hours with me.

"I mean, it really wasn't for me," I say, snuggling deeper into the throw. "The whole thing was just a cute way to make giving to charity fun. But then Nathan's grumpy friend started bidding on me, like these insane amounts and that didn't feel fun at all until Nathan got protective and started bidding on me too. But!" I whirl, caught up in the drama of the moment, the blanket fanning out with my skirt like I'm a bohemian goddess twirling in a meadow. "It was Benjamin Bancroft who won. He called me his hundred-thousand-dollar girl the rest of the night."

Fallon's entire demeanor changes. A slow smile melts the frost in her eyes, and I realize it's been a long time since she hasn't looked like a watchdog on alert. "You spent the evening with Benjamin Bancroft?" she asks, her smile still growing, the ice still melting. "Meens! This is big. No wonder you're in such a good mood!"

"Believe me. I'm just getting started on why I'm in such a good mood." I tell her about Benjamin parading me around like a prize, then the two of us sitting alone while he offered me a dream come true. "Bancroft and Blake Design! Benjamin freaking Bancroft wants to partner with me! Of course, we still need to hash out the details. There's a lot to consider before I'm ready to commit, but just the fact that a man like that wants to work with a nobody like me..." I trail off, overcome with awe over my life. Mom's getting better. I'm with a wonderful man. My money worries might be over. I want to go back to young me and tell her to just keep on keepin' on because it gets better. It gets so much better.

"You're not a nobody," Fallon retorts with a ferocious shake of her head that sends her silky locks swinging.

"I know, I know. You're gonna say a bunch of positive 'ra ra go Mina go' stuff, but in the scheme of things, Benjamin has made a name for himself, and I haven't. Not yet anyway. He's established. He wins awards. I work for a tiny firm here in the Keys. There's a difference. Just like there's a difference between me and Nathan. His entire family is dripping with money and stability and opportunity and I haven't experienced much of that. Like ever. Not to mention they break every single stereotype I have of the rich and famous. They're kind and generous and welcoming…"

"Too bad Nathan doesn't fit that description," growls the watchdog.

"He might be the best of them," I retort with a warning arch of my brow. Again, if she'd been paying attention to anything I've said over the last five or six months, she'd know this.

I tell Fallon about his plans to expand the foundation, leaving out the whole Blossom story as the catalyst. I won't share Nathan's tragedies. Fallon has proven I can't trust her with the juicy bits.

"Are you gonna use your connection with him to apply to the foundation and get your mom's medical bills taken care of?" Fallon asks, crossing her arms and stalking to the window to stare at the sky. "Like pull some strings and jump to the front of the line?"

"What?" The suggestion is so shocking I actually step back. "No. Why would I do that?"

"Why wouldn't you?" Fallon sounds disgusted with me, and I can't for the life of me figure out why. If anyone should be disgusted, it should be me, seeing as I now have to explain how not to take advantage of a person you care about to someone I thought knew better.

"Nathan and I just started dating. What we are is brand spankin' new—"

"You've been together for six months, Mina."

"But it didn't get real until recently." I furrow my brow. "There's no way I'm going to him with my hand out, expecting him to solve my financial problems. That's just not how you handle relationships."

"So now it's a relationship." Fallon looks like she wants to choke on the word. "Isn't the whole thing supposed to be fake?"

Is she really calling me out on *not* being in a relationship when just five seconds ago, she suggested we've been together long enough to ask him for money?

What am I missing?

How are we miscommunicating?

"It was fake. But now it isn't. If you'd just listen,

you'd know that, especially because I haven't gotten to the best part. I was at Nathan's house last night. This morning too," I finish with a grin that feels a tad forced.

"You slept with him?" Fallon leans against the window and the grim set of her jaw says she hasn't been listening at all. She's too busy being protective. Given what she thinks she knows about Nathan, I can understand.

Time to remedy her misconceptions.

"We had *that night,* Fal. You know the one. There's talking and making love and it's intimate and sweaty and beautiful and you know, just connecting with another human being on this personal level with all the physical stuff thrown in to make it real and raw and..." I trail off because Fallon's just standing there. Staring at me.

No...*glaring* at me.

"Are you done?" she barks, and I recoil.

"I am now. Why do you look like I just force fed you garbage?"

"Because you did!" Fallon's jaw drops like I'm an idiot for asking. "For God's sake, Mina! What were you thinking?"

"I was thinking I'd share the best night of my life with my friend, and she'd be happy for me."

"How can I be happy when you're being a damn fool?" Fallon closes her eyes, exhaling slowly, then softens her tone. "We talked about this. Nathan is using you."

She emphasizes the last sentence, speaking deliberately, enunciating every messed-up syllable.

Now I'm genuinely annoyed. She's obviously not heard anything I've said lately.

"We did talk about this." I enunciate even harder than she did. "And I informed you that you're wrong about him."

"Yet you still can't talk about money. Or your mom. Or any of the things that matter. Did you tell him about me? That we're friends?" She holds out her hands, like she's begging me to see her point, but all I see is someone who's too proud to admit she might have been wrong.

"I'm sorry but you weren't exactly top of mind last night. We were at an event—"

"Ohhhh, an event. How very bougie of you. Can you hear yourself right now?"

"Would it be different if he'd taken me to a dive bar and fucked me in the back of a pickup? Would you be happy for me then? Because Nathan's rich, that makes all this bad?"

"What makes this bad is who he is and who you are. You guys don't live in the same world. People like him? They see opportunities and they take them. They don't worry who gets hurt. Or who they use. Or if what they're doing is right or wrong. That's how they get ahead. It's why they're rich and the rest of us struggle."

"Funny. His creepy friend said people like *me* see people like *him* as opportunities. That all I saw when I looked at him was a dollar sign. Maybe it says more about you and Dom than me and Nathan."

Fallon takes my shoulders and the intensity in her eyes begs me to see her point. "I make a living following the lives of people like this. I know them better than you. You need to slow down because Nathan West will chew you up and spit you out."

"I'm good, Fallon. Better than good. I've never felt anything like this before and I know you think he's faking it to use me for some diabolical plot, but you're wrong. He's not a villain."

"Then what is he?"

"He makes me feel safe to be who I really am." I flash to last night, curled up in his lap on his couch. "And I think he feels safe with me too."

"Funny thing about con men. They're pretty good at making you think and feel exactly what they want you to. Facts, Mina. Not feelings. If Nathan West isn't a villain, what is he?"

"He's none of your damn business, that's what." I unfurl the throw from around my shoulders, fold it carefully and drape it over the back of the couch. "I don't know if you're upset because you were wrong about him and will have to stop telling everyone he's a bad guy or—"

Fallon gasps. "You don't have to get mean just because you don't like when I'm right."

Getting mean? That wasn't mean. That was me, telling her what I'm thinking, just like she's been telling me. So, she's allowed to speak without a filter, but I'm not?

Has our friendship always been this off balance?

Dear God. Feeling a little blindsided right about now. Clarity would be a blessing. Yours forever, Mina Blake.

"You know what." I hold up my hands in defeat. "I'm gonna go."

"Mina..."

"We're not getting anywhere, and I don't want to go round and round with you. Thank you for looking out for me, but stop, Fallon. Just stop."

I leave, but don't want to go home. There's only one place I want to be, one person I want to be with. I make the drive to Nathan's house with Fallon's arguments circling my head. Does she really think now is the time to ask him for favors? I can't wrap my mind around that. Sure, I haven't told him she's my friend yet. I keep meaning to, but the time is never right. And now we've come so far, and he hates her so much, I can't imagine his reaction when I finally do tell him.

Scratch that. I can totally imagine his reaction.

It won't be pretty.

I haven't intentionally kept it a secret, and last night was not the time to drop that bomb.

But maybe now is.

And I can tell him everything she said about him, about us, and he can assure me she's wrong and all will feel right with the world again.

I park in the driveway, then knock on the door, tapping my fingers against my thigh as I wait.

And then Nathan appears in the doorway, looking just as happy to see me as I am to see him, and I take my first full breath since leaving Fallon's apartment.

"I was just thinking of you." He draws a knuckle across my cheekbone, and I shiver in delight.

"I'm just now realizing I probably should have called or something. I was out and wanted to see you and here I am."

Nathan draws me inside, wrapping his arms around me and kissing me deeply. "Don't be silly," he whispers, his lips brushing mine. "You've made my evening. I was just about to have a drink and enjoy the sky." He jerks his chin in that direction. "Join me?"

I nod and follow him through the living room and onto the deck. The setting sun sends golden light shimmering over the ocean, and I take a moment to lean against the rail and breathe it in. The wind rustles my hair and my skirt brushes against my legs while Nathan presses a kiss to the back of my neck, my shoulder, my throat.

Maybe I don't need to say anything about Fallon.

Or maybe now isn't the time.

Or maybe I need to stop making that excuse and get it over with.

"Are you okay?" Nathan asks, resting a hip on the rail beside me. "You seem tense."

"I'm fine. I had a strange conversation with my friend and just needed...you."

"Me?"

"Yeah. You make everything better and—"

Nathan silences me with a kiss. His lips are charged, electricity releasing from his body to mine as his hand lifts my skirt and slides up my thigh. "Funny. I've been thinking the same thing about you."

I pull back because I need to tell him about Fallon before I get distracted by his touch. "Nathan, I—"

"Tell me after," he growls, his voice sending a shiver of delight down my spine.

After, I think as he nuzzles my neck.

After, I think as his teeth graze my lips.

And then he palms the tight bundle of nerves between my thighs and I stop thinking altogether.

His fingers fumble with his pants and he bends me over the rail. I'm staring at the ocean as he kicks at my feet, spreading my thighs. I glance over my shoulder to find him watching as he enters me, his face transforming in ecstasy as his cock slides inside. With one thrust he has me weak in the knees. With another I'm little more than the night sky, hanging somewhere near the moon and glimmering with the stars. He grabs my hair, wrapping it around his fist as he pulls my face skyward, changing the angle while I grunt and moan each time our bodies collide.

"You're so beautiful," he murmurs. "So perfect. So exactly what I needed."

And then he's beyond speaking and it's just his hands on my body. His fist in my hair.

The rush of the water blends with my moans and then there's nothing but sensation. Nothing but Nathan.

Nothing but us.

THIRTY-ONE

Nathan

As of the charity auction last week, we officially overshot our financial goal for the adult side of the Reversal of Fortune Foundation. The board gave its perfunctory okay and Aunt Maisie is as excited as I am about this new venture. Next is community outreach and marketing and we'll finally be able to offer some relief to the people drowning in this hard new world.

My family isn't worried about me anymore. The concerned glances and fake smiles are gone, as is my general mistrust for humanity at large.

I pull open my closet and flick through a few shirts before a realization stops all movement.

I'm happy. I'm actually happy.

Who would have thought several months with

Mina Blake, Hot Mess Express, would give me my life back? I feel comfortable in my skin again. I don't have to be the villain or learn to play the hand I was dealt. I can just be me. The guy who feels best when he's giving. And I don't have to worry about being lied to or taken advantage of. Mina doesn't want my money. Or my notoriety. She doesn't want anything from me except me.

I haven't regretted one thing about letting her into my life. Not one thing. These last six months have been the best of my life.

My phone pings and I smile expectantly.

It's probably Mina, informing me she's running late for our dinner date. She and Benjamin have been going over the final plans for my house before we send them to the builders and start purchasing materials.

That right there might be one thing I regret.

That damn lair on a secluded stretch of beach.

I don't need that much space. Even if I wasn't living alone.

But Mina and Benjamin are ecstatic about the build, and he swears it's going to be *the thing* that gets their business noticed. If that's true—and I think it might be—then I can't regret it. Not if it's the first step to Mina realizing her dreams.

Satisfied, I check my phone.

Fuck.

Not a text from Mina.

It's another alert on my name. Another article by Fallon fucking Mae. I read the headline and my heart trips, stumbles, and falls flat on its face.

It's Fake Folks. Nathan West Strikes Again, and Buckle Up, This One is a Doozy.

It's fake?

It's fake?

There's only one thing that article could be about. My relationship with Mina.

Which is not only exceptionally real, thank you very fucking much, but there's no way Fallon should know about it. Not unless she's some kind of super sleuth or paid off Mina's ridiculously good-looking assistant for weekly updates.

Maybe there's some other part of my life Fallon's grossly misrepresenting. Unlikely, but a man can hope.

I scan the article and there it is. Laid out in black and white. Everything from the fact that Mina is my interior designer, to the twenty percent increase in payment she negotiated before she agreed to the whole thing in the first place. There's speculation I bought the dress for the gala because I was embarrassed for Mina to show up in what she could afford followed by innuendo about our dressing room antics. As if that isn't bad enough, Fallon doubles down on douchebaggery and outright says I've been taking advantage of my fame and fortune to cajole Mina into bed, all while keeping my heart at a distance so I can get out of paying her for the fake relationship.

I'm dumbfounded.

The only person who would know so many details is Mina, but this didn't come from her. There's no way, especially considering that last part, a gross mistruth if I've ever seen one. Maybe someone hacked her diary or eavesdropped on a phone call or…something.

There has to be something.

I refuse to believe Mina would tell anyone this much about our life together. Specifically, a someone she knows I despise.

That's a Blossom move, and Mina is not Blossom.

"Fuck." I stand and pace, fists clenching. "Fuck, fuck, fuck."

I'm going to ruin Fallon Mae. I'm going to find her and make her personally apologize to Mina for spreading lies, then to my family for making them believe something that isn't true.

I mean it *was* true.

It isn't anymore.

There is nothing fake about the way I feel when I'm with Mina. Nothing fake about what I feel *for* Mina. Nothing at all.

Damn it. This doesn't help me believe the trust I'm rebuilding in the world is justified. When I find out who's responsible—

My phone buzzes with a call from Dad and I hurl curse words at the screen.

I can't talk to him right now. I'm too pissed off. Too confused. Too ready to blow. How in the fuck does Fallon know what she knows? Who's to blame? Where can I direct my anger? Maybe it's Dom feeding her information...

I entertain the idea for a minute or two, but no, that's too despicable, even for him.

The call goes to voicemail and I take half a breath of relief before my phone starts ringing again.

Fuck...

This couldn't be about the article.

Could it?

With a heavy sigh and my head in my hand, I accept the call. "Hey, Dad."

"Where are you?"

My father has always been kind and patient. After growing up in a series of foster homes—some good, some terrible—he knew his job as a parent was the most important thing he'd undertake in his life. He drew hard lines when we needed them and wouldn't let us cross boundaries, but he's never been harsh. Never made me feel like my slipups meant I was a failure. According to Collin West, missteps are part of the human experience. He made sure all three of his children knew it's not our mistakes that define us, but what we learn from them.

Tonight, Dad's voice is sharper than it's ever been. Clipped and tight and concerned.

"I'm at home," I say, pinching the bridge of my nose. "For now, anyway. I'm taking Mina to dinner soon."

Oh, shit. Do I really want to be out in public right now? How many people have read that article? I might lose my shit if I caught anyone staring, or whispering, or laughing…

"What's up?" I ask, shaking my head and pinching the bridge of my nose.

"There's something I need to tell you and well…"

There's an urgency about my dad. Something that has my hair standing on end as goose bumps flare across my skin. A rock settles in the pit of my stomach. My heart races.

"Is everything okay?"

Dad swallows hard. "Nick's missing."

"Nick?" My ass hits my mattress before I realized I needed to sit. "Missing…"

"Kara and Wyatt just got the call."

"When did…how…what do we know?"

"Not much. His unit disappeared sometime last night."

Disappeared.

So fucking ominous. There's no certainty. Nothing to do. Nowhere to start looking. He's just...gone.

"I see," I say, as calmly as if I was going over an application with one of the ROF caseworkers.

But I'm not calm.

I'm numb. I'm terrified. I'm angry. My heart gallops and my jaw tightens and I want to punch something or break something or fly out to wherever he is and lead the search and rescue team myself. It's what he'd do for me.

"What can I do?" I'm up, patrolling my room. To the window. Pivot. Pass the bed. To the door. Pivot. To the window...

Nick's missing.

It's Fake, Folks!

Nick...

Mina...

Fallon...

It's Fake...

Fuck! Make it stop!

"The family's meeting at The Hut," Dad says, jarring me off the merry-go-round in my head. "There's not much to do, but we want Kara and Wyatt to know they're not alone. Maybe answer some questions with everyone together so the rumor mill doesn't distort the truth. But you know, mostly we just want to be together. If you want to help, that's the best way."

"I'll be there," I say, my voice echoing through the shock numbing my body, then text Mina to let her know I won't make dinner tonight, explaining that family stuff came up.

I pause just before I hit send. Could it be her? Is she the one who told Fallon everything? Anger tightens my fists. Fury clenches my jaw. Rage tenses my shoulders and I'm ready to punch and curse and kick and swear. A hurricane of emotion demolishing everything in my path. Mina being Fallon's source makes too much sense…

Except that would mean Dom's right and I've been an asshole, falling for the same shit twice in a row. And I know in my heart that's not true.

It's just not.

"Focus on one disaster at a time," I murmur to myself.

With a terse nod, I press send then make the drive to The Hutton Hotel, my knuckles white as I grip the wheel.

THIRTY-TWO

Mina

After my argument with Fallon last week, I set an alert on Nathan's name because I want to know anything and everything she says about him from now on.

I honestly didn't expect it to go off.

I grit my teeth, preparing for the worst, but hoping for the best.

Fallon is my friend. She might not like Nathan, but she loves me. That should be enough for her to slow down and process what I've told her about us. Nathan isn't a villain. He's the hero. He's good for me. Hell, he's good for anyone who crosses his path. From little kids needing a pep talk before a talent show to full blown adults who need a helping hand, Nathan West is the one reaching out. Maybe Fallon finally heard me.

But then I see the headline.

It's Fake Folks...

Jaw dropped, I forget all about getting ready for my date with Nathan and scan the story then scan it again. What I read can't be real.

It's the article she suggested we write as leverage all those months ago. The one I absolutely didn't agree to.

As I continue to read, my heart stops. This is worse than I thought. So much worse.

Fallon didn't just give details of my life, my relationship, things I only shared because I thought they were protected by best friend code.

She embellished.

First, she betrayed my trust, then she doubled down and added speculation as if it were truth. I look bad, but Nathan looks like Asshole of the Year.

My heart pounds so hard I feel my pulse in my ears.

Fallon just ruined everything. My relationship. Our friendship. Hell, maybe even my career. Will Benjamin want anything to do with me after this? They say there's no such thing as bad publicity, but I'm not sure he operates like that.

I don't know who to call first, Nathan to apologize

or Fallon to rip her a new one. He's sure to be a mess, but she deserves to feel my outrage while it's fresh.

A text comes in just as I pick up my phone to call her.

> **NATHAN**
> Can't make dinner. Family stuff. I'm sorry.

Family stuff.

I stare at my reflection in my vanity mirror, distress tightening my brows, my jaw, my lips.

Not only is the text vague, but those choppy sentences end in periods.

Everyone knows a period is bad news.

Shaking my head, I stand and pace my room in frustration. There's a chance family stuff really did come up. There's also a chance Nathan read the article and is freaking out and doesn't want me around.

Shit.

With my anger doubling by the second, I call Fallon. She answers on the first ring.

"How dare you!" My jaw is so tight, my voice comes out thin and hissing and weak. It's a terrible indicator of the rage boiling through my bloodstream. I stalk out of my bedroom and down the hall, unable to stay still.

"Mina...listen..."

"No, you listen." I stab the air like I'm poking her in the chest, then huff a sigh. "Actually? No. I want you talking. What the hell were you thinking?"

"This is for your own good."

"My own...?" I swipe a hand over my face as if that'll help Fallon's statement make more sense. "My own good? Who are you to decide what's good for me and what's not good for me?"

"I'm your best friend." She sounds so sure. So final. So confident that I'll hear her excuse and be completely okay that she might have blown up my relationship with Nathan right as it got off the ground.

It was already going to be hard telling him that Fallon is my friend. And I am a weak asshole for not doing it when I went over there for that express purpose.

But now? After this? He'll never forgive me.

There's only one way she could know so much about everything.

Because I told her.

Dear God. I know I asked for clarity, but did it have to come like this? Tearfully, Mina Blake.

I sink to the floor where I stand, my head in my hand, my heart in my throat. "You *were* my best friend."

"You don't mean that."

"Give me a reason not to."

"I published that story for you, Mina. To help you. You're falling in love with someone that doesn't exist. This guy is playing a role for you. The real Nathan West will chew you up and spit you out."

He will after I tell him the truth. If only I hadn't been such a coward. If only I told him Fallon is my friend the first time he mentioned her name...

"If I want to get chewed up and spit out, that's for me to decide. Not you. I feel physically sick, Fallon. You have no idea what you've done."

"Meens..."

"Don't Meens me. Nathan canceled dinner. Your article goes live and seconds later, he's dealing with 'family stuff.'" I make air quotes even though no one's around to see.

"Don't you think that should tell you something?" Her voice is too soft. Like she's trying to lead me to a realization she had weeks ago. Like she feels sad and sorry and knows I've been foolish.

It relights the fire of my rage.

"I'm not going to assume it means anything until I talk to him. See, that's what you do when you care about someone. You take them at their word until they prove you wrong." I'm up and pacing again, appalled that Fallon had the balls to publish that article. That she actually believed she was helping me by dropping a bomb on my life. She had no right to make this decision for me. None at all.

This is such an awful feeling, being exposed for the world to see. Not just exposed. *Misrepresented.* It's more than a violation of trust. It's a defilement of my sovereignty. It amazes me that Nathan didn't go completely insane under this much scrutiny. He has every right to hate Fallon as much as he does.

"Mina..." Fallon starts to make more excuses for herself, but I've heard all I care to.

I end the call because I can't stand the sound of her voice, then throw the damn phone onto the couch with a fist clenching, body shaking growl. I don't know if I've ever felt this betrayed. Fallon? I trusted her with my life.

And then there's Nathan, who may or may not be dealing with a family emergency, who may or may not mean more to me than he should, who definitely trusted me more than he should and has every right to blame me for what just happened.

I growl again, my hands in fists, my eyes squeezed tight, my teeth bared.

These are murky waters and I don't know how to navigate them. At the very least, Nathan deserves a response, so I find my phone, tell him all is well, then perch on the arm of my couch and hope that's true.

THIRTY-THREE

Nathan

The parking lot at The Hut overflows with cars—all belonging to my family. I climb the steps to the wraparound porch of The Hutton Hotel, with the pristine white paint and the ferns drooping over their hanging pots. Sometimes it's hard to believe my mother grew up here. That this was her home for most of her childhood. That the kitchen where my family waits is where she sat to do her homework. Where she ate dinner with her brothers, my grandmother, and the grandfather who died before I was born.

I pull open the front door and step inside. With tension lighting up my neck and shoulders, I enter the kitchen and pull up short. Aunt Kara sits at the table, shoulders shaking as she quietly cries. Uncle Wyatt stands behind her, a hand on her back, head bowed. His face is drawn and pinched. His eyes closed. Wyatt Hutton always has a smile ready for everyone but today, sadness hovers over him like ash blocking the sun.

Mom sees me and her face contorts with emotion. She rushes across the room, wrapping me in her arms, burying her face in my chest. I cup the back of her head as my gut twists with concern.

"Hey. Hey now," I whisper, quiet. Afraid. Dad places a heavy hand on my shoulder and the weight of something terrible descends along with it.

My sister Maren arrives with her twin Joshua, and they hurry to join our little clump. Angela meets my gaze from across the room. She covers her heart with her hand, shaking her head and closing her eyes. Two fat tears trail down her cheeks and she swipes them away. Finally, after several more of us press into the kitchen, Uncle Lucas stands. As Grandma's firstborn, he's the spokesman of the family. The one we turn to for guidance. A former Marine who nearly lost his life, only to return home and find it again with his wife and family. He clears his throat and the soft murmurs of conversation die away. Not like people were talking much anyway.

"Thank you all for dropping everything to come here tonight." Uncle Lucas casts a worried glance to his brother. Aunt Kara's head drops even lower. Aunt Cat sits on one side while Grandma sits on the other, taking her son's hand while she whispers in her daughter-in-law's ear. Grandma's second husband, Brendan, stands behind her, his hands on her shoulders.

"There's not a lot of information," Lucas continues, "but Nick disappeared last night during a top-secret mission. As soon as they know more, we'll know more." His gaze travels over the occupants of the room, solemn but hopeful. "Remember though. Missing means he can be found. It's easy to assume worse news is coming, but that won't help Nick, and it certainly won't be good for you. Avoid conjecture and stick with certainty."

Tears prick my eyes as Maren sags against her twin, who wraps an arm around her shoulder and presses his head to hers.

Missing.

One of my worst fears realized.

Every time Nick deploys. Every time he's silent for too long. Every time he misses a call, there's a part of me that doesn't rest until we hear from him again. His safety isn't guaranteed. His luck won't last forever.

And here we are. It's happened.

Missing.

"He'll be back." Micah bobs his head as if he's never been more certain of something in his life. His eyes crackle with an intensity that's almost crazed as he drapes an arm around his wife's shoulder and pulls his daughter close. "You can't keep that guy down. Nick's fine."

Aunt Cat grips Kara's hand while Grandma sighs deeply. Her heart is big enough to hold the whole world. Strong enough to bring her family together after my grandfather ripped them apart. If anyone knows what to say, it'll be her.

"Kara. Kara, my love," she croons. "My darling Wyatt, too. Listen to me. I know you're hurting. We're all hurting with you. But you can't give in to your fears. The day I learned Lucas was injured was one of the worst days of my life. When they told me his heart stopped, mine did too. And for three infinite minutes I wasn't sure it would start again. But there he is. Right here with us. He's strong. He's happier and healthier than I ever could have hoped for."

Kara looks up, falling into Grandma's eyes like she's desperate for a lifeline. "Nick isn't injured. He's missing." She chokes on the word and Uncle Wyatt lets loose a shuddering breath.

Injured is finite. It's determined. It comes with answers and understanding, no matter how terrible.

But missing? It's ephemeral. There's no knowing. No certainty. Only hope and fear and the awareness that both are useless.

Grandma nods, accepting Kara's feelings without

hesitation. "You've been part of this family long enough to know Huttons are a tough breed. Even when it seems all is lost, we put up a hell of a fight. Everyone in this room has faced devastating odds, yourself included, but here we are. Nick is strong. He's smart. He's made of the kind of stuff you can't keep down."

Aunt Kara's gaze lands on Grandma's, wide and searching. "But what if—"

"There's no room for 'what if.' Don't even think 'what if.' Think about how good Nick is. How much you love him. Think about how you'll feel when they find him. And remember, you're not alone. You are surrounded by people who love you. People who will hold you up when you're too tired to do it yourself."

Murmurs of agreement sound through the room. An army of Huttons standing behind my aunt and uncle on one of the hardest days of their lives. All of us sharing the pain of not knowing but determined not to give up on Nick because Grandma's right. You can't bring a Hutton down. And Nick? He might be the best of us.

I swallow hard, swiping at tears filling my eyes, then cross the room to stand with my aunt and uncle, my hands on their shoulders, a physical reminder that I'm here with them. One by one, the rest of the family crowds in, heads bowed with worry, hearts heavy with concern, but stronger because we're together.

THIRTY-FOUR

Mina

Hours pass without word from Nathan. Dinnertime comes and goes, but I'm too nervous to eat. I try to read, but stare at the same page for ten minutes without digesting one word. I turn on the TV as a last resort. It's never been good at holding my attention. Tonight, though? With my thoughts firmly glued on Nathan and whether or not he's avoiding me because of Fallon's stupid ass article? There's no chance the TV will help.

Fallon calls and texts, over and over, desperate to apologize for something she knew was wrong. There's no way she believes a betrayal like that was right. She did what she did to get more views, certain I love her enough to forgive her. Or that I'm stupid enough to think she truly sabotaged my relationship because it's good for me.

If I'd known she was one of those 'better to ask for forgiveness than permission' people, I would have valued her friendship differently. Life is hard enough without having to second-guess motives and protect yourself from selfish assholes who only care about themselves.

After living through the aftermath of Dad, I thought my screening process was airtight.

Looks like Fallon was right about one thing anyway. I see kindness where it doesn't exist.

I ignore every buzz of my phone with her name attached.

I have nothing to say to Fallon fucking Mae. Not yet. Not until I've processed what she did. Not until I tell Nathan that she's my friend. Not until I've seen what kind of damage that does to our relationship—assuming there still is one.

And with that bright and sunny thought, I'm up and pacing again. Picking up my phone to check on Nathan only to put it right back down for the hundredth time. He'll reach out when he's ready. So what if I've been a mess since he canceled tonight? That's on me. On Fallon. Not him.

Or maybe it's on the family stuff he said he was dealing with. Which is yet another reason to let him reach out when he's ready.

Though, isn't communication the cornerstone of any good relationship? If I'm worried, shouldn't he know? Is there really a problem if I text him to say I'm thinking of him and hope everything's okay?

I swipe my phone off the coffee table and draft a text, then read it three times to check for neediness, pushiness, clinginess…

…really any kind of 'ness' that might be construed as negative.

"For shit's sake, Mina," I mutter with a growl. "Less thinking. More doing." With a shake of my head, I send the text, then watch for a sign of a response. My heart sinks when nothing happens.

Well, hell. There's that, then. Whatever it means.

I lock the phone and put it down when a knock sounds at my door. My gaze whips up and I stare, confused. It's too late for deliveries. Mom used to drop by unannounced, but she's tucked into bed at Shady Cove. It could be the frat boys, drunk, lost and confused again, but this knock is too gentle to be them. Maybe it's Fallon, desperate to have the discussion I'm not ready for, but that doesn't ring true either. She knows me well enough to wait until I've cooled down before forcing me into a conversation. Of course, I thought she knew me well enough not to publish that article.

And then, this sense of knowing overcomes me.

It's him.

It's Nathan.

He's here. Right there on my porch. No call. No text. Just here. That feels important somehow. It speaks of urgency. Of desperation. Of emotional decisions, not rational ones.

With a smile on my face and worry in my heart, I stride to the door and throw it open. Nathan stands there, bowed under the weight of the world. His shoulders are slumped. His chin dropped. His eyes downcast. When he looks at me, I fall into an abyss of sadness. Like he's holding my hands and plunging us into the depths of the ocean, bubbles rushing against our skin, hair drifting upwards in a languid dance as we sink farther and farther from the light.

"What's wrong?" I reach for him, my hands gripping his biceps, sliding up and around his shoulders, until my palms rest on his chest.

The worst of me worries he's here to break things off. He read the article and now that the world knows how we started, he's too embarrassed to keep going. The rest of me knows this is more than that. Something truly terrible has happened.

Nathan steps into my embrace, tucking his face

into the crook of my neck, his arms limp at his sides. His shoulders shake as he inhales a stuttering breath, then lets it loose with a low sob. I run my hand in circles along his back, holding him while he cries.

"It's okay," I murmur. "I'm here."

I whisper to him as we stand in the doorway, the wind rustling in the palms, the sky black on black on black. After minutes of stillness, he wraps his arms around me, pulling me close, so close. As if he can steal safety just by being near me. I do my best to give it to him.

"It's Nick," he says hoarsely. "Nick's missing."

A long sigh escapes me. Dread weighs on my heart. This was the beginning of the end for my father. Missing. Then injured. Then discharged. Mom used to say he would have been better off if he'd died. That the man she knew and loved was killed that night and a stranger sent home in his place.

"Oh, Nathan..."

"My family called a meeting at The Hut so we could be with my aunt and uncle. We were all just sitting in that room, desperate for more information. Waiting to hear if Nick's gone forever or coming home or hurt or lost or what?" Nathan holds out his hands, lifting his shoulders and closing his eyes. "All of us, hoping for something certain. Something solid. But there isn't anything real to grab onto. That's all we know. He's missing."

"Come inside," I say, oh so quietly. "Come in and be with me." With gentle hands on his shoulders, I pull Nathan into my apartment, then close the door. He's aimless. Standing in the foyer, waiting for direction. I lead him to the couch. He sits, elbows on knees, hands limp, gaze on the floor as he shakes his head.

I bring him a glass of water then sit beside him. He immediately drops his head into my lap, curling up like a little boy. I run a hand through those dark locks, hints of mahogany and gold shooting through them. He's silent for a long time and I honor that. Holding him. Letting him know I'm here, but not pressuring him to say or be or do anything more than he can. And in this moment that doesn't seem to be much. I imagine myself pulling the fear and worry out of him like sticky, black threads and sending it up to the universe to be cleansed. It's a silly thing, but I feel called to do something.

"Would it feel good to talk about it?" I ask. "Or do you need quiet? Either way, I'm here."

Nathan is still and silent for several long moments, and then, "Nick isn't just a cousin. He's one of my best friends."

"The best big brother ever," I say, remembering the conversation on the boat.

Nathan nods, pressing his lips together in a sad smile. "Nick listens. You know? And he doesn't judge, and he won't spread rumors. And he always has good advice. He's a protector."

"The kind of man who joins the Marines."

Pride ripples off Nathan as he settles into silence for another couple minutes. "Uncle Lucas told us not to worry, not to focus on all the what ifs, but it's hard. My brain won't put it down."

"Tell me about him. Focus on everything good about Nick Hutton. Maybe then your brain won't have a chance to worry."

Nathan shares several stories of Nick when they were younger. He's nostalgic. Laughing. Shaking his head as he gets caught up in the memories. He tells me about a man who spent a lifetime protecting the people who matter to him. A friend. A confidant. Someone who always knows exactly what to say. Someone who goes out of his way to take care of everyone else. Someone who's strong and kind and funny.

Nick sounds a lot like Nathan.

Maybe it's a Hutton thing.

Eventually he sits up, gesturing and smiling as he shares a few more stories. They sound so close. Cousins, but also the kind of friends I always wished I had when I was younger. The kind who are there no matter what. Someone who knows the worst of you but sees the best and does everything they can to make sure you see it too.

The kind of friend I thought I had in Fallon.

The kind of friend I know I have in Nathan.

I swipe a hand through my hair to brush away thoughts of my so-called friend and that horrible article. They'll be there, lurking, waiting to pounce when this tragedy is over.

"Once, when we were kids," Nathan says, "Nick and Angela disappeared for most of a day. They didn't go far. Just down the beach, but they didn't tell anybody where they were going and we weren't old enough to be gone that long. Turns out, Angela had a really bad day at school and Nick thought he would give her all the time she needed to get it off her chest. And when they finally came home, his arm wrapped around her shoulder and the two of them just beaming, I felt so left out. They were always close and I wanted that, you know? I was so furious they didn't include me that I wouldn't speak to them for the rest of the day. This time, I won't be mad when he comes back. I'll wrap that bastard in a hug and thank God he's okay."

I want to promise Nick will come home. That they'll find him and whatever's happened will be just as easy as the day he took care of Angela.

But Nathan isn't the kind of man who takes comfort in false hope.

"He sounds like an amazing person," I say instead.

"If the situation were reversed, he'd be halfway to finding me by now," Nathan says with a sad smile. He stands, pacing to the window and then back again. "I feel so powerless."

That makes two of us. I want so desperately to make it better but can't think of anything to do other than be here, listen, and find a way to take his mind off things once he's had a chance to process.

"What would Nick tell you to do?" I ask and Nathan pauses, staring at me like he's had an epiphany. Everything about him softens and for the first time since he knocked on my door, the clouds of sadness lingering over him lift. Just a little. But it's a start.

"He'd tell me to stop worrying about things I can't control. Especially when there's a beautiful woman looking at me the way you are right now."

The warmth in his voice brings a blush to my cheeks. "And how am I looking at you?"

"Like you'd do anything to make me feel better. Like you understand everything I'm going through. Like you like me. And you're not just with me for the fun times. You're *with me*."

I sit there, on the couch, stunned into silence by his words.

Everything he said is true.

I don't just like being with him.

I'm *with* Nathan West.
With my body.
My mind.
And in my heart.
I've never felt anything more real in my life.

THIRTY-FIVE

Nathan

I left The Hut and drove straight to Mina's apartment. I needed her. I couldn't imagine going through this without her.

She comforted me for who knows how long, running her hand through my hair while I rambled, lost in my pain. Lost in uncertainty. She listened to my past, my present, and my fear of the future all jumbled up and spilling past my lips in an incoherent stream of consciousness. And now here I am, smiling. Totally aware that she is the 'something good' Nick told me to look for when he was standing in my office at the foundation six months ago.

That conversation feels like another life.

One where I was hurting and receding, pulling inward and losing trust in the world.

Mina resuscitated me. She helped me remember who I am. She reminded me the world has enough assholes who are only out for themselves, and I shouldn't be so quick to add my name to that list.

She's a damn miracle. An answer to questions I didn't know needed answered.

I am better with her. I feel safe to be myself with her. Mina won't take advantage of me. She isn't with me for personal gain...

I almost laugh out loud at the thought. The only reason we're together at all is because I'm paying her to pretend to be my girlfriend.

But a pretend girlfriend wouldn't have invited me in tonight. She wouldn't have listened to me talk and held me patiently when I couldn't. Blossom would have told me I was making too big a deal. That I was wallowing. That she couldn't be around me until I was in a better place.

Mina opened her arms to it all.

That damn article blazes through my mind, the headline lit up in flashing neon. *It's Fake, Folks!*

She would have invited me in if she were gathering more info for Fallon fucking Mae...

I banish the thought and pull Mina into my embrace, my heart full for the first time in maybe my whole life. I'm wide open and vulnerable to her. It scares me to death but I'm safe. I know she sees me. I know she cares about me.

I know that she's with me for me.

Not what she can get out of me.

My jaw drops at the thought and Mina narrows her eyes. "You look like you just thought of something important."

"I think I did." I smooth her hair back, cupping her face and getting lost in her eyes. Blue like the clearest parts of the ocean, streaked with the gray of a foggy morning with hints of green grass poking through. The same colors in my favorite of Mom's paintings hanging in my living room, like she saw into my future and knew Mina would be here.

Waiting.

Mine.

I angle my head, leaning closer, eager to kiss her, to taste her, to erase any distance between us so it's just her and me and me and her, closer and closer until we're one. Her presence erases my pain and I need her. In my heart. In my life. She's already taken up a full time residence in my brain, she might as well claim everything else as well.

"What?" Her lips whisper against mine. Gaze fluttering to my eyes and then back to my mouth. Her hands swooping up my arms, along my neck and into my hair, pulling me close like she's read my thoughts and agrees.

I brush her lips with a kiss. Her chest heaves. Her fingers clench. So ready for more, but I pull back, smiling down at this woman I wasn't prepared for. "I think I'm falling in love with you."

The words are hoarse and rough, slow and faltering, refugees stepping into the light of day after being trapped underground.

"I crave you, Mina," I say, cupping her cheeks and gazing into her beautiful eyes. "I don't know how to be without you. You've brought me back to life."

"Nathan..." she begins with a smile, but I haven't gotten it quite right yet and I need her to know what's in my heart.

"It's more than that, though." I brush my thumb across her cheek. "You didn't just bring me back to life. You've shown me what it means to truly live."

A soft smile plays across Mina's face. "I'm falling in love with you too, Nathan. I think I have been for a long time."

My name, from those lips. It's medicine for my heart. It's a jolt of need straight to my dick.

My mouth finds hers. My hands travel her body. There is solace here. With her. I stop thinking and start feeling. Pulling her to her feet. Tugging at clothes until she's bare. Pressing her against a wall, pinning her wrists above her head and freeing my throbbing cock.

I will give her all of me.

The best of me.

The worst of me.

My hopes and dreams and fears and sadness.

I am safe with her and will keep her safe from the world. She will have everything she ever wanted because that's what I found in her.

Mina's breasts press against my chest, and I bend to take her into my mouth. Licking. Sucking. Teeth grazing her rose-colored peaks.

She moans my name, her hands in my hair, head tossed back, chest heaving.

"I love you, Mina," I whisper at her throat, kissing the delicate skin below her ear.

"I love you too," she whispers back and then I'm past speaking, past thinking. I slide my aching dick into her sweet warmth and lose myself to her.

THIRTY-SIX

Nathan

Someone's in Mina's apartment. My eyes blink open and I push up on my elbow, listening to the squeak and bump of the front door quietly being closed. Mina sleeps beside me, one arm thrown over her head, blissfully unaware as a stranger creeps down the hallway, ever closer to where we lay naked and vulnerable. Judging by the whisper of light slipping through the blinds, it's barely morning, though the jolt of adrenaline sizzling in my veins has me wide awake.

I yank back the covers and slip out of bed, swipe my underwear off the floor and nearly fall over yanking them up, struggling to get them over my thighs, but wrenching them in place anyway. I'm not confronting an intruder with my dick out.

The bedroom door creaks open.

"Mina?"

It's a soft voice. Not the roughened rasp of a burglar, but the gentle probe of a friend.

"Meens?"

A woman steps through the door. Judging by her silhouette, she's small. And judging by her use of Mina's name, she's been here before.

She flips on the light, sees me crouching in my underwear and unleashes a scream of pure terror.

"Oh my fucking God and everything holy!" shrieks the intruder. "What the fuckity fuck is happening right now?"

Mina bolts upright and looses a scream of her own, hands up and shaking with the force of it leaving her body. There's a moment of silence as everyone processes. Then relief on Mina's face followed by, "Jesus! Fallon! What the hell are you doing in my bedroom?"

I'm sorry...Fallon?

Did she say *Fallon?*

As in *Fallon fucking Mae?*

That's not possible. This has to be a different Fallon.

But it's an unusual name. How many of them can there be?

"You wouldn't answer my calls or texts," the

intruder says with a glance my way, "so I used the key you gave me for emergencies. I thought I'd catch you before you left for work—"

"Just hold on one fucking second." I hold up both hands and pray to God that Mina has an explanation other than the most obvious one. "Fallon?"

There's so much hanging on that question, the air grows thick. This moment out of time. Before the hammer has dropped and the truth has slapped me in the face. There's still a chance for the worst not to happen, though the look on Mina's face doesn't make me hopeful.

"Fallon Mae. Pleased to finally meet the dreaded Prince of Darkness." The intruder extends a hand, smirking as her gaze rakes over my body so harshly I want to cover myself. "Huge fan of the undies, by the way."

I glance down and discover why my underwear put up such a fight. They're not mine. They're Mina's. And they don't leave much to the imagination. I swoop my pants off the floor and step into them, still not quite processing what the fuck is going on. I look at Mina who's clutching her blanket to her breasts, her eyes filled with absolute dread.

And so, the hammer drops.

"That's Fallon Mae," I bark at Mina, my lips pressed together, like there's a chance I can hold in what wants out. "You're *friends* with Fallon fucking Mae? Like 'let me give you a key to my house' friends?"

Mina's face is slack. Her hair mussed from sleep, her eyes wild. She opens her mouth to respond, closes it, then tries again, only nothing comes out. Her silence is the truth slapping me in the face.

"I'm so sorry, Nathan," she finally says, her voice cracking. "So unbelievably sorry."

Fallon backs toward the door. "I can see this isn't a good time."

"Damn straight it's not a good time." I bite off the words with barely a glance toward the woman who's made it her mission to ruin my life. My energy is focused on Mina and hers on me.

"I was going to tell you." Her voice is low. Her eyes filled with shame. If her words hadn't confirmed she's been lying to me, her face finishes the job.

"It's probably best if I leave." Fallon reaches for the door, then pauses as if she expects some sort of award for recognizing she doesn't fucking belong here.

I level a finger at Mina. "You're friends with Fallon fucking Mae and you didn't think that was something I should have known from the very beginning?" My voice is low and level, while anger and betrayal riot in my veins like twin wildfires. My jaw clenches against the spite I want to hurl at the woman I let myself love.

The woman I let myself trust.

The woman I thought was different from the rest.

"I know; I'm sorry. It was such a mistake not to say anything. I didn't know she was a problem for you at first." Mina's face falls, like she can hear how shitty she sounds.

And in case she doesn't, I reiterate the most important point of her sentence. "*At first.*"

"I'll just show myself out then," Fallon says, and I turn to glare, all the shit I'm not spewing at Mina aimed at my nemesis. She recoils, whispers a quick, "Sorry!" then slips out the door.

"I kept promising myself I'd tell you, but there was never a good time." Mina holds out a hand, then balls it into a fist, squeezing her eyes shut, grimacing like she's so fucking annoyed with herself she doesn't know what to do.

Which makes two of us.

"I'm damn sure there were better times than this!"

The front door squeaks open then bangs shut, and it feels like the perfect metaphor for my time with Mina. What was open is now closed. Maybe permanently.

"Nathan, please..."

"Don't 'please' me."

And suddenly I can't ignore the truth that's been flashing like a neon sign since last night.

My jaw drops and I step back. "You're the one

who's been telling her everything. Oh, fuck me. It's been you this whole time!"

Mina presses up onto her knees, the blanket still clutched to her chest. "Last night's article she did on her own. Against my will."

I scrub a hand over my mouth as that one sinks in. "But the ones before that you were fine with."

"No! I asked her to stop so many times. Fallon thought she was doing you a favor and I told her it wasn't working the way she thought it would. She said if you were angry, her plan must be working."

"A favor." The words drop like an anchor, thudding to the floor at my feet. "How delusional do you have to be to think those articles were a positive experience for me on any level?"

"She thought by showing you how much you've changed, it would help you remember who you used to be. And until recently, I didn't have a lot of reason *not* to believe what Fallon said about you. But after I got to know you, I could see how terribly wrong she was. I told her who you really are, I swear. I'm sorry I didn't tell you about her..." Mina's voice trembles. Tears wobble in her eyes. Her little deception is crumbling around her and she's clinging to hope that something is salvageable. Why? Because she cares about me?

I highly doubt that.

"And you didn't think that by misrepresenting my

every move, she made things worse for me? Not better! You know this! For fuck's sake, Mina! I told you everything!"

Jesus Christ. Dom was right. Mina didn't see me. She saw an opportunity to help her friend. What a sick joke.

"And I *didn't* tell her all of it!" Mina stands, dragging the sheet off the bed with her. "Nathan, please..."

I back away from her outstretched hand. "Has any of this been real? Any of it?"

"All of it!" she cries, letting her arm drop to her side.

"And how am I supposed to take your word on that? Just when I let my guard down and started to think maybe the world wasn't a shitty place filled with shitty people, I find out you've been lying to me this whole time. I stopped faking, Mina. I fell in love with you!"

"And I love you back!"

My heart clenches, begging me to stop retreating, to pull her into my arms because that's where she belongs. But my heart is kind and easy to manipulate. It shouldn't have a say in this situation. It's time to start listening to my mind.

"Love doesn't keep secrets." My head bows from the weight of the truth. "Not like this."

"Nathan..."

"I am so tired of being used so other people can get ahead. All I want is for someone to see me. Me! Not my money. Not my fame. Not what I can do for them."

"I do see you, Nathan." Mina frowns, her voice quiet, the desperation leaving her eyes as my voice rises.

"If you did, then you would have told me you were friends with Fallon fucking Mae. Even if it was hard. Even if the timing wasn't perfect. You would have told me."

"You're right. I should have told you. And I really am sorry this is how you found out." Her jaw tightens. Her eyes flash. "But come on. At this point, you know me well enough to trust I haven't been using you. I mean, what am I getting out of this relationship?"

"Designer dresses? Invitations to galas you wouldn't normally step foot into? Multiple fucking orgasms? Twenty percent over your design fee? Shit, Mina. When were you going to start working me so the foundation would take care of your mom's medical bills?"

"Nice, Nathan." Mina sneers. "You offered to buy the dress. You required I go to the gala. You initiated the orgasms. And you haven't fucking paid me yet."

"You asked for an advance." I stab the air with my finger. "You cashed the check."

We stare at each other for several terrible seconds before Mina finally breaks the silence.

"Do you know why I wouldn't answer Fallon's calls or texts?"

I swipe my underwear off the floor, step out of my pants so I can remove Mina's panties and pull mine into place. It's time to get the fuck out of here. "Not sure I care, but I'm positive you'll enlighten me anyway," I say, hunting down my pants, only to find them clutched in my fist.

"Fallon published that article yesterday because she knows I'm falling in love with you and had the balls to think telling the world how we started would help me see why that was a stupid idea. And after this—" she waves her hand in my direction "—I'm starting to see her point."

"That makes three of us." I sneer as I step back into my pants, tug the zipper up, and shove the button through the hole. "Everything about this was a mistake."

"You won't hear me fight you on that one."

I snag my shirt off the floor and yank it over my head. Turn to Mina then realize there's nothing I can say that will make this better. I trusted her with all of me, and she didn't trust me enough to tell me the truth.

She's been Blossoming me this whole time. Everything between us has been about Fallon fucking Mae and her blog.

The fact that I don't quite believe it even though Fallon was here as proof enrages me.

"Tell me how much of this was contrived," I demand, anger pulling me deeper into the room. "Was that text really an accident? The one that started everything? Or were you and your bitch friend plotting against me the entire time? Did you two dream this whole thing up to feed that cunt information for her stupid clickbait gossip bullshit?"

"Get out." Mina stabs a finger at the door.

I step closer, tutting in disapproval. "Did you whore yourself out for clicks, HM?"

"Get out!" Her voice shakes. Her eyes flash. Her finger trembles as her jaws clench.

I take one last lingering look, savoring the taste of her rage while my chest clenches and my throat tightens.

"You better believe I'm out," I say, shaking my head and reaching for the door.

"I don't want to see you or your Prince of Darkness smirk again."

I turn over my shoulder, smirking for her benefit, then about face and leave the Hot Mess Express in my rearview like I should have from the start.

THIRTY-SEVEN

Mina

Fury mixes with sorrow as Nathan marches out of my room. I stand, panting, chest heaving, brain whirling. I've been awake all of ten minutes and everything has changed. Everything.

Last night he told me he loved me.

This morning he called me a whore.

He thinks I used him for personal gain when he was the one who came to me about faking a relationship.

If I'm a whore, it's because you made me one! I think, then scurry down the hallway, intent on hurling the statement his way. Instead, I watch through the window as Nathan lowers himself into his car, then clutch the wall for support as my knees go weak.

Tears gather and my fists clench and fuck him for making me feel like this. Fuck him for talking about love only to throw horrible words in my face. Fuck him for running away instead of sticking around for a hard conversation. Fuck him for giving me a glimpse of a dream come true, then slapping me in the face with reality.

And fuck me for being too much of a coward to be honest with him in the first place.

Dear God. What have I done? Regretfully, Mina Blake.

Shortly after Nathan leaves, I call the office and inform them I'll be working from home, which is definitely an overstatement of what will be happening. The chances of me actually working are small. I can't think clearly. My emotions are all over the place. I desperately need someone to talk to, but my support system is gone.

I can't talk to Fallon; she's part of the problem.

I'm not ready to talk to Nathan, and I'm gonna bet the feeling is mutual.

Mom has enough on her plate and isn't strong

enough to handle my emotional turmoil. Since that sums up my list of trusted confidants, it looks like I'm on my own for this one.

With a wry twist of my head, I pull on my sweats, go to the store to stock up on ice cream, and hunker down for the weekend.

The day fades and so does my anger, leaving a queasy trail of guilt in its wake.

This fiasco is on me.

I knew I needed to tell Nathan Fallon was my friend. And I knew it was going to be ugly when I did, which is why I kept putting it off. But instead of hearing it from me, he finds her in my bedroom first thing in the morning *while wearing* my underwear *after* discovering his cousin is missing.

That's ugly stacked on ugly stacked on ugly, compliments of yours truly.

Nathan reacted badly, but who could blame him? Considering the circumstances, a saint wouldn't have done better.

With a sigh, I swipe my phone off the table.

> I'm so so so so so sorry. I can't stop thinking about you. I miss you. I'd love to talk when you're feeling up to it

NATHAN

I'm not feeling up to it.

> For what it's worth, I haven't been manipulating you

If that's true, I'm sorry I called you a whore for clicks.

> It is true.

> And I just now realized you said you're not feeling up to talking and I'm making you talk anyway.

> When you're ready, I'm here.

I wait for signs of a response that never come, then lock my phone with a sigh and head to the freezer for another pint of ice cream.

THIRTY-EIGHT

Nathan

I glare at my phone as the last text from Mina comes in.

> **MINA**
> When you're ready, I'm here.

I'm not fucking ready to talk to her and I don't know if I ever will be. She knew how I felt about Fallon. She knew! I should have been made aware of their friendship from the very beginning.

All those articles.

All those terrible things Fallon said about me.

And Mina just let it happen.

Or worse, she was in on the game.

How many times do I need to get my heart trampled before I fix this idealistic streak of mine? I'm a prime target for manipulators. First Blossom. Now Mina. I'm so ready to believe people are mostly good that all they have to do is pretend to be decent and I'm hooked. I even defended her to Dom when he was trying to keep me from making this very mistake.

Fuck!

I run my hands into my hair and pull.

I wish Nick were here…

The thought is a nuclear blast of anxiety. Nick's lost. Maybe hurt or dying. Maybe already dead…

And here I am wishing he could make me feel better. How pathetic can you get?

I check my phone in case I missed a call or text with news, then toss the thing onto my coffee table when there's nothing to see, only to pick it right back up to call Micah.

"What?" my cousin barks, just before the call goes to voicemail.

I lean forward, grimacing. Micah doesn't bark greetings. "Wow. Okay. Hello to you, too."

"What do you want Nathan?" Again with the clipped tone. Something's crawled up his butt and made itself comfortable.

"Why are you being such an ass?" I grumble when what I should have said is *what's wrong?*

It's like I've gone back in time and am everyone's

favorite villain again. If I'm not careful, I'll start spouting the dreaded barbed wire speech again.

Micah scoffs and it's like anger shoots through the phone to slap me in the face. "Maybe because I'm pissed with you? Your timing could be better, you know. Nick going missing is a lot to deal with. I haven't slept since we found out. Now we find out you've been lying to us about falling in love, faking a relationship. And *how* did we find out about it? Because some stranger posted about it on the internet."

"I wasn't lying." Even I hear how defensive I sound, so I take it down a notch. "I was genuinely falling in love with Mina."

Micah sucks his teeth. "So the relationship wasn't fake?"

This is not how I expected the conversation to go. For some reason, I thought I'd be able to fill Micah in on the story from my point of view. It never occurred to me that he might have already read it. Now, I have to battle his preconceived ideas about how it all went down. I stand and pace to the sliding glass doors. One hand on the glass. Gaze on the horizon.

"I'll take your silence to mean it was a hundred percent fake."

Fuck me...

No...

Fuck *Fallon*.

"It was at first but—"

"Shit, Nathan." Micah lets out an angry growl. "You are the last person I expected to do something this dumb. I actually thought you'd found something good with Mina. I like her so much, I told Ivy I'd be stoked if you guys got married. And now, since everything was a lie, I'm not sure if I know the real her."

"That makes two of us." I press my forehead to the glass and close my eyes, then I'm pacing into the kitchen for no reason other than I can't stay still.

"What's that even supposed to mean?"

I explain Mina's connection to Fallon. My words come out jumbled, one on top of the other as the story rushes forth. "I'm just..."

Lost.

Scared.

Alone.

Hurting.

Drowning.

I scrub my face. "I just don't know what to do."

Micah sighs. A long, sad thing that cuts me to the bone. "Man, look." Another sigh. "I love you. You know I do. But I don't have bandwidth for this right now. You pulling this kind of shit would be a lot all by itself, but with Nick gone? And no news for days? You got yourself into this mess. You've gotta be the one to get yourself out of it."

The line goes dead and I stare at my phone, jaw dropped. There has never been a time when a Hutton wouldn't step up for family. I consider calling Angela but pull up Dom's contact info instead.

"Why didn't you tell me the whole thing was fake?" he asks in lieu of hello. "I would have backed off with all the 'she's playing her role so you should play yours' shit. I didn't know you had it in you."

"It started fake but didn't end that way. At least not on my part, but that's because I think you were right the whole damn time." I explain the whole story one more time. Dom huffs in indignation at every point along the way, feeding my righteous fury.

"That's fucked up, brother," he says when I tell him about finding myself face-to-face with Fallon fucking Mae in Mina's bedroom.

"So fucked up." I bob my head, thrilled to have someone take my side.

There's the clicking of a keyboard on Dom's end. "You doing okay?" he asks, mildly distracted.

"No. I'm not doing okay. I'm pissed. And I swore I'd take down Fallon and everyone who was connected with her and now that includes Mina and that is seriously fucking with my head."

"I hate to say I told you so, but...no, actually I don't. I love saying 'I told you so.'" It's the best feeling ever." Dom laughs. "People play their roles, Nathan. I'll say it 'til I'm blue in the face if that's what it takes for you to hear me. Mina played hers. Now you should play yours."

"Whatever that means..." I grip the counter, shaking my head, then push off and head for another lap around the living room.

"I've got something for you. You can thank me later."

Dom ends the call before I can ask what the hell he's talking about. A text comes in a second later.

> DOM
>
> Fallon Mae
>
> 22 Bay Breeze Dr
>
> Don't ask me how I got it

While I'm staring at the address, trying to decide what the hell I'm supposed to do with that information, one last text comes in.

> DOM
>
> Take her down, brother.

THIRTY-NINE

Mina

Monday morning hits like a freight train. Between the emotional roller coaster of the weekend, about four pounds of ice cream mixed with a *Friends* marathon, and crappy, broken sleep, I'm feeling like a character in a post-apocalyptic movie the day after the world ends. Not even a super sweet, super creamy coffee hand-delivered by my too hot to be real assistant gets me moving. If anything, it makes me sicker to my stomach than I already was.

I never did hear from Nathan and I'm trying to be okay with that. We all process things at our own pace. His pace might be a tad slower than I'd like, but that's okay.

To a point, adds the snarky voice eager for a resolution, and I agree. After a while, he becomes the asshole for avoiding the situation.

But we aren't there yet.

"Coffee not doing it for you?" asks Tad from my doorway. The man's a genius when it comes to reading my moods, but I think even a stranger off the street could figure out I'm not doing great. My hair is brushed but not styled. My outfit is a basic black pant paired with a white blouse and flats. And no matter how much attention I paid to my makeup, it couldn't hide the circles under my eyes.

"The fact I'm here at all is a miracle." I slide the coffee out of reach and Tad gives me that sad smile reserved for people who look as bad as they feel.

"How can I be the best help to you today?" he asks. "Do you need to bury yourself in work? Or do you want me to tell everyone who calls that you're in a meeting and buffer you from the world so you can take a catnap in that armchair over there?" Tad jerks his head toward the chair with a look that says he'll hunt down a blanket and pillow if I so much as yawn.

And that right there is why I hired him. As much as I love to joke about it being because he's so pretty, it really comes down to his kindness and his innate ability to read the room, not to mention he's damn good at his job.

I sigh and shake my head. "Any chance you could

go back in time a few months and give me some advice?"

"If only I had that power." Tad holds up his hand in a silent hallelujah. "I'd make the world a better place one time jump at a time and wouldn't even charge for the service. The good vibes would be payment enough."

I nod knowingly, imagining the bliss of a world without regret. Why are we all so intent on making things harder than they need to be?

"I wouldn't worry about that article, you know," Tad says from his place in the doorway. "Nathan comes off worse than you do. He paid you to fake a relationship? That's freakin' dodgy, if you ask me, and fits a profile. The rich never miss a chance to take advantage of us little folks."

Dear God. I'm willing to forget all previous unanswered prayers—this time is serious. Send in SEAL Team Six. Best, Mina Blake.

I reach for my coffee and stare balefully at the contents. "The only thing fake was that article. Nathan's a good man and he wasn't taking advantage of me. I wish everyone could know him like I do."

"As long as he didn't pay you to say that too." Tad dips his chin as I fire up my rebuttal. "I'm sure he didn't, but I'd be remiss if I didn't put that out there.

You know where to find me," he finishes, then quietly closes the door.

I immediately consider calling Nathan. It's been two days since we spoke. How much space can he possibly need? But one look at my calendar reminds me that life didn't grind to a halt because I had a fight with my boyfriend. I have a meeting with a potential client in an hour, with Benjamin coming in after to hammer out the details on our business venture. I can't control how Nathan handles his shit, but I can control how I handle mine.

Right now, I need to show up for me.

With a deep cleansing breath, I brush my hair back, chug my coffee and ask Tad to help me bury my feelings with work.

FORTY

Mina

Benjamin arrives just as the coffee wears off. My previous meeting went well, but this is the one that matters and I'm in a fatigue spiral.

Go figure.

His smile is bright, and his messenger bag bounces off a pair of beige pants that fit like they were designed for him. A dark blue button up with the sleeves rolled to his elbows completes the outfit, reminding me of one of the reasons I had a crush on the man in the first place. He's very, *very* pretty.

I force a smile and shake his hand, then do my best to focus as we discuss LLCs versus LLPs, contracts, payment structure, and marketing. Everything seems fair. Generous even, considering it'll be his name that draws clients at first. I say as much, and Benjamin waves the statement away.

"What kind of partner would I be if I lock you into a contract that favors me just because in this moment, I'm farther along the career path?" Benjamin sits back in his chair, his fingers steepled under his chin. "You're every bit as talented, if not more so."

I swallow a yawn and fight the urge to slap my cheeks. "Some might call you business savvy if you went that direction."

"We need less people thinking that way, not more. I have my eyes on the future, Mina. If I leverage my name for bigger gains in the short term, I risk you resenting me in the long term. That's not a great foundation for what I hope is a lasting relationship."

Given how well the conversation is going, I should be giddy, but I can barely muster a hell yeah.

Benjamin frowns, studying me for a long moment before cocking his head and drawing his brows together. "Do you have reservations about us working together?"

"What? No! I'm incredibly excited."

Damn this fatigue spiral! Surely, I can muster enough energy from somewhere to appear enthusiastic about one of the most important conversations in my life. I blink rapidly, hoping that might shake some liveliness loose.

"Excited is not the word I'd use to describe the person sitting across from me." Benjamin sits back and crosses his ankle over his knee just as the sun dips behind a cloud, dimming the energy in my office even further. I can't catch a break.

Dear God. Throw a girl a bone here! Yours, Mina Blake.

"I'm sorry. I had a difficult weekend and tried to caffeinate my way through the day and that clearly didn't work as planned."

Benjamin studies me for a long moment, then nods like he's come to an understanding. "Your difficult weekend wouldn't have anything to do with a certain article about a mutual friend, would it?"

I blink in surprise. How the hell have so many people read Fallon's blog? I was furious when I thought she was small potatoes, but if her reach extends far enough for Benjamin and Tad to be reading, I'm more than furious.

I'm...

I'm...

I'm so angry there isn't a word for it!

Benjamin holds up his hands. "Forgive my bluntness. A few people find it endearing, and by few I mostly mean my mother, but the majority prefer a level of sugarcoating I'm just not good at. I probably should have elegantly segued into that question."

"No, no, no. Put me in your mom's camp. I like it too. I'm just not used to it yet." I puff out my cheeks.

Am I really going to talk about my personal life with Benjamin?

After too many emotionally constipated days, it appears I am.

"My bad weekend has everything to do with that article." I add a sad head bob of resigned annoyance.

Benjamin takes the statement in stride. "Is it true? The relationship's fake?"

"No," I say emphatically, then dip my chin in concession. "I mean it was, but it isn't anymore."

The statement unlocks a weekend's worth of turmoil I've been trying to rationalize away. I'm tired of hunkering in on myself. I want to explode. To expand. To let my feelings take up space because I am too small to contain them. I'm not sure people are meant to contain them in the first place. Maybe emotion should be expressed so it doesn't linger and fester.

If Benjamin digs bluntness, I hope he likes to get as much as he gives, because it's been a long, quiet weekend and I have a lot to say.

"My friend published that article."

He grimaces, catching the less than favorable implications right away. Not like they were difficult to see.

"And you didn't approve?"

I huff in exasperation and cross my arms over my chest. "I most certainly did not. She is so in the wrong."

"But she wasn't lying?"

"Not about the way things started. But the way things were going?" The look on Nathan's face when he realized who was standing in my room flashes through my mind and my heart spasms. "Although I have no idea where they're going now."

I explain that stupid text to the group chat, my even stupider request to Nathan, and him bargaining himself a sixty percent discount to pretend my message was for him.

"Sixty percent?" Benjamin looks sufficiently shocked. "That's predatory!"

"It's why I called him The Prince of Darkness. We *negotiated* that price."

"Predatory or not, you accepted." Benjamin shrugs. "No judgment, I promise."

"I was drunk, and I had a pretty big crush on you. I didn't want that text to be the way you found out."

How's that for blunt?

Benjamin looks touched and I hurry on, explaining the lunch meeting where Nathan asked me to pretend to date him and how proud I was to renegotiate myself into a financial gain.

He steeples his hands under his chin as if he's studying blueprints and watching a building come together. "This explains why I was so worried about your relationship in the beginning. It was every bit as toxic as I feared."

"Fallon was just as concerned. She suggested we write an article as leverage, or you know, protection, and she'd publish it if Nathan ended up taking advantage of me or whatever. I said no, of course, but she wouldn't drop it. The other night, I told her I was falling in love, and she told the world we were fake. And then, when I wouldn't accept her apology, she breaks into my apartment and that's how Nathan discovered we're friends. He hates her by the way. Ruthlessly."

"For the shitty articles she's posted for months now, I assume."

"Exactly." I cock my head, trying to figure out why Benjamin knows so much about a gossip and entertainment blog.

"I researched Nathan when he initially contacted me. Your friend's articles turned into a giant rubbernecking rabbit hole. She's vicious. I understand why Nathan hates her. How did he react to learning you knew her?"

"He immediately assumed I was pretending to date him so I could feed Fallon info."

"Ooof." Benjamin scrunches up his nose. "So, you're best friends with Nathan's archenemy, you know how he feels about her, but somehow get far enough into a relationship to fall in love before he finds out. Are you sure you're in my mom's camp?"

"Sure am," I reply, with more confidence than I feel.

Benjamin huffs a laugh and shakes his head. "We'll see how you feel about that in a minute. Mina?" he says, leaning his elbows on my desk and cocking his head.

I mimic his posture. "Yes?"

"You're kind of being an asshole."

I'd already come to that conclusion, but hearing it from someone else stings.

I sit back and drop my jaw. "So is he!"

"I never said he wasn't. Fake relationships. Hidden friendships. Nothing about what you two have been doing is up front and honest."

"I used to joke that we didn't bring out the best in each other."

Benjamin licks his lips and bobs his head. "That's not a great foundation for a relationship. At least not the way I'd build one. But what do I know? I prefer blueprints to people."

"Seems to me, you know quite a lot." I reach for my coffee mug, then sigh in frustration to find all that's left is the last bitter swallow. "What do you think I should do?" I ask as I push the mug away.

"At the very least, you owe Nathan an apology and you owe each other a bullshit free conversation."

"I've tried that, but he's not ready to talk."

"If he's worth it, you'll find a way to make him hear you. And if he's the kind of man you want him to be, he'll listen."

I replay the last few days one more time. Nathan arriving Friday night, heartbroken over his cousin Nick. Telling me he was falling in love with me and then after an emotional rollercoaster of a night, waking up to discover I've been hiding something big from him…

Not my best moment.

But then he lashed out when I tried to apologize and explain…

Not *his* best moment.

But after wasting years with a woman who was using him for her own benefit, I guess I see why.

Damn it.

I really don't look good in this situation.

I meet Benjamin's eyes with a long sigh. "I appreciate you listening to me and giving your honest opinion. I hope I didn't strain the boundaries of our relationship."

"I don't feel strained at all." He looks pleasantly surprised. "Honestly, it's usually the other way around."

We finish the meeting and I feel more energized than I have in days. While I don't exactly feel better about the Nathan situation, I do feel more solid. Admitting to myself that he has a genuine reason to be angry doesn't feel great, but it gives me something to work with. The last thing I wanted was to make him feel taken advantage of. While that's not what I was doing, I understand why he feels that way.

Now I just need to figure out how to help him see.

FORTY-ONE

Mina

I leave the office, intending to head home, but make an unscheduled stop when a Help Wanted sign in the front window of a bar catches my attention. With the advance I got from Nathan, my finances are fine. Tight. But fine. But given where we are? Using that money seems wrong. When he was The Prince of Darkness and I was the Hot Mess Express and everything between us was a show we put on for others, it only seemed right to be paid for my efforts. But now that he's Nathan and I'm Mina and we were falling in love, spending that money feels dirty. Considering he called me a whore for clicks, it feels downright filthy.

So.

I should give it back.

Except I can't pay Mom's bills without it.

Unless I get that second job I've been thinking about—hence my interest in the Help Wanted sign.

Working two jobs will be hard, especially given the extra clients I've added to my roster. And I'll be tired. But I'll be able to take care of Mom and maybe help Nathan realize I didn't think of him as an opportunity like his friend Dom swears I did.

With a resigned sigh, I pull into the bar's parking lot and walk inside to ask for an application.

Twenty minutes later, I walk back to my car with a job and an idea. Benjamin and Tad helped me realize how bad Fallon has made Nathan look. I don't know where he and I stand and that sucks. I wish he'd talk to me so I can apologize and try to make things right. Until then, the very least I can do is some damage control on his reputation.

Instead of driving home, I go to Fallon's house. It's small, but impeccably maintained, with flowerpots lining the steps leading to the porch she sweeps every day. I used to think she had great taste and wasn't afraid of hard work, but I'm starting to believe image means more to her than it should. That the impeccable clothing and hair and landscaping speak more to her need to feel better than other people than an innate sense of style or self-worth.

I'm not in the mood for the conversation she wants, but I'll negate my irritation long enough to see if she'll help me do right by Nathan. A man like him deserves a little discomfort on my part if it will help show the world who he really is.

With a bracing sigh, I knock on my friend's freshly painted red door. Seconds later, it cracks open.

Fallon peeks out, then throws the door wide with a grin. "I knew you'd forgive me!"

I step out of hug range, hands up, warding her off. "We have a long way to go before we're there."

Fallon huffs and draws up short. Her gold-shadowed eyes flicker with annoyance. "Then why are you here?"

"I want you to do something for me."

"Anything. You name it. I'll do it." She steps forward again, hands out, eager to put our friendship back together. If she's the person I thought she was before all this, then I am too. But if she's the person I think I'm starting to see, then I'm not sure I want anything to do with her.

"I want you to publish an apology article on your blog for Nathan."

"An apology?" Fallon physically retreats, shaking her head like she smells something nasty. "That'll ruin my credibility."

And there it is. Her first thought is her damn blog. Not her impact on Nathan's life or her supposed best friend. She's seen firsthand how her choices affected me. That should mean something.

"Seems fair," I say, inwardly begging her to think about someone other than herself for a second. "You ruined his reputation. And our relationship."

"He ruined his reputation." Fallon steps outside and closes the door, then crosses her arms over her chest. "How is that my fault?"

How can she even ask that question?

"You grossly misrepresented his every move."

She scoffs. "For his own good."

The fact that she didn't deny the misrepresentation suggests she knew exactly what she was doing the whole time. My heart sinks to my stomach.

"Just like you told everyone we were fake for my own good?" I place a hand to my chest as Fallon triumphantly lifts her chin.

"Exactly."

She thinks I'm finally understanding her, and in a way, she's right. I think I'm seeing the real Fallon Mae for the first time, without the assumption of kindness and goodwill I naturally apply to everyone. It's not a good look.

I reach out to take her hand. "If you value our friendship at all, I need you to do this for me. For Nathan. I'll even write the article. You just need to hit publish."

A storm cloud darkens her eyes. "That blog pays my bills." Her voice rolls like thunder, warning me of impending danger.

I'm stunned by her resistance, despite what I'm coming to understand.

I don't know why I didn't see it before, but it's clear now. Helping Nathan realize how much he changed was never the point of Fallon's articles. Maybe, *maybe* she wrote the first one with that intention, but those that followed? She was harnessing the energy of his name for personal gain.

God, I hope I'm wrong.

"You told me Nathan sees me as an opportunity, but you need to take a long hard look at yourself." I brace myself as I channel Benjamin's bluntness. "I think you've been writing these articles about him to grow your subscriber count. This was never about him. It's about likes and clicks and money."

"Wow, Mina. Tell me what you really think." Fallon tosses her hair and breaks eye contact, staring blankly at the sky. "Come on, though. You know this.

You know me. I was showing Nathan how much he'd changed so he'd pick himself up and put himself back together. The growth in subscribers was an unexpected bonus."

"Maybe that's how you started, but that's not how it ended. Nathan isn't the man you made him out to be and if you didn't know that before I got together with him, you certainly did after. Even then, you obliterated best friend code, publishing things I told you in confidence, and still managed to misrepresent his every move. *You* made him sound like a villain when he is so not. Imagine how infuriating it is to have someone lie about you and know people believe the lies? Put yourself in his shoes. Just for a minute. And then, when you're done, put yourself in mine. I'm furious, Fallon! Furious!"

She smooths her hair and shakes her head, still not able to look me in the eyes. "I'm so small, Nathan probably doesn't even know I exist."

That's all she has to say? After I initiate the conversation I wasn't ready to have in the first place, she has the balls to brush off my feelings with an excuse she knows isn't true? Fallon's been saying it this whole time. I only need to see a glimmer of goodness in someone to forgive a whole lot of bad. She just had the target wrong. She's the one I needed to look out for. Not Nathan.

"You saw how he reacted to you in my bedroom, which, by the way, shows he definitely knows you exist." I grimace as the truth of the woman in front of me crystallizes. "I told you how frustrated he was because of your articles. You just doubled down and said that meant your plan was working. Even when I asked you to stop, you kept going. How are *you* not the one seeing *him* as an opportunity? Explain to me how you didn't take advantage of me, of our friendship, for personal gain. I'm desperate for a reason to forgive you, here. You gotta give me something."

There's a long moment with the two of us just standing there, silently staring. An older couple walks by on the sidewalk in front of the house, both lifting hands in greeting when we glance their way. A week ago, I could have seen that as a possible future for me and Nathan. Now, I'm waiting to discover if I've been friends with the real villain all along. Life sure does love its surprises.

"You make me sound like such an asshole," Fallon says, but her face is so closed, I can't tell if she's coming around to my point of view or victimizing herself.

I raise my brows. "You have one thousand percent been an asshole. Profiting off someone's misery? You're better than that."

Or at least I hope you are, I think, then wait several uncomfortable seconds for Fallon to respond.

"Fine," she finally says. "You can write that article, but I get final say over whether I publish it. And just to set a boundary up front, if you make me sound this bad in your post, this goes no further. I won't let you publicly humiliate me."

"Says the woman who was fine to publicly humiliate everyone else."

"Do you want this or not?"

The look on Fallon's face is hard to read. She's not happy, that much is clear. And I'm not sure how honest she'll let me be, but I have to try. I don't know if what I want to say will be enough for Nathan to understand I wasn't in cahoots with Fallon, but I have to tell the world who he really is.

At the very least, I owe him that.

FORTY-TWO

THE ARTICLE

It Wasn't Fake, Folks. Nathan West Is Not the Man You Think He Is.

There are times in life when it's necessary to pause and take stock of who you are and what you're doing. To judge your actions, choices, and thoughts against who you want to be and see if they align, then make Big Scary Changes if they don't.

My name is Mina Blake and I've come to one of those moments.

As you may have read on this blog, I entered into a fake relationship with Nathan West.

He offered to pay me to pretend to be his girlfriend. I needed the money so I accepted, even though, at the time, I didn't like him. I'd built my opinion of him off things I saw online and never slowed down to wonder how much was exaggerated, blown out of proportion, or just plain wrong.

I'm sure you expect me to apologize. To tell you I'm ashamed of what we did and then spin a story about a rich man taking advantage of an underprivileged woman.

But that's not what happened. I wasn't taken advantage of by a villain. And I'm not going to apologize for a choice that led me to fall in love with an amazing person.

I'm here to set the record straight.

I willingly entered into a fake relationship with Nathan West, but that's where the truth in the article you read last week ends. He wasn't using me. He didn't seduce me for personal gain. Yes, he's rich and sure, I'm poor, but he made me feel like a treasure, not an embarrassment.

When I first met Nathan, I called him The Prince of Darkness and thought I was cute. I'm sure many of you judge him based on the things you think you know and believe he's a rich asshole building a villain's lair, living in excess while the rest of us struggle to put food on the table and pay our bills.

But know this.

Nathan West is not that man.

Period. Full stop. The end.

He's not drinking too much. He's not with a new

woman every night. He's not sipping champagne in exclusive hotels, enjoying luxury at the expense of the little guy.

Nathan cares deeply about the world and the people in it. He dedicated his life to charity and kindness, not to impress anyone, but because that's what he's called to do. He's a protector. A provider. Someone who gives freely. Who sees the best in people even when they do him wrong. He's dedicated to his family and strives to make life easier for everyone. He does what's right, even when it's hard. When you meet the man, the whole man, the human being who has good days and bad days instead of the caricatures of him you see online, he will inspire you to live as your best self because that's what he's doing every day.

I thought the hardest thing about pretending to date Nathan West would be making people believe I liked spending time with The Prince of Darkness.

Turns out the hardest thing is that I fell head over heels with a wonderful man, and when push came to shove, I'm not sure I deserved him.

I ask all of you to rewrite what you think you know. When you see the name Nathan West, don't think about a playboy or a villain or a trust-fund-asshole.

See the man for who he is:

A philanthropist dead set on leaving the world better than he found it.

FORTY-THREE

NATHAN

Nick's missing. My girlfriend is a liar. My cousins won't talk to me. And everyone at work keeps staring and whispering when they think I'm not paying attention. Life took a hard right turn and I fucking hate it. I want to go back to a week ago when everything was beautiful, and I thought I was healing and falling in love with the woman of my dreams. Except maybe it never was fine, at least according to Dom, who's gloating like a motherfucker while pretending he's oh so sad to have been right about Mina's motivations. Even Rita had a hard time making eye contact this morning and I'd pegged her as unflappable.

Mina hasn't texted since Saturday, probably giving me the space I said I needed. The petulant child that lives in my head swears it's proof she was using me. That she'd fight harder if she genuinely cared. The adult knows she's being respectful of my wishes.

I'm the reason we haven't talked.

I just can't deal with it all right now.

I'm simmering in stress.

The Nick situation would be enough on its own. But to find out he's missing the same day my nemesis told the world my relationship was fake? Only to find her in Mina's bedroom the next day?

It's too much stacked on too much stacked on too much.

I've lost the respect of my family. My colleagues. I can't talk to Micah or Angela or my brothers or sister about it. I can't even think about Nick without a jolt of panic scattering common sense.

I've lost Mina.

Or maybe I haven't.

One conversation might solve everything, but therein lies the problem. I don't trust her anymore. What if Dom is right to gloat? What if Mina being friends with Fallon Mae was just the tip of the iceberg. What if she *was* pretending to love me because of her mom's medical bills? Being my girlfriend would be a hell of a solution, either because she applies for assistance through ROF and asks me to grease the wheels on the application, or I just pay the damn things off myself.

I should talk to her.

I miss her.

But worse than not trusting her, I don't trust myself. I'll hear what I want to hear, not what she's actually saying. Just like I did with Blossom.

I am too gullible for my own damn good.

But I should have called her days ago. Letting this drag on so long is an asshole move.

I'm better than this.

I groan, leaning my elbows on my desk and threading my fingers through my hair, begging to get off this damn merry-go-round. "Come on, West. You're here to work. Buck the fuck up and work already."

Lifting my head, I stare at the email I opened who knows how long ago. I've read it four times and still have no idea what it says. I scrub my face, realize I probably should have shaved before coming in this morning, then lean in for one last attempt at reading when my phone pings. An alert on my name...from Fallon's blog.

Damn it.

She had the balls to post another article?

Really?

Has she not done enough damage?

Seriously, what did I do to her?

I tap on the alert and the blog opens to the article, but you know what? I don't have the bandwidth to care. My thumb moves to close the browser, but I pause when I see Mina's name. With my heart in my throat, I read the first few lines, then the whole damn thing, then sit back, chewing my bottom lip. Before I've had time to figure out how I feel, my office door opens.

"Mr. West?" Rita crosses her arms like a palace guard. "Your interior designer is here." She places an unusual amount of emphasis on Mina's job description.

My jaw sets.

I'm not prepared for this. I still haven't processed her apology—assuming that's what that was. She never actually said the words, but they were strongly implied. But what was Mina's motivation for the article? Was she genuine? Does she want something? Fuck me. I should have stayed home.

I scrub my face again because damn it, I need to get a grip. All this whining and 'what-ifing' is a waste of energy.

"Would you like me to tell her where exactly she can go?" Rita asks, lifting her chin and squaring her shoulders.

The ferocity in her eyes brings a ghost of a smile to my lips. It's quite possibly the first time I've not frowned in the last three days.

"There's no need for that." I wave off my self-appointed bodyguard. "I appreciate you for looking out for me, but go ahead and send her in."

Rita gives a bob of her head and gestures for Mina to enter, mean-mugging her as she steps into my office.

There's this moment. My gaze lands on hers and joy riots through me. A weekend apart is too much because all is right with the world when we're together. I want to rush to her, wrap her in my arms and apologize over and over for going so long without talking.

But I don't. I will myself still until I know why she's here. I watch as Mina closes the door and takes a seat.

Her hair is down. She looks paler than usual. Her eyes are sad and her smile is weak and my heart stutters at the sight of her.

"I'm sorry to barge in like this." Mina tucks her hair behind her ears, tightens her hands into fists, then places them in her lap. "I know I promised I'd give you space, but there are things I need to say and I can't wait any longer."

She meets my eyes with so much trepidation, I feel like even more of an asshole for the distance I've maintained. Unless, of course, Dom was right. In that case, I've done exactly what I should have.

I hate myself for being this suspicious.

Why is nothing in life cut and dry and easy?

"I should have told you I was friends with Fallon," Mina continues, her bottom lip trembling, her voice reedy and thin. "Any time in the last several weeks would have been better than letting you find out the way you did. I promise you; I wasn't keeping the secret intentionally nor did my involvement with you have anything to do with my friendship with her."

Her words are rehearsed. She's nearly in tears. I hate to see her like this.

"Mina, I—" I start the sentence with no idea how to finish it, but Mina holds up her hand.

"I understand it seems that way," she continues. "I really do. And I also understand why you think I was trying to take advantage of you. I wasn't. I'm not. But what I need you to hear most is that I'm deeply, incredibly sorry for not being honest, especially knowing how Blossom treated you."

I close my eyes at the parallel and Mina hurries on.

"I went to see Fallon the other day and…" She closes her eyes and huffs a laugh. "I think I met the real her for the first time. I guess I have blinders when it comes to people and their motivations. I assume the best in everyone, and I was wrong to put my trust in her. She's not a good person and I don't want her in my life anymore, but I made her post a clarification about you on her blog. It should go live sometime today, and I only tell you so you don't get upset when you get the alert on your name. I figured the least I could do was tell her readers who you really are, maybe undo some of the damage to your reputation. As soon as that article goes live though, I'm officially done with Fallon fucking Mae."

Mina holds my gaze, smiling weakly as she emulates my intonation every time I say my archenemy's name.

I muster a weak, "Thank you," and Mina swallows hard.

"There's a few more reasons I came to see you today." She ruffles in her purse and pulls out a check, places it on the table and slides it my way. "I'm returning the advance you gave me. And the extra twenty percent we agreed on for..." She drops her gaze with a sigh, then brings those soulful blues back to me. "For this whole thing?"

Her voice breaks and every instinct I have is to close the distance between us, to cup her cheeks, to hold her close...but I'm glued to my chair, still and waiting.

"I won't be accepting the extra money," Mina finishes. "I can't accept it."

I glower at the check and slide it back across the desk. "I don't want your money."

"It's not mine. I shouldn't have taken it in the first

place. I like being with you, Nathan. It's weird to be paid for it."

A million thoughts fight for dominance, all of them conflicting. My jaw clenches while I decide which to listen to.

I swallow hard before, "I like being with you too."

A smile warms Mina's face. It's the first time she's looked like the woman I know since she walked in. "That's gonna make what I have to say even harder. Everything we're built on is flimsy and fake, Nathan. We flirted because we signed a contract. Because we negotiated a price on our affections."

I huff in disgust. "I flirted because I wanted to."

Mina lifts a brow. "At first, you flirted because you wanted to sell a story about a relationship that didn't exist. I have to wonder; did we get so caught up in faking it that we fell for our own lies?"

"No." The answer is simple. Powerful, and right there. I don't have to think to find it. "I fell for you because of who you are."

"Then why is finding out I was friends with Fallon enough to make you hide for a whole weekend? And why was knowing you'd be mad we were friends enough to keep me from telling you in the first place? Maybe we don't trust each other as much as we should."

I sit back with a growl.

Mina reaches across the desk to take my hand. "A man like you deserves something real and honest and true. You deserve to be with someone you trust. Someone who makes you happy. Whole."

A man like me. Blossom's favorite phrase. Only this time, it doesn't feel like manipulation. It feels like a compliment.

"You made me happy."

Mina's practiced demeanor cracks and a river of pain ripples across her face. "Then why didn't you call me back? Why did I have to come to you, here, at work, and force you to hear me?"

"Because I'm a petulant child." I scoff and look away. "Is that what you want me to say?"

"No, Nathan. I'm not here to toss around blame. I've recently come to respect a certain measure of blunt honesty and...well...I'm just trying to be real with you. Because that's what a good relationship needs. Real emotions. Real thoughts. Honesty in all things, even when it's scary. Even when it might break us. Otherwise, we're built on lies."

I stare so long, weighing everything she says against my bullshit meter, that Mina starts to fidget. It's endearing. And heartbreaking.

"So anyway, I guess I'll just get to the hard part. I don't think we should see each other until I'm financially stable. So you can trust I'm with you for *you* and not what I can get from you."

"You don't want to see me anymore?"

Mina sags, eyes sliding closed, brows drawing tight. When she meets my gaze again, it looks like her heart is breaking. "I think we need to take a break so we can unravel what was real and what was fake."

"I don't want to take a break."

"I don't either, but I think you and me, us together, I think it could be special. There's a chance for it to be as real and true and as beautiful as it felt, but if you can't trust me, we'll never get there. The only way I can think to do this is to show you I can stand on my own two feet. To be strong separately so we can be even stronger together."

"I don't want to take a break." I cross my arms and shake my head, frustrated enough to repeat myself.

"Then tell me how to fix this!" Mina cries. "Because going a whole weekend without talking is a lot. Yes, I messed up, but if I can't even have a conversation with you to apologize, what does that mean? I've been going crazy, beating myself up, wondering what you're thinking, missing you like...like I don't know how to breathe when you're not around, but it's just been silence on your end. How long am I supposed to be okay with that before you're just as much the asshole as I am? What do you need, Nathan? Just tell me what you need!"

"If I knew what I needed I would have done it!" I bark, then consciously lower my voice. "I'm juggling a lot. Nick. You. Fallon fucking Mae in your bedroom." I close my eyes against that particular image. "My family is furious with me. Angela won't talk to me. Micah basically told me to fuck off. My parents are more disappointed than ever. The whole crew loves you as much as I do and then some stranger on the internet says it's fake..." I close my eyes and grit my teeth and clench my fists because everything I feel for Mina is real. How dare Fallon Mae say otherwise? "Or it started out fake and then it wasn't," I say, opening my eyes with a sigh. "I don't know, Mina. I just don't know."

Mina's shoulders slump and she releases a long, slow breath. "Which is why I think it's best if I remove myself from the equation for a bit. Just until we do know."

"I'm sorry I didn't call you. I'm sorry I'm human and imperfect and I don't always know what to do or say." I throw up my hands then let them drop to my lap. "A week ago, I was so happy..."

Mina stands, fighting tears. "I was too. And this isn't goodbye forever. Just...for now. Until we know."

Until we know.

Whatever the fuck that means.

Part of me dies at the thought of goodbye, but if this is what she thinks is best…

"A little distance might be a good thing."

Mina nods. Frowns. Blows a short puff of breath past her lips. "Okay, then. I guess that's it, then. Goodbye, Sweet Prince," she whispers, one hand on the doorframe.

The nickname is a blast of regret, nostalgia, fondness, all tangled in an impenetrable knot in my stomach.

I sit back in my chair and scrub my hand over my mouth as she turns and walks away. "Goodbye, Mina," I mumble, then slam my laptop shut with a growl.

FORTY-FOUR

Mina

I hold it together long enough to navigate the halls of the Reversal of Fortune Foundation, but as the front doors whoosh shut behind me, tears roll down my face. By the time I'm safely seated in my Honda, I'm hiccupping back sobs, my forehead leaning on the steering wheel as the Florida heat swelters out the open door. Walking out of Nathan's office, unsure as to whether I'll see him again, was the hardest thing I've ever done.

But it was the right choice.

If he can't trust me, our relationship has no foundation and I'm not in the market for what Mom had with Dad. A lack of trust leads to bitterness, resentment, and decay.

I don't want to live like that.

I'm worth the real deal and so is Nathan.

If I have to walk away now so we can be better later, so be it.

I slam my hand against the steering wheel and silently scream until white-hot rage gives way to icy sorrow. I breathe through it, giving myself space to feel whatever comes up. When the tears stop, I take a few deep breaths, then angle the rearview to wipe my red-rimmed eyes.

"You're gonna be okay," I say to the woman in the mirror. "You're no stranger to hard work. You'll keep the job at The Depot until Bancroft and Blake starts earning money. It'll be tight and your days will be long, but you know how to do that. You've done it before. You're strong. You're capable. It's just one foot in front of the other for a little longer."

But what if Nathan never comes back? she asks, not at all concerned about money or long hours.

"You'll pick yourself up and dust yourself off. You're not really built for relationships anyway."

The woman in the mirror doesn't look convinced.

FORTY-FIVE

Nathan

When Dom sent me Fallon's address, I didn't think I'd do anything with it. I'm not the guy that shows up at a stranger's house to...what? Tell her off? Make sure she knows how much I hate her? Who does that? I'm so not that guy, I can't even come up with an action plan.

But the more I think about what Mina said, the more I want to believe she wasn't conspiring with Fallon to bring me down. Sharing secrets with a woman who so clearly has it out for me was a bad call on Mina's part, but it's easy to give a friend more credit than they're due. I did it with Blossom, then again with Dom. Mina could have fallen into the same trap, which means there's a chance everything she did was totally innocent.

It's that chance that has me standing on Fallon Mae's front porch. The house is small, tucked into a quaint neighborhood with kids rolling down the sidewalks on bikes and neighbors strolling by, waving as they pass. Despite all that, Fallon's home still manages to appear grandiose. Luxurious planters line the steps with tropical plants waving in the breeze. The landscaping is meticulous and expensive, every tree, bush, shrub, and flower trimmed into submission. It's bigger, bolder, brighter than every other house on the block, like it's screaming for attention. It doesn't help my opinion of the woman.

I knock.

Fallon answers.

We stare in mutual loathing, her brow slowly arching in disbelief, my jaw setting tighter and tighter.

"What are you doing here?" she asks, in a voice that would make polar bears shiver.

"I need to talk to you," I reply, with enough heat to melt the ice caps.

"I'm not inviting you in." Fallon steps outside and pulls the door closed to make her point, then glances over my shoulder. Her face transforms into the friendliest of smiles as she waves at a woman walking her dog, only for her features to harden again when she refocuses on me.

"I'm happy to have this conversation out here." I

retreat a few steps to lean against the porch rail and Fallon lifts her chin.

"Just so we're clear, I have my phone and won't hesitate to call for emergency services." She waves the device in question. She doesn't look at all concerned that I might have something nefarious in mind, but seems like she's dying to make that call anyway.

I shake my head in disgust. "You don't actually think I'm here to hurt you."

"I wouldn't put anything past Nathan 'Villain Era' West. Plus, my subscribers would eat that headline up." Fallon's lips twitch into a cruel smile. It's nearly identical to the way Blossom looked when she told me she was using me for my money. Like she takes pride in being nasty. How was Mina ever friends with this person? Though, my family said the same of me and Dom. Sometimes good people get caught up with bad people and don't realize until too late.

"What did I do to you, Fallon?"

She recoils. Scoffs. Takes a few steps in my direction only to shrug off my question with disdain. "You didn't do anything to me," she replies, picking her fingernails with practiced nonchalance.

"Then why did you post all those terrible things about me?"

"I was holding up a mirror." Fallon extends her hands like a priest to his flock. "Showing you how much you changed. It's not always comfortable to look our bad choices in the face and admit to our faults, but it's an important part of being human."

I've never disliked a person as much as I dislike the woman in front of me. It's taking every ounce of restraint not to loosen the leash on my anger, but I'm playing the long game. Blowing up now won't do me any good. Patience, grace, and a little vulnerability on my part will reveal everything I need to know about Fallon fucking Mae.

"They weren't my bad choices though," I say as a little girl rolls by on a scooter. "You were publishing lies."

Fallon looks unimpressed. "Was I though? Are you sure?"

"A hundred percent you were." I cross my arms over my chest, and she wobbles her head back and forth like she's conceding my point.

"Maybe some of my early stuff was conjecture..."

"That you stated as fact." I swallow a smile. She doesn't know it yet, but I have her dead to rights with that admission.

Fallon brushes off the statement. "But most of my latest articles are true."

"Because Mina started feeding you information." The statement grinds past a clenched jaw.

Easy now, Nathan. Don't lose control now.

"You make it sound so duplicitous." Fallon scoffs in disgust. "Mina wasn't feeding me information. She was talking to her best friend."

"A best friend she knew was publishing lies about me!" I close my eyes and purposefully loosen my fists. This conversation requires a clear head. Patience will serve me better than anger.

"You were rude to her for weeks! Of course she's gonna vent to her best friend! Who wouldn't vent about fake relationships and rich assholes negotiating most of her paycheck away just to send a text?" Fallon stalks to the other end of her porch, sighing when she notices her neighbor watering her garden, pretending not to listen.

"So it was Mina who said I was using sex as a weapon."

"No." Fallon's quieter now. Closer now. "That was me, seeing through your lies to your true motivation."

"My true...? I was actively falling in love and doing everything I could to make Mina feel special! You *interpreted my* actions as manipulative. That doesn't mean they were."

And it says more about the woman in front of me than anything yet. The people who manipulate expect manipulation, while the people who are genuine give credit to those who don't deserve it.

Fallon shrugs. "What can I say? I understand how

people work. Poor Mina, though. Her rose-colored glasses just beg someone to take advantage of her. She needed me to help her see what was going on and the only reason she shared anything was because she made me swear not to publish any of it."

I grab onto that nugget of information like a lifeline. If Mina made Fallon promise not to use what she shared, she couldn't be Fallon's secret agent.

"But you published it anyway."

"I was trying to protect her."

"Bullshit."

"Fine." Fallon throws up her hands. "My career took off when I started talking about you and I couldn't help myself. Is that what you want to hear?"

"You couldn't help yourself? My family and friends and colleagues won't talk to me because of the things you've said. You don't know anything about me or what was really happening or what I was actually doing, but oh no! Don't let a few facts get in the way of a good story, and certainly not when it's good for your career. People actually think I'm a villain because of you and Mina. Do you have any idea what you've done to me? I'm a real person with real feelings."

"Not Mina." Fallon shakes her head. "Just me. She asked me to stop multiple times. She told me I had you wrong more than that. She said I was misrepresenting you—"

"And you kept going? Knowing you were publishing lies as fact?"

She shrugs. "The money was good. What can I say?"

"Maybe start with I'm sorry for lying about you. I'm sorry I told the world you were a villain—"

"Show me proof you're not a villain! Where is it, Nathan?"

"How about my work for charity? Or the fact that I haven't sued you for libel?"

Fallon cocks her head, jaw thrust forward, eyes narrowing. "You wouldn't dare."

"After this conversation, I would. See, I had my phone ready to go at a moment's notice, too." I reach into my pocket and pull out the device, brandishing the open and active recording app like a weapon.

"That recording is illegal." Fallon crosses her arms and lifts her chin. She should be panicking, but she's too proud and cocksure. "The state of Florida requires consent from all parties to record a conversation."

I click my tongue. "Unless there is no reasonable expectation of privacy. You yelling at me on your front porch with neighbors in earshot doesn't seem all that private to me."

"That's..." Fallon's panicking now. "That's weak and you know it."

"I don't think it is, but I can afford the best lawyers to fight it out in court for as long as it takes. Can you?"

"Fine. You've got me by the balls. What do you want out of me?"

"I want you to stop posting lies about me. You stop, I won't sue."

Panic gives way to sheer terror. "That'll ruin me! If all I can talk about is how good you are, I'll lose subscribers."

"I didn't say you had to talk about how good I am. I simply said you had to tell the truth."

Fallon rolls her eyes. "So I can either stop writing about you and lose my livelihood, or write about you and get sued."

I click my tongue again. "If those are the only two options you see, then I've learned all I need to know about Fallon fucking Mae." Sliding my phone back in my pocket, I turn my back on the woman once and for all.

"Have a lovely day," I say, then lift my middle finger and strut down the steps.

FORTY-SIX

Mina

A few days after my conversation with Nathan, I'm sitting in the physical therapy room at Shady Cove, watching Mom walk on a treadmill. Her pace is improving. As is her stamina. When she checked in, they had to bring a wheelchair to get her from the car to her room. The woman in front of me wouldn't need it. She notices me watching and waves, grinning like an Olympian taking gold, before giving her attention to her therapist, a beefy man with peewee football coach vibes.

"How long you been on?" he asks.

Mom checks the readout on her machine. "Ten minutes now."

Another giant smile.

"What's your pace?" asks Beefcake McGee.

"Up to a three!" Mom pumps a triumphant fist.

"And your exertion level?"

"I'd say a five or a six," she replies. "A little out of breath but not that bad. Legs are starting to burn."

The grin on her therapist's face says he recognizes the improvement as much as I do. "Why don't you go another minute and call it a day. That's great work, Ms. Blake."

Mom finishes up and does her seated cooldown exercises, then turns down a wheelchair escort to her room. "I don't have anything else to do today and my daughter's here. We'll go slow and I'll lean on her for support, then take a nap when she leaves."

Her therapist gives the thumbs up, and Mom threads her arm in mine. I kiss the top of her head then set that slow pace she promised. Fatigue has a way of sneaking up on her. I don't want excitement to trick her into overdoing it.

"Looks like you're leaving here to go to work at The Depot." Mom frowns at my black slacks and black fitted tee.

Returning the advance Nathan gave me definitely put me in a financial pickle. The clientele at my new job is swanky, so the tips are good, but I'm going to be late paying Shady Cove. Thankfully, they were willing to work with me. Glenda, the woman in charge of the finance office, is also a fan of Fallon's blog. When she saw me walk in, her jaw hit the floor. After some awkward fangirling, she was eager to give me some grace 'after my ordeal.'

"You promised you wouldn't feel guilty about me working evenings and weekends," I say, adjusting my grip on Mom's arm. "It's only temporary. Besides, I kind of like it."

Interior design is mental. I sit in a chair and stare at screens or fabric swatches, daydreaming new color and texture combinations. Waitressing is movement. I'm running from one table to the next all night long. It's the perfect outlet for my nervous energy.

"I wanted better for you than working so much you barely have time to sleep." Mom sighs like the weight of the world is settling on her shoulders—an early sign fatigue is setting in. The sooner I get her back to her room, the better, but I don't dare pick up the pace or I'll wear her out. Managing her energy is a constant balancing act, but at least she has energy to manage now.

I pat her hand. "There is nothing better than knowing my time and energy are going towards your health and wellbeing. You should know that, considering you worked yourself to the bone for me when I was a kid."

"That's just motherhood, Meena Bean."

The return of my childhood nickname sets off a burst of embarrassed warmth in my heart. "You went above and beyond, and you know it. I'm honored to return the favor. Our family is small, but boy are we mighty."

"That we are, Meens. That we are." Mom presses a hand to the wall, and I slow our pace a little more. "Have you heard from Nathan?"

She's working hard to sound casual, like she didn't just poke a tender bruise.

"Not really," I reply, aiming to match her tone and failing. "A little for work, but with the plans for his house finalized, I'm pretty much out of the picture. We haven't talked about anything real. Nothing about us."

"I'm sorry, Mina. I so wanted all those red flags to be false." Her eyes hit mine with the kind of understanding that only exists between mother and daughter, with decades of real, honest talk connecting them.

"You and me both."

"Have you thought about calling him again?" she asks, smiling at a handsome older man trundling past with an IV stand as we turn the corner to her hallway. He grins, lifting a hand and dipping his chin in a gentlemanly bow. I widen my eyes at Mom after he passes and she waves the topic away, blushing furiously.

If I didn't know better, I'd say my mother has a

crush she's trying to hide. She must be feeling even better than I thought.

"I didn't give Nathan the time and space he said he needed the last time," I say, honoring her need not to talk about Mr. Silverfox with great effort. "I'm giving it to him now. If he's ready to try again, he'll call."

We make it back to Mom's room and I help her into bed. The walk has tired her out enough that frustration tightens her features. There was a time when walking down a hallway was something she took for granted. There was also a time when we weren't sure she'd ever manage it again. The stronger she gets, the more she wants what she once had, the easier it is to take her progress for granted.

"You're doing great," I say, brushing the hair back from her face. "Making good strides week after week."

"That's what they say." Mom's eyes slide closed as she sinks into her pillows.

"Listen to 'em, Mom. Your first doctors said you'd never get your life back and look at you, walking to and from PT like a boss."

She cocks her head and tuts, a sure sign she knows I'm right, but isn't in the mood to admit it. Mom's attitude slips when she's tired, so I make an excuse about needing to get to The Depot early to fill out some paperwork and make my exit to let her rest.

The drive to the bar is easy and I sit in the parking

lot, digesting my conversation with Mom. I miss Nathan. A lot. I'd love to tell him about Mom's progress, even take him to meet her so he can be just as impressed as I am. But he never saw her at her worst, and I was so busy being strong and trying to prove I wasn't using him, that I never shared those stories. He was real with me, but I wasn't with him.

What a shame.

FORTY-SEVEN

Nathan

I pull open the door to The Depot and sigh. It's everything The Pact is not, which is exactly why Dom chose to meet here. The lighting is dramatic, the tables a gleaming black lacquer with warm brown inlays. The customers are dressed in clothes so expensive, the cost of an outfit could buy a few weeks of groceries for a foundation family, while the servers wear the black on black typical of luxury customer service.

I scan the crowd and find Dom at a table in the middle of the room, sitting back in his chair like he owns the place. There's a light fixture directly over his head, casting warmth down on him like a spotlight. He probably chose the table himself for that reason alone.

He waves me over, grinning wolfishly as I approach. "What's good, brother?"

"Can't complain." I pull out my seat with a shrug. "The expansion at ROF is rolling along smoothly. We've successfully approved our first round of applications and can start bringing much needed relief to people in the area."

Dom nods even though he doesn't give a shit. "You heard from Mina?"

"Nope. But she hasn't heard from me, either. We left things kind of ambiguous."

I've missed her every day and thought about calling her twice an hour. But she said we shouldn't see each other until she's financially stable, and I don't know how I'm supposed to know if that happened. With work so busy and Nick still missing, I don't have the bandwidth to figure it out. But if I wait too long, she'll slip through my fingers and the one thing I'm sure of with each passing day is that I can't let that happen.

Something behind me catches Dom's attention. He arches a brow and smirks before leaning his elbows on the table. "You're better off without her."

"Right." I fight the urge to turn and see what caught his attention. Probably a dazzling and spectacular woman, and I couldn't care less about those. "Dollar signs and opportunities and all that."

"You can't deny your life improved since you started taking my advice."

"I'm gonna have a giant ass house that's too much space for one person. Does that count as an improvement?" As beautiful as that home is going to be, it's a lot of house for one person.

"I can introduce you to all kinds of women who'd love to fill that extra space for a while." Dom's gaze darts over my shoulder again.

"What are you looking at?"

I turn and there she is. My Mina. Hair slicked back into a tight bun, black slacks, black tee, red lips. Tray in hand...

She fucking works here?

Our eyes meet and she draws up short.

A smile brightens her face for an instant before dismay takes its place. Her brows knit and she sighs, looking around as if desperate for an escape.

"Ouch," murmurs Dom but I don't care because Mina's heading this way, shoulders square, chin proud, eyes blazing.

"Hello and welcome to The Depot. I'm Mina and I'll be your server this evening. Did I give you enough time to decide?" Her tone is polite, though her eyes are panicked. Or pissed. Or...fuck. I don't know.

"If it isn't the hundred-thousand-dollar girl.'" Dom throws an arm over the back of the chair and looks downright gleeful at the change in her fortune. "I'll take a scotch on the rocks, doll."

"What are you doing here?" I ask.

Mina brandishes her tray. "I work here."

"Yes," I growl. "But why do you work here?"

When she returned the advance, I assumed she had money coming in to take its place. But if she took a second job, I must be missing pieces of the puzzle.

"The same reason anyone works anywhere," Mina replies dryly. "Some of us have boring lives that need to be maintained. I'll be right back with the scotch and whiskey neat."

Mina pivots and practically runs away before I realize I didn't place my order. She simply knew what I wanted.

And just like that, I know what I want too. Her. Not a break. Not time apart so she can work herself to the bone to prove something I already know. I want her in my life. In my arms. In my bed. In my heart.

Where she belongs.

"That had to be awkward for poor Ms. Blake, don't you think?" Dom asks, tutting like he actually cares. "From designer dresses and bidding wars to 'can I take your order.'"

"Do you ever listen to yourself?" I shake my head. "You're such a fucking asshole."

"Never up for debate, brother."

I stare for a moment. Dominick Taylor was a means to an end. A way to get the backing and donations I needed as quickly as possible. Given that last statement, I think his time in my life has come to its natural conclusion.

"No," I say with a frown. "I guess it wasn't."

I'm out of my chair and squeezing between tables before I know where I'm going, just following Mina's path because I have to talk to her. She's standing at the bar with her back to me, tapping her foot on the floor and her fingers on her thigh. I grab her arm and she squeals.

"Nathan!" She places a hand to her heart and exhales. "Are you trying to give me a heart attack?"

How have I gone so long without touching her? Without seeing her? Hearing her? I should have chased her down the second she left my office. I never should have let her leave.

"What happened to opening a business with Benjamin?" I bark, when what I want to know is what do I have to do to get you back in my life?

"Nothing happened." Mina draws her brows together and turns back to the bar. "We're moving ahead as planned."

I step closer—only a whisper of space between us—and lean in to make eye contact, forcing her to look at me. "Then why are you working here?"

A blonde woman with broad shoulders and watchful eyes drapes a towel over her shoulder as she approaches from the other side of the bar. Her gaze rakes me over and she doesn't look impressed. "Everything good, Mina?"

"It's fine, Nat." Mina waves her away. "We're good. I know him."

"Is there somewhere we can talk?" I lean even closer. "Privately?"

"I'm at work, Nathan. If you wanted to talk, you could have called or texted or stopped by my apartment or hell, even sent a letter. But now?" Mina shakes her head. "Now's not a good time."

I open my mouth to tell her I don't care about money, that I don't think she was in league with Fallon and I don't want her working as a waitress just to make ends meet, but my phone rings with a call.

Mina smiles sadly. "Saved by the bell."

I pull my phone out to silence it, but see Dad on the caller ID. Anyone else would have gone straight to voicemail but...

"I have to take this," I say to Mina. "It could be about Nick."

The defensiveness melts from Mina's posture. She reaches for me but pauses and crosses her arms instead. "Has there been any news?"

Her eyes meet mine and there she is. The woman I

love. The woman I'm tired of living without. The woman who seems more and more like she's been telling the truth.

"This could be it," I say, then accept the call, turning to lean my back to the bar. "Dad?"

"They found him, Nathan. They found Nick."

Relief washes over me and I sag, one hand to my heart as I exhale shakily. "Do we know anything? Is he okay?"

I hold Mina's gaze like a lifeline. She's smiling for me, looking as hopeful as I feel. The distance between us erased that easily.

"He's alive, but he's hurt pretty badly," Dad says. "Mom and I are on our way to Wyatt and Kara's if you want to meet us there."

I agree then end the call, releasing a long breath.

Mina puts a hand to my shoulder and I sigh, grateful for the comfort. "That doesn't look like completely good news."

"They found Nick," I murmur, eyes closed. "But he's hurt. Dad wants me to go to my uncle's..."

I'm pulled in two directions. I need to know more about Nick but I'm not ready to leave Mina. I never want to leave her again.

"Go," she urges. "You need to be with your family. I'll let Dom know what happened. You and me? We can talk when you're done."

I nod. "I'll call you as soon as I can," I promise, then rush for the door.

I leave The Depot and drive straight to Nick's parents' house, arriving at almost the same time as Angela, Garrett, Micah, and Ivy. We park behind my parents' car, share a quick greeting, then race up the steps to the front door. Uncle Wyatt lets us in, while Aunt Kara paces back and forth across the living room, phone to ear. "Okay," she says. "Okay. Thank you."

Her face is pale as she ends the call.

"They're rushing him to Bethesda instead of stopping in Germany." Her hands shake as she brushes hair out of her face. "His truck drove over a landmine and he was taken behind enemy lines. He's the only one that survived." Her voice falters and she seems older and smaller than I remember.

"When will he arrive in Bethesda?" asks Uncle Wyatt.

"Soon. I don't know. We can book a flight ourselves or maybe the military wants to pay for our tickets, which is silly but he was talking fast and I'm not—"

Aunt Kara covers her face, choking on sobs and her husband rushes to her side, pulling her close.

I turn to Angela, who looks stricken. Uncle Lucas strides through the door, back straight, shoulders square. "What do we know?"

"It's not good," Angela murmurs, then explains what we overheard to her father.

Lucas's face falls, his mouth going taut as he closes his eyes and nods. He pulls his daughter to him and presses a kiss to her forehead before crossing the room to place his hands on his brother's shoulder. "Don't worry about a thing. Forward me the name and number of your contact with the Marines. I'll be the liaison so all you have to do is take care of Nick. Let me handle everything else."

It's such a Hutton thing to do. Rush in. Take charge. Protect. Provide. It's the way we're built. All of us.

It's what I did with Blossom, what I wanted to do the second I learned Nick was missing. It's what I kept myself from doing with Mina at first. It wasn't until I accepted my need to take care of the people who matter that things started to feel real between us.

Suddenly, I feel less like a fool for the mistakes I made with Blossom. I did my best for her and maybe, someday, it'll mean something. Or maybe it won't. But in the meantime, I can take comfort knowing I was true to myself.

Mina's hopeful face flashes through my mind. I promised I'd call when I'm done with my family, and I have every intention of following through, but she was right when she said we need to be real and true and honest if this is going to work between us.

So, before I call her, there's something I have to do first.

FORTY-EIGHT

Mina

To say I'm distracted is an understatement. My mind is on Nathan. On how my heart spasmed when I realized he was the man sitting across from Dom. On the intensity surging between us when our eyes met. On the hope followed by fear dashing across his face when he answered the call from his father.

Nathan said he'd call as soon as he could, and my heart took him literally. Half my attention is on my phone while I fill orders even though I know he's too busy with family to be thinking of me.

As it should be.

Nat, the owner of The Depot who prefers to spend her evenings tending bar, stops me as I return from my last table. She's got Mama Bear energy and that is so what I need right now. "You doing okay, Mina?"

"I'm fine." I slide my tray onto the tray spot and do my best to conjure a convincing aura of fine as I grab the tubs of salt and pepper to refill the shakers in my section.

"You've been rattled since that man cornered you earlier." Nat leans her elbows on the bar, the picture of nonchalance. "Which is an understandable response. Being hemmed in by a man that big who looks at you the way he did. Anyone would be off after that."

"I'm sorry. I've had a hard time getting our conversation off my mind. He..." What am I supposed to say? Nat might be the first person I've talked to who doesn't seem like she's a fan of Fallon's blog. "He's kind of my boyfriend and we had a fight and we're not handling it well."

I'd say that about sums it up.

Nat waves off my apology. "Don't sweat it. We all have off days, especially when you're fighting with someone that intense." She leans against the bar with an understanding smile. "Tell you what. Why don't you stop by the office, grab your paycheck, and head on out. I'll finish your sidework for you."

That's the most welcome thing I've heard all night, but I don't want to take advantage of Nat's kindness. I refuse to be that person, so I grab a saltshaker off the bar and give it a shake to see if it needs filled. Yup. This one's definitely low.

"I don't want to be a problem," I say, twisting the lid off the big tub of salt. "I can finish my own stuff."

"Considering how distracted you've been, it'll be more of a problem if you stay," she replies with a pointed look at my hands. I glance down to discover I've poured pepper from the shaker in my hand into the large tub of salt. There isn't one thing I got right.

I'd love to argue with Nat, but don't really have a leg to stand on, so I thank her, then head home and climb into bed, replaying my conversation with Nathan while I fruitlessly chase sleep.

After a long night, I spend yet another distracted day at the office, then skedaddle on over to Shady Cove. Nat's Mama Bear energy is nice, but nowhere near a substitute for my actual mom. With everything going on, I really need her right now. I stop in the financial office to spend my first paycheck from The Depot on my way in. The walls are painted a cheery lemon with well-loved motivational posters hanging in sporadic intervals. Cats telling me to hang in there.

Prancing goats reminding me to live, laugh, and love, or to hope, believe, and dream.

"Hello, Glenda!" I singsong as I walk through the door. "I've got money for you!"

Instead of the insta-grin I'm used to, Glenda looks concerned. "Well, hey there," she says, her perfectly shaped brows drawing together. "I didn't expect to see you today."

I'm not sure what to do with that statement. "Just thought I'd keep chiseling away at that bill," I offer weakly.

"Oh. Right." Glenda gives me a look I can't decipher. "There's, uh...there's nothing to chisel at."

I scrunch up my brow. "There's definitely lots to..." In my confusion I mime a hammer and chisel. "I still owe you guys a ton of money."

Dear God. Why am I this way? Yours truly, Mina Blake.

"Not as of this morning." Glenda shakes her head and stabs her keyboard to wake up her computer, then leans close as her fingers fly over the keys. "I'm definitely seeing a zero balance. You won't owe anything for...three months." The corners of her mouth twitch, like she's holding back a smile.

What in the name of fairy godmother guardian angels is going on? Did Glenda work some magic on my behalf?

"How is that possible?" I lean over her desk, trying to read the numbers on her screen for myself. "I was significantly behind..."

"If I were you, I'd count your lucky stars for...um... accounting errors, yeah, accounting errors, and come see me in three months." The gleam in Glenda's eyes makes me think I'm missing something, but I'm too stunned to ask. I say my goodbyes and wander into the hallway, pausing to look over my shoulder at the woman who's definitely grinning from ear to ear.

Something's going on. And whatever it is, she's in on it. Or in charge of the whole thing.

"Don't forget to stop in and see your mother," she adds with a wink.

What a strange thing to say. Why would I forget the whole reason I'm here?

"I won't," I mumble, lifting a hand before heading down the maze of halls to find Mom's room, then pull up short when I hear her laughing.

"That's not the best part though!" she says, between giggles. Actual giggles! Who is she talking to? That handsome man we passed in the hallway? The one who made her blush?

I lean a little closer, hoping for a peek.

"If that's not the best part," replies...*Nathan?!* "You need to finish the story now."

I poke my head through the doorway, so dazed I

can't speak. Mom and Nathan are sitting at her table, each cradling a mug she made in art therapy. She has her hand on his arm and the biggest smile on her face while she giggles, wiping tears from her eyes. And him? He looks completely at home sitting next to my mother. Was everything that happened over the last couple months a set up? Were the two of them in cahoots the entire time? That doesn't make any sense, but neither does what I've walked into.

"Hello?" I manage and my two favorite faces in the world turn to me with matching grins.

"Speak of the devil," Mom says, smiling widely.

"Why didn't I know you were afraid of the teacup ride at carnivals?" Nathan's eyes are warm like springtime and feel like coming home.

"Why didn't I know you were friends with my mother?" I ask in return, then glare at Mom. "And why are you telling him the teacup ride story? So I was scared and hugged a tree when the ride ended. It's not that big of a deal."

Mom waves off my concerns about a story she finds charming and I find mortifying. "Nathan stopped by to introduce himself and let me tell you what, you have yourself a wonderful man here."

Hold on.

Wonderful?

I have a wonderful man?

"How did we get to wonderful?" I wander a little deeper into the room, still epically confused. "Wasn't it just yesterday you were sorry to be right about all his red flags?"

"We talked about those." Mom pats Nathan's hand with the motherly understanding I came here to receive. "And now that I understand, well, my last statement stands. You have a wonderful man."

The last I heard, I didn't *have* anything.

I pull up a chair and sit at the table, my hands in my lap, my heart in my stomach, and my eyes on Nathan. "I thought we called a time out until I got my finances in order."

"We did." He nods confidently. "But that shouldn't be a problem anymore."

Suddenly, Glenda's not-so-poker-face makes sense. "Did you pay my mother's medical bills?"

I don't know whether I'm frustrated or relieved. Knowing Mom is taken care of is a weight off my shoulders, but I was in the middle of solving the problem myself...to prove to Nathan I wasn't using him for his money, no less. How does him paying off her medical bills get us any closer to okay?

"I spoke to your mom about it first," he says, like that clears it all up. "I didn't want to overstep."

"Oh, well." I throw up my hands and sit back. "That fixes everything then.

Mom cradles her mug with a knowing smile. "After he explained, I really couldn't put up much of a fight."

"Anyone feel like sharing that explanation with me?" My gaze bounces between two smiling faces before I finally settle on Nathan's. "Walking out of your office, not knowing if I would see you again, that was the hardest thing I've ever done, but it was right. I know that down to my core. I needed to solve my financial problems myself to prove your friend was wrong about me. Why are you solving them for me anyway?"

Nathan takes my hand, elbows on knees, eyes on mine. "Last night, with my family, it was hard. Nick's hurt pretty badly and his parents were an absolute mess, trying to make sense of it all. Then my uncle Lucas showed up. He spoke calmly. Acted decisively. His brother needed him, and he stepped right up and took care of everything. That's just what my family does. We protect. We provide. We do for others when they can't do for themselves. And that's the way it should be, as long as you have the right people in your life. If I'm being true to myself, that's who I want to be for you."

"But the whole Blossom thing, and then the Fallon thing, making it look like I was doing the whole Blossom thing…"

"This is nothing like that." Nathan brings my hand to his lips. "Blossom is a user and a taker. You are a giver. Even down to the space you keep giving me to get my shit together. I'm better with you. You feel like sunshine, like warmth and goodness and I can be true to myself with you. While everything about our break made logical sense, it didn't take those details into account. I love you, Mina. I can't spend another day without you."

"See what I mean about you having a wonderful man?" Mom pats my hand in that motherly way I've been craving.

Tears well in my eyes. The room shimmers before one rolls down my cheek. My hands are still. My heart pounding. My brain filled with the static of confusion. And then I meet Nathan's eyes and see his love for me shining through.

"I don't know what to say. I love you too. And I miss you. But I can't let you pay for Mom's treatments. It's just not right."

"I only paid for the next three months. Just enough to give you some breathing room while you decide what you want to do. If I had my way, you'd quit the waitressing job tonight, but I'm going to leave that up to you."

"I can pay you back as soon as—"

Nathan puts a finger to my lips. "Let's not worry about that. Not yet. Let's just agree that we're good for each other and be happy we've survived our first fight."

"I'm not sure I can stop worrying about that," I mumble against the weight of his finger. "This is all happening too fast—"

Nathan presses his palm to my mouth. "I overreacted, Mina. You're jumping through hoops to prove something I already know, so it's really not too fast at all. If you ask me, it took way too long for me to get here and I'm sorry for that."

I glance at Mom who bobs her head, then back to Nathan.

"When I remove my hand," he says, "I'm going to kiss you, something I've been wanting to do since this all happened. Will you please stop arguing with me and kiss me back?"

I nod, my eyes on his. And then he stands, takes my hands to pull me into his arms and presses his lips to mine, while my mother claps and cheers.

EPILOGUE

Mina

"Your family get togethers are super casual," I say to Nathan from the depths of our closet. "Why are we dressing up tonight?"

I poke my head through the doorway and catch my boyfriend grinning to himself as he lifts his shirt collar and drapes a red tie around his neck. When we first met, I wondered how The Prince of Darkness grew up in a family that feels like sunshine. In the last year, he's become the light of my life. The two of us moved into his villain's lair on the cove as soon as it was finished and have done our best to fill it with the best feelings, the best memories, the best energy ever since. It's a massive improvement from my apartment at Lime Tree

Bay, with its outdated tile and chipped grout. Sometimes I still can't believe I live here. Nathan gave his old house to Mom, who protested, then cried, and now drinks a glass of wine on the patio every night, texting me pictures of the sunset like a proud momma.

"It's my birthday. If I want to dress up, we dress up." Nathan's gaze wanders my body, and he smirks appreciatively. "You should wear your black dress. The one with the neckline I like."

"You mean the one that shows all the cleavage?" I ask with an arch to my brow.

"I've never felt more understood." Nathan drops a wink my way, his deft fingers working his tie into place. "What can I say, HM? You get me and I like it." He takes my hands and pulls me into his arms, his palms trailing down my back to cup my ass.

I lean into him, smiling against his chest as I remember last year's birthday party. "I can't believe there was a time I was offended by that move."

"Hey, now." Nathan pulls back, jaw dropped. "Don't you dare rewrite history. You were the one who grabbed my butt. Not the other way around."

I snake my hands down to squeeze both delicious butt cheeks. "Can you blame me?"

He nuzzles my neck, going straight for that place below my jaw that sends shivers of delight down my spine. "On second thought," he says, sliding his hands under my shirt, "I don't think you should be wearing anything at all,"

"I'm not sure your family would appreciate that."

"Like I said, it's my birthday. I get what I want."

We arrive at Nathan's parents' a little late and a touch disheveled. He wraps an arm around my waist and guides me up the walk and I can't help but smile to myself. A year ago, I was shocked by the simple elegance of the home, then utterly embarrassed to be the only one who dressed up for the evening. I couldn't stand the thought of touching the man beside me and now, I can't stand the thought of not touching him.

A lot can change in a year.

Nathan pulls the door open for me and we step through the foyer to find his family waiting. Everyone's in red. Dresses, ties, shoes, earrings, bracelets, jewelry. They're dressed to kill, with me in my simple black dress. Even Mom is wearing red, standing with Collin and Harlow West, her new best friends, and her boyfriend, John McFadden, Mr. Silverfox from the hallway at Shady Cove.

"I thought we'd mix it up this year," Nathan whispers. "Especially after I was such a dick last year."

Before I can reply, we're surrounded by his family. Everyone's talking at once, wishing Nathan happy birthday and passing out hugs like candy.

Nathan's cousin Nick thumps him on the back, with his latest girlfriend Amanda waiting to give a hug of her own. She's sweet and funny, but Nick's track record suggests it's best not to get attached.

Nicholas Hutton is not the man he was.

Dark circles stand out under his eyes and his smile seems forced. While his body is mostly healed, his spirit seems muted. He's never complained. He's never said much of anything really, other than to insist he's fine and tell us to stop worrying. After his medical discharge, Nick's been untethered and unsure. Nathan's sure he'll find his way again, but I can't help but think of my dad.

"Another year older," Nick says with a wry twist of his lips.

"And wiser." Nathan waggles his eyebrows.

"Let's not put the cart before the horse on that one." Nick gives a weak smile then disappears with Amanda in search of a drink.

"I wish you'd gotten to know him better before the accident," Nathan says to me once he's out of earshot.

Garrett crosses his arms over his chest. "I keep hoping Amanda will help get him back on track."

"And Tillie before her, and Aisya before her." Micah sighs, hands in pockets, shoulders slumped.

Angela stares after Nick, shaking her head with a long, sad smile. "I was shocked when he started dating anyone who wasn't your sister." She glances at her husband, obviously distraught.

"I don't know why everyone thought they'd end up together." Garrett huffs an exasperated laugh. "Charlie lives across the country."

"So did you when we first met." Angela gives him a look that says, 'so there.'

"Well, he's seeing someone. She's seeing someone. And at the rate he's going through girlfriends, I think it's time everyone stops being surprised they're not seeing each other and be happy Charlie dodged a Nick-shaped bullet. I love the guy. I do. But he needs to get his shit together before he's good enough for my little sister."

We talk. We eat. We sing happy birthday and laugh until we cry when they bring out a cake with so many candles the smoke alarm goes off. Once that hubbub dies down, Nathan stands and clears his throat.

"So many of you asked what I wanted for my birthday this year," he begins. "And I replied the way I always do. I have everything I could ever want," he says, and half the crowd recites the words with him.

"I have a wonderful family and a job that gives me purpose, a beautiful girlfriend." Nathan looks at me with those soulful eyes. A dreamy sigh floats through those listening with a quiet "Awww..." coming from my mother.

"This year, though?" Nathan continues. "I find myself in the strange position of wanting something I don't have." He smiles softly at me with so much love and respect on his face, tears unexpectedly well in my eyes. "A wife. A family of my own. A future with the love of my life bringing out the best in me day after day. At Micah's wedding, I was sure love was a trap and I'd never be stupid enough to get married. But now, after you, that's the only thing I want in the world."

Gasps sound around the room and somewhere, Micah whispers, "I knew it!"

I place a hand to my heart as Nathan kneels beside me.

"Mina," he says in a quiet voice, just for me. "Will you marry me?"

In his hand is a black box, opened to show an exquisite ring, simple yet dazzling, shimmering spectacularly in the light.

Tears well in my eyes and I glance up to see my

mother grinning through tears of her own. Nathan's dad wraps an arm around his wife's shoulders and pulls her close, both smiling proudly.

I slide out of my chair and kneel beside Nathan, nodding as I throw my arms around him and nuzzle into his neck. "I don't know what I did to deserve you," I whisper, "but I'll spend the rest of my life trying to earn it."

"Is that a yes?"

I nod into his shoulder and then he's sliding the ring onto my finger and kissing me while his family claps and cheers.

The first time Nathan kissed me, it was like my favorite time of day, gentle and unassuming, but filled with expectation and the promise of something wonderful. I didn't want to like it as much as I did.

The second time he kissed me, it was inevitable. We were drawn to each other like magnets, incapable of ignoring the pull. It broke the definition of what we were and as much as I loved it, it left me confused.

Today, his kiss is sunshine after a hurricane. The first cool breeze on a humid August evening. It's sweet and welcome and something I never knew I needed but don't want to live without.

Just like him.

After all that's happened between us, there's one thing I know for sure:

I'll never stop loving Nathan West.

Want more time with Nathan and Mina? Sign up for my newsletter using the QR code or tapping this link and I'll send you a bonus scene right away! Already subscribed? Find a link to bonus content at the bottom of my latest newsletter.

BONUS SCENE

Mina

"Oh my God! Babe!" I lurch to my feet, propelled out of my office chair by excitement, then stop and reread the email to make sure I'm not dreaming. Or hallucinating. Or have somehow become untethered from reality.

Dear Mrs. West,

I'm delighted to inform

you that you've been selected as Architectural Digest's "One to Watch"...

Nope.

Not hallucinating.

I pinch myself.

Definitely felt that.

Not dreaming either.

And unless Nathan shows up wearing a kilt or with the head of a talking cat, it's safe to assume I'm still tethered to reality.

Dear God. Are you freaking kidding me with all the blessings?! Yours always and forever, Mina West.

"Babe!" My hands shake. I take one step forward then pause to reread the first line. You know. Just in case.

Nathan appears in my studio doorway, eyes wild. "Mina! What's wrong? Are you okay?"

"It's happening. Or I guess, it's happened!" I wave my phone in my husband's direction. "I didn't...I mean...who woulda thought?"

"Who woulda thought what?

Mina, you're scaring me a little." Nathan's face contorts through a memorable performance of half smile, half concern. "I can't tell if you're excited or dying."

"I'm so excited I might die. I just got an email from *Architectural Digest*. They..." I open my phone and start to read from the screen, but then thrust the thing into his hands instead. "Here. You read. Tell me I'm not losing my mind."

Nathan takes the phone like he's afraid a bomb might go off, then reads. Concern gives way to amazement, then his eyes meet mine. The pride shining in them has my hands covering my swelling heart.

"It's about damn time!" He crosses the room and wraps me in his strong embrace, swaying ever so slightly as his hands press into my back. "I am so proud of you. So happy for you. Not at all surprised, but so damn proud."

"To the fabulous Mina West!" Angela raises her glass, and the rest of the crew follows suit. "We've known she was one to watch since the day she showed up to your birthday in that red dress. It's about damn time the rest of the world sees her the way we do!"

"That's what I said!" Nathan cries amidst a chorus of "here, heres," "hell yeahs," and lifted drinks.

I beam from my place at the head of a huge table at The Pact. Angela, Garrett, Micah, Ivy, Nick and his latest girlfriend Sabrina smile back at me. Since the wedding, I've gotten incredibly close with Nathan's cousins. These people aren't just family, they're my best friends. Though I expect poor Sabrina won't be around much longer.

"Oh!" Angela puts her hand on her swollen tummy. "The baby's kicking. She must be excited for Mina too!"

Garrett puts his drink down and places his hand on his wife's belly. The smile that lifts his lips is pure bliss, which says a lot because Garrett isn't a pure bliss kind of guy. "I didn't think fatherhood would be my thing," he says, reverently, "but this has been the coolest experience. I can't wait for the day I finally get to meet my little girl."

Micah nods knowingly. "I've loved every minute of being a dad."

"Come on." Nick rolls his eyes and sits back, huffing in disgust. "Every minute? The diapers? The crying? The snot and drool? You like the late nights and loss of freedom, do you?"

The rest of us exchange worried glances. Once Nick gets on a roll, it can be hard to switch him off.

"It's worth it, man." Micah leans forward, like maybe he can show Nick what he's feeling through proximity. "I know it doesn't sound like it, but it is. You'll understand once you're a father."

Nick scoffs. "Not gonna hold my breath on that one."

There's a moment of awkward silence while everyone worries about what to say next. Dancing around his moods can be like walking a tightrope. One wrong move can have disastrous results. I've found it's best to move the conversation away from him when he's like this.

"What about you guys?" Angela asks, physically turning away from Nick to look at me, clearly having read my mind. "Are there any pregnancy plans in your future? Nathan always did want a big family."

While I understand the reason she chose this topic, I wish she'd have gone in a different direction. Nathan and I have talked about kids and I know he's ready to start our family, but my career is just starting to take off. I want a baby too, but not when I'd have to split my attention between motherhood and Bancroft and Blake.

Nathan gives an angelic smile and takes my hand, patting it gently. "The timing's not right for us," he says to his cousin, while silently communicating to me that he's totally okay with our decision to wait.

"What are you talking about?" Angela squawks. "The timing's perfect! If you start now, all the cousins can be close, like we were."

Never one to skip an opportunity to pile on Nathan, Micah leans his elbows on the table with the shit-eatingest grin. "You know how much you hated being the youngest. Never being as fast or tall as the rest of us. Always feeling left out..."

"I wasn't the youngest for long," Nathan says. "I had brothers and a sister and so many younger cousins to boss around. Besides. A little humility was good for me."

"Like you were the one with the ego problem." Ivy laughs gently and jerks her chin at her husband.

"I want kids," I blurt, eager to take the focus off Nathan since I'm the reason we're waiting. "I always wished I had a big family growing up and after being part of this one, I'd love a kid or three. It's just..."

Bancroft and Blake Design has taken off. We have people reaching out for our services from all over the country. Benjamin and I have actually discussed starting a waitlist. After this story about me in *Architectural Digest*, we'll probably have to implement it. Which is wonderful. It's more than wonderful. It's a dream come true. As it stands, I'm traveling a lot. Sometimes Nathan comes with, and we sightsee when I'm not with a client or at a job site. Sometimes he stays home and focuses on work or hangs out with his cousins, trying to snap Nick out of his funk.

All of this is great, except I don't see how I can do the whole pregnancy and mommy thing without sacrificing work. And I'm currently a big fan of my life. Am I ready to give up on all that?

"It's just not the right time for us to start a family." Nathan finishes my sentence for me, pats my hand, and brings it to his lips. Something in the gesture sets off a chain reaction of epiphanies around the table. I watch understanding pop off on face after face until we get to poor Sabrina who's staring at Nick's grimacing profile, probably concluding that his sour attitude doesn't fit into her vision for her life.

Angela shoots us an apologetic glance. "The timing has to be right," she says with an understanding smile. "It's not like adopting kittens. Parenthood is a big commitment."

We finish the night laughing and stumble out of the bar into a gorgeous night. The moon is full and high and bright, casting everything in shimmering silver. Nathan's hand is warm and strong on my back. There's nothing to do. Nowhere to be. It's just the two of us in this perfect moment where anything could happen. I turn my face skywards and inhale deeply, like I can breathe in the perfection.

Nathan slides his hand from my back to my wrist then tugs me closer. "This is one of my most favorite memories," he says, brushing my cheek with his thumb.

"What's that?" I lean into his touch and close my eyes. He is the best feeling I've ever had. I just want to be here a while and revel in it. When I open my eyes, I find my husband staring down at me with warmth glittering in his gaze. Gone is the frozen barbed wire and steel skyscrapers I added to his mood board when we first met. Gone are the thorns and brambles. He's warm and golden and sweet and wonderful.

Not the villain. The prince.

"This is where we had our first kiss," Nathan says with a smile.

"Does it count though? Since it was just for show?"

"Of course it counts!" His eyes go wide. "Remember the whole, 'I'm not paying you for the kiss, the kiss was for me, speech I gave the next day? I played it off like I did it because we had an audience, but I had been wanting to do that for days."

I grin. "I was so confused after that. It was like the perfect kiss. A million-dollar kiss." I wave my hand through the air. "But you showed up so grumpy and rude the next morning."

"We've had a lot of perfect kisses since then."

"Maybe because we're the perfect couple."

"I wonder if we could do it again?" Nathan leans close, brushing his nose against mine. "Another million-dollar kiss."

"I've been standing here for the last ten minutes hoping you'd try," I murmur, then press my lips to his as Angela wolf whistles on her way out of the bar.

"I've been thinking," I say, plonking a cup of coffee on the table for Nathan. "About what Angela and Micah were saying at The Pact the other night."

"About you being awesome?"

"No, the other thing." I pour a little milk into my mug. Then a little more. Then a dash more. "About starting a family," I say, reaching for the sugar like I didn't just open the door on a topic we both agreed was closed.

"Mina." Nathan sits back, shaking his head. "Honey..."

"No. Let me say this." I lift my chin and fold my hands on the counter. "I've heard the family legends. Little Nator Tot decreeing he wants seven kids and holding onto that dream for years. You're a caregiver by nature. Of course you want a family. You deserve a family. And I want one too. A little you running around here? I mean..." I give in to a crooked smile as I imagine chubby legs and bare feet slapping against the tile in a wobbly toddly dash through the kitchen.

I hurry on before Nathan can remind me we decided the time's not right. "The cool thing about my job is that it's super flexible. I do most of my work out of the studio here at home, so I can juggle mamahood and work. Because you know, Angela is right. The best time to start is now. Everyone else is having babies, so there will be lots of cousins to play with. Sure, it'll be difficult to balance everything, but I'm used to doing hard things. And knowing how happy it'd make you? Plus, the fact that I want a family too? That'll make it worth it."

Nathan swipes his coffee off the table and sits back, an odd look on his face. "Are you finished?"

I can't read his expression.

I can't decipher his tone.

I expected some pushback, but...did I actually make him mad?

I clear my throat. "No. I have one more thing to add. Thank you for your time and consideration." I wink at the line I used the night I drunk-texted the group chat and hope he catches the reference. The soft chuckle and slow shake of his head says he does.

"Now that you've said your piece, I'd like to ask for your time and consideration on my vision for this whole starting a family thing." Nathan takes a long swig of coffee, eying me over the rim of his mug. "Are you ready for this?" he asks after he swallows.

He looks so serious. So intense. So not like the easygoing version of Nathan West I've come to expect.

"I don't know." I tuck a lock of hair behind my ear, then swipe my coffee off the counter and join my husband at the table. "Am I?"

"Let's just jump in there and see. I also get a little

misty-eyed at the thought of a miniature version of you running around here. As everyone has been so quick to remind me lately, being a father to a herd of children has been high on my list since I was a little boy. And, like you, I agree with Angela. With my cousins starting families of their own, and my brothers and sister sure to follow suit soon, now is the right time to join in the fun. But that's where we stop agreeing and start disagreeing."

I cock my head in question. "What else is there to agree about? We both want kids. We both think it would be a good time to start on the cousin front. Help me out here. What do you disagree with?"

"I disagree with you being the one to sacrifice your life, your wants, your dreams. I disagree with you thinking you can work from home and be a mom and be happy with the amount of time you can give either venture."

I hold up my hands, shaking my head in defeat. "I don't know what else to do then, my love."

"I'll be the one to pare down my career." Nathan grins as his statement hangs between us. I exhale, jaw dropped, trying to decipher how real he's being. He's devoted his life to the foundation.

"I can work from home just as easily as you can." Nathan leans forward, elbows on table, eyes lighting up as he grips his coffee mug in both hands. "Easier even, since I don't have to fly out to meet clients. I can lean on Rita a lot more. I might even promote someone to take my place."

I shake my head, like that will help me rattle some processing power loose. "But Maisie—"

"Is thrilled with the idea. I've been thinking about this for a while and brought it up to her after our conversation at The Pact."

"Are you sure this is what you want? I know how important your job is."

"A thousand percent sure. I'm ready for kids. I've accomplished what I set out to accomplish career-wise. You still have a lot of kickin' ass and takin' names ahead of you. Of course, you'd still have to do the whole pregnancy thing, which can be a lot. So, if the timing still isn't right, that's fine. And if you want to wait until you can do the whole primary caregiver thing, that's fine too. We can talk about it. We can postpone until you're really ready. This has to be right for both of us."

"I kind of always saw myself doing the mommy thing—"

"That's fine." Nathan sits back, holding out his hands, so sure he knows what I'm about to say. "We can wait until your ready—"

"I'm ready now." Tears shimmer in my vision as I feel the truth of those words down to my roots. I want to start a family with Nathan. Enough that I'm willing to step back from work to make it happen. The fact that he's just as willing proves how perfect he is for me.

"You promise me this is what you want to do?" I ask. "You're sure?"

"So sure." Nathan's grin reminds me of Garrett's the other night at The Pact. Pure bliss. Coming from the man I once referred to as The Prince of Darkness, that says all I need to know.

"Then I'm onboard with the idea, as long as this isn't a sacrifice." I hold his gaze, begging him to be honest with me.

Nathan steeples his fingers under his chin. "Let's see, just as the entry to this little project I get to make love to you. Score one for me."

"That's a point in my favor too," I say with a grin.

Nathan nods his agreement. "Then, I get to watch you do the whole glowy pregnancy thing and I can be the doting husband who renovates a spare room into a nursery in between trips to the store for ice cream."

"Again, that sounds like another win for me. Doting husband. Unlimited ice cream…"

"Then, as if that's not enough, there's a tiny little person who looks like you and me who I get to take care of and teach to play the guitar and take to the beach and burp and feed and…" Nathan shakes his head. "Does that sound like a sacrifice to you? Because it doesn't to me."

"Every time I think I couldn't possibly love you more, you show me another facet of yourself and I'm left awestruck. You're an amazing man, Nathan West."

"Whatever I am, I'm better with you. Now. Are we a go on our entry to parenthood?"

"I'm ready if you are." My husband takes my hand and pulls me into his arms. His fingers thread into my hair as his lips press to mine. I drape my arms over his shoulders and press my body to his and feel the long length of his erection growing between us.

"You better fucking believe I'm ready, HM," Nathan growls.

And then his mouth finds mine and my fingers fumble with his pants and it's just him and me raw and honest and real, stepping into the next phase of life together.

NATHAN'S PARENTS AND FAMILY

Did you love Nathan and Mina? You'll adore his parents' story!

Meet Nathan's parents in BEYOND DREAMS.

You know that feeling when the famous musician you're totally crushing on shows up at your brother's wedding dressed as Elvis?

Really? Huh. Guess it's just me...

Collin West isn't just hot. And he's not just 'the next big thing,' either. He's the biggest thing to happen to music since...music. He's got heart. And soul. And the most adorable ginger hair that's somehow always a little mussed. Add in his bangin' body and bedroom eyes and it's easy to see why the whole world loves him.

And he wants me.

Harlow Hutton. Not-so-secret lover of all things Collin West. Dreamer of big dreams. Thinker of deep thoughts. He falls into my life like a fairy tale, whisking me away on a champagne and glitter adventure around the world. London. Paris. Rome. It's a dream come true...

But every princess has a villain. Throw in some demons from Collin's past and our dream might actually be a nightmare...

One thing's for sure, hiding in the swirl of music and passion, is the glimmer of a happily-ever-after bigger than I ever imagined possible.

I only hope we don't get burned in the process...

This standalone contemporary romance is chock full of heart, soul, and all the feels you're looking for!

If you love strong characters who fight for what they believe in, hot musicians in cheap disguises, and four, scowlingly sexy, protective older brothers in tuxedos, one-click now!

Check out BEYOND DREAMS now!

Meet Angela and Garrett in FATE.

He shouldn't have kissed me. But I shouldn't have liked it.

Garrett Cooper is grumpy. Bossy. Rude. Sparks fly every time we're in the same room—and not the good kind. While I'm trying to brighten the mood, he's dismissing me with a roll of his eyes.

One thing's for sure. Garrett and me? We would never work.

But there's the problem...

He's my last, best chance to save my family's hotel. He waltzes into our business meeting—grinning like a Bond villain—and verbally eviscerates me in front of my father and uncle. I try to see the good in everyone, but the only thing this guy has going for him is dark hair, a rugged jawline, and black slacks that hug a fantastic rear end.

I convince him to one last meeting. Just the two of us. A do-over, if you will. Instead of focusing on business, the sparks between us catch fire.

Tall, dark, and evil has never been my thing, but staring into those stormy eyes makes me feel equal parts alive and uncomfortable. Nothing good comes from mixing business with pleasure, especially not with a man like this. Intense. Glowering. And holding the lifeline for my family.

Before I know it, inappropriate text conversations become an X-rated phone call I will never forget. Suddenly, this grumpy, growly man is feeding me strawberries in bed and what am I supposed to do with that?

He doesn't do relationships. He doesn't even do connection.

And I'm supposed to be closing a deal, not enjoying that trick he does with his belt.

I have to put an end to this.

I will put an end to this.

Maybe after one last kiss...

Check out FATE now!

Meet Micah and Ivy in FIRE

He was my first and I thought he'd be my last. Now he's asking for a second chance.

Micah Hutton is charming. Sweet. Confident. And his page in the shirtless fireman calendar for charity? Trust me, November has never been hotter. But like Grandma says: it's never the angels who look like sin.

Micah promised he'd love me forever. And I believed him, enough to give myself to him the night before my parents dragged me across the country, tearing us apart. He broke my heart—and his promise—by disappearing the moment I learned I was pregnant.

Seven years later, I'm back in my hometown, staring at my first love, watching his heart break as he meets a little girl who looks just like him. A little girl he swears he never knew existed.

He thinks I kept our baby a secret, but why would I do that? I told him as soon as I found out, certain he'd be at my side the very next day.

Micah says he's ready to be a father, but am I ready to open my heart and let him back in? Does he deserve that second chance?

Check out FIRE now!

THE HUTTONS

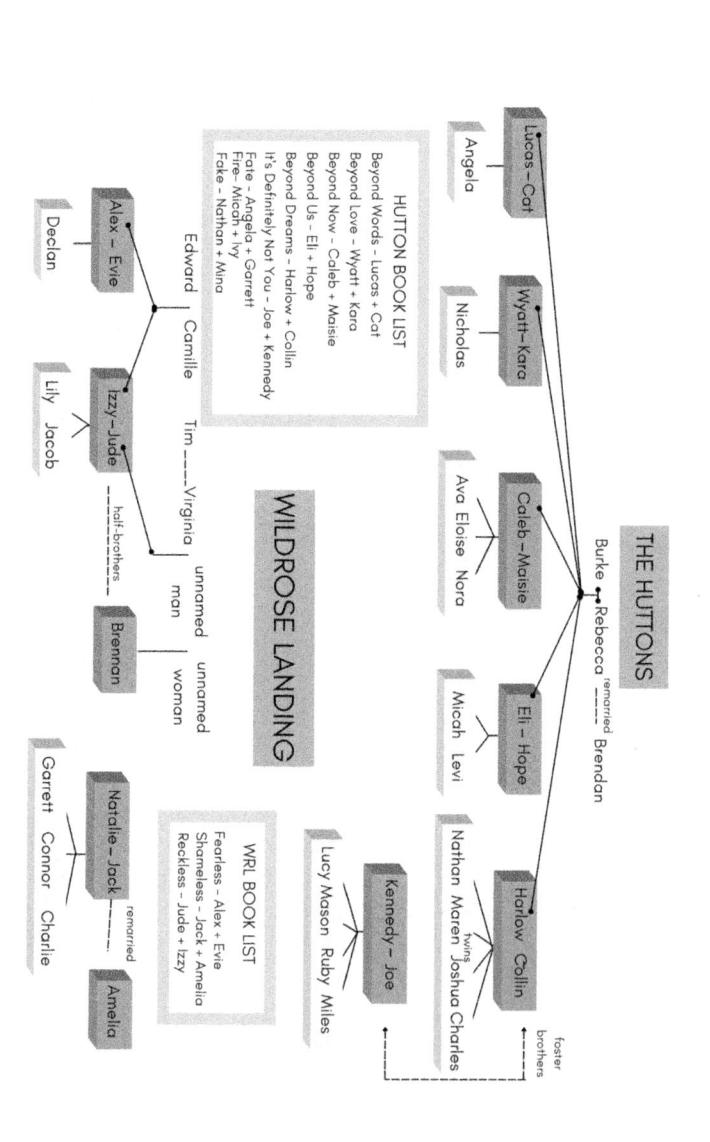

Burke ↔ Rebecca —remarried— Brendan

Lucas — Cat
- Angela
- Nicholas

Wyatt — Kara

Caleb — Maisie
- Ava
- Eloise
- Nora

Eli — Hope
- Micah
- Levi

Harlow — Collin
- Nathan, Maren (twins)
- Joshua
- Charles

HUTTON BOOK LIST
- Beyond Words – Lucas + Cat
- Beyond Love – Wyatt + Kara
- Beyond Now – Caleb + Maisie
- Beyond Us – Eli + Hope
- Beyond Dreams – Harlow + Collin
- It's Definitely Not You – Joe + Kennedy
- Fate – Angela + Garrett
- Fire – Micah + Ivy
- Fate – Nathan + Mina

WILDROSE LANDING

Edward — Camille
Tim ----- Virginia — unnamed man

Alex — Evie
- Declan

Izzy — Jude
- Lily
- Jacob

Brenan (half-brothers with Izzy-Jude's children) — unnamed woman

Natalie — Jack —remarried— Amelia
- Garrett
- Connor
- Charlie

Kennedy — Joe
- Lucy
- Mason
- Ruby
- Miles

foster brothers (Kennedy/Joe ↔ Harlow/Collin)

WRL BOOK LIST
- Fearless – Alex + Evie
- Shameless – Jack + Amelia
- Reckless – Jude + Izzy

A NOTE ON CHRONIC FATIGUE SYNDROME

A younger version of me used to hear people talk about Chronic Fatigue Syndrome and think, "Yeah. So? I've been really frickin' tired before too."

Then, at the beginning of 2023, I found myself bedbound. Unable to think. Incapable of holding a conversation or watching TV.

'Fatigue' is a woefully inadequate descriptor for this profoundly debilitating disease.

We've all been really frickin' tired.

Not all of us have been completely disabled by it.

Let's start with some dreary data:

Myalgic encephalomyelitis/chronic fatigue syndrome (ME/CFS), is a serious, chronic, complex, and systemic disease associated with neurological, immunological, autonomic, and energy metabolism dysfunction

The late William Reeves, MD, former head of Viral Diseases at the CDC said, "The level of functional impairment in people who suffer from CFS is comparable to multiple sclerosis, AIDS, end-stage renal failure and chronic obstructive pulmonary disease."

According to Yale Medicine, 75% of ME/CFS patients are too ill to work, and a quarter of patients are unable to leave their homes or, in some cases, their beds. Some physicians caring for ME/CFS patients say it's one of the most disabling illnesses <u>they've ever seen</u>.

836,000 to 2.5 million Americans have ME/CFS. At least one-quarter of individuals with ME/CFS are bedbound or housebound at some point in the disease and most never regain their pre-disease level of functioning.

To date, research into ME/CFS has been dramatically underfunded. <u>One paper</u> suggests the disease burden of ME/CFS is double that of HIV/AIDS and over half that of breast cancer. The authors of the papers also found that to be commensurate with disease burden, NIH funding would need to increase roughly 14-fold.

If you'd like more information on the signs and symptoms of ME/CFS, start here:

https://www.cdc.gov/me-cfs/hcp/clinical-overview/index.html

https://www.cdc.gov/me-cfs/signs-symptoms/index.html

In my personal experience, receiving a diagnosis was difficult, as there isn't a test to confirm ME/CFS. It's more a diagnosis of exclusion. There also isn't a known cure, and when a strongly independent woman suddenly finds herself unable to drive to her own doctor appointments hears something like that, it can be a tad disheartening.

However, under the supervision of my doctor and specialists, and with the damn near heroic support of my husband, I've come a long way, baby.

Between physical therapy under the careful eye of a specialist, slowly increasing my activity level (at one point, this meant adding 10 minutes of writing or reading every week or two), overhauling my diet and supplementation, and embracing therapy even when it brought up things I didn't like, I've completely overhauled my life.

A year ago, I couldn't drive. I couldn't walk to the end of my street. I couldn't follow the plot of a television show. I spent my days in bed, away from my husband and children, deeply lonely and completely dependent on others.

Now, I've driven to other states. I've written a book. I've gone on bike rides and started jogging—then stopped, because yuck! I'm learning French and how to play the guitar. I've made two quilts and some terribly misshapen pants.

I can't say I have my life back. There are too many changes to say that.

But I have made myself a new life.

And it's a good one.

The people who consider themselves cured of ME/CFS/long COVID recognized they wouldn't come through this without profound change, both internally and externally.

Diet.

Exercise.

Medication.

Supplementation.

Breathwork.

Meditation.

Spirituality/religion.

The removal of toxic people.

Therapy.

Recognizing limitations.

If you are suffering from cfs, long Covid, or this strange assortment of symptoms that no one understands, you can live again. You'll have to fight for it. You'll have to change for it. But you can do it.

There are places on the internet that talk about this disease as if it will forever hold you back. They say there's no cure and will fight anyone who claims otherwise.

Stay away from those places and listen to the recovery stories.

After all, you become who you surround yourself with.

Looking for help?

These resources positively impacted my progress. Please take everything with a grain of salt and talk to your doctor before implementing anything new.

https://www.youtube.com/@RaelanAgle
https://www.youtube.com/@cfsrecovery
Never Finished by David Goggins

Would you like to learn more?

Watch the documentary Unrest here: https://www.unrest.film/watch

Popular YouTuber Physics Girl has chronicled her battle with CFS.

Find her videos here:
https://www.youtube.com/@physicsgirl/videos

ACKNOWLEDGMENTS

To my husband—My love. My life. My reason. There are no words to express the appreciation I have for you. The way you've supported me. Challenged me. Loved me. Last year tested us. My health failed and you did not. You held me up while supporting our family and helped me put the pieces of myself back together again. Each year I think I've come to understand the true power of love and vulnerability and then you show me that there's more, more, more... Your fingerprints are all over this book. Like me, it's better because of it.

To my children—I love you deeply. Thank you for showing me how much you love me in return.

To Dr. Sandra Small—I deeply appreciate your impact on my life. Thank you for showing up for me week after week.

To—Linda, Nickiann, Kieran, Candy, and Suzanne. You ladies are brilliant. And you somehow manage to deal with me and all my complexities. So, you know, you deserve an award or something.

ABOUT THE AUTHOR

Abby Brooks writes contemporary romance about real people in relatable situations. With equal parts humor and heat, her books provide an emotional smorgasbord readers love. You'll laugh, cry, and cheer her characters on as they chase down their happily ever after.

Raised in a small town in the mid-west, Abby always leaned creative. She discovered her love of stories early, writing her first book at the tender age of four. As her passion developed, Abby explored poetry as well as storytelling, leading to many school and local awards.

After high school, Abby pursued her other passion, ballet. First working with Dayton Ballet and later Pittsburgh Ballet Theatre, she appeared in numerous works, including Balanchine's *Jewels* and *Serenade*, and other full-length ballets such as *Romeo and Juliet* and *Coppelia*. After an injury cut short Abby's performing career, she transitioned to teaching, where she founded a successful ballet school and pre-professional ballet company and earned accolades for her cutting-edge choreography. Some of her former students now grace stages with renowned companies like American Ballet Theatre and Cirque du Soleil.

Abby's transition to writing full-time began with the publication of her debut novel, *Blown Away* in 2016, which was instantly loved for its hopeful narrative and endearing characters.

With a portfolio of 25 novels to her credit, including the top 25 Amazon bestseller *Beyond Words*, and top 15 Amazon bestseller *Fire*, her novel *Beyond Love* continues to stand out as one of her personal favorites. Delving into the generational trauma caused by family conflict, the story ultimately explores the unstoppable healing power of love, and the pain often hiding behind a smile.

Abby believes romance is the genre of hope. We all need to believe there's someone who will see the best and worst of who we are and love us anyway, and there's a happily-ever-after waiting at the end of it all.

Currently, Abby lives in Ohio with her amazing husband and their three cats. In her spare time you'll find her messing around outside, dancing in the kitchen when she should be paying attention to cooking, and enjoying the company of her family.

For more books and updates:
abbybrooksfiction.com

facebook.com/abbybrooksauthor
instagram.com/xo_abbybrooks
tiktok.com/@abbybrooksauthor

Books by

ABBY BROOKS

THE HUTTON FAMILY SECOND GENERATION

Fate

Fire

Fake

WILDROSE LANDING

Fearless

Shameless

Reckless

THE HUTTON FAMILY

Beyond Words

Beyond Love

Beyond Now

Beyond Us

Beyond Dreams

It's Definitely Not You

The Hutton Family Series - Part 1

The Hutton Family Series - Part 2

A BROOKSIDE ROMANCE

Wounded

Inevitably You

This Is Why

Along Comes Trouble

Come Home To Me

A Brookside Romance - the Complete Series

WILDE BOYS WITH WILL WRIGHT

Taking What Is Mine

Claiming What Is Mine

Protecting What Is Mine

Defending What Is Mine

Wilde

THE MOORE FAMILY

Finding Bliss

Faking Bliss

Instant Bliss

Enemies-to-Bliss

THE LONDON SISTERS

Love Is Crazy (Dakota & Dominic)

Love Is Beautiful (Chelsea & Max)

Love Is Everything (Maya & Hudson)

The London Sisters - the Complete Series

IMMORTAL MEMORIES

Immortal Memories Part 1

Immortal Memories Part 2

AS WREN WILLIAMS

Bad, Bad Prince

Woodsman

Printed in Great Britain
by Amazon